EX LIBRIS

VINTAGE **CLASSICS**

THE MONARCH OF THE GLEN

Compton Mackenzie was born in West Hartlepool in 1883, and educated at St Paul's School and Magdalen College, Oxford. During the First World War he rose to the rank of Captain in the Royal Marines, and he was made Director of the Aegean Intelligence Service. He wrote more than ninety books – novels, history and biography, essays and criticism, children's stories and verse – and was also an outstanding broadcaster. He founded and edited the magazine *The Gramophone*, and was President of the Siamese Cat Club. He lived for many years on the Island of Barra in the Outer Hebrides, but later settled in Edinburgh. He was knighted in 1952.

Compton Mackenzie died in 1972.

OTHER WORKS BY COMPTON MACKENZIE

Whisky Galore

COMPTON MACKENZIE

The Monarch of the Glen

VINTAGE BOOKS
London

Published by Vintage 2009

11

Copyright © Compton Mackenzie 1941

Compton Mackenzie has asserted his right under the Copyright,
Designs and Patents Act 1988 to be identified as the author of this work

First published in Great Britain in 1941
by Chatto & Windus

Vintage
Random House, 20 Vauxhall Bridge Road,
London SW1V 2SA

www.vintage-classics.info

Addresses for companies within The Random House Group Limited
can be found at: www.randomhouse.co.uk/offices.htm

The Random House Group Limited Reg. No. 954009

A CIP catalogue record for this book
is available from the British Library

ISBN 9780099529545

Penguin Random House is committed to a sustainable future for
our business, our readers and our planet. This book is made from
Forest Stewardship Council® certified paper.

Printed and bound in Great Britain by Clays Ltd, Elcograf S.p.A.

To
Pilot Officer Robert Boothby, M.P., R.A.F.

My dear Bob,

I do not propose to involve myself with any institution or any individual by saying why I particularly choose this moment to dedicate to you a farce ; but I want to commemorate a friendship of twenty years, and this dedication gives me a chance to say how precious that friendship has been, is and always will be to

Yours ever,

COMPTON MACKENZIE.

SUIDHEACHAN,
ISLAND OF BARRA,
JULY 14, 1941.

CONTENTS

Chapter 1

GLENBOGLE

INADEQUATE indeed would be the guidebook or traveller's tale that did not accord to Glenbogle a place of honour in the very forefront of Highland scenery and romance, and it is a tribute to Scottish thoroughness that no such guidebook exists. Here are a page or two from *Summer Days Among the Heather:*

" Nobody who can spare the time should omit to explore Glenbogle. Apart from the wild magnificence of the natural scene Glenbogle literally teems with historic memories and romantic legends. It was in a cave in the rocky fastnesses of Ben Booey, the yellow mountain, that Bonny Prince Charlie spent several nights hidden from the ' redcoats.' Ben Booey (3,100 ft.) with Ben Glass (2,890 ft.), the grey mountain, and Ben Gorm (3,055 ft.), the blue mountain, are the famous Three Sisters of Glenbogle celebrated in many a poem and many a picture. Loch na Craosnaich (the loch of the spear) will be noticed on the left-hand side of the road five miles up the glen from the main road between Fort William and Fort Augustus. It was here that the famous Hector MacDonald of Ben Nevis, known as Hector of the Great Jaw, speared eleven Macintoshes and drowned them in the waters of the loch. A further two hours' walk from Loch na Craosnaich will bring the visitor to the gates of Glenbogle Castle, the seat of MacDonald of Ben Nevis. The present Chieftain, Donald MacDonald of Ben Nevis, is the twenty-third of the famous line of Mac 'ic Eachainn (pron. *Mack 'ick Yacken*), and it is one of the boasts of the ' true and tender North ' that a MacDonald of Ben Nevis in the direct male line still occupies the stronghold of the ' sons of Hector.'

" The Castle itself is not shown to visitors, but permission to wander about the well-wooded policies is readily granted on application at the lodge by the main entrance-gate, on the pillars of which will be noticed the two stone water-horses mordant of the MacDonalds of Ben Nevis. Legend says that the first Mac 'ic Eachainn was pursued by two water-horses from sunrise till sunset all over Glenbogle and its guardian bens, and that at sunset, having found a claymore embedded in a granite boulder, he drew the weapon and immediately slew the two monsters. Thereupon a fairy woman appeared and promised that all the land within the line along which he had been pursued by the two waterhorses should be his and his heirs, until the day of the seven whirlwinds or, as the more prosiac Sassenach would say, the end of the world. Tradition goes on to relate that the granite boulder in which the claymore was embedded is the actual cornerstone of Glenbogle Castle. Everybody who is privileged to gaze upon this stately pile, portions of which date back to the first half of the fourteenth century, will give a fervid assent to the motto of this branch of the great Clan Donald, *Beinn Nibheis Gu Brath* (*Anglicé* Ben Nevis For Ever).

" Those who have promised themselves the pleasure of passing a summer's day exploring dark Glenbogle or wild Glenbogle as it is variously called, will do well to provide beforehand for the refreshment of the inner man. The grandeur and desolation which greet the eye on every side from the moment the wayfarer enters Glenbogle will amply compensate for the absence of any dwelling-place until the immediate surroundings of the Castle are reached. No, gentle reader, Glenbogle has no hotel, and the sophisticated traveller who expects teashops and restaurants should not wend his steps towards this historic spot. For him, however, who is content with a mossy bank for his resting-place, with water from the burn, and with the simple fare he carries in his knapsack, Glenbogle is ' Paradise enow.' Many a long summer's day has the present scribe dreamed away in that delectable spot 'far from the madding crowd,' pondering upon the lore of the misty past and recapturing with the mind's eye the stirring scenes of auld lang syne. The scent of the bell-heather and the bog-myrtle, the buzzing of honeybees, the babbling of the peaty burn, the solemn shapes of the old brooding bens, are not these better than the superficial luxury of our so-called civilisation? If we go to Glenbogle when ' the world is too much with us ' there is no doubt what our answer will be."

With a romantic sigh young Mrs Chester Royde laid down *Summer Days Among the Heather* and gazed out of the window in the North Tower of Glenbogle Castle at the Three Sisters of Glenbogle dreaming majestically in the flickering haze of a fine morning on the twelfth of August.

She had some reason to sigh romantically, for this was her
first visit to the home of her forefathers, one of whom, much
against his will, had been deported to Canada by the
twentieth MacDonald of Ben Nevis, the great-grandfather
of the present laird. As a girl Caroline Macdonald had
suffered from the Lone Shieling complex. She had seen the
fairies in a peach-orchard on the shores of Lake Ontario.
She had repined at not having been christened Flora, but
had derived a measure of consolation from the thought that
Caroline was the feminine of Charles. Then Chester Royde
Jr., who was in Canada on business for his father's great
financial house in New York, had met Caroline Macdonald
at a Toronto ball and she was persuaded to become Mrs
Chester Royde Jr. Chester was no Prince Charlie. Indeed,
Carrie's friends all said they were surprised, after the way
Carrie Macdonald had talked so much about Celtic romance
and second-sight and Mrs Kennedy-Fraser's Hebridean
songs, she should go and marry a fat pug-nosed New
Yorker with a double chin already at twenty-five and a
complexion like a marsh-mallow. Yet Carrie's friends
weren't so much surprised as they pretended: Chester Royde
Jr. was the heir to the Royde millions, and well they knew it.

That was last year, and the honeymoon had been cut
short on account of a crisis in the money market. So they
had had a supplementary honeymoon this year in Europe
and in London they had met Mrs MacDonald of Ben Nevis,
who was down there with her two hefty daughters, Catriona
and Mary. They were known to the ribald as the Three
Sisters of Glenbogle, but this was an injustice to Mrs
MacDonald, who was as large as her two girls put together
and English at that. The yearly matrimonial campaign of
Mrs MacDonald was short and sharp. They were always
back in Glenbogle by the beginning of June.

The knowledge that a clanswoman of his was married to
the heir of the Royde millions had filled Donald MacDonald,
twenty-third of Ben Nevis, with the liveliest patriarchal
emotions. Blood of an unusually disproportionate thickness
compared with water coursed through his arteries, and the
little veins upon his eagle's beak glowed like neon round a
shop-window.

"You must come and visit Glenbogle," he declared.
"Home of your forefathers, what? And we must work out
our exact relationship."

" But my great-great-grandfather was just a simple
crofter. He left Glenbogle during the first clearance. In
fact I'm afraid he was put out by the Ben Nevis of the time."

" That was my great-grandfather Hector, twentieth of
Ben Nevis. Yes, a bad business. Well, well, that's what
comes of loyalty."

" Loyalty ? " Carrie Royde repeated, perplexed.

" Loyalty to the old Stuarts. We managed to keep the
land, but it was only by raising regiments for the Government. And then of course once Highlanders had started
settling in Canada the only sound economic policy was to
settle as many more of them as possible. That was why my
grandfather had to make a second clearance. He hated
doing it of course, but it was for their own good, and where
would the Empire be to-day if people like my great-grandfather and grandfather hadn't taken the bull by the horns
and faced up to hard facts ? Yes, I'm sure we must be
related. Distantly of course. But if you and your husband
come up to Glenbogle we'll work it out."

" Chester's young sister is coming over to us at the end of
July."

" Is she married ? "

" Oh, no, Myrtle's only twenty. And one of the sweetest
girls in the world."

" Look here, Mrs Royde," said the Chieftain earnestly,
" you and your husband and your sister-in-law simply must
come up for the Twelfth and put in at least six weeks with
us at Glenbogle. My eldest boy Hector's unfortunately out
in India with his regiment, but my second boy Murdoch
expects to be with us for part of August. He's in the Navy.
And Iain, my youngest boy, who's at Cambridge, will be
with us the whole of his vacation. In fact we shall be a very
jolly party of young people."

Thus it was that Mrs Chester Royde Jr. found herself
gazing from the window in the North Tower of Glenbogle
Castle at the shapes of the Three Sisters of Glenbogle,
dreaming majestically in the flickering haze of a fine Twelfth
of August morning.

When the rest of the party had been mustered by their
host to shoot the grouse or watch them being shot on his most
prolific moors which swept between the braes of Strathdun
and the braes of Strathdiddle, Carrie Royde, surrendering
to the Lone Shieling complex of her youth, had expressed a

desire to enjoy by herself the solitude of Glenbogle.

" I just want to make the most of this lovely weather, Ben Nevis," she told the Chieftain. " And I'm feeling kind of remote and mysterious. I feel as if anything might happen to me if I go and search for it alone."

" Well, don't go and sprain your ankle or anything," said Ben Nevis, who believed that a heavy bag of grouse was the way to make the most of the weather but had too much respect for the Royde millions to discourage anybody in close touch with them from the utmost extravagance of emotional self-indulgence.

" Carrie and I will find plenty to do to amuse ourselves," Mrs MacDonald boomed confidently.

Carrie Royde threw a slanting glance from greenish eyes at her monumental hostess and said quickly that the very last thing she should think of being was the least responsibility.

" I know you have lots and lots to do without bothering yourself about me, dear Mrs MacDonald. So please, if I may just have a little packet of sandwiches and a few crackers I'll go wandering off by myself and spend the day with my dreams."

" But won't that be rather dull for you ? " the hostess suggested anxiously.

" You let her do as she likes, Trixie," Ben Nevis adjured. " She's going to look for the fairies. I can see it in her eye."

Carrie put a finger to her lips and flashed a glance at the Chieftain, who went charging from the room to see that the party from the moors had gathered in the courtyard of the Castle, convinced that between him and that pretty little red-haired American-Canadian with her roots in the peat of his own moors there existed a secret understanding. Well, so much the better. If Murdoch could manage to make the running with that attractive little sister-in-law of hers, the closer the understanding between him and Mrs Chester Royde Jr. there was the better. As he climbed up into the big pre-war Daimler (there was only one war to date fashion at the time of this tale) which was to drive him and most of his house-party to the Ballochy Pass where the ponies would be waiting for them, he wished regretfully that the Clanranalds were not in India, because after all Hector as the Younger of Ben Nevis was the son of his most entitled to benefit from the share of the Royde millions that would be Miss Myrtle Royde's portion. He looked round to where the engagingly plump little heiress was seated beside his second son Murdoch in the sports car whose noisiness and vulgarity he had hitherto deplored and reflected that after all there might be something in these foul products of the post-war age—sometimes.

He turned to his principal guest, Chester Royde Jr., who in his costume for the moors looked like a full-page colour advertisement in the pages of *Esquire* or *Vanity Fair* designed to haunt, to startle and waylay the most casual reader.

" And this is really your first experience of our Twelfth, Royde ? " he asked.

The cork-pop with which his guest answered him Ben Nevis had learnt by now to recognize as an affirmative.

" We're expecting plenty of birds this year."

"That's fine," the young financier twanged enthusiastically.

Up in the North Tower of the Castle Carrie Royde watched the cars down the glen turn off to the right and start winding slowly up the narrow road that led toward the Pass of Ballochy. Her Macdonald heart beat faster at the memories the name brought back. She opened *Summer Days Among the Heather* again:

" It was in the Pass of Ballochy that in the year 1546 a party of marauding Macintoshes were surprised by the Macdonalds of Ben Nevis led by Mac 'ic Eachainn in person and every single one of them killed. Some years later Clan Chattan took its revenge for this defeat by descending into Strathdiddle, when the young men were raiding the Cameron country to the south, and baking thirty-two old and infirm Macdonalds in an oven. For this Hector the ninth of Ben Nevis exacted a terrible penalty from Clan Chattan when after marching from Glenbogle with his Macdonalds through a stormy December night in the year 1549 he caught the Macintoshes unawares on a Sunday morning and burned forty-five of them in church. While the unfortunate victims of Hector's vengeance were burning, Hector's piper Angus MacQuat improvised a tune and played it to drown their shrieks. This tune, called Mac 'ic Eachainn's Return to Glenbogle, is still played by a MacQuat whenever Mac-Donald of Ben Nevis returns after spending even a single night away from his Castle.

" A poem by an unknown Gaelic bard of the sixteenth century celebrating the battle in the Pass of Ballochy was rendered into spirited English verse by the late lamented

Reverend Colin MacKellaig, D.D., whose translations from
the vernacular rendered a service to the ' land of bens and
glens and heroes ' second only to his faithful service for over
sixty years as a Minister of the Gospel at first in his own
Inverness-shire and then at the United Free Church in
Dudden Gardens, Glasgow.

" THE BATTLE OF THE PASS OF BALLOCHY

Sound the loud pibroch, ye sons of great Hector,
Lift your claymores and strike hard at the foe,
Hurry as fast as ye can from Glenbogle,
Clansmen of Hector, cry shame on the slow!

Whistle, ye winds, ' Mac 'ic Eachainn for ever! '
Roar, ye wild waters, ' Ben Nevis gu brath! '
Swift as the Bogle in spate, ye MacDonalds,
Fall on the Macintosh, drive him awa'.

Sharp are the claws of the cat of Clan Chattan,
Gleam their claymores in the Ballochy Pass;
But sharper the talons of Hector's own eagles
. That swoop from Ben Booey, Ben Gorm and Ben Glass.

Swoop on the Macintosh, rend him in pieces,
None of Clan Chattan this day shall survive,
Sons of Clan Donald, salute your great Chieftain;
Dead is the Macintosh, Hector's alive!

Faithful and fair is my own Mac 'ic Eachainn,
Mighty and mettlesome, stalwart and true,
Lord of Ben Nevis, Glenbogle, Glenbristle,
Strathdiddle, Strathdun, Loch Hoch and Loch Hoo."

Mrs Chester Royde tossed her red locks. The echoes of
ancestral voices prophesying war were ringing in her ears
when she took from the butler the packet of sandwiches and
set out to commune with her forefathers, the nettle-grown
tumbled stones of whose cottages were strewn about the
emptiness of wild Glenbogle. In one pocket of her green
coat were the sandwiches, in the other a copy of *Gaelic
Without Tears*.

Seldom can the long winding drive of Glenbogle Castle
have been graced by a more becoming figure than that
presented by Mrs Chester Royde Jr. when she set out that
morning to commune with her ancestors. She was wearing
a skirt of the tartan of the Ben Nevis MacDonalds, the
predominance of red in which did not detract from her own

red hair, thanks to the judicious interposition of the green coat, and her green bonnet was brooched with the eagle's head of the Ben Nevis MacDonalds. Her host had presented her with a cromag as dainty as the crook of a Dresden shepherdess. The dark pines that bordered the drive seemed to light up when she passed as if touched by a fleeting sunbeam.

She paused a moment at the gate and looked up at the two water-horses mordant gnashing their teeth at one another from the lichen-covered pillars on either side. She turned to the vocabulary of her *Gaelic Without Tears* to see if she could find the Gaelic for water-horse, but it was evidently too difficult a word for such an elementary instructor and was not to be found. Just beyond the gate a Glenbogle estate painter was admiring the result of some recent work on a large notice-board:

> GLENBOGLE CASTLE. NO CAMPING.

Thus the inscription ran in large black letters on a white ground. The spread of hiking had soured the milk of human kindness. No longer was permission readily granted on application at the lodge by the main entrance-gate to wander in the well-wooded policies of the Castle, as recorded by the author of *Summer Days Among the Heather*.

Carrie debated with herself for a moment whether she should venture to give the painter ' good day ' in Gaelic, decided that one had to begin some time, looked up the phrase in her little brown volume, muttered her phonetics over to herself once or twice, and gulped:

" La math."

There are few joys accessible to human beings more grateful than the joy of trying out a phrase from a conversation manual according to the pronunciation indicated in brackets alongside and finding that the subject of the experiment understands and responds. This joy was denied to Mrs Chester Royde. It was clear from the expression on the painter's face as he touched his cap that he was respectfully hoping the Castle guest would amplify her question if it was a question or if she had not really addressed him at all relieve his embarrassment by doing so.

Carrie Royde did not like being beaten. She turned back to *Gaelic Without Tears*. Yes, there it was. Good day. La math (*lah mah*). She tried again.

" La math."

" I couldn't tell you, mistress, I'm afraid. I only came here from Glasgow two weeks ago."

" Aren't you a Gaelic speaker ? "

" No, mistress; I have nae a word of Gaelic."

The Macdonald in Carrie was shocked by this revelation of Glenbogle's decline, but her disappointment was lightened by the reflection that the virginity of ' la math ' was still intact and that the phonetics of *Gaelic Without Tears* had not betrayed her.

" What is the meaning of that notice ? " she asked. For all this painter knew that might have been what ' la math ' had meant.

" It's Mr MacDonald's orders," she was told.

" Ben Nevis's orders ? " she enquired, with a note of rebuke in her voice.

" Ay, mistress, that's right. Ben Nevis himself, as they call him up here. They've been plagued a lot by these hikers, as they call them, and I have orders to paint a couple of dozen of these notice-boards all about the estate."

" Well, you have lovely weather for your painting."

" Ay, it hasna rained for nearly a week. Most extra-ordinar', the fellows on the estate tell me. Begging your pardon, mistress, are you from London ? "

" No; I'm an American Macdonald."

" Well, well, is that so ? I'm a Macdonald mysel'."

" You must be very happy working in this part of the country, aren't you ? "

" Och ay, I like it well enough. But it's no' Glasgow, ye ken. Were you never in Glasgow, mistress ? "

" No, I never was."

The painter shook his head sympathetically.

" Dinna fash yoursel', mistress. Och ay, you'll visit Glasgow one of these days. It's a bonny bonny city. Full of life, and the trams are sae convenient. I'll be back there mysel' in October. It's unco dreich in Glenbogle."

Carrie Royde walked on along the road down the glen, and lightly though she swung her cromag her heart was heavy awhile to think of a Macdonald in this ancestral stronghold sighing for a city to which neither beauty nor romance ever accorded a testimonial. However, the bad taste of one degenerate Highlander was not enough to spoil the magic of the natural scene for long. Beside the road the

2

Bogle babbling gently after nearly a week without rain kept
her company. On the other side of the glen Ben Booey,
Ben Gorm and Ben Glass towered, their lower slopes
empurpled as richly by heather as the nose of Mac 'ic
Eachainn himself by wrath. Two buzzards which she had
the pleasure of supposing were eagles hovered in the crystal-
line air. A bobbing stonechat clicked at her from a boulder.
A lanky blue mountain-hare scampered up the brae on the
left of the road. A shaggy Highland bull eyed her from a
field on the other side of the little river, and with that and a
barbed-wire fence between him and her she waved her cromag
at him as carelessly as if he were in the foreground of a
picture by Peter Graham.

For some three or four miles she followed the road down
the glen until she came to a narrow grass-grown turning
where a mouldering signpost pointed to GLENBRISTLE and
beside it a freshly painted notice-board nailed to a larch-pole
proclaimed No CAMPING. Carrie Royde decided to follow
this even wilder-looking road. Mrs MacDonald had suggested driving along Glenbogle to pick her up and bring her
back to lunch in case she grew tired of her own company.
She was delighted by her own company and in no mood to be
dragged out of ancestral reveries by her hostess. She was
anxious to eradicate the belief prevalent in Glenbogle Castle
that American visitors expected to be assiduously entertained
all the time. Besides, she wasn't feeling at all American
at this moment. She was feeling more like Deirdre than
anybody since Deirdre said farewell to Scotland.

> *Dearest Albyn,*
> *Land o'er yonder,*
> *Thou dear land of wood and wave.*

These were as much of the words as she could remember,
but she hummed to herself the tune in an ecstasy of romantic
emotion, such an ecstasy that she kept quickening the
tempo, and before she came to the end of the first verse
Deirdre's Farewell had turned into *Oh, my darling, oh, my
darling, oh, my darling Clementine*.

Soon, however, the profound silence of Glenbristle, un-
broken even by the babble of the smallest burn, made even
the humming of a tune correctly seem a sacrilegious interruption of the stillness.

Carrie became obsessed by an urgent intuition that the

home of her great-great-grandfather before it was pulled down and he was sent away in an emigrant ship to Canada had been in Glenbristle and that his spirit was leading her to its site. Besides her own Celtic origins she had dabbled a bit in Yogi. So she took several very deep breaths and surrendered her will to the influence she felt all round her. Her corporeal response was immediate. She seemed to be floating over rather than walking on the rough grass-grown road, and then on a green knoll about fifty yards up the brae on her right she saw the strewn stones and luxuriant nettles which still mark, sometimes centuries later, where once a human habitation stood. She had no doubt whatever that this knoll was the site of her ancestral home, and in high elation of spirit she made her way up to the top of it; and after meditating piously for a moment or two on the foundations of the cottage that were still clearly visible, this daughter of Glenbristle returning to it across a wide gulf of time and sea looked at her delicately diamonded wrist-watch, saw that it was high noon, and decided to eat her lunch.

" But there ought to be a burn close by," she said aloud.

There was a burn close by, and convinced this was a clear case of ancestral memory Carrie Royde sat down on the grass cropped close by rabbits and untied the parcel of sandwiches the butler had made up for her.

"Yes," she murmured, "I certainly have been here before."

When she had finished her lunch and drunk of the water of the burn from cupped hands she stuck a cigarette in a long tortoiseshell holder ringed with diamonds and studied *Gaelic Without Tears*. The boat is here. The boat is there. Is the boat here? Is the boat there? The boat is not here. The boat is not there. Is not the boat here? Is not the boat there? The boy says that the boat is here. The boy says that the boat is there. The boy says that the boat is not here. The boy says . . .

The boy's information about the boat's whereabouts became vaguer and vaguer as the outline of the hills opposite flickered in the heat of the sun, and beyond the tobacco-smoke the landscape lost all definite form, blending in a rich blur of purple and green and grey and blue and receding from her as she floated back into the past. Wrapped in a plaid and barelegged, she was gazing anxiously up the glen for signs of the redcoats searching for her Prince, when she fell fast asleep.

Chapter 2

THE SCUFFLE IN THE HEATHER

WHILE Mrs Chester Royde Jr. was asleep on that green knoll in Glenbristle the members of the house party together with two or three of the neighbouring shots the Chieftain of Ben Nevis considered worthy of his best moor were enjoying their lunch after the most satisfactory bag registered on any morning of the Twelfth for six years.

" If we do as well this afternoon on Drumcockie, Hugh, we might lower the '22 record."

This remark was addressed by the Chieftain to Hugh Cameron of Kilwhillie, a small button-headed man with long thin drooping moustaches, a faded kilt and a faded eye. Although some ten years junior to Ben Nevis, he was his prime favourite among the Inverness-shire lairds. Their land nowhere marched together. Kilwhillie was a better fisherman; but Ben Nevis preferred the gun, and Kilwhillie was no match for him with a gun. Both were fond of whisky and both flattered themselves they could carry as much of it without a slip of the tongue or a trip of the toe as any two lairds on either side of the Great Glen. You could not call them boon companions, for there was a touch of Celtic melancholy about Kilwhillie, attributed by some to liver, which forbade the epithet; but their intimacy was as close as men in their class can achieve. It was beautifully expressed once by Mrs MacDonald when she said that Donald never slept so soundly and so peacefully as when Hughie Cameron had dined at Glenbogle. The laird of Kilwhillie was unmarried, not from misogyny but because he had failed to persuade either of the two young women to whom he had proposed to accept him.

" And I don't intend to try again," he used to assure Ben Nevis. " I don't think this Bruce and the spider business has any bearing on marriage."

And Ben Nevis, who always called it a pity when a good fellow got married, used to agree warmly with his friend, though sometimes he would remind him about the succession.

" There's not so much to succeed to now," Kilwhillie would

say, swallowing a dram recklessly. "Let the Department of Agriculture take over what's left."

But this was the kind of talk which suited a dying fire and an empty decanter. Up here in the heather on a fine Twelfth of August the mood was different.

"Splendid view, isn't it?" Ben Nevis exclaimed to his guests, with a justifiable touch of Highland pride, for indeed it was a splendid view over the wide level of Strathdun away to where flashed the silver of Loch Hoch, whose farthest bank marked the boundaries of Mac 'ic Eachainn's land.

Chester Royde eyed the chieftain thoughtfully as he chewed slowly on a mouthful of chicken and ham. Then he turned to Kilwhillie, who was reclining next him on the heather:

"What exactly lets anybody in on wearing kilts?" he asked. "I mean to say, suppose I took a fancy to wearing kilts, would that strike a low note in Scotland?"

Kilwhillie, who was also chewing on a mouthful of chicken and ham, gulped it down and murmured, "Kilt not kilts," with a hint of reproachful pedantry.

"Are you only allowed one then?" the young financier asked. He did not like this kind of restriction.

"Only one at a time."

"I got you. But what would happen if I were to wear one of these kilts? Would I be run out of the country on a rail or lynched or anything like that?"

"There's no objection to anybody's wearing the kilt," said Kilwhillie. "But there's always the question of the tartan. Some people who haven't themselves the right to a tartan wear their mother's tartan. But I'm against that. I believe it to be contrary to the best tradition. There's a tendency nowadays to introduce alien notions of female descent into the clan system, so that you actually get women claiming a chiefship, which is preposterous."

"I suppose now we have women lawyers and preachers and doctors they don't see why they shouldn't be Highland Chiefs. So you'd be against me wearing my wife's tartan, which by the way is the same as our host's. I tell you I was tickled to death when I found that out."

"Personally I am strongly against wearing the tartan of one's wife. Some people without a tartan of their own who want to wear a tartan wear the Stewart tartan as subjects of King George."

" But I'm not a subject of King George. And I guess George Washington never had a tartan."

" The solution for you is to wear a kilt of hodden grey."

" Grey ? Is that the best you can do for me ? " Royde exclaimed indignantly. " I guess I'm better off as I am." He contemplated his own polychromatic tweediness with frank admiration.

" Boswell in his account of his trip with Johnson through the Hebrides describes Malcolm Macleod as wearing a purple kilt."

" Purple ? Say, that's an idea."

" But I've never seen a purple kilt in these days," Kilwhillie added hastily.

" You will," the young financier promised with fervour. " But see here, this purple kilt is a secret between you and me. I want to give Carrie a surprise."

" I shan't say a word about it," Kilwhillie vowed.

And he meant it. A fine subject for Inverness-shire gossip if it leaked out that he was responsible for an American financier in a purple kilt ! Why, it would be conspicuous even at the Oban Gathering.

" That's bully," said Chester Royde in a tone of the deepest satisfaction. " I'm crazy about the Highlands, Kilwhillie. I used to laugh at Carrie, but I tell you I've been bitten by this Highland bug myself. Now, see here, let me get this right, old man. Provided I stick to plain colours I'm O.K. ? I mean to say purple, blue, green, anything I like so long as I keep off lines and checks and any kind of pattern ? "

" It's unusual, of course, but . . ."

" I don't give a darn about it being unusual provided I'm not muscling in on somebody else's property."

" You certainly wouldn't be doing that."

" That's all I wanted to know. I mean to say, when I was in Canada I was adopted into the Carroway tribe of Indians with the name of Butting Moose. That's Chester Royde Jr. among the Carroways, and that's the way I want to feel in the Highlands. The romance of the whole business has gotten a hold of me, Kilwhillie. I aim to buy a place up here."

Kilwhillie's faded eyes were lighted up with that strange light which never was on sea or land, but is only to be seen in the eyes of a landed proprietor in the Highlands who hopes he has found a buyer for an overtaxed forest of twelve heads and a shooting-lodge that looks like a bunch of tarnished pepper-pots.

" I could probably help you with my advice over that," he murmured. " I think I know the kind of place you want. When you've definitely made up your mind let me know. And if I may venture to offer a word of advice, don't talk about it till you have. Otherwise you'll be pestered with all sorts of shooting-properties you don't want to waste time looking at. I think Miss Royde's enjoying it up here with us."

" Oh, Myrtle's enjoying herself fine."

Myrtle Royde was seated between the two beefy sons of Ben Nevis—Murdoch the sailor and Iain the undergraduate. They, like their sisters Mary and Catriona, had inherited size and weight from their mother; they could indeed be called massive, particularly Iain, who was the heaviest Five that ever rowed in the Trinity Hall boat. It had been the impressive showing they made in the kilt which had prompted Chester Royde's emulation more than the superb appearance of Ben Nevis himself upon his native heath, with which he would probably never have dreamed of competing.

Myrtle undoubtedly was enjoying herself, but an observer would have been right in dissociating her enjoyment from the company of the two young men, whose conversation indeed was hardly more enlivening than a couple of megaliths. Ben Nevis had noticed optimistically the opportunities a two-seater sports car offered to develop an understanding between two young people. He forgot his second son's lack of conversation and was also unaware of the American point of view which makes dumbness and stupidity synonymous. Iain had more to say than Murdoch, but Myrtle Royde was twenty, and a month or two past the final stage when College boys are interesting to the majority of the female sex.

" Well, I envy you your lovely country," she had exclaimed when Kilwhillie had commented to her brother on the enjoyment he had fancied in the brightness of her dark-brown eyes and the rosy flush upon her cheeks.

" It's not bad," the sailor agreed.

" Not bad, indeed ? Why, Lieutenant MacDonald, it's divine."

Murdoch knitted his brows. He wished she would not call him Lieutenant MacDonald, and that if she must she would not pronounce it " Lootenant! "

" I used to think my sister-in-law Carrie crazy when she was always on at Chester to take her to Scotland, but I understand it now. I wish I had Scotch ancestors myself. Look at that lovely lake shining away down there. We used sometimes to spend the summer in Vermont when we were children, and that's lovely, too. But I think it's the romance here that gets me. Look at your father now. What a wonderful figure of a man he is! You can fancy him leading his clan into battle, can't you? Oh, I tell you I'm just in a sort of dream state. And so's Carrie. And I think Chester's pretty taken with it. I noticed a look in his eye I've never seen before when the pipers came in at dinner last night."

" I think they're rather boring as a matter of fact," said Iain.

" Mr MacDonald, how can you say that? Why, I was getting thrills all down my back every time they passed behind my chair."

But Myrtle was spared further disillusionment by the voice of Ben Nevis asking if the guns were ready to move off.

" Drumcockie this afternoon, eh, Ben Nevis? " asked a thin elderly man in plus fours, with a white toothbrush moustache, his countenance dyed an indelible brownish-yellow by the Indian sun.

" Yes, and if we do as well as we did this morning, we ought to make a record."

" Hope we do," said the thin man.

Chester Royde asked Kilwhillie who the thin man was. He had not caught his name when they were introduced.

" Colonel Lindsay-Wolseley of Tummie."

" Say, I don't have to call.him Tummie, do I? " the young financier enquired anxiously.

" You can if you like, but he only bought Tummie after the war. I should call him ' Colonel ' if I were you."

Chester Royde sighed his relief as he threw a leg across the hill pony that was to bear him to the grouse-teeming moor of Drumcockie.

Alas, for the high hopes of Ben Nevis! His dearest moor failed him. There were some birds. There could not fail to be some birds on Drumcockie. But compared with the

number of birds there ought to have been the few that
whirred toward the butts and death were nothing.

" What the devil are the beaters playing at, Duncan ? "
he demanded wrathfully, his eagle's beak darkening to the
tint of an Anglican prelate's evening apron.

Big Duncan Macdonald, who looked like a major prophet
in tweeds, shook his head.

" I'm thinking it's some of these hikers, Ben Nevis."

" You think it's what ? " the chieftain gasped.

" Hikers."

" Hikers ?   Hikers on Drumcockie ? "

" They're after frightening every bird in the neighbourhood," he declared, with a muttered imprecation in
Gaelic.

" You're not seriously telling me, Duncan, that some of
these abominable hikers have dared to defile Drumcockie on
the Twelfth of August ? "

" There were a party of sixteen of them camping in
Strathdiddle last night."

" In defiance of these notice-boards I've just had freshly
painted ? "

" My grandson Willie says they were camping right round
the notice-board on the north bank of the loch."

Mac 'ic Eachainn glared across Drumcockie Moor away
to where the fair expanse of Loch Hoo crowned the head of
Strathdiddle with gleaming silver.

" Why wasn't I told of this outrage before, Duncan ? "

" Because I was not so anxious to spoil your eye, Ben Nevis.
You should not have hit a bird this morning if you were
after hearing about those hikers in Strathdiddle. I was
hoping no harm would have been done, but there you are.
While we were shooting Clacknaclock these hikers were
at their devilment on Drumcockie."

" Duncan," his chief asked, " how long have you been in
my service ? "

" Thirty-two years last June, Ben Nevis."

" In the whole of that time have you ever known me go
back on my word ? "

" No, I don't believe you ever went back on your word,
Ben Nevis."

" Then when I tell you that whatever it costs me I am
determined to rid my land of hikers you know I mean what
I say."

" You said the very same thing about rabbits, Ben Nevis, three years back," his old henchman reminded him.

" Hikers don't breed like rabbits."

" But you cannot trap hikers, Ben Nevis."

" No, I can't trap them, thanks to the grandmotherly laws under which we suffer, but I can clear them off my land, and I will too. They're a fouler pest than rabbits. They're worse than bracken. Are hikers going to be able to do what the Macintoshes were never able to do ? Am I or am I not the twenty-third MacDonald of Ben Nevis ? "

" Gently now, gently, Ben Nevis. You're getting very red in the face. You mustn't excite yourself too much. It's very annoying, right enough. Och, it's terrible. But you mustn't let it boil your blood too much. If I call in the beaters we might move along to the Derrybeg. It's not too late at all."

" I'm not going to shoot another bird to-day. The morning bag was the best for six years. I'm not going to spoil it. I want to find these hikers. Go and get hold of my two boys and Kilwhillie. I can't ask my other guests . . . no, stay where you are and I'll speak to them myself."

The Chieftain strode across the moor, his kilt swinging, his sporran jigging, his amaranthine nose cleaving the air. He came to the butt at which Colonel Lindsay-Wolseley was standing.

" Look here, Wolseley, you had a lot of experience on the North-West Frontier. I want your help. There's a band of filthy hikers loose in Strathdiddle."

Colonel Wolseley looked a little apprehensive. He did not immediately perceive the link between Inverness-shire and Waziristan.

" What action exactly were you proposing to take, Ben Nevis ? "

" I'm going to round the brutes up. They've ruined any hope of good sport on Drumcockie for to-day. And I *don't* see why they should get away with it."

" You mean you're going to turn them off your land ? "

" I'm going to lock them up in Glenbogle for a couple of nights and see if that'll give them the lesson they deserve."

" You're proposing to use force ? " the Colonel asked, amazement only kept in check by the traditions of his caste and calling.

" When these savages see themselves covered by half a

dozen guns I don't assume they'll offer any resistance," the Chieftain barked.

"But you can't threaten to shoot trespassers, Ben Nevis. You really can't."

"I can and I will," he declared.

"Well, I'm sorry, but I'm afraid I cannot take any part in such a proceeding. You must remember that I am Convener of the Police Committee of the County Council. It would put me in an impossible position. And if you'll take the advice of a friend, Ben Nevis, you'll avoid putting yourself in an impossible position by taking any such action as you contemplate. The proper course is to ask for their names and addresses and institute legal proceedings. If you take the law into your own hands you'll expose yourself to an action for assault and false imprisonment. You may get heavy damages against you."

"Look here, Lindsay-Wolseley,. I don't want you to take what I'm going to say personally. I've no desire to be offensive. But I'm not in the mood to be lectured about my actions. This band of miscreants camped last night on the banks of Loch Hoo, actually right round one of my freshly-painted No CAMPING notice-boards. Not content with that they've evidently been careering about all over Drum-cockie this morning, and our Twelfth has been wrecked."

"My dear Ben Nevis, do not misunderstand me. I sympathize profoundly over this beastly business. But when you ask me to take part with you in what amounts to a punitive expedition I should be no true friend of yours if I didn't try to dissuade you from such an action. I suppose you'll call me a cold-blooded Lowlander, but I do beg you to think twice before you embark upon a course of action the consequences of which may be . . . I mean to say, Ben Nevis, we landed proprietors cannot afford to stir up popular feeling in these democratic days."

"Clap-trap!"

"What?"

"I said clap-trap, Lindsay-Wolseley. You're talking Bolshie clap-trap."

"You are allowing your feelings to get the better of you, Ben Nevis," the Colonel observed, a dull flush asserting itself beneath the brownish-yellow dye of the Indian sun.

"I have no desire to quarrel with you, Lindsay-Wolseley."

"I accept that, Ben Nevis. So let us say no more about

it," the Colonel replied, with a gesture of old-world courtliness. " I'm very sorry that the splendid sport you've been giving us has been interfered with by uninvited guests."

" I suppose Bottley won't be any more anxious than you to round up these filthy hikers," Ben Nevis growled, with a glance in the direction of Sir Hubert Bottley, the owner of the famous forest of Cloy which had been bought by his father, the first baronet, out of Bottley's Bottled Beans.

" I won't answer for him," said the Colonel hurriedly. " Bottley must decide for himself."

" I shan't try to involve him or Rawstorne or Jack Fraser," Ben Nevis said proudly. " I think I can manage with my own people. We've managed for a good many years now. I only asked you, Wolseley, because I thought you might enjoy the kind of sport you must often have enjoyed at Peshawar. Well, I'm sorry to break up our day like this, but I must get my forces together."

The Colonel saw it was useless to argue further with his friend. At any rate, he was glad to hear himself addressed again as " Wolseley." It indicated that his refusal to take part in the punitive expedition against the hikers was no longer resented. Lindsay-Wolseley was what Ben Nevis always called him when they found themselves in disagreement at a meeting of the County Council.

" That was the kind of thing which wrecked the 'Forty-five, Hugh," the Chieftain observed to the laird of Kilwhillie when the ponies with the four recreant guns were lost to sight in a dip of the moor on the way back to the Pass of Ballochy and the waiting cars. " However, thank God, the old loyalties haven't entirely disappeared! "

" You can't expect newcomers to feel as we do, Donald." Then Hugh Cameron remembered his plan to sell Knocknacolly and its dilapidated lodge to Chester Royde Jr. " Not *all* newcomers, that is."

" Well, I'll say I'm enjoying myself," the young financier declared. " But what do we do if these hoodlums won't put their hands up, Ben Nevis ? "

" I'm sending the beaters round to cut off their retreat. I don't think they'll resist. They're a weedy type. And there are some women with them. Extraordinary class of people altogether. I'm relying on you, Mary, and you, Catriona, to deal with these women. And what about you, Miss Royde ? "

" Oh, please don't call me that, Ben Nevis. I don't feel a little bit like a daughter of the clan when you call me Miss Royde."

" Very nice of you. Appreciate it very much. Well, what are you going to do, Myrtle ? I think Murdoch had better look after you."

" No, I know just what I'm going to do," said Myrtle firmly. " I'm going to stay right by you, Ben Nevis. I'm going to be your vivandière."

The imaginative observer capable of rejecting the materialistic explanation that it was a sporting party walking up any game that was about would have derived from the spectacle of Mac 'ic Eachainn's line of battle the deepest romantic gratification. On the right as befitted MacDonalds was the Chieftain himself, a hefty son on either side of him, a daughter not less hefty on either side of their brothers, the tartan of the kilts and skirts in which red predominated recalling a dozen poems of battles fought by the Mac-Donalds of Ben Nevis. A few yards behind this line of red and immediately behind Mac 'ic Eachainn himself marched Myrtle Royde carrying a flask of whisky.

A pity Hector was out with his regiment in India, his father reflected. This was the very girl for him. Murdoch was too much of a slowcoach. He ought to have done better with the chances he had already had. And after all this jolly little girl with so much money in prospect would want an eldest son. She'd be sure to cotton on to Hector. He had a good mind to send an urgent cable telling Hector to apply for leave at once and fly home. It would cost a bit, but nothing venture nothing win. Ben Nevis looked round and smiled benignly at his vivandière, and the answering smile dimpling those cheeks decided him. He would cable Hector to obtain leave for urgent family reasons and come by plane.

The centre of Mac 'ic Eachainn's line of battle consisted of Chester Royde, whose fat face had taken on the severe lines of an Arizona sheriff riding after a gang of rustlers in the timeless air of Wild West romance, and his head-keeper, Duncan Macdonald, who looked like Elijah hot upon the trail of the priests of Baal. The left was commanded by Hugh Cameron of Kilwhillie, who had a couple of gillies with him.

For a quarter of an hour the line advanced steadily across

Drumcockie's heather. Then as the moorland began to
slope toward the braes of Strathdiddle Mac 'ic Eachainn
uttered a shout.

" There they are! "

Yes, there they were in green corduroy shorts and brown
corduroy shorts, in pink shirts and pale green shirts and
coffee-coloured shirts, hatless, towzled, with long sticks and
crêpe-soled shoes and knapsacks, there they were sitting
round a fire they had just lighted to make tea and listening to
a portable wireless, female hikers and male hikers to the
number of sixteen.

Ben Nevis charged ahead of the others, and five of the
hikers dived for their cameras to get snapshots of this
magnificent specimen of the native fauna striding through
the heather in the sun's eye. One young woman with
smoked glasses and very short green corduroy shorts whose
fat flaming thighs looked as if they were melting at the knees
held up her hand when the Chieftain was almost on top of
the party and asked him to stand still for a moment while she
altered the focus of her Kodak.

" Who is in command of this party ? " Ben Nevis bellowed.

The hikers looked at one another. The spirit of comrade-
ship which had animated them ever since they had got out
of the train from London at Perth and hiked their way to the
bonny banks of Loch Hoo had made a leader superfluous.

" Who is in command of this party ? " Ben Nevis bellowed
again.

The loudness of his voice had by now convincd the hikers
that the first specimen of the native fauna they had seen
between Perth and Inverness was angry about something.
They turned to the only member of the party over twenty-
four. This was a dark desiccated little man of anything
between forty and fifty with legs as thin and hairy as a spider's
and the eyes of a kindly old maid, the sort of eyes one so often
sees in confirmed scoutmasters.

" I am the Secretary of the N.U.H., sir," he told Ben
Nevis in a prim voice. " Were you wanting information
about anything ? "

" I don't know what the N.U.H. is, but you must be aware
that you are . . ."

" Excuse me, sir, the initials N.U.H. stand for National
Union of Hikers. We are now a very large organization

with branches in every one of our great cities. My name is Prew, Sydney Prew. I'm afraid I haven't a card with me. One disembarrasses oneself of such urban paraphernalia, does one not, when one takes to the open road ? "

The combination of some peculiarly irritating quality in the timbre of Mr Prew's spinsterish voice, of the sight of his own armed forces closing in upon the hikers and a dozen beaters advancing upon them from the rear, and of the recollection of his ruined Twelfth of August was too much for Donald MacDonald, the Twenty-third of Ben Nevis. He was suddenly seized with an access of rage that must have been similar to the convulsion which had seized his ancestor Hector of the Great Jaw when in the year 1482 he speared eleven Macintoshes beside Loch na Craosnaich and drowned them in it one after another. Grasping the secretary of the N.U.H. by the collar of his khaki shirt, he shook him as a conscientious housemaid shakes a mat.

" This is assault and battery," protested Mr Prew. " I call on all you boys and girls to observe what this gentleman is doing. He is assaulting me. And please note I am making no resistance whatever. May I ask what is the meaning of this outrage ? "

The sight of Mr Prew's enquiring face turned round with some difficulty owing to the grip upon his shirt-collar seemed to rouse Ben Nevis to fresh fury, and he shook him more violently than ever.

" I'll teach you to run amok among my birds. I'll teach you to camp out round one of my notice-boards forbidding camping. I'll teach you to light fires in the heather."

By this time the shaker and the shaken were both so much out of breath that neither could speak, and the only sound that broke the heathery silence of the braes of Strathdiddle was the voice of a crooner coming from the portable wireless. Even those who disapprove of Mac 'ic Eachainn's assault upon Mr Prew will not blame him for dropping Mr Prew and giving the crooner the contents of his gun's two barrels.

" Look here, that's my portable," a tall pink-faced young man expostulated. Whereupon Ben Nevis seized him by the front of his mauve shirt and shook him as violently as he had shaken Mr Prew. The young woman with the melting knees screamed in a rage and banged away at Ben Nevis with her hiker's staff. Catriona MacDonald caught hold of her by the back of her shorts and put a hefty arm round her neck.

There was a general mêlée, but the male hikers, severely handicapped by the attempts of the female hikers to help them, were no match for Clan Donald.

" What will we do with them, Ben Nevis ? " Duncan asked when the invaders were disarmed and surrounded.

" Bring them along to Ballochy, and I'll send the lorry for them when we get back to the Castle.   You want to camp on my land, do you ? " he snarled at Mr Prew.   " Very well, then you shall camp in the dungeons of Glenbogle Castle and see how you like that."

" This is going to be a serious matter for you, Mr Mac-Donald," said the Secretary of the N.U.H., his prim voice trembling with indignation, " for I presume you are the Mr MacDonald who owns this land."

Mac 'ic Eachainn turned away with a look of utter disgust.   A gardener would as soon think of arguing with a slug as he would with Sydney Prew.

Chapter 3

ANCESTRAL VOICES

WHILE such stirring events were happening on Drum-cockie moor and the braes of Strathdiddle, Mrs Chester Royde Jr. was asleep on that green knoll in the perfumed silence of Glenbristle.

When she awoke with a start about three o'clock to find two kilted forms gazing at her it is no matter for wonderment that she should have failed to disentangle them immediately from the romantic dream in which she had been wrapped and that for two or three all too brief moments she should have fancied that her attempt, with the help of Yogi, *Gaelic Without Tears* and dormant ancestral memories, to spirit herself back into the past had been successful, and that the young men, one in the vivid red and yellow of the Macmillan tartan, the other in the kaleidoscopic tartan of the Buchanans, were ancestral visions, their garb shining with celestial radiance. She recalled reading somewhere that Gaelic was the language of Eden, and thought it another good opportunity to murmur, " La math."

This time the phrase worked. The young man in the Macmillan tartan at once replied:

" La math. Tha è blath."

" Blah ? " Mrs Chester Royde echoed to herself. Was this fair shock-headed young man trying to be rude ? The celestial radiance faded from the red and yellow of his kilt, for she had now perceived that the nimbus was caused by the newness of the material.

" Tha è blath," the fair shock-headed young man repeated, feeling in the pocket of his doublet and drawing forth a copy of *Gaelic Without Tears* at the same instant as Mrs Royde discovered her copy and began turning over the pages.

" You'd better both speak English," the second young man mumbled severely in the accent of Glasgow. " Blah's just about what you're talking, Alan."

" I've found ' blath,' " Carrie Royde exclaimed. " It means warm. Yes, it is very warm indeed, isn't it ? I see you're learning Gaelic from the same book as I'm using. But you're two exercises ahead of me."

" I've been right through it once," said the red and yellow
kilt, with a touch of loftiness.

His companion grinned.

" What are you laughing at, James ? " the red and yellow
kilt demanded.

" I was not laughing, Alan. I was thinking to myself."

Carrie did not want the peace of Glenbristle disturbed by
a brawl, and she said quickly that Gaelic was a very difficult
language.

" I thought at first it was because I was American," she
went on. " But it seems to me just as difficult for English
people."

" I'm not English," said the red and yellow kilt hotly, his
shock of light-brown hair billowing with indignation at the
disgraceful slur.

" Well, I'm not really American," Carrie said soothingly.
" I'm a Canadian Scot married to an American. Royde is
my name. But I was a Macdonald," she added proudly.

" My name's Alan Macmillan, and this is my friend James
Buchanan."

" I'm so very pleased to meet you both. Are you staying
near here ? "

" We're camping further up the glen," said Macmillan.

" Oh, you're camping, are you ? I suppose you didn't
see the notice-board ? " Carrie asked.

" We saw the notice-board right enough," Buchanan said.
" That's *why* we are camping in Glenbristle."

" We don't recognize the right of lairds like Ben Nevis who
have stolen the land from their clansmen to treat it as their
own private property," Macmillan explained.

" Why is Glenbristle a wilderness ? " Buchanan asked in
his best Glasgow University Union manner. " I'll tell you
why. It's because the grandfather and great-grandfather
of the present owner cleared out the crofters and drove them
to Canada."

" It's strange you should say that," Carrie Royde remarked pensively. " You see those stones and nettles over
there ? "

" They show that there was a cottage here once,"
Buchanan said.

" There certainly was," Carrie declared impressively.
" The cottage of my great-great-grandfather who was
evicted from Glenbristle in the first clearance."

" That's interesting," Alan Macmillan commented.

" It is very very interesting," Mrs Chester Royde Jr. agreed emphatically.

" How do you know this was where your great-great-grandfather lived ? " James Buchanan asked,

Carrie would have liked to say that the site had been revealed to her in a dream by the spirit of an ancestor, and if Alan Macmillan had been alone she might have succumbed to the temptation; but she felt that James Buchanan's bullet-head was too hard for such a tale, and instead attributed her knowledge of the evicted crofter's site to family tradition.

" I used to dream about Glenbristle when I was a little girl living on the shores of Lake Ontario. Once upon a time in a peach-orchard I saw . . .," she hesitated. It was a pity that a man privileged to wear that Joseph's coat of a tartan should be so evidently drab in his point of view about existence. Alan Macmillan might easily have seen the fairies himself, but of course he would never admit it in front of his prosaic friend.

" Are you camping round here ? " Buchanan asked her.

" No; I'm staying at Glenbogle Castle."

The two young men stiffened.

" Oh, please don't look so ferocious, both of you. If you knew Ben Nevis you'd think him most terribly kind."

" We're not likely to have the honour of making his acquaintance," said Alan Macmillan proudly.

" I wouldn't make it if we had," Buchanan avowed. " It's men like MacDonald of Ben Nevis who've brought Scotland to the position it's in to-day."

" But surely Scotland is in a perfectly wonderful position," the returned exile ejaculated.

" Practically dead," Buchanan declared firmly.

" But that's not at all what we Canadians think. We think Scotland is the moving spirit of the British Empire."

The two young men shook their heads compassionately.

" That's a sublimation of the libido," Alan Macmillan asserted. " Canadian Scots being mostly descendants of evicted Gaels long to score off their oppressors, and they sublimate this longing by being more imperialist than the imperialists who first exploited them a hundred years ago. I'm afraid James is right. Scotland is practically dead."

" That's very discouraging news to hear on coming back

to the land of one's forefathers. It certainly is. But why
do you blame a nice man like Ben Nevis ? "

"You needn't look beyond these empty glens for the
answer to that one," said Buchanan.

" Can't anything be done about it ? " Carrie asked.

" We are doing our best," he told her.

" Who are you ? " she asked, piqued by the slight suggestion of portentousness in the emphasis on the first person
plural.

The two young men looked at one another, each with a
question in his eyes. Both almost imperceptibly shook their
heads.

" It's a society we belong to," said Alan Macmillan,
after an awkward pause. He was upset by the thought that
this pleasant red-haired Canadian should be fancying he
and James distrusted her.

" A secret society," James Buchanan added quickly.

" Isn't that thrilling ? " Carrie exclaimed. " I do wish
you'd tell me more about it."

" I'm afraid we can't very well," Alan Macmillan said
apologetically. " You see, it's a political secret society.
Look here, would you like to come up the glen to our camp ?
It's about a mile from here. We can give you some tea."

" Why, I'd love a cup of tea. Aren't you an angel
child ? "

Buchanan's dark eyebrows beetled in his bullet head.
He did not trust Alan Macmillan's imperviousness to feminine wiles. However, if she thought she was going to be able
to secure a tête-à-tête with Alan by pleading the view from
up there as an excuse she was mistaken.

" Well, I must say I never expected to find two Highland
beaux in Glenbristle," Carrie said, when she and the two
young men were walking up the glen toward their camp.
And to herself she added the reflection that only in dreams
had she ventured to hope she should behold anything so
attractive as Alan Macmillan with his fair wavy hair and his
melting blue eyes and clear-cut rose-browned features.

" What a gay tartan the Macmillan is," she exclaimed.
" It makes my Ben Nevis MacDonald look quite dingy.
My husband would go crazy about that. He just worships
colour."

" Is your husband staying at Glenbogle Castle ? " Alan
asked.

" Yes, he's away up on the moors to-day shooting grouse with our host."

Had Carrie but known it, this was the very moment when on the braes of Strathdiddle Ben Nevis had just silenced the crooner with the contents of both barrels.

" The Twelfth of August, eh ? " James Buchanan growled. " That's all these lairds think about. Shooting stags and grouse and salmon . . ."

" You don't shoot salmon, James," said his friend, a little irritably. He was inclined to deplore James's manners in criticizing lairds like this when the guest of the one on whose land they were camping was their guest.

" Salmon fishing I was going to say if you hadn't chipped in so smartly," James Buchanan snapped.

" And your tartan is even more gay than Mr Mac-millan's," Carrie interposed. " It has every colour imaginable in it."

" Too many, I think," said Alan.

" Not one too many," James declared passionately. " Just because the Macmillans can't think beyond two colours that doesn't say the Buchanans are to be bound by *them*. We let you have your red and yellow and kept a few of our own besides."

" A few! " Alan exclaimed. " You have the whole spectrum."

" Look here, Alan Macmillan, I'd be glad to hear the reasons on which you base your right to sneer at the Buchanan tartan."

" I was not sneering at it. I simply said I thought it was too polychromatic."

" Alan, you're awful fond of trying to skate out of rash statements on long words. But that won't work with me. You sneered at the Buchanan tartan. I want to know why."

" I was not sneering. I merely expressed my personal preference for fewer colours."

" So our clan tartans are all to be re-designed to fit in with your private taste in colours. Well, that's a good one, right enough. Gosh! You really are the limit, Alan."

Carrie felt it was time to intervene again.

" I'm sure Mr Macmillan would never think of changing that very lovely tartan of yours, Mr Buchanan."

" He'd better try," James muttered.

" Personally, I think they're both beautiful tartans.
And, as I said just now, they make my own Ben Nevis
MacDonald look quite drab.   But I wish you'd tell me some
more about this terrible condition of Scotland, because I
assure you I do feel so distressed about it."

For the rest of the way to the camp James Buchanan
rattled off statistics, a confusing business always but rendered
more confusing in his case by the indistinctness of his
enunciation.

" So I think you'll admit, Mistress Royde, that I was not
exaggerating when I said a while back that Scotland was
practically dead," he concluded.

Carrie came back to consciousness with a start.

" Indeed you certainly did not, Mr. Buchanan.   But I
feel they ought to know all that in Canada . . . why, there
are your tents I do declare.   Aren't they cute ? . . . Yes,
I think you and Mr Macmillan ought to come over to
Canada and explain about the state of affairs in Scotland.
I'm sure you'd have a most sympathetic audience.   And I
could give you letters of introduction to so many people
who would be helpful."

James Buchanan began to consider Mrs Chester Royde
from a new angle.   A visit to Canada with letters of intro-
duction to the right people might lead to a good opening
in business.

" I'm much obliged to you, Mistress Royde.   I'll certainly think seriously about your offer."

By now they had reached a grassy level at the foot of a
steep rocky escarpment in the shelter of which were pitched
the low green tents of her hosts.

" I feel I'm being entertained by two Jacobite fugitives,"
Carrie declared, with a sigh of gratified romance.

" They wouldn't have been able to offer you tea," Alan
Macmillan reminded her.

" No, that's true.   And I just can't tell you how much
I'm looking forward to a cup of tea."

Nor was Carrie disappointed by that cup of tea brewed
with water from a near-by stream.   It seemed the most
delicious cup of tea she had ever drunk and afterwards
when she sat smoking in the mellow afternoon sunshine, her
back supported by a ledge of warm granite, she was confirmed in her belief that this glen welcomed her as a child of
its own.

" I wish you two boys would tell me more about yourselves," she said. " And more about what you're going to do for Scotland. I can't help feeling I was brought to Glenbristle to-day for some purpose. I am aware of a most mysterious sort of psychic atmosphere all around me. I couldn't hope to put it into words, because of course if the atmosphere really is psychic you just can't put it into words. Yes, it's a very strange sensation. If I were a poet I would want to write a wonderful poem right now."

" You'd better get Alan to write one for you," said James Buchanan. " He's a poet."

" He is? Why, Alan, isn't that . . . oh dear, I hope you don't mind my calling you Alan ? "

" Not at all," Alan replied, scowling through a rich blush because he noticed what he fancied was a slightly derisive expression in James Buchanan's eyes.

" And what are you, Mr James ? Are you a poet too ? "

" No, I'm a lawyer," said James Buchanan in the voice of a future Lord Justice Clerk.

" Ah, that's why you're so good at figures," Carrie observed brightly. And she turned round to gaze reverently at the bard. " I suppose your poetry is full of Celtic mysticism ? "

" I hope not," said the bard distastefully, who from what he and the young poets of the Scottish Renaissance believed was the sunny summit of Parnassus had been hurling savage epigrams at the Celtic twilight since his first term at Glasgow University.

" You hope not ? " Carrie exclaimed in surprise. " But surely that's the great gift we Celts can offer the world to-day ? "

" If that's all we have to offer we won't get very far. What we have to teach the world is how to make the best of itself."

" But isn't that a mystical message of spiritual hope ? "

" Not at all," the bard replied, with a hint of petulance. " We have to teach the world how to make the best *practical* use of itself."

" Ay, that's what the world has to learn," James Buchanan agreed. " And that's what a free Scotland could teach it."

" Well, I must say you both puzzle me. I thought your idea for a free Scotland was to restore the spirit of the past and so set an example to the world of to-day. Surely spiritual values are what we all so badly need ? "

" We don't object to spiritual values *quâ se*," said the bard.
" But we have realized the danger of putting thought
before action. Therefore although I write a good deal of
poetry I know that what I call poetic action is the only
poetry really worth while. For instance I consider that
when James and myself camp here in Glenbristle in defiance
of a notice-board forbidding camping that is more truly
poetry than for me to write verse about deserted glens and
lone shielings in the misty islands. That's just stale emo-
tionalism. James and I are strictly practical people."

" In every way," James agreed.

" We told you about our secret society," Alan went on.

" You didn't tell me very much about it," Carrie put in
reproachfully.

" That's another example of poetic action," the bard
insisted. " It's an extremely practical society."

" Well, of course I can't pass an opinion about that,"
Carrie said, " because I don't know what your aims are
except what Mr James told me about statistics. I know
you want to change all those statistics."

The bard looked at the lawyer.

" I think we might tell Mistress Royde a few of our ideas,
for instance that one about kidnapping MacDonald of Ben
Nevis. Obviously we can't do that now because it would
involve her."

" You weren't going to kidnap Ben Nevis ? " Carrie
gasped.

" Only as part of a general campaign for kidnapping
lairds," the bard explained. " But don't worry, Mistress
Royde. There are plenty of others. We'll leave Ben Nevis
out of the general campaign, at any rate for this year."

" I'm afraid you'll think me terribly dense," said Carrie.
" But I wish you'd explain just exactly what would be the
practical value of kidnapping lairds."

" The creation of a state of uneasiness among the landed
class," James informed her. " The same with the rich
business men. We aim to kidnap quite a few of them.
Trades-union leaders too. Ministers. Sheriffs. Schoolmasters.
The Editor of the *Glasgow Herald*. The Editor of the
Scotsman. The general idea is to shake up complacency."

" Take a man like MacDonald of Ben Nevis," Alan urged.
" He's a friend of yours. But you must see how fatal that

kind of stodgy comfortable existence is to any display of
national energy. A man like that could do so much to give
a lead to the country. But what does he do? Shoots,
stalks, fishes, forbids camping on his land and thinks he has
fulfilled his political duty if he votes against a measure of
reform which will put a halfpenny on the Inverness-shire
rates. We're not going to kidnap him. I give you my
word about that. But think how much being kidnapped
would widen the point of view of a landed proprietor like
that. Men of his type require mental shocks imaginatively
applied. They move in a rut."

"The whole country's moving in a rut," said James
solemnly. "And the whole country's got to be jolted out
of it."

"By poetic action," the bard insisted, rising to his feet
and apparently ready to begin such action immediately.

"I'm so glad I chose to-day to visit Glenbristle," Carrie
said. "I'm still a little hazy about just what you *are* going
to do, but it's so wonderful to feel that something really is
going to be done. I feel more positive than ever that I was
guided to Glenbristle to-day by some higher power for a
purpose. Do you have women in your secret society?"

"We have women members, yes," James Buchanan
answered doubtfully.

"Well, won't you accept me as a member? I'd be so
happy to help you kidnap anybody except Ben Nevis. I
think I'd have to make him an exception because he has
been so intensely hospitable, and I should feel a little mean
about helping to kidnap him."

"Well, of course personally, Mistress Royde, I would
welcome you as a member," said James, who had not forgotten that promise of hers to give him introductions to the
right people in Canada. "But I think it'll have to be re-
ferred to the Inner Council."

"Of which James and I are both members," the bard
added encouragingly.

"I suppose you have an annual subscription?" Carrie
asked.

"We have voluntary donations," James replied. "The
trouble with annual subscriptions was that if a member got
in arrears with his we couldn't expel him. It's not like a
club or an ordinary society. Once you've admitted somebody to a secret society he knows too much. So we had to

substitute voluntary donations for a regular subscription."

" I hope you found that satisfactory," Carrie asked.

" Oh, it's not too bad. We've had to spend a good deal on paint, but there's still a small balance in hand."

" On paint ? "

" Imphm! Painting slogans in Gaelic and English on public buildings."

" I'm against that, James, don't forget," said the bard sternly. " It's pandering to words, and we can't afford to waste any energy on words."

" Well, whether I'm admitted to your secret society or not," said Carrie, " I'd like to make a voluntary donation right away. There's no rule against that, I hope."

" No, there's no rule against that," James Buchanan admitted.

Carrie took out her vanity bag, pressed a spring, and from behind the mirror produced a hundred-dollar bill, which she offered to James. He looked at it, and his eyes were suddenly glazed as though by a well-timed upper cut.

" Losh, Alan," he murmured, " we'll be able to . . ." He put a hand up to his brow as if to shut out the too dazzling prospect conjured by this hundred-dollar bill. Then he turned to Carrie. " But, look here, Mistress Royde, this is too much, at any rate before you're a member. We won't be able to convene the Inner Council before the end of next month at the earliest."

" Oh, dear! Why, I'll probably be back in America by then," Carrie sighed.

" I think we ought to take the responsibility of admitting Mistress Royde ourselves, James," said the bard.

" But we're not a quorum, Alan."

" This is a clear case for poetic action, in my opinion."

" If we even had a third," James Buchanan lamented.

" Well, we haven't," said Alan Macmillan. " And I'm positive this is a case for poetic action. If the rest of the Inner Council make a row about it I'll clear out of the S.B.A. and start another society."

" Look here, Alan, if Mistress Royde doesn't mind I'd like to talk the matter over with you alone," James suggested.

" Sure," said Carrie. " I'll walk back to where you found me by the ruins of my great-great-grandfather's cottage and you can come along and tell me what you've

decided." She smiled at the young men. " Somehow I
feel you'll discover a way."

Carrie's presentiment was right. She had hardly been
seated ten minutes on the knoll where she had fallen asleep
after lunch than the red and yellow of the Macmillan and
the rainbow of the Buchanan tartan came flashing down
Glenbristle's grass-grown rocky road.

" Well ? " she asked when the young men rejoined her.

" We're taking it upon ourselves to admit you to the
Scottish Brotherhood of Action," Alan Macmillan announced
gravely. " Will you please repeat the oath after me ? "

" I think that's a very wonderful oath," Carrie declared
when she had echoed the bard's words and been initiated
into the secret sign and countersign by which members of
the Brotherhood recognized one another. " Did you
compose that oath, Alan ? "

" Yes, I composed it, Mistress Royde," said the bard
modestly.

" I was positive you did. And listen, please don't call me
Mrs Royde when we're just ourselves among the Brotherhood. Please call me ' Carrie ' then. How long do you
expect to be camping in Glenbristle ? "

" We were planning to move on nearer to Fort William
to-morrow," said James. " I have to be back in Glasgow
by the end of the week."

" Isn't that too bad! And you, Alan ? "

" I'll find a place to camp by myself for a week. I want
to do some work."

" I believe you're going to write a poem," Carrie exclaimed.

The bard looked embarrassed. He felt such an admission
might sound feeble after his stern words about action.

" I'm going to revise some poems I've already written."

" Well, why don't you come back to Glenbristle when
James goes to Glasgow ? "

" Ach, you'd better stay where you are, Alan," said James,
who had been prepared for this development from long
experience of the bard's effect on women and their effect on
him. He had always found much to deplore in these
effects, but that voluntary donation had made for an unusual
tolerance. " I'll stay another night and catch the bus to
Fort William on Saturday."

" I think I ought to be going back to the Castle now," said

Carrie. "Will you both walk with me as far as Glen-bogle?"

The Brotherhood was temporarily dissolved where the mouldering signpost hinted at Glenbristle and the garish new notice-board proclaimed No CAMPING.

The two young men turned back along the rocky grass-grown road whence they had come. Mrs Chester Royde turned up Glenbogle in the direction of the Castle.

She had just entered the pine-darkened drive when she was passed by a lorry and saw to her astonishment that it was packed with young men and young women all shouting what sounded like abusive expressions at the tops of their voices.

" Ah, there you are, Mrs Royde," her host shouted when she came into the Great Hall covered with targes and Lochaber axes, old muskets and stags' heads and the por-traits of the kilted chieftains of Hector's race. " Have you heard about our bag?"

" No, did you have good sport?"

" Sixteen camping hikers. We've got the women locked up in the dungeon under the North Tower and the men, if you can call them men, safely stowed away in the dungeon under the Raven's Tower—the one we call Mac 'ic Eachainn's Cradle."

Carrie turned to her husband, who was standing in front of a welcome evening fire in the great hooded hearth, a whisky and soda in his hand.

" Chester, is this a joke?"

" Joke?" he echoed enthusiastically. " No joke at all. Finest day's sport I ever had. Carrie, this little old country of yours is some country. I'm crazy about the way they do things here."

And Ben Nevis, reflected Carrie, was the man whom the Scottish Brotherhood of Action wanted to shake out of a humdrum complacency and forcibly extricate from a rut.

Chapter 4

DINNER POSTPONED

IT was the Lady of Ben Nevis among his immediate
entourage who first ventured to question the wisdom of the
Chieftain's high-handed action, catching him at the moment
when he reached his dressing-room from the bath, herself
already dressed for dinner. He found her there in black
satin, a great catafalque occupying valuable space required
for his own toilet.

"What do you want, Trixie?" he asked, a touch of slightly
querulous apprehension in his tone which the consciousness
that he had nothing on beneath his flowered-silk dressing-
gown did not allow him to neutralize by a masterful gesture
of patriarchal authority.

"I want to have a little talk with you, Donald, before
dinner," the Lady of Ben Nevis boomed placidly. Dame
Clara Butt answering the diapason of the Albert Hall organ
was never more sure of herself. Mrs MacDonald's sway
over her husband was a miniature (though perhaps miniature
is an infelicitous word to use in her connection) of the sway
which England exerts over Scotland. Mrs MacDonald, to
put it shortly, had the money. Her father, a magnate of
English business, had invested a considerable amount in the
marriage of his only daughter to the Highland Chieftain,
and he had taken care to see that his money was not lost by
leaving a large sum in trust for her and her children after he
had presented his son-in-law with enough to put the estate in
order.

"Look at the time, Trixie," said her husband reproachfully. "And I have to shave as well as dress."

"You can get on with your shaving and dressing while we
have our little talk, Donald. You shouldn't have dallied so
long talking to Hugh Cameron."

Ben Nevis puffed out a sigh for feminine obstinacy and
began to strop his razor.

"You know what I want to talk about, Donald?"

"Haven't the ghost of a notion," he replied, with what
they both knew was but a feeble simulation of defiance.

"It's this business on the moors this afternoon."

45

"Oh, these hikers, you mean. Well, why are you worrying yourself about them?"

"I am worrying about them for many reasons, Donald, but chiefly on your account."

"There's nothing to worry about on my account, as I told Lindsay-Wolseley this afternoon," said Ben Nevis.

"Oh, Colonel Wolseley was worried, was he? I can't say I'm surprised, Donald. He's such a nice sensible man, and Mrs. Wolseley is a very nice sensible woman. And such a good gardener. Her primulas are always a joy. What did Colonel Wolseley say?"

"Talked a lot of nonsense. These fellows who've spent half their lives in India always do. I suppose the sun affects them."

"But what did he say, Donald?"

"I don't know exactly what he said, but he seemed to have some idea that my action wasn't legal. Well, if it isn't, all I've got to say is there's something very radically wrong with the law. Things have come to a pretty pass if bands of hikers can camp round notice-boards forbidding camping, and light fires on grouse-moors, and scare the birds, and sit listening to all this beastly jazz on the wireless in the middle of a landowner's preserves. I told Lindsay-Wolseley I was determined to give them a lesson and when I've made up my mind, Trixie, you know nothing will change it."

"Yes; that's why I thought it wiser for us to have this little talk. I'm sure you already realize you've been too hasty."

"I don't realize anything of the kind," the Chieftain contradicted loudly. "And I do wish you'd let me get on with my shaving. I'll be late for dinner, and you know what a point I make about punctuality. I've always tried to set an example. You have to in the West Highlands. We'd be starting dinner at midnight before we knew where we were if I didn't set an example."

"There's no need for you to be late, Donald. If you'll give me the keys of the dungeons I'll try to arrange matters."

The indignant swing round of the Chieftain's head at this request was too quick for the shaving-brush, which missed his cheek and profusely lathered the inside of his right ear.

"Arrange matters?" he fumed. "How are you proposing to arrange matters?"

" Why, I shall tell Mrs Parsall to give them supper, and
then they can be driven back to where they were camping
beside Loch Hoo. Duncan told me you'd given him orders to
throw all their camping outfit into the loch. But I said you'd
changed your mind and did not wish the tents disturbed."

Ben Nevis stared at his Lady. Had the lather in his ear
affected his hearing ?

" You countermanded orders I'd given to Duncan ? "

" Yes, dear, and now let me have the keys. I shall have
plenty of time to put matters right before dinner," she assured
him tranquilly.

" Look here, Trixie, when I rounded up these hikers I
didn't bring them to Glenbogle to be entertained. I brought
them here to show them that they can't play fast and loose
with a man like myself. They are going to remain in the
dungeons at any rate for to-night. I may release them to-
morrow with a warning. I shall decide about that to-
morrow. Royde thinks I ought to keep them shut up for at
least a week."

" What *does* Mr Royde know about such matters ? " Mrs
MacDonald asked, the bitter-sweetness of the oboe audible
for a moment in her tone. " I'm sure Hugh doesn't think
you ought to keep them here a week."

" Hugh agrees with me that the time has come for landowners to take a firm stand. Ever since the Lloyd George
Budget before the war we've allowed ourselves to be harried
and bullied and persecuted and robbed right and left. Hugh
agrees with me that a lead is required."

" If Hugh Cameron thinks any good will come of your
imprisoning hikers and campers on your own he certainly
should be on a lead." The oboe was reinforced by the
bassoon.

" I don't mean that kind of a lead, Trixie. I mean the
lead given by a leader."

" Nobody is fonder of Hugh than I am, but if he's going to
fill your head with all these extravagant ideas I shall not be
fond of him any longer." The deep rich diapason was again
flooding the Chieftain's dressing-room.

" Hugh is loyal, Trixie. He holds fast to the old loyalties.
Our ancestors stood back to back against the Macintoshes,
and we don't intend to be bullyragged by hikers. Lindsay-
Wolseley can't understand that kind of loyalty. He's a
Lowlander."

"And I am English, Donald, and I think there are occasions when common sense is more valuable in a friendship than loyalty."

"Now, look here, Trixie," he protested. "I must ask you not to sneer at the old clan loyalties. And do let me get on with my dressing."

"Very well, give me the keys and I'll leave you to yourself."

"I will not give you the keys. If you go and let those hikers out and offer them supper they'll think I'm afraid of them. Before I know where I am they'll be threatening me with an action for assault and false imprisonment and I don't know what not."

"Well," said the Lady of Ben Nevis with dignified firmness, "even if you keep the men of the party shut up I insist, Donald, I insist on your releasing the girls."

This was no Queen Philippa humbling herself in tears to beg the lives of the burghers of Calais from an angry monarch. This was a woman who had frequently had her own way before and was determined to have it again.

"Girls!" Ben Nevis scoffed. "I don't call a lot of unsexed young females in corduroy shorts girls. To be shut up in a dungeon for a bit without any jazz is just what they require."

"The dungeon under the North Tower is no place for girls to spend the night in, Donald, however scantily they may be clothed. There's no kind of accommodation."

"The decencies of a civilized existence are wasted on women like that," Ben Nevis declared. "They fought like wild cats. One of them went for me with her stick. And Catriona and Mary set about them."

"I have already spoken to Catriona and Mary and expressed my surprise at their allowing themselves to be mixed up in such a disgraceful brawl," Mrs MacDonald boomed.

"Disgraceful brawl?"

"Disgraceful brawl, Donald," his wife boomed on a steady note.

"A short scuffle in the heather with sixteen male and female hikers is not a disgraceful brawl."

"That is what people will call it, especially when they hear you encouraged your own daughters to take part in it. Now please give me the keys and I shall endeavour to undo a little of the harm you have done."

" I should be much obliged if you would have the goodness to allow me to finish my dressing first," said the Chieftain, grasping at haughtiness but landing in pomposity.

" I am not going to move from here, Donald, until you
give me the key of the dungeon in which these girls have
been shut up. I presume you will not attempt to use force
with me."

Mac 'ic Eachainn looked at his wife. Her eyes were
steady as an owl's. He hesitated. Then he produced from
the pocket of his dressing-gown a bunch of very large keys.

" If you're going to let the women out you may as well
let the men out too," he said sulkily. His wife rose with a
sigh of relief. " But you are not to offer them supper," he
added. " I refuse to have them fed. You hear that,
Trixie ? "

" I shall certainly offer them supper, Donald. And I
shall be extremely relieved in my mind if they accept the
invitation, for in that case we might hope they would be
willing to consider the incident closed."

" *They* would be willing ? " Ben Nevis exploded. " Let
them think themselves lucky that I don't keep them locked
up for a week on bread and water as I'd intended."

" Donald! " his wife boomed.

" What is it now ? "

" Don't be childish. It detracts from your dignity."

With this the Lady of Ben Nevis swept from her lord's
dressing-room, and retired to her own stronghold, which
was still known as the Yellow Drawing-room, though it
had not been either yellow or a drawing-room since twenty-
five years ago Hector, the Twenty-second of Ben Nevis,
died and was succeeded by the present Chieftain, who was
the second son, his elder brother Hector having died in
boyhood. Mrs MacDonald had devoted herself loyally
to the customs of her adopted country from the moment
her dowry had enabled Ben Nevis to put his castle and his
land in order, but she had felt the need of having at least
one room in the castle that apart from the view from the
windows of the Three Sisters of Glenbogle might have been
a room in the Grosvenor Square house of her father. She
had seen that her proposal to substitute for the carpet and
curtains of the bridal chamber a softer design and more
becoming colour than the Ben Nevis MacDonald tartan
had wounded Donald, and she had abandoned the notion

at once. She would have liked to strip from the walls their
frieze of substantial Victorian wallpaper depicting stags in
every attitude a stag can put itself into, and when the
attitudes were exhausted no less than eight sets of stags
repeating the same set of attitudes all round the room.
There were moments when the steel-engravings of Mac-
Donalds overwhelming Macintoshes in battle palled upon
her and when views in water-colour of the Three Sisters of
Glenbogle, with that perpetual view of them from the
windows, seemed superfluous. However, she always recognized that they were dear to the heart of the chieftain she
had married and she had never complained. Only to the
Yellow Drawing-room had she left nothing except its name,
and of its chintzy privacy made for herself a refuge that was
for ever England.

Mrs MacDonald laid the keys of the dungeon door upon
a small table which shivered under the impact and when a
kilted gillie that was the equivalent of a footman answered
her bell she bade him send Toker to her.

The butler was not kilted. He was as English as his
mistress.

"Toker, tell Mrs Parsall I wish to speak to her. And,
Toker," she added as he neared the door, "dinner must be
postponed until half-past eight."

Not even Toker's impassivity was proof against the slight
tremor that shook him, so slight that only the most delicate
seismograph would have registered it, but still a perceptible
tremor.

"Until half-past eight, madam," he repeated in case his
ears had deceived him.

"Yes, and tell Mr Fletcher I should like to speak to him
when he comes down."

"Mr Fletcher is now in the Great Hall, madam."

"Is Duncan still here?"

"Mr MacDonald is in Mrs Parsall's room, madam."

"Tell him to come with Mrs Parsall."

"Very good, madam. Pardon me, madam, but is Ben
Nevis aware that dinner has been postponed until half-past
eight?"

"No; you had better tell him at once."

This time a definitely sharp tremour ran through Toker's
solid shape.

"I will inform Ben Nevis, madam," he said gloomily.

The Reverend Ninian Fletcher was a venerable clergyman who for the last twelve years had been the private chaplain at the Castle, an unexacting spiritual task to which had been added the somewhat more exacting mental task of coaching the sons of Ben Nevis in their holidays.

" Ah, Mr Fletcher, I'm so sorry to disturb you," said Mrs MacDonald when he came into her room. " But I need your help."

" It is always at your service," said the old Episcopalian divine.

" You have heard about these hikers whom Donald has shut up in the dungeons ? "

" I have indeed. May I say that I was a little startled by the news ? "

" You couldn't have been more startled by it than I was, Mr Fletcher. However, I am glad to say Donald at once realized that his original plan to keep them shut up for a week on bread and water was not feasible."

" Dear me, was that his original plan ? "

" It was. However, he has now entrusted their release to me."

" A very wise move, I venture to think."

" Yes, if it is not too late."

" Too late ? "

" To bring the matter to a pleasant conclusion," Mrs MacDonald explained. " Obviously, if these people desire to make themselves unpleasant, Ben Nevis has given them the opportunity. I understand Colonel Lindsay-Wolseley pointed out to my husband that he was exposing himself to all kinds of unpleasantness in the way of actions for damages, but he was in one of his headstrong moods and refused to listen to Colonel Wolseley's advice."

Mr Fletcher shook his venerable head.

" I gather that Kilwhillie encouraged him," Mrs Mac-Donald went on.

" Dear me, I'm sorry to hear that."

" Yes, it was extremely selfish of Kilwhillie. As you know, Mr Fletcher, nobody is more grateful than I am to Hugh Cameron for his devotion to Donald, but on this occasion I think he made his devotion an excuse to indulge his own Highland intolerance. However, that's beside the point at the moment. Where I want your help is in trying to persuade these people to take the business in good part.

I have the keys of the dungeons, but I do not want to unlock the prisoners myself because I do not want to give the impression that there has been the slightest disagreement between myself and Donald. Therefore I am enlisting your help, Mr Fletcher. I want you to do the actual unlocking, or rather as I know the locks are very stiff I'll tell Duncan to do the actual unlocking, but I want you to let the prisoners know that they are free. I'm arranging with Mrs Parsall to give them supper in the old dining-hall, and afterwards the lorry can take them back to the nearest point in the road to their camp."

" But suppose they refuse to accept your hospitality, Mrs MacDonald ? If they are bent on some form of retaliatory action in the shape of a lawsuit against Ben Nevis they might consider it prejudicial to their case to eat, drink and make merry with an enemy."

" That is exactly what I fear may happen, and I am relying on your ability to put before them the Christian point of view. I won't venture to suggest what line you take. You will know far better than myself how to present that side. You've always been so tactful about religion and never rammed it down the children's throats ever since you came to live at Glenbogle. I do feel that you are the only person who can hope to adjust this unfortunate affair."

The chaplain looked a little doubtful.

" I must confess I'm not as confident as I should wish to be of influencing this motley gathering. I fear that all this hiking is closely bound up with the new paganism which is such a distressing feature of contemporary life. The clergyman *quâ* clergyman merely represents to these young people an old-fashioned person wearing too many stuffy clothes. Some of my fellow-clergy have tried to keep pace with modernity by holding special hikers' services at convenient hours. The vicar of a church on the outskirts of London went so far as to conduct a breezy little service every Sunday at a convenient hour in a surplice and black corduroy shorts. He received for a while some publicity in the popular Press as the Hikers' Parson, but I should surmise any success he may have attained owed more to the itch of curiosity than the urge of religion."

" Oh, I was not suggesting for one moment, Mr Fletcher, that you should try to ram religion down their throats. No, no. As I was trying to explain just now, I'm sure you

can rouse their better feelings without the very slightest
suggestion of religion. I do feel, however, that even hikers
will pay some respect to a clergyman. I don't know if you
heard what they were shouting when the lorry drove up
with them to the Castle."

" I heard only a confused noise."

" Well, I heard what they were calling Donald, and I
must say it was very unpleasant and uncomfortable and not
a little alarming. By this time after nearly a couple of hours
in these dark, damp, grubby dungeons their temper is
bound to be even worse, and I feel sure they would be exasperated by the sight of anybody except perhaps a clergyman.
I feel a little guilty in leaving you to tackle them without me,
but you do understand, don't you, my dread of creating the
least suspicion of any difference of opinion between myself
and Donald ? "

" Perfectly. Well, I'll do my best to adjust matters in
the dungeons."

At this moment Mrs Parsall the housekeeper came in with
Duncan.

" Duncan," Mrs MacDonald said, " Ben Nevis has decided to release the hikers."

" I'm very glad, my lady. They'll be more trouble than
they're worth, locked up here. It was very annoying the
way they spoilt the afternoon on us. But they're after being
given a good lesson and I don't think we will be troubled
with them again."

" I hope we shan't indeed," said Mrs MacDonald without
any warmth of conviction. " And now, Mrs Parsall, I'm
afraid I shall have to give you the trouble of arranging for
the prisoners to have supper before they go off in the lorry."

" Very good, ma'am. I shall make the necessary arrangements. Excuse me, ma'am, but Mr Toker was not mistook
in giving orders for dinner to be kept back till half-past
eight ? "

" No; I wanted to give Mr Fletcher plenty of time. You
will go down to the dungeons, Duncan, with Mr Fletcher,
who wishes to say a few words to the prisoners. And after
they have had supper you will see that the lorry puts them
down at the nearest point to where they are camping."

" Oh, well, well, he's a very fine gentleman right enough
is Ben Nevis," said the old head-keeper. " There's few
gentlemen would be served as he was served to-day over

Drumcockie and then turn round and treat the culprits like lords. Och, it's wonderful, right enough. A very noble godly gentleman."

As his ancient henchman followed Mr Fletcher toward the dungeons, the noble and godly gentleman himself was being told by his butler in the very middle of the delicate operation of tying his lace jabot that dinner would not be served until half-past eight. The effect of the rush of blood to the head provoked by this announcement was intensified by the fact that under the shock of the news he pulled the knot of the jabot much too tight. The indignant bellow was stifled in his throat and petered out in a low gurgle.

" Can I be of any assistance, sir ? " Toker enquired solicitously.

The Chieftain managed to loosen the knot and breathe again.

" Did you say dinner would not be served until half-past eight ? "

" By Mrs MacDonald's orders, sir," Toker made haste to add hastily. His master glared at him.

" What are you jigging about like that for, you ninny ? "

" I beg pardon, sir. The action was not deliberate. Is there anything I can get you, sir ? "

" Yes, you can get out."

The Chieftain spent some minutes composing his nerves after the shock administered to them by Toker's news about the postponement of dinner for a quarter of an hour by debating with himself which of his doublets he should wear this evening. In the end he chose a tartan one buttoned to the neck with eagles' heads of silver. He looked at himself in the glass. Serenity once more enfolded him as he left his dressing-room and descended to the Great Hall. Outside the massive doors his piper Angus MacQuat stepped forward to ask if there was any special tune he would like this evening.

" No, I leave it to you, Angus."

" I was thinking if perhaps you would like *Mac 'ic Eachainn's March Against Moy*."

" Ah, to celebrate our little scuffle in the heather this afternoon ? "

" That was my idea, Ben Nevis."

" Well, Angus, I don't think it's quite fair to put even Macintoshes on a level with hikers."

" No, perhaps it is a little strong, Ben Nevis."

" I really think it is, Angus. You'd better give us some Jacobite tunes to-night. Mrs Royde is a very keen Jacobite."

" Very good, Ben Nevis. To-morrow night I will be playing my new pibroch."

" Ah, what's that called ? "

" The Braes of Strathdiddle."

" In celebration of our little scuffle in the heather, eh ? "

" That is so, Ben Nevis."

" Capital, Angus. I shall look forward to that. You missed a grand afternoon."

The Chieftain passed on into the Great Hall, and barked at his assembled guests like an immensely friendly dog.

" Ah, there you all are! Dinner's not till half-past. I had to postpone it to give Mr Fletcher a chance to finish a reprimand he is giving to the hikers on my behalf. I'm setting them free after that. They've had their lesson."

Chapter 5

THE DUNGEONS

"WELL, I call this properly chronic, Ethel."
"You're right. It *is* chronic."
"It's worse than chronic. It's shocking."
"It's bloody awful."
"What language, Elsie!"
"Leave her alone, Mabel. It's nothing to what I'll say in a minute if they don't let us out of this dark hole. So it is bloody awful. Elsie's right."

A shriek rang out.

"Oh, my god, girls, there's something walking up the inside of my leg."

Seven shrieks of sympathy shrilled through the murk of the dungeon.

"What are *you* all screaming about? It isn't walking up you, is it?"

Seven shrieks shrilled again.

"Strike a match, one of you. Oh, my god, it's biting my behind now. Oh, whatever is it? Strike a match, I say."

Trembling fingers fumbled in the pockets of shorts. By the light of two matches simultaneously struck the young woman with fat legs who had asked Ben Nevis to stand still while she focussed her camera was revealed with her green corduroy shorts round her ankles.

"Look what it is, somebody," she adjured, wringing her hands.

A young woman with the thin nose of the born investigator inspected the posterior condition of the appellant and declared it must have been her imagination. There was no sign of snake or toad or rat or bat or beetle or mouse.

At this last word another young woman released a shuddering wail which would have made a banshee jealous. The young woman with the thin nose, startled by the sound, threw away the lighted match, which rested for a moment on the behind of the young woman who had thought something was biting her and who now by a scream comparable to the whistle of an express proclaimed her conviction that she had been right.

And that of course set off all the other young women screaming again at one another like sopranos trying to annihilate contraltos in a Mendelssohn oratorio.

It was at this moment that the chaplain and the gamekeeper reached the iron-studded oaken door of the dungeon beneath the North Tower.

" Look at that now," said Duncan. " They were singing songs before and now they are screaming. What a lesson to human vanity! What a lesson, Mr Fletcher! "

" We mustn't be too ready to note the effect of human vanity in others, Duncan, in case we fail to detect the effect of it in ourselves."

This rebuke from Mr Fletcher was inspired partly by the pleasure which he as an Episcopalian clergyman took in putting a Presbyterian elder in his place, partly by his having slipped on one of the damp stones in the passage that led to the dungeon and turned his ankle rather painfully.

" Ay, ay, that's very true, Mr Fletcher. Yes, yes, indeed. We are all as creeping things in the sight of the Lord."

" I hope those unhappy young women have not been driven mad by terror," said the chaplain, who was distressed by the sounds on the other side of the door.

Duncan banged on it with the bunch of keys.

" Keep quiet in there unless you want to stay there," he shouted sternly.

The screaming stopped.

" Oh, my god, girls, it's a man," cried the young woman who thought she had been bitten. " Don't let him in till I'm presentable."

She had just zipped up her shorts when the great lock turned to admit the chaplain and the gamekeeper, the latter carrying a stable-lantern the beams of which illuminated the group of eight young women, but made the vaulted glooms beyond seem more profound.

Mr Fletcher had time to utter only the word ' ladies ' when by far the most piercing shriek yet emitted came from the lips of the young woman who thought she had been bitten as with a frantic gesture of horror she unzipped her shorts again. A second later a mouse leapt for freedom. Poor Winifred Gosnay, who was an assistant in one of the great London stores, had not let down her shorts for nothing. Something *had* been walking up the inside of her leg.

Something *may* have bitten her behind. And that something
actually *was* a mouse.

" Come along, ladies," said the chaplain in soothing
accents. " You will soon be in more comfortable quarters
if you follow me."

In all his ordained life Mr Fletcher had never been so
supremely the shepherd of his flock as when he shepherded a
titubation of young women to the great dining-hall of Glenbogle Castle that August evening.

" Supper is being prepared for you, and after supper it
has been arranged to drive you back as near as possible to
your camp, with the proviso that you will move from the
land of MacDonald of Ben Nevis at the earliest possible
moment to-morrow. Is that understood ? "

The female hikers muttered what sounded like an affirmative, but they were still too much shaken by the memory of
that mouse leaping into the lantern-light from Winifred
Gosnay's unzipped shorts to express anything except
reminiscent shudders.

" I am now going to fetch the gentlemen of your party,"
Mr Fletcher went on. " Ah, here is Mrs Parsall the house-
keeper. Mrs Parsall, these are the young ladies whom Ben
Nevis has invited to supper."

Mrs Parsall eyed them coldly. She and Mrs Ablewhite
the cook had long ago made up their minds what they would
give these shameless half-naked hussies. And it was not
supper.

The dungeon beneath the Raven's Tower was a more
formidable place of detention than the dungeon under the
North Tower. Originally the only access to it was by a
trapdoor in the floor of what had been the guardroom of the
keep. Down this the victims of MacDonald ferocity had
been dropped into what was really a large pit, the sloping
walls of which left a comparatively small level space at the
bottom and thus inspired the name of Mac 'ic Eachainn's
Cradle. Such air and light as reached the dungeon came
through a few loopholes above the massive sloping walls.
At the end of the eighteenth century when the power of the
chiefs had been broken and they had degenerated into mere
landowners an entrance had been constructed to the Cradle
from the stable-yard and it had served for many years as an
outhouse, accumulating rubbish all the time. It was the
present laird who when putting his estate in order with his

wife's dowry cleared out the Cradle, gave it an iron-studded oaken door two inches thick, and entertained his guests with tales of MacDonald prowess, which it would seem had kept Mac 'ic Eachainn's Cradle as full of Macintoshes as a larder of game.

"You'd better put on a coat and hat, Mr Fletcher," the old gamekeeper advised. "There's a chill in the night air. Run, Alec, and bring Mr Fletcher's coat and hat," he told a gillie who was standing by one of the doors at the back of the Castle.

"Oh, we only have to cross the stable-yard," said the chaplain. "Come along, Duncan. We can bring them in this way to the dining-hall."

"If they'll come quietly," said Duncan.

"Why should they not? The girls came quietly enough."

"Listen to that, Mr Fletcher."

Across the yard reverberated a muffled thudding sound.

"What is it?" the chaplain asked. "It sounds like somebody chopping wood."

"It will be the hikers banging on the Cradle door," Duncan replied. "Och, they did not like it at all when we pushed them into the Cradle. Oh, indeed, no, not at all. They were threatening what they would do when they got out."

"You're not anticipating trouble are you, Duncan?"

"I'm not anticipating it, but I think we will have trouble with them. They're very fierce, these London people. Wild savage people they are. We had quite a big business to get them into the Cradle."

"Oh, I think they'll have cooled down by now," said the chaplain.

"They don't sound very cool at all. They sound very hot. Ah, here's Alec with your hat and coat. You'd better put them on, Mr Fletcher."

The chaplain surrendered to Duncan's solicitude and they crossed the yard together to the Raven's Tower.

"Did you have a great deal of difficulty in persuading them to go into the dungeon?" the chaplain asked.

"We didn't persuade them at all, Mr Fletcher. We just pushed them in and locked the door upon them. Any kind of persuading would have been wasted upon such trash."

They had reached the door of Mac 'ic Eachainn's Cradle by now.

" You'd better knock on the door with the keys, Duncan. I'll never make myself heard above this banging."

Duncan did so. The banging stopped.

" I am speaking on behalf of MacDonald of Ben Nevis," the chaplain began; but no sooner did the prisoners hear the name of their captor than the banging started again with thrice the vigour.

" We'll have to go inside and speak to them," he decided. " My voice is no longer strong enough, I'm afraid, to compete with such a noise. Will you unlock the door, Duncan ? "

The old keeper inserted the key and with what was an effort even for his strong fingers turned it.

Of what exactly happened then neither Mr Fletcher nor old Duncan was ever able to give a clear account. The result of whatever did happen was that the chaplain and the gamekeeper found themselves locked up in Mac 'ic Eachainn's Cradle and that the eight hikers were at large.

" Did you get a bang, Mr Fletcher ? "

" No, I didn't get a bang, but somebody butted me very heavily in the stomach and knocked my wind out."

" There you are. I wondered what kind of a queer noise you were making, but I thought it must be your prayers you were saying. They're very different from our prayers, these Episcopalian prayers. Quite another kind of worship altogether."

" Well, passing from the study of comparative religion to the position in which we find ourselves, what do we do now ? " Mr Fletcher asked a little irritably. Few men recovering their breath after being winded are able to combine sweetness with dignity. If they can sustain their dignity after making the idiotic noises winded people do make they are lucky.

" We'll just have to wait until they come and let us out again," Duncan replied.

" Who ? "

" The hikers."

" I'm afraid we'll have to wait a very long time before the hikers let us out. They made on me a strong impression of being out for revenge. I don't suppose they saw I was a clergyman."

" No, they did not see a thing. They just put their heads down and rushed at us like bulls. Oh, well, we'll just have to wait until somebody does come and let us out."

" If anybody knows we're here," said the chaplain gloomily. " And if anybody has the key."

" You're looking too much on the dark side of things, Mr Fletcher. When you don't come in for dinner Ben Nevis will send somebody to look for you."

" What good will that be if he hasn't a key to unlock the door ? I think we'll be very lucky indeed if we don't spend the night in this dungeon. Was your lantern broken ? "

The chaplain and the gamekeeper were standing at the top of the steps that led down into the dungeon from the outside door. Duncan struck a match, which lit up the bottom of the Cradle dimly enough, but sufficiently to show that his lantern was lying at the bottom of it.

" I'll go down and see if it can be lighted," he said. " Have you any matches, Mr Fletcher ? "

" No, I haven't any. Why ? Haven't you plenty ? "

" I have only two left. It's a great pity I didn't get another box. Wait you where you are, Mr Fletcher. I'll go down the steps." Presently he called up from below. " The glass is broken all to pieces, but there's a little oil left in it. There you are," he said when he had used one of his matches to light the wick of the lantern, which smoked a good deal but did at least banish the oppressive blackness of Mac 'ic Eachainn's Cradle.

" This really is not a suitable place in which to shut anybody up," said the chaplain. " I wonder where those hikers have gone ? "

It was at this moment that they rushed into the Great Hall just as Ben Nevis had noted that the long hand of the clock stood at a minute from half-past eight and was wondering what the deuce was keeping his chaplain now.

" Look here, what does this mean ? " demanded Mr Sydney Prew, any lack of impressiveness in his own prim voice being supplied by the snarls of the seven younger hikers which provided a menacing accompaniment.

The Chieftain drew himself up to his full height.

" It means that I have decided to release you and I hope the experience will be a lesson not to disturb my birds again, and not to light fires in my heather."

" And also," Mrs MacDonald put in, " that supper is waiting for you in the old dining-hall. Didn't Mr Fletcher make that clear ? "

The Secretary of the National Union of Hikers stepped

forward, held up his hand to quell the snarling of his seven companions, and thus addressed Ben Nevis:

" If you think, Mr MacDonald, that you can escape the consequences of your fascist behaviour . . ."

Yowls, boohs and hisses from his followers caused Mr Sydney Prew to raise his hand again.

" I repeat, Mr MacDonald, you cannot escape the consequences of the disgraceful assault you and your fascist . . ." Once again the word was too much for the feelings of the representatives of democracy. Their yowls, boohs and hisses were redoubled.

" Please, boys," said Mr Prew, turning round reproachfully, " please, please! I repeat, Mr MacDonald . . ."

" Well, don't," the Chieftain bellowed. " If you call me that any more I'll lock you up again."

" I repeat, you cannot escape the consequences of the assault you have committed by trying to bribe us with supper. What legal action some members of our party may wish to take against you I do not know, but speaking for the National Union of Hikers as a whole I warn you that we reserve to ourselves the right to take any such reprisals as the Governing Body may judge suitable. We are a great democratic body, Mr MacDonald, and we are not to be bullied out of collective security by fascist insolence."

At this the yowls, boohs and hisses of the hikers became so passionate that Chester Royde climbed upon a chair and took down a Lochaber axe from the wall.

" Am I to understand you are threatening me ? " the Chieftain demanded, that nose a Caesar might have envied stained with rich Tyrian.

" I am warning you, Mr MacDonald, that you have not heard the last of this," said Mr Prew. " And now where are the young ladies of our party ? "

" The ladies are at supper, Mr . . . I'm afraid I do not know your name," Mrs MacDonald boomed amiably.

" My name is Prew, madam. I am the Secretary of the National Union of Hikers."

" Well, Mr Prew, if you will follow me I will take you to the ladies. The lorry in which you arrived at the Castle is waiting to drive you back, as no doubt Mr Fletcher informed you."

" One of my rules, Mrs MacDonald, for I presume you are Mrs MacDonald, is never to be rude to a lady, and so you mustn't think me rude when I say that we must flatly decline to eat supper in your house and also to be driven back to our camp in the lorry. We prefer to walk."

" But you are not going to leave the ladies behind, are you ? Of course I shall be happy to put them up at Glenbogle, but . . ."

" Thank you, no. We will wait for the ladies outside. I am sorry to hear they have been persuaded into accepting supper, but that must not be taken to imply the slightest condonation of Mr MacDonald's behaviour."

" And what about my portable wireless ? " the owner of it called out. " Mr Prew can do what he likes, but I'm sueing you over that."

The future of the portable wireless was left in abeyance, for at that moment Toker flung open the doors of the Great Hall and announced that dinner was served. Almost simultaneously three pipers started off at full blast with the stirring march *Beinn Nibheis Gu Brath* by which from time immemorial the Lord of Ben Nevis had been piped in to dinner.

The hikers looked at one another in dismay. They thought it was a signal for violence of some kind. In a panic they rushed out of the Great Hall and along the corridor toward the front-door, carrying with them Toker as the Bogle in spate will carry upon its waters the broken branch of a pine. Luckily the table in the entrance hall on which the bonnets of the MacDonalds were always parked gave Toker something to which he could cling and thus escape being swept down the front-door steps and out into the courtyard of the Castle. In fact he was back in the dining-room in time to push in the great chair of his master, who took his seat at the head of the table when the pipes retired to avoid interrupting grace with the odd noises pipes make when a tune expires.

" Dash it, where *is* Mr Fletcher ? " the Chieftain asked when from his seat the chaplain did not rise to ask a blessing upon the food.

" Mr Fletcher is probably arranging matters in the old dining-hall," Mrs MacDonald boomed from her end of the table. " Won't you say grace yourself, Donald ? "

" Oh, very well. For what we are going to receive may the Lord make us truly thankful," he barked.

The pipers now came in again and began to march slowly

round the dining-room to the strains of *Will Ye No' Come Back Again?*, the first of the Jacobite airs Angus MacQuat had chosen for the delectation of Mrs Chester Royde.

"Fine old song, eh?" Ben Nevis said to his honoured guest who was sitting on his right.

"Oh, but of course, it's one of my very very favourite songs," Carrie declared fervently.

"Yes, I thought you'd like it. I expect he'll give us *Over the Sea to Skye* next."

Carrie's thoughts were in Glenbristle. Her host's treatment of the hikers had made her a little anxious for those two campers with whom she had spent so delightful an afternoon.

"Tell me, Ben Nevis," she asked, taking advantage of the pipers being at the end of the room for a moment or two, "what do you think of Scottish Nationalists?"

The tints of the dying dolphin at their most vivid and most varied would have seemed drab compared with the tints that displayed themselves upon the countenance of the Chieftain when he heard this question. The hats of cardinals, the shirts of Garibaldi's legionaries, the flags of the World Revolution, the ribbons of O.B.E.s, the plumes of flamingoes, the tails of redstarts, the breasts of robins, the skies that warn or delight shepherds according to the time, the tunics of grenadiers and the tape of the Civil Service mingled and melted, flamed and faltered, and flamed again in his cheeks.

"Scottish Nationalists? I regard Scottish Nationalists as worse than hikers. To me they hardly appear human. They should be stamped out like vermin. But what do *you* want to know about Scottish Nationalists?" he asked, suspicion suddenly dimming his choleric blue eyes.

"Why, I was reading somewhere the other day about their objects, and I wondered if you had interested yourself in the movement at all."

"Movement? Did you say movement, Mrs Royde? If you call foul subterranean squirming movement, well, I suppose you can call Scottish Nationalism movement. But it's not my idea of movement. I like something healthy and above ground."

Carrie became pensive. If Ben Nevis was capable of treating sixteen male and female hikers as he had, what was he capable of doing to these two members of the Scottish

Brotherhood of Action now camping in Glenbristle? She must warn them to-morrow. She ought to warn them to-night, but that was hardly feasible. She looked across the table at Myrtle, who was evidently not at all interested by Murdoch MacDonald's company next her. If she took Myrtle into her confidence . . . at that moment Ben Nevis gulped down the rest of his soup and turned to Myrtle.

" I'm sending a cable to my boy Hector to-morrow morning, urging him to get a spot of leave and fly home. I want you to meet him very much. The trouble is I'm not sure whether he's stationed at Tallulahgabad or Bundalpore. I know he expected to be moved from Tallulahgabad to Bundalpore pretty shortly. Do you think the Clanranalds will have moved to Bundalpore yet, Murdoch? "

" Don't know at all," said the naval Lieutenant.

" If you send it to Tallulahgabad they'll probably forward it on to Bundalpore, Dad," Iain suggested.

" That's a good idea of yours, Iain. What do you think of that, Murdoch? "

" I think it's quite sound," the naval Lieutenant allowed cautiously.

" I mean to say, it would be jolly to get old Hector back here for a little stalking, wouldn't it? Well, I'll cable to Tallulahgabad. You approve of that idea of Iain's, Myrtle? "

" Why, surely," said Myrtle, with what Carrie thought was too obvious a wink at herself.

" You think that's a good idea, Mrs Royde? "

" I think it's a terribly good idea, Ben Nevis. But what I don't think is at all a good idea is for you to call Myrtle Myrtle and me Mrs Royde. What has poor Carrie done? "

" That's very nice of you, Mrs . . . I mean, Carrie," said the Chieftain, gurgling benignly.

" I was afraid I'd offended you by asking about Scottish Nationalists."

" What are they? " Murdoch asked.

" Ghastly people," said Iain. " I saw two of them hiking up the glen the day before yesterday."

" You saw two Scottish Nationalists hiking up Glenbogle? " Ben Nevis gasped.

" Well, they were rigged up in reach-me-down kilts and had that awful earnest Highland look," said Iain. " Ghastly tartans too, neither of which ought to be allowed outside

5

a music-hall. I'm sure they were Scottish Nationalists."

"But they weren't proposing to camp in Glenbogle?" Ben Nevis pressed incredulously.

"Couldn't say," his youngest son replied. "But if they do, those tartans will scare every bird and stag in the neighbourhood. They'll scare the salmon back to the sea."

"Do you hear that, MacIsaac? You missed our little scuffle in the heather this afternoon. Here's a chance for you."

This remark was addressed by Ben Nevis to his Chamberlain, Major Norman MacIsaac, late of the 8th Service Battalion of The Duke of Clarence's Own Clanranald Highlanders (The Inverness-shire Greens). If the White Knight had worn a kilt instead of armour he would have looked much like Major Norman MacIsaac. And the Chamberlain of Ben Nevis had a similar gentle melancholy which most people attributed to the boisterous energy of the Chief he served, but which was his natural disposition. The Chamberlain, to say truth, had been delighted that urgent business in Fort William had kept him off the moors to-day and therefore relieved him of any responsibility in the matter of that little scuffle in the heather.

"You'd better give orders to keep a sharp look out for these two fellows," Ben Nevis continued. "And if they are Scottish Nationalists I'll teach 'em what real Scottish Nationalism means."

The savage guffaw with which the Chieftain adorned this threat seriously disturbed Carrie, who was convinced that the two kilted figures seen by Iain MacDonald were her fellow-members of the Scottish Brotherhood of Action. At all costs they must be warned somehow. The pipers were skirling *Over the Sea to Skye* now. It was an appropriate melody for the heroine's mood in which Carrie found herself.

When the pipers' music was finished and they had withdrawn from the dining-room, above what seemed the almost deathly quiet that succeeded, there was heard from the direction of the courtyard on which the windows of the dining-room faced a series of calls resembling the kind of noises made by Red Indians gathering to attack the logwood house of a settler.

"What the deuce is that?" Ben Nevis exclaimed, tossing his head like one of his own stags on Ben Booey challenging a rival on Ben Glass in the misty moonlight of October.

" Cooee! Cooee! Wolla-wolla-wolla-wolla! Oo-hoo! Oo-hoo! "

" That's mighty like the war-cry of the Carroways," said Chester Royde. " Well, perhaps the Carroway war-cry is more ' Oo-ha ' than ' Oo-hoo.' Still, it is mighty like it."

Toker eyed the guest of honour nervously. He had not yet perfectly recovered from that mad rush which had swept him helplessly along the corridor and but for the bonnet table would have swept him right out of the Castle altogether.

Mrs MacDonald reduced the mysterious sounds to the level of commonplace experience.

" It must be the hikers, Donald, getting their party together before they walk home. Now poor Mr Fletcher will be able to get his dinner."

" Oo-hoo! Oo-hoo! Gertie! Elsie! Winnie! "

" I never heard such vile sounds," Ben Nevis declared. " There you are, MacIsaac. That's the kind of noise these brutes must have been making on Drumcockie to scare the birds like that."

The Chamberlain eyed the Chieftain a little nervously. He had kept clear of this hikers' business by good luck, and he did not want to be involved in it now by being asked to go out and disperse the offenders. However, the next ' coo-ee ' was less loud, and presently a faint ' wolla-wolla-wolla-wolla ' floating back from far down the drive warranted the belief that at last the intruders were definitely bound for their camp.

A few more minutes passed.

" What *is* Mr Fletcher doing ? " Ben Nevis asked fretfully. " Doesn't he *want* any dinner ? "

" I do hope he didn't feel bound to eat the supper I arranged for those young women," Mrs MacDonald boomed anxiously. " The good man is so very conscientious. He may have felt that his kindly advice would be listened to more attentively if he joined in their cold meat and bread and cheese."

" I never heard such rank nonsense," Ben Nevis spluttered. " Rory, go and tell Mr Fletcher that we're at dinner."

The gillie retired and presently communicated the result of his errand to Toker.

The butler stepped forward.

" Mrs Parsall, sir, says Mr Fletcher did not return to the

dining-hall where the young persons were feeding. It would appear that he and Mr Macdonald busied themselves with the persons in the Raven's Tower, and nobody has seen either Mr Fletcher or Mr Macdonald since that intrusion before dinner."

" Where are they, then ? " Ben Nevis asked.

" Oh dear," Mrs MacDonald sighed vastly, " I expect poor Mr Fletcher had difficulty with that nasty little Mr Prew and has been wrestling with him."

" Nonsense, Trixie. Mr Fletcher's much too old to start wrestling with people at his age," her husband declared.

" I mean arguing with him, Donald. I do hope he won't feel he has to walk too far. He is so very conscientious."

Toker stepped forward again.

" I understand from Alec, madam, that Mr Fletcher sent for his hat and coat, and which Alec brought him."

" Oh dear, oh dear, that's what he must have done. And the poor man's had no dinner. We'd better send Johnnie after him."

A quarter of an hour later word came that Johnnie Macpherson had brought back the Daimler empty. He had overtaken the hikers singing on their way back, but there had been no sign either of Mr Fletcher or Duncan.

Ben Nevis had been inclined to discount his wife's alarm about the chaplain, but when he heard that his head-keeper was also missing he himself became alarmed.

" Look here, MacIsaac, we'll have to organize a search-party. And if there's been any dirty work, you'll have to take a few guns and round up these ruffians."

The Chamberlain sighed. He had known all the while, he told himself, that the luck which had taken him to Fort William would not hold.

Once again Toker stepped forward.

" Excuse me, sir, but Alec reports that it's generally believed in the staff quarters that Mr Fletcher and Mr Macdonald were shut up in the dungeon under the Raven's Tower."

" Well, why doesn't one of the ninnies go and let them out ? "

" That was the intention, sir, but it was frustrated by the absence of the necessary keys."

" Trixie, I gave you the keys," said Ben Nevis reproachfully.

" Donald dear, Duncan had the keys."

" Well, for Heaven's sake, somebody go and find out what is happening." the Chieftain said irritably. " This sort of vagueness is wrecking our dinner."

Another messenger from the back of the Castle brought word that banging on the door of Mac 'ic Eachainn's Cradle and what sounded like the voice of Duncan Macdonald indicated definitely that somebody was shut up in the dungeon. The keys, however, were nowhere to be found.

" They must be found," bellowed the Lord of Ben Nevis, Glenbogle, Glenbristle, Strathdiddle, Strathdun, Loch Hoch and Loch Hoo. " I expect these keys to have been found by the time we've finished dinner. I expect them to be brought to me with the coffee."

Chapter 6

MAC 'IC EACHAINN'S CRADLE

ALAS, when the Chieftain was handed his coffee he was
not handed the keys of the dungeons. The most widely
accepted theory was that the hikers had carried them off,
but when Ben Nevis proposed to dispatch a party to demand
the return of them it was pointed out that by this time the
keys had probably been flung into the Bogle.

"And we cannot leave poor Mr Fletcher in that horrid
place indefinitely," Mrs MacDonald urged.

"Oh, well, we shall have to break in the door of the Cradle.
That's all there is to it," Ben Nevis ruled.

But it turned out that there was a good deal more than
that to it. The lock defied any attempt to force it, and the
iron-studded door two inches thick stolidly resisted the repeated assaults of the three heavy-weights that flung themselves against it, now one at a time, now all together.

"Some door," declared Chester Royde, rubbing his
shoulder.

The two hefty sons of Ben Nevis shook their heads, dazed
by the ability of any substance to stand up against them for so
long.

"We must try a battering ram," the Chieftain decided.
"Go and fetch a caber," he shouted.

A caber was fetched, and the three heavy-weights reinforced by the blacksmith and a couple of other strong men
drove it at the door. The noise was considerable, but the
result was nil. Ben Nevis was divided between admiration
of the door he had installed and annoyance with it for failing
to appreciate that one could have too much of a good thing.
The caber was replaced by a beam which required eight men
to give it any propulsive force but was no more successful in
disturbing the door than the caber had been.

Catriona and Mary MacDonald had made one or two
attempts to enlist in the battering-parties, but every time
their brothers had told them not to get in the way. This
had rankled. They were such hefty young women that they
had long ago decided to make the best of it and build up their
sex-appeal on this very heftiness. Neither ever lost an

opportunity to move something or lift something or over-throw something which would have been beyond the strength of the average woman. Both had distinguished themselves in the mêlée with the hikers, particularly Catriona, who had rescued her father from the hiker's staff of the young woman roused to frenzy by his treatment of the mauve-shirted owner of the portable. In fact the success-ful imprisonment of the female hikers in the dungeon under the North Tower had been largely due to the competent way in which Catriona and Mary had handled them by the backs of their shorts. For this they had received no thanks. Indeed all they had received was a lecture from their mother for taking part in the battle.

Catriona and Mary MacDonald might despise women like Carrie and Myrtle Royde for their appalling femininity and disgusting coquetry, but they recognized bitterly that the sex-appeal of heftiness stood no chance against the odious wiles of small slim women prepared to be shamelessly provocative. Catriona had confessed it puzzled her why such a fuss was made about Myrtle Royde's dark eyes and crimson cheeks, and Mary's imagination was baffled to explain why the greenish eyes and red hair of Carrie Royde should attract so much attention.

" I do think men are extraordinary," Catriona growled to her sister. " Just because the two Royde women have come out to watch the proceedings all the men are making the most tremendous business of pretending they're performing feats of superhuman strength."

" Father's just as bad as any of them," Mary growled on an even deeper note, for she was just a little bit heftier than her sister.

" He's worse," Catriona growled, " because he doesn't lift anything himself but keeps telling everybody else how to lift it."

" Catriona! "

" What's the matter ? "

" I've just remembered something," Mary twanged in tones that resembled an excited pizzicato on the violoncello.

" What ? "

" I've just remembered the trap-door."

" What trap-door ? "

" The trap-door down into the Cradle from the Raven's Tower."

" But that's been closed for a hundred years or more,"
Catriona said.

" I know, but you and I might manage to open it. I
expect it will be a pretty hefty job, but I don't see why you
and I shouldn't be able to manage it. And if we could it
would be a pretty good score," Mary said, gruffly gloating.

The Chieftain had just ordered an attempt to be made on
the door, with a crowbar, and the males one after another
were trying their strength, each no doubt hoping he would
be the lucky one to force an entrance and win the applause of
Carrie and Myrtle Royde.

" Come on, Catriona," her sister urged. " If we don't
succeed nobody will know and if we do we really will have a
hot score."

The old guardroom of the Raven's Tower was cluttered,
not only with the rubbish which had been removed from the
Cradle when Ben Nevis fitted it up as a show dungeon some
twenty-odd years ago but with the rubbish which had
accumulated in it ever since. The Glenbogle Castle of this
date had not heard the broadcast appeal of the Minister of
Waste. When it did the contents of the old guardroom would
make one of the most notable contributions in the country
to the nationwide effort to save its rubbish.

While caber, beam and crowbar assaulted the door of the
Cradle below, up in the old guardroom Catriona and Mary
worked strenuously to clear away the rubbish from that
part of the floor where they judged the trap-door was likely
to be found. They made a good deal of noise, but people
outside heard nothing, so much louder were the operations
in the yard that Ben Nevis was directing.

" Eureka," Catriona suddenly growled.

" Well, it's pretty hot work," her sister answered. " One's
bound to reek a bit."

" You ass, I mean I've found it."

" Found what ? "

" Good lord, Mary, you are a thickhead. The trap-door,
of course."

" Oh, the trap-door? Oh, stout stuff ! " Mary exclaimed.

The joy of flinging sacks about and shifting a chaff-
cutter which had been waiting in a West Highland dream for
eleven years to be mended had taken possession of her. In
the zest of being hefty she had forgotten for a moment why
she was being hefty.

" Well, seeing it was your idea to find this trap-door,"
Catriona growled, " you are a bit absent-minded." She
bent down and gave a tug at the iron ring of the trap-door.
" Phew! This blighter *is* going to take some shifting."

The eyes of Mary lighted up as with a grunt of determination she plunged down to grasp the ring. She knew that
the trap-door hoped to prove itself a worthy antagonist of
her heftiest heftiness.

" Come up, you brute," she growled. " Come up, will
you. Get a grip on it, Catriona, you slacker."

Catriona got a grip on it, and the two sisters tugged and
pulled, growling like a couple of sabre-toothed tigresses over
the body of a palæolithic man. The trap-door had forgotten
the days when it was opened for captured Macintoshes to be
dropped into the safe keeping of Mac 'ic Eachainn's Cradle.
Years of idleness beneath gradually accumulating rubbish
had sapped its morale. It lacked the resistance of the oaken
door put in by Ben Nevis. The combined heftiness of
Catriona and Mary MacDonald was too much for it. Five
minutes after they had seized its iron ring the trap-door
revealed the dungeon, on the floor of which Mr Fletcher and
Duncan were sitting, a broken lantern between them, their
heads buried between their knees in an attempt to muffle
the deafening noise that caber, beam and crowbar were
making in their assault upon the oaken door.

" Mr Fletcher! " Catriona called down triumphantly.

" Duncan! " cried Mary.

Neither of the bowed figures on the floor of the Cradle
gave a sign of having heard the voices of their rescuers.

" Yoicks! " Catriona boomed.

" Yoicks! " her sister echoed.

The bowed figures some fifteen feet below remained
unresponsive.

" They can't hear us," Mary said.

" I'm not surprised," said Catriona. " I can hardly
hear what you're saying in my ear. The noise of that
battering is pretty hefty."

" Wait a jiffy," Mary growled. She dropped an old
sack to attract the attention of the prisoners. Unfortunately
it fell on the broken lantern and extinguished it.

" That's torn it," Catriona observed severely. " Where's
the torch ? "

Mary flashed the electric torch down into the dungeon.

"Look up, Mr Fletcher. The Lord has sent an angel to deliver us," Duncan proclaimed. "Isn't that wonderful? I was saying to myself like Daniel, 'My God hath sent his angel, and hath shut the lions' mouths,' and right enough the Lord has sent an angel."

"It isn't an angel, Duncan," Mary shouted down. "It's Catriona and Mary MacDonald."

"Well, well, it isn't an angel at all, Mr Fletcher. It's Miss Catriona and Miss Mary."

The venerable chaplain peered up, shading his eyes against the glare of the torch.

"If we let down a rope, do you think you can climb up?" Catriona asked.

"No, I'm afraid that's rather beyond me," the chaplain replied. "And anyway I don't think it's worth while now. That door is bound to give way soon. It can't hold out indefinitely against such battering."

Catriona and Mary were not at all anxious to lose the honour of having rescued the prisoners and they pressed upon the chaplain the advantage of escaping from the Cradle by means of a rope.

"It'll be quite easy," Catriona assured him.

"Easy as pie," Mary declared.

They had found what they thought was a suitable rope and having tied it fast to the iron ring of the trap-door they threw it down into the dungeon.

"Come on, Duncan," Catriona urged, "show Mr Fletcher the way. Hand over hand."

But the old gamekeeper demurred.

"Go on, Duncan, put some beef into it and you'll be up in a jiffy," Mary promised.

But the old gamekeeper still demurred.

"Look here, I'll show you how easy it is," Catriona volunteered.

She gripped the rope and dived down through the opening like the heroine of the poem *Curfew shall not ring to-night*.

"Oh, good-oh, Catriona!" Mary commented. "I'm coming too."

Whether it was the extra swing her weight gave to the rope or whether it was the removal of that weight from the trap-door that caused it to rise from the floor and shut itself with a bang might be hard to say. But that is what it did. Catriona was nearly at the bottom when the rope snapped,

but even so she winded Mr Fletcher for the second time
that evening, only to be winded herself by Mary who had
farther to fall.

" I'm awfully sorry, Mr Fletcher," said Catriona when she
had recovered her breath. " Hope I didn't hurt you. It
was the fault of that goof, Mary."

" No, no, I'm—ah—hah—hah—hah—quite—ah—hah—
all right—ah—hah—hah—just a little winded—ah—hah—
that's all."

" I hope you didn't hurt yourself, Miss Mary," the old
keeper enquired anxiously, for Mary was his favourite.

" Mary hurt herself!" Catriona growled indignantly.
" Why, she fell on Mr Fletcher and me."

" I'm all right," said Mary. " But where's the torch?
Wow! it's smashed. Strike a light, somebody."

" I've only one match left," Duncan said.

" You would have," Catriona growled.

However, that solitary match just managed to light the
smoky lantern when it had been released from the sack
which had extinguished it.

" The more I think of it the more of an absolute coot
you are, Mary," her sister declared. " We should have had a
tophole score over the others if you hadn't muffed it by
barging in with that rope."

" Never mind," said the chaplain, who had recovered
from the *peine forte et dure* of both sisters being on top of him
at once. " Never mind, you both did your best."

" If Duncan hadn't funked climbing up the rope," said
Mary, " it would have been perfectly good-oh. We could
have hauled Mr Fletcher up between us."

" I'm very thankful I did not climb up the rope," said
Duncan. " I might never have fallen on Mr Fletcher at all,
and that would not have been very enjoyable. I wonder
what they're doing outside now."

This speculation was prompted by a lull which had lasted
for two or three minutes. The answer came almost at once
with a most terrific crash as the oaken door gave way before
the impact of a beam twice the size of any yet used and pro-
pelled by ten stalwart batterers at the double.

" I knew it could be done," Ben Nevis was heard pro-
claiming with a triumphant roar. " Duncan, are you
there? You're all right, I hope? And Mr. Fletcher, is he
all right?"

The batterers puffing with their supreme effort stood aside to let Mac 'ic Eachainn enter his Cradle, lantern in hand. Macbeth confronted by the three witches on the blasted heath probably looked much less startled than Ben Nevis when he beheld his two hefty daughters in their black silk evening gowns stained with the rust and dust and must of the accumulated rubbish in the old guardroom.

For a moment or two he could only bark wildly in utter bewilderment. Then he found his voice.

" How in the name of all that's . . . in fact how the deuce *did* you get into the Cradle ? "

" We came down through the trap-door in the old guard-room," Catriona growled. " We'd have had both the prisoners out if the rope hadn't gone phut when we were on it."

" I should think the rope would go phut," observed Iain, with a brother's kindly sympathy. " Any rope would."

" Less of it from you, fat boy," Mary rumbled. " Something had to be done while you Lady Janes were all pecking at that door."

" Now don't start bickering together," the patriarch commanded. " I want to hear how Mr Fletcher and Duncan found themselves in the Cradle."

" That's a very difficult question to answer, Ben Nevis," his head-keeper replied. " But before we knew where we were that's where we were."

" But where were you ? "

" That's what I'm after telling you, Ben Nevis," said Duncan severely. " We didn't know where we were till we were where we were. That's how it was, wasn't it, Mr Fletcher ? "

" It was certainly all very sudden," the chaplain agreed. " Something in the nature of a rush took place when Duncan unlocked the door, but I was unfortunately butted in the wind and that temporarily deprived me of any ability to see what happened."

" And I had a big bang on the nose," Duncan added.

" Good lord, I should think you did," Ben Nevis exclaimed. " You'd better go in and get Mrs Ablewhite to clap a beefsteak on it. Well, I'm sorry you both got knocked about, but in a way it's just as well because it will give me a chance of bringing a counter-charge against these brutes if they try to sue me for assault."

The voice of Mrs MacDonald was heard over her husband's shoulder.

" Donald dear, don't you think it will be more comfortable for Mr Fletcher and Duncan if these questions are discussed indoors ? Poor Mr Fletcher must be famished. He was expecting dinner over two hours ago when he so kindly offered to attend to the hikers. Come along, Mr Fletcher. Dinner's waiting for you. Catriona! Mary! I'm glad you were able to be of little some assistance to poor Mr Fletcher, but I think you ought to go in now and tidy yourselves. In fact I think the sooner we all go indoors the better. You agree, don't you, Donald ? "

The Chieftain led the way back to the Great Hall, where long after the rest of the party had gone off to bed tired out by exercise, excitement and the strong air of Glenbogle he and the laird of Kilwhillie sat with their whisky, going over the events of this great day.

" By the way, Hugh,", he said as he poured out the *deoch an doruis* or drink at the door to speed Kilwhillie on the road to bed, " I don't know if you heard Iain saying at dinner that he had seen two Scottish Nationalists in Glenbogle the day before yesterday."

Kilwhillie tugged at the ends of his long moustache, which by this time of the day met in a droop over his chin.

" No, I didn't hear that," he said gravely.

" I wouldn't bet much they aren't camping somewhere around," Ben Nevis went on.

" Oh, they'd hardly have the impudence to do that, Donald."

" Wouldn't they ? Hugh, my boy, these Scottish Nationalists have impudence enough for anything. They're worse than hikers. They're worse than Bolshies. In fact they are Bolshies, only worse, if you see what I mean."

" Yes, I see what you mean," said Kilwhillie, disentangling the ends of his moustache which showed signs of twining round one another like two strands of badly-trained honeysuckle. " Well, we don't want these fellows upsetting people in Inverness-shire. It's difficult enough to keep the rates within reasonable bounds as it is without a lot of Bolshie agitators from Glasgow."

" Quite," Ben Nevis agreed. " Well, I've discovered a way to deal with hikers and I'm not going to be defied by

Scottish Nationalists. Look here, you'd better have another jockendorrus."

" Well, perhaps one more."

Mac 'ic Eachainn raised his glass solemnly.

" If I find these Scottish Nationalists have been camping on my land, Hugh, I'll tell you what I shall do. I shall have them thrown into the nearest loch."

" Suppose they were drowned ? "

Mac 'ic.Eachainn drank down his second *deoch an doruis*.

" Well, that's that, if you see what I mean."

" Yes, I see what you mean," Kilwhillie admitted, swallowing his second *deoch an doruis*. " But I think Beatrice mightn't like it."

" Why not ? "

" Well, she spoke to me after dinner while you were super-intending that door business . . ."

" Wait a moment, Hugh. What about another jocken-dorrus ? "

" Well, this really must be the last, Donald."

" Go on, what did Trixie say ? " asked Ben Nevis when he had refilled Kilwhillie's glass.

" She seemed to think I had egged you on to shut up these hikers. She was very cross about it really. She said if that kind of thing happened again her pleasure in our friendship would be destroyed. I was a bit upset. So I'd rather not be brought into this drowning business if you don't mind, Donald. Of course, so far as I'm concerned the more Scottish Nationalists you drown the better I should be pleased. But I'm very fond of Beatrice as you know. And I do think it might upset her if you drowned these fellows."

" Well, of course, if you make it a personal matter, Hugh, I'm not going to do anything to upset you. After all there are other ways of dealing with Scottish Nationalists besides drowning them."

" Quite, that's what I feel."

" One more jockendorrus ? "

" No really, Donald. It's bed for me."

" Well, I suppose it's bed for both of us. Don't worry, Hugh. I'll put things right with Trixie. It's a pity women never appreciate loyalty."

" Oh, I think Beatrice does, Donald, but she said there were times when she put common sense before loyalty."

" Dreadful! " the Chieftain groaned. " Well, I'll never understand women if I live to be a hundred."

On this reflection the Twenty-third MacDonald of Ben Nevis switched on as he thought the electric light for the stairway but in point of fact plunged the Great Hall into darkness.

" I wish I'd never given way to Trixie about installing this damned electric-light at Glenbogle," he exclaimed fretfully. " We were much better off with lamps. The beastly contraption never works properly."

However, after clicking away for some moments he found the switch for the stairway, and the two lairds went off to bed.

While they had been discussing the future of Scottish Nationalists downstairs, the same topic had been started by Carrie Royde when she went along to her sister-in-law's room for one of those little chats which women find such efficacious sleeping-draughts. Myrtle was already in bed, a great mahogany four-poster, on which Carrie in a pastel rose dressing-gown was sitting with her feet up and her back against one of the posts at the foot. The charming contrast of her red hair with the colour of her dressing-gown was slightly marred by the wallpaper on which life-size flamingoes, whose roseate plumes had been turned by the mists of Glenbogle into a revolting shade of washed-out magenta, were stalking about among greenish-yellow tuffets of boggy vegetation or arching their necks apparently to smell the butter-coloured water-lilies that were scattered about the marsh these antipathetic birds frequented.

" Myrtle, you heard what Ben Nevis said at dinner about Scottish Nationalists ? "

" They seemed to worry him a whole lot. But what are Scottish Nationalists, anyway ? " asked Myrtle, who looked as small and merry as Puck in that great mahogany four-poster.

" They believe in the independence of Scotland."

" Good for them. Give me independence every time. But I don't see why you're worrying, Carrie."

" You know I'm crazy about Scotland."

" And how! But what of it ? I'm crazy about Scotland myself. So's Chester. That's why he's going to get himself a kilt."

" Chester's going to get himself a kilt ? " Carrie repeated in amazement.

" Oh, don't tell Chester I told you. He wants it to be a surprise for you."

" It'll be a surprise all right whether I know beforehand or not," said Carrie, with conviction.

" I don't know. I think Chester'll look kind of cute in a kilt. He's pretty serious about it because when I said ' kilts ' instead of ' kilt ' he eyed me as if I was eating peas with a knife. But promise you won't let him know I told you. And don't try to discourage him. After all, it's a compliment to you."

" I'll wait and see what he does look like in it before I agree to that theory. And oh, Myrtle, before I forget don't wink at me again across the table like that. I'm sure Iain MacDonald noticed it."

· " Don't worry, my dear. Iain wouldn't notice it if I dropped an eye in the soup. Dumb ? Why, there's only one thing dumber than Iain, and that's his brother the Lieutenant."

" Ben Nevis isn't dumb."

" You're telling me. Why, Carrie, I think Ben Nevis is the brightest sixty-year-old I've met in all my young life. If Hector's only half as bright as the Monarch of the Glen I'm going to make the Monarch of the Glen my father-in-law. I sure am. I guess I'd make a pretty good chieftainess. You didn't see Ben Nevis with those hikers, Carrie. He kept picking them up by the collar one after another and shaking them. You missed that. Well, if he's taken a dislike to Scottish Nationalists it's going to be just too bad for the Scottish Nationalists."

" You surely don't agree with letting your prejudices run away with you, Myrtle ? "

" I don't know. I think I'd kind of admire any prejudice that could run away with Ben Nevis."

" Yes, but if you knew a very nice—two very nice Scottish Nationalists—you wouldn't want Ben Nevis to treat them like these hikers ? "

" They'd have to be mighty nice before I got between them and Ben Nevis."

" But you wouldn't take Iain MacDonald's opinion ? And it was Iain who was being so high hat about those Scottish Nationalists he saw. As a matter of fact I know them."

" You do ? " Myrtle exclaimed.

" That is, I met them to-day in Glenbristle.   It was rather romantic really."

" Tell sister all about it."

" Well, you know I was terribly anxious to find the exact site of my great-great-grandfather's cottage."

" I didn't know, but I'm sure you were."

" He was put out of Glenbristle by the great-grandfather of Ben Nevis."

" He was, was he ? Well, if great-grandpa was anything like great-grandson I bet your relation went out of Glenbristle with a bang."

" It was he who emigrated to Canada."

" Uh-huh, that's about where he would land if great-grandpa shook him up the way great-grandson shook up those hikers."

" Well, I think I've found the site of the old place.   There's a family tradition about it.   Of course, I can't be absolutely sure, but I felt a very strange unearthly sort of feeling when I came to this place.   Some unseen presence seemed to be telling me I had come home.   So I sat down on the grass."

" Didn't the unseen presence offer you a chair ? "

" No, please, Myrtle, don't laugh at me.   To-day was a terribly solemn experience.   I sat down on the grass and ate my sandwiches and smoked a cigarette and fell fast asleep. I must have slept for quite two hours."

" I'll say you did.   I never knew you so wide-awake at this hour before."

" And when I woke up, two young men in kilts were looking down at me.   I thought at first they were fairies."

" So you felt kind of safe and didn't scream for help," Myrtle teased.

" You have no poetry in you, Myrtle.   I mean supernatural beings.   And then I realized that they were two perfectly good young men and we talked for awhile and they were very interesting about Scottish Nationalism, which is why I asked Ben Nevis about it at dinner.   And now here's my problem, Myrtle.   These two young men are camping in Glenbristle.   In fact they gave me tea at their camp.   I must warn them.   They know I'm staying with Ben Nevis and if he treats them the way he treated those hikers they'll think I betrayed them.   You see the very difficult position I'm in ? "

Myrtle nodded; and encouraged by what she thought was

6

the dawn of sympathy in her sister-in-law Carrie became
more confidential.

" And that's not the only thing. One of their ideas in
coming to Glenbristle was a plan they had to kidnap Ben
Nevis."

" Kidnap Ben Nevis ? " Myrtle exclaimed in amazement.

" Yes; but as soon as I said he was a friend of mine they
said at once they wouldn't dream of kidnapping him.
They'd kidnap somebody else instead."

" They sound tough guys, your two boy friends."

" Oh no, it's all political. It isn't kidnapping the way
we kidnap in the United States. Oh no, money doesn't
come into it. It's a political gesture. Well, what I want
you to do, Myrtle, is to say you'd like to go for a walk with
me to-morrow morning instead of going out with the guns.
I'm afraid if I go off alone again I'll make Ben Nevis
suspicious. Will you do this for me, Myrtle ? "

" Why, of course I will."

" Oh, that's lovely of you. But when you see this young
man—these young men—I'm sure you'll be just as anxious
as I am that nothing should happen to him—to them. Well,
I'm not going to keep you awake any longer. Chester'll be
wondering where I am."

" Don't tell him you've heard he's going to get a kilt."

" Why, certainly I won't tell him, Myrtle. You will come
with me to-morrow ? "

" Sure."

" Oh, perhaps I ought to have told you that one of these
boys is a poet. Well, honey, I won't keep you any longer.
Sweet dreams."

Carrie blew a kiss to her sister-in-law and went back to her
own room.

" What have you been talking about ? " her husband
asked from a mahogany four-poster even larger than the one
which held Myrtle. " I wanted to tell you something
before I went to sleep."

" What is it, Chester ? "

" I've fallen for your country, Carrie. They know how
to live up here. I'm going to buy a little place in Scotland."

" Why, that's lovely news, Chester."

" Yes, and Kilwhillie's going to show us a lodge of his
that he's anxious to sell. Of course, he says he isn't so
anxious, but that's hooey. Knocknacolly it's called.

About ten miles from Glenbogle across the hills, but nearer thirty by road."

" When are we going, Chester ? "

" He's going to drive us over to-morrow morning."

" To-morrow morning ? "

" What's the matter with to-morrow morning ? "

" Well, I'd promised to take Myrtle for a walk.   I thought you'd be out shooting."

" You can take Myrtle for a walk any time. We'll be back by the afternoon. Ben Nevis is going to have a drive for some Scottish Nationalists, whatever they are, and throw them into a loch. But he's coming with us in the morning."

Chapter 7

KNOCKNACOLLY

IN spite of having been the last of the party to leave the
Great Hall of Glenbogle on the previous night Ben Nevis
and Kilwhillie were the first to appear in the dining-room
next morning for breakfast. They ladled generous helpings
of porridge into their bowls and walked about blowing it.

"Another good day, Hugh," Ben Nevis observed enthusiastically.

"Yes, and it looks like lasting."

"This is the eighth consecutive day without rain. Must
be a record for August I should think."

"We had nine days running without rain in 1911,"
Kilwhillie reminded him.

"Did we? Well, if we get a fine day to-morrow that will
equal the 1911 record," Ben Nevis observed, after a scarcely
perceptible pause to be sure his calculation was correct.

"Quite."

"And by Jove, if we don't have rain to-morrow we shall
beat it," he went on.

Delighted with the establishment of this mathematical
fact, Ben Nevis stamped across to the side-table and ladled
another couple of spoonfuls into his porringer.

"I don't think I'll say too much about this record in
front of Royde," Kilwhillie remarked pensively, "if you see
what I mean."

"Knocknacolly, eh?" Ben Nevis asked, an expression of
tremendous sagacity playing about his florid weatherbeaten
countenance.

"Quite. That's why I'm anxious he should see the place
as soon as possible. I think places always look better when
the sun is shining. Particularly Knocknacolly. It's very
good of you, Donald, to come with us this morning."

"Not a bit, Hugh, not a bit. I mean to say I think I can
be helpful, and I do want you to get Knocknacolly off your
hands at a fair price. Besides, I think the Roydes will be
an asset, what? The more money we can get into Inverness-shire the better for everybody. I'll send a cable to
Hector from the post-office at Kenspeckle. I don't see why

he shouldn't be able to get home in ten days from now."

"I should think he would. Wonderful thing, this flying. I'm really extremely obliged to you, Donald, for coming along with us this morning. If I can sell Knocknacolly at a fair price it will be helpful. But it's rather an interruption to sport."

"Oh, that's all right, Hugh. Besides, I've given up that idea of throwing those hikers into a loch. I don't want them to cause any friction between you and Trixie. I put things right last night, and she's very pleased I'm going to drive over with you to Knocknacolly instead of rounding up these Scottish Nationalists. By the way, I think we'll take the Daimler. It's more comfortable than your old Austin."

"If I manage to sell Knocknacolly I'll get a new car," said Kilwhillie hopefully.

"I've told MacIsaac to arrange for the beaters to get round Glenbristle and Glenbogle this morning and I propose to round up the Scottish Nationalists this afternoon, put them in the lorry, and have them deposited at the railway station in Fort William. It's a pity not to use the dungeons, but Trixie's got this old idea into her head that it'll cause trouble. So I'm humouring her. You've got to humour women, Hugh."

"Yes, my mother required a lot of humouring during the last ten years of her life," said Kilwhillie. "I know what it is."

"I'm afraid Royde will be disappointed. I told him about throwing any Scottish Nationalists we caught into the nearest loch, and he was very pleased with the idea. What are you going to ask for Knocknacolly?"

"I thought of asking ten thousand and taking eight. Well, as a matter of fact I'd take seven."

"Ask fifteen and take twelve."

"Well, of course if I could get twelve thousand, I could pay off the mortgage on Kilwhillie and have enough to do it up. But what's the use of dreaming?" The Laird of Kilwhillie shook his head sadly.

"Look here, Hugh, you leave this to me . . . by the way, look out, the end of your moustache has got into your porridge . . . that's it, it's out now . . . yes, you leave this to me. I'm going for fifteen. After all, what's fifteen thousand to a man like Royde? His father has over twenty

million, and he's the only son. Twenty million pound
a lot of money, Hugh."

" Yes, it is a lot of money."

" I suppose his sister will have at least a couple of million
one day. By the way, don't let me forget I have to send that
cable to Hector. Oh yes, I'm going for fifteen thousand
pounds. After all, if you had twenty millions you wouldn't
be worrying about the difference between fifteen thousand
pounds and twelve thousand pounds. Look out, Hugh, the
end of your moustache has got back into your porridge."

The laird of Kilwhillie was trying not to feel optimistic and
so kept shaking his head to express a determined defeatism.
Hence the erratic behaviour of his moustache.

" The lodge will want a lot doing to it," he said gloomily.

" Well, that's what these people like, Hugh. Now, don't
you worry. I'm going for fifteen thousand. And I shall get it."

Kilwhillie's hopes and fears were presently left to fend for
themselves because the rest of the party were coming in to
breakfast.

Carrie had already consulted with her sister-in-law about
the problem created by this expedition to Knocknacolly,
which she had not expected.

" Keep smiling. I'll go along and warn your two beaux
that the monarch of the glen's out for their scalps," Myrtle
volunteered.

" It's terribly sweet of you, Myrtle, but suppose Chester
wants you to drive over to Knocknacolly too. And even if
Chester doesn't, Ben Nevis will be peeved if you don't come,
that's a sure thing."

" Well, the monarch will just have to be peeved," said
Myrtle. " Now, what do I say to your two beaux ? "

" I've written a note warning them to flee. James
Buchanan—that's the lawyer—was going anyway on
Saturday, but Alan Macmillan—that's the poet—was going
to camp on for another few days. But I don't think it's safe
for him to stay around here. This is what I've written:

" *Dear Mr Buchanan . . .*"

" That's the lawyer ? " Myrtle interrupted.

" Yes."

" What's the poet done that you don't write to him ? "

" Why, I think the lawyer will pay more attention to my
warning. Lawyers are kind of practical folk compared with
poets."

" I see," said Myrtle thoughtfully.

"*Dear Mr Buchanan*," Carrie went on reading, "*This is to introduce my sister-in-law Miss Myrtle Royde who will explain to you how very necessary it is for you and Mr Macmillan to leave Glenbristle at once.*"

She broke off. " I thought you could explain better than by my trying to write all about Ben Nevis. They think he's in a rut."

" Oh, they think he's in a rut, do they ? "

" Yes, and you've got to convince them that he's not." Carrie went on reading—" *to leave Glenbristle at once on account of the attitude of the owner towards camping . . .*" She broke off again. " I think it's wiser to concentrate on the camping side of it. I'm afraid if I make too much of a point about the political side of it they may feel bound to stay and fight it out." She went on reading: " *It is a great disappointment not to meet you and Mr Macmillan again but I have to drive over with my husband to inspect a property in the neighbourhood. Should we be lucky enough to secure it I need hardly say how glad we shall be to have you camp on our land whenever you feel inclined. Should you decide to make that visit to Canada which we discussed, be sure to write and let me know so that I can give you a few letters of intro-duction. Mrs Chester Royde Jr., 10, Green House, Park Lane, London, W.1, is my London address and letters will always be forwarded. But I hope to have an address in Scotland soon, and if you will give Miss Royde your address and Mr Macmillan's I will write and let you know what that is. . . .*"

She stopped reading. " I think that says all I can say in a letter, but I'm relying on you, Myrtle, to impress on them how very fierce Ben Nevis can be. Chester told me his idea was to throw these young men into the nearest loch. Well, I believe he's quite capable of doing it."

" He certainly is," Myrtle agreed.

" Then be an angel, Myrtle, and try to get that into their heads."

" I'll do my best."

Ben Nevis, as Carrie had expected, was definitely peeved when Myrtle announced her intention of spending a quiet morning by herself instead of driving in the Daimler to Knocknacolly.

" But what will you do with yourself by yourself ? " he asked.

" Oh, I'll amuse myself."

The patriarch eyed his two sons farther down the table. They had just banked up their plates with bacon, eggs, kidneys and sausages, and were apparently oblivious of anything else. However, he was going to send that cable to Hector and therefore it was a waste of time bothering about Murdoch or Iain. He had given them their chance. They had failed to grasp it.

" Well, I'm sorry you won't come and give your opinion of Knocknacolly, Myrtle. It's the best twelve-head forest in Inverness-shire. The lodge is a bit old-fashioned, but it could easily be turned into a delightful place. You've not done any stalking yet. I'm looking forward to a day on Ben Booey with you soon."

He turned to Chester Royde.

" What you'll like about Knocknacolly, Royde, is its remoteness, and as for you, Carrie, I think Knocknacolly is going to be the dream of your childhood come true, if I may express myself rather poetically, what ? "

" It sounds wonderful, Ben Nevis."

" Well, it is a wonderful place. I never knew you thought of selling it, Hugh."

Kilwhillie, who for the last ten years had been thinking almost incessantly of selling Knocknacolly, tried to look startled by his own recklessness.

" Oh, of course, we none of us like parting with land, Donald. Still, when you find the ideal purchaser . . . however, perhaps Royde won't like Knocknacolly."

" Like it ? Of course he'll like it," Ben Nevis shouted. " Nobody could help liking Knocknacolly. Ah, by Jove, Hugh, we've had some great days in that forest. Do you remember when . . ." and for the rest of breakfast he talked of the stags he and Kilwhillie had stalked over thirty years. Carrie encouraged him whenever his reminiscences showed signs of flagging. She thought he was much better occupied stalking stags than Scottish Nationalists.

At ten o'clock Johnnie Macpherson drove to the front courtyard with the pre-1914 Daimler, riding in which was like riding in a Victorian boudoir on the back of an elephant. That it still appeared spacious when loaded with Ben Nevis, his two hefty daughters, the Roydes, Kilwhillie and Johnnie Macpherson the chauffeur was a tribute to life as it was once lived.

Catriona and Mary MacDonald were to desert the party

at the entrance of Glenbogle. They wanted the pleasure of what they described as a little jog back to the Castle for lunch by way of the bridle-path across Glenbristle. This meant as a preliminary footing it along five miles of road long out of repair, because Ben Nevis with all his territorial influence had failed as yet to become a member of the Roads Committee of the County Council.

"I can't understand why they don't ask me to be Convener of the Roads Committee," he used to declare from time to time.

Yet the explanation was simple enough. His fellow-councillors were determined to save the ratepayers the expense of putting the Glenbogle road in good order merely for the benefit of Ben Nevis, his castle and the cottages of his dependants being all that it served.

"Stop a moment, Johnnie," he bellowed to his driver when the Daimler reached the turning that crossed the bridge over the Bogle and wound up the Pass of Ballochy. "What about finding out if these hikers have cleared away from Loch Hoo?" he suggested to his guests.

"If we do that, Donald," Kilwhillie demurred nervously, "we may be rather late getting back for lunch." He was determined that Beatrice MacDonald should not be given the slightest excuse to lecture him again on his encouragement of her husband's autocratic violence.

"Perhaps you're right, Hugh. All right, Johnnie. Drive on. I do want to be back in good time," he admitted, "in case my beaters have spotted the whereabouts of these Scottish Nationalists. I told MacIsaac to get a report in by two o'clock, and then after lunch, if there's any prospect of good sport, we'll have a jolly afternoon."

"Your idea is to throw them into the nearest loch, isn't it?" Chester Royde asked.

"Ah well, I'm afraid I've got a disappointment for you, Royde, over that. Yes, the suggestion seemed to worry my wife rather. She seemed to think they might be drowned. So I promised her I wouldn't throw them into the loch."

"That's a pity," said Chester Royde.

"Yes, it is a pity, but it can't be helped. However, we'll think of something else to do to them."

"Sure thing."

"I don't know why you're such a smarty over Scottish

Nationalists, Chester Royde," his wife snapped crossly. " You don't even know what they are."

" I certainly don't," the young financier admitted. " But if our friend Ben Nevis thinks they ought to be bumped off, that goes with me."

" They're a kind of tartan Bolshie, if you know what I mean," the Chieftain explained.

" Communists, eh ? " said Royde.

" That sort of thing, only rather worse because they ought to know better. I mean to say they don't come from lower classes. They're agitators. Their great grievance is that Scotland isn't independent of England. Well, of course the idea is ludicrous. If there was the slightest reason for Scotland to be independent, people like Kilwhillie and myself would have sent the fiery cross round long ago and called out the clans."

" But are there any clans left to call out ? " Carrie asked, a noticeable tartness in her tone. " I thought that people like Kilwhillie and you drove them out of Scotland long ago."

" Oh, for the love of Mike, Carrie, don't start a political argument," her husband begged.

" Oh, she's not arguing," said Ben Nevis. " That's her MacDonald blood asserting itself. But look here, Carrie, if my great-grandfather hadn't forced your great-great-grandfather to go to Canada you wouldn't be driving to look at Knocknacolly with a view to buying it. You'd still be living in Glenbristle. You haven't seen Glenbristle yet, Royde, have you ? Johnnie, you can turn the car at the end of the road in Glenbristle ? "

" Oh yes, Ben Nevis."

" Well, I'll run you up Glenbristle as far as the road goes. It's only about three miles."

" No, no, please, Ben Nevis," Carrie begged. " Chester and I can go there to-morrow or any time. I do think we ought to concentrate on Knocknacolly this morning."

Kilwhillie's moustache, which had flagged at the proposal to explore Glenbristle, recovered itself as he acknowledged Carrie's firmness with a grateful if slightly melancholy smile.

" All right, Johnnie, keep right on," said the Chieftain. " I'm glad you're so interested in Knocknacolly. I won't deny I've set my heart on you two charming people having a place not too far away from Glenbogle. I mean to say, if

you take the bridle-paths you'll hardly be ten miles from us.
How long do you reckon it takes you to walk to Knocknacolly
by bridle-path, Mary ? "

" Three hours if it hasn't been raining for a day or two,"
she growled.

" About five if it has," her sister added.

" Which it usually has," Mary growled.

There was a curious resemblance between the expression
of Ben Nevis at that moment and the expression of one of the
water-horses mordant that surmounted the pillars of the
Castle gates.

" Now don't exaggerate about our rain, Mary," he said,
directing this expression at his daughter. " People *will*
exaggerate about our weather, Royde," he added. " What
could you want better than to-day ? And this is typical of
the West Highlands in August."

Mary and Catriona turned round and looked at their
father in amazement. They had heard him tell tall stories
about stags and salmon, about the prowess of the Ben Nevis
Macdonalds in clan feuds with the Macintoshes, and about
orations he had made at meetings of the County Council;
but they had never heard a story the tallness of which came
within measurable distance of the one he had just told about
West Highland weather in August.

" You'd call to-day a typical August day, wouldn't you,
Hugh ? " he went on.

Kilwhillie grabbed his moustache as a drowning man
clutches at a straw.

" Oh yes, Donald. I should call this a typical fine
August day," he replied.

Ben Nevis's countenance had reverted to that water-horse
mordant expression as he glared at his daughters, defying
them to contribute any further to the discussion.

" Well, of course over in America we've always had the
idea that it rained a whole lot in Scotland all the time,"
said Royde. " But this is great weather."

" Mind you, I'm not going to pretend it never rains in the
West Highlands," said Ben Nevis with a generous frankness.
" Oh no, it does rain sometimes. By Jove, Hugh, look at
Loch na Craosnaich. I've never seen it so low—this year,
I mean," he added quickly. " That's where our ancestor
Hector of the Great Jaw drowned eleven Macintoshes in
the year 1482, Carrie." He indicated a stretch of water

menacingly dark even upon this fine day. " I call him our ancestor because he's pretty sure to be an ancestor of yours. He had twenty-two sons. One of them, Murdoch Ruadh, was famous for the violent red of his hair, and his descendants known as Clan Vurich lived in Glenbristle. I dare say that jolly hair of yours was inherited from Murdoch Ruadh."

" Why, that's great, Carrie," her husband exclaimed. " That's a name for us to remember some happy day."

Carrie blushed.

" You'll have to drop a fly on Loch na Craosnaich, Carrie, one of these days. I don't fish much myself nowadays. Too slow for me. But Kilwhillie's a great hand with a rod. Yes, I more or less gave up fishing after I caught that forty-eight pounder in Loch Hoo five years ago. What a battle! He took a Blue and Yellow Flying Dutchman which I used quite by accident, because I'd always used Simpson's Green Boobytrap on Loch Hoo until then. But I hadn't a Boobytrap with me that morning and I used this Blue and Yellow Flying Dutchman which Bertie Bottley was always plaguing me to try. I'd no faith in it at all. None whatever. But I was wrong. Yes, extraordinary thing, I was wrong. Well, to cut a tall story short—ha-ha —this fellow took the Blue and Yellow Flying Dutchman at five minutes past eleven on a beautiful fishing morning and I played him till three o'clock that afternoon. What a battle! Forty-eight pounds, five ounces and a half. And as clean-run a salmon as ever I saw. Of course I had plenty of other fish after that, but they didn't give me the fights I wanted and so gradually I more or less gave up the rod. Always know when to stop, that's been my motto, ever since I left Harrow."

Soon after this cautionary tale the entrance to Glenbogle was reached and the Daimler stopped for Catriona and Mary to alight. The two young women gave an unemotional wave over their hefty shoulders and then immediately set out to walk back up the glen at four miles an hour.

" What a dust those two girls of mine are kicking up," Ben Nevis exclaimed. " That shows you how dry it is, Hugh. Stop at the post-office in Kenspeckle, Johnnie."

The small village of Kenspeckle lay about a mile along the main road westward from the entrance to Glenbogle. Ben Nevis strode into the post-office and demanded a form on which to write a cablegram to India. He was supplied by an old lady of about eighty with bright eyes and gold spectacles.

" Wonderful weather we're having, Mrs. Macdonald."

" Oh, it's beautiful weather indeed, Ben Nevis. I don't remember the like of such weather in August since I left school."

" Where's Willie ? "

" Willie's away out, Ben Nevis. He had to see a traveller in Fort Augustus about some biscuits which never reached us."

" When's he coming back ? "

" Och, he'll be coming back some time, Ben Nevis."

" Well, I'm anxious for this cable to go off as soon as possible."

" That will be quite all right, Ben Nevis. He'll send it as soon as he comes back from Fort Augustus."

The Chieftain wrote his cablegram:

> *Lieutenant Hector MacDonald*
> *Clanranald Highlanders*
> *Tallulahgabad*
> *Punjab*

> *Ask Colonel Rose-Ross as special favour to self to give you month's leave for urgent family business impossible to specify in cablegram stop if leave granted come by plane earliest possible moment. Ben Nevis.*

" How much is that, Mrs Macdonald ? "

The old lady shook her head.

" I don't know at all, Ben Nevis. Willie will know. But what does that matter ? Next time anybody from the glen is passing will be time enough to pay for the telegram. So Master Hector's coming home ? Isn't that splendid, now ? "

" Yes, we'll all be glad to see him."

" Indeed, yes. Such a fine young gentleman. Very like yourself, Ben Nevis."

A compliment from a woman was to Ben Nevis always agreeable whatever her age. He beamed.

" Well, good morning, Mrs Macdonald. And mind Willie sends that cablegram as soon as he comes in."

" Oh indeed, yes, Ben Nevis. Willie will be wanting to see Master Hector back himself as soon as possible."

The Chieftain strode from the post-office and climbed back into the Daimler.

" Well, I hope with any luck Hector will be home for the Gathering."

" The Gathering ?   What's that ? " Chester Royde asked.

" Our little Glenbogle Gathering.   We hold it on August 28th this year.   Quite a humble affair, of course.   We don't compete with Inverness or Oban or Braemar.   But we preserve the old spirit."

" But what's the gathering for ? "

" Oh, tossing the caber and running and dancing and piping.   Friendly rivalry and all that sort of thing.   It's the only day in the year I encourage trippers.   They come in buses.   You'll enjoy it, Royde.   You'll see a fine display of tartan."

Chester Royde looked thoughtful.   He was wondering if he could get his kilt in time for what sounded like an appropriate occasion for the début of that costume.

About four miles after Kenspeckle the bastions of Glenbore came into sight, and the Daimler turned off from the main road to make up Glenbore a journey similar to the one it had already made down Glenbogle.   Kilwhillie had parted some time ago now with most of Glenbore to a rich stockbroker called Dutton, who had pulled down the old Glenbore Lodge and built himself a concrete palace designed by an architect of the modern school.   It looked like a frozen cheese lying about in a rockery, and was considered unsuitable to Inverness-shire.   So it was, but not more unsuitable than some of the new bridges put up by the Inverness-shire County Council.

" Ghastly-looking place, what ? " Ben Nevis said as they passed the new Glenbore Lodge.   " Gives me the creeps whenever I see it."

Kilwhillie was reflecting that the prospective purchaser of Knocknacolly might share Dutton's taste in architecture and therefore refrained from savage criticism.

" Every man to his own taste where a house is concerned," he observed tolerantly.

" I don't agree with you at all, Hugh," Ben Nevis argued. " Nobody has a right to defile one of our glorious Highland glens with a building like that."

" What I object to much more than his house is his calling himself Dutton of Glenbore," said Kilwhillie.   " Glenbore was part of Kilwhillie till I sold it and I think it's rather bad form calling himself Glenbore."

" So if I buy Knocknacolly," Chester Royde asked, " I wouldn't be called Knocknacolly ? "

Kilwhillie was in a painful quandary. He did not want to risk losing a purchaser for Knocknacolly by denying him the right to use it as a name. At the same time he did feel very strongly about these rich fellows who bought sporting estates in the Highlands and supposed that by doing so they could turn themselves into lairds of long lineage and ancient territorial privileges. He had an equal objection to lairds of long lineage who put a ' The ' in front of Macintosh or Macleod or Macneil, always excepting The Chisholm. Kilwhillie in fact was a stickler for tradition, and it says much for his sincerity that he preferred to risk losing a purchaser than to mislead him by letting him suppose that if he bought Knocknacolly he would be justified in expecting to be addressed as Knocknacolly.

" Well, I dare say some people would call you Knocknacolly if they thought you liked it," said Kilwhillie. " But I could not undertake to call you Knocknacolly myself."

" What do you want to call yourself Knocknacolly for, Chester ? " his wife asked. " There's no point in you calling yourself Knocknacolly."

" I don't want to call myself Knocknacolly," Chester Royde replied, a little huffily. " Can't I ask a perfectly good question without being accused of wanting to change my name ? "

Kilwhillie tried to reassure himself by hanging on to his moustache, but he felt that the prospect of a successful sale had clouded over since they entered Glenbore. Indeed he felt inclined to give up the business altogether and instead of taking the Roydes to Knocknacolly to take them to Kilwhillie House and show them his relics of the 'Fifteen and the 'Forty-five.

Luckily Ben Nevis himself had made up his mind to sell Knocknacolly at a good price, and when Kilwhillie asked if they would not like to turn aside and see his Jacobite relics he condemned the notion as ridiculous.

" You can show our friends Kilwhillie House another day, Hugh. If we're going to be back in Glenbogle for lunch, we have our time cut out."

Presently the car turned off to the left and began to climb

among majestic scenery. Then it dipped down again on a
corkscrew descent, crossed a small stream and went on
for five miles over as desolate a stretch of level moorland as
might be found in all Scotland, at the end of which on a
slight elevation surrounded by dense plantations of Scots
firs and backed by a savage range of bens stood Knocknacolly
Lodge like a stained and faded frontispiece to a novel by
Sir Walter Scott.

" Why, I think it's perfectly gorgeous," Carrie exclaimed.
" It's the house I've prayed for all my life."

Kilwhillie had received two sharp rebuffs from women in
his day. He believed himself asbestos where the female sex
was concerned. Yet at that moment he was on the verge of
kneeling down in the Daimler and kissing the hem of Carrie's
extremely smart skirt.

" Knew you'd like it," Ben Nevis shouted exultantly.
" It's the best twelve-head forest in Inverness-shire, not to
mention quite a pretty little grouse moor on your doorstep
as you might say."

As in most Scottish shooting-lodges the rooms at Knocknacolly tried to make up with quantity for their lack of size
and absence of any kind of architectural proportion. The
kitchen-quarters were designed to pay out the domestic staff
for all the waste and breakages and bad meals of the rest of
the year, by making the annual migration to Scotland the
equivalent of two months' hard labour in the days before
prison reform. But why continue? It is more cheerful to
hear Chester Royde assert that Knocknacolly Lodge will
want a hell of a lot doing to it inside and out before it
remotely resembles anything he calls a house. The mouldering blinds, the dry rot in the attics, the corrugated-iron
bothy built along one side, the kennels with their rusty
railings, the dead bluebottles on the window-sills, the dead
tortoiseshell butterflies on the floors—one knows that all
these will vanish if Chester Royde decides to buy Knocknacolly.

But will he?

" I would just adore this place, Chester," said his wife.

" I knew you'd like it. I am so glad," Ben Nevis barked.
" And as I say it's the best twelve-head forest in Inverness-
shire."

Kilwhillie said nothing. He just let his moustache nuzzle
his hand and comforted himself with its dumb sympathy.

" How much are you asking for it, Kilwhillie ? " Chester Royde snapped suddenly.

" Fifteen thousand pounds," Ben Nevis replied for his friend.

" I'll give you six thousand pounds, Kilwhillie," Chester Royde said in a voice as hard as the rock of Manhattan.

" I'd hoped to get at least seven thousand," Kilwhillie murmured.

" That's O.K. by me. I'll give seven thousand," Chester Royde snapped. " Do you accept that offer ? "

" Why, yes, I'll accept that."

After all he had always told himself he would take seven thousand for Knocknacolly, and he had taken it.

" You've got a bargain, Royde," Ben Nevis said. " You wouldn't have had Knocknacolly from me for seven thousand."

" No, I guess I wouldn't," Chester Royde agreed, with a contented smile.

Chapter 8

GLENBRISTLE

THE reflections of Miss Myrtle Royde when she set out
that morning to Glenbristle were very different from
those of her sister-in-law the previous morning. Carrie had
been animated by a dreamy interest in the past; Myrtle was
inspired entirely by a lively curiosity about the present.
She found her sister-in-law's Scottish origin an inadequate
explanation of her so evident anxiety about the welfare of
these young men she had met, and she was looking forward
to ascertaining for herself just how attractive this poet was.
With the advantage of three years' sophisticated juniority
she was tolerantly amused by Carrie's naïvety in supposing
she had covered her tracks by addressing the letter to the
lawyer.

When Myrtle appeared in the front courtyard about a
quarter of an hour after the Daimler had started for Knocknacolly the trimness of her check cream and brown skirt,
the turnery of her legs, the deep carnation of her cheeks, the
flash of her dark eyes, and the particularly provocative tilt
of her hat combined to quicken faintly the muscle-bound
heart of Lieutenant Murdoch MacDonald, R.N., who was
receiving from a cocker spaniel the only kind of emotional
response by which he was not embarrassed. Myrtle
realized at once that he was mustering the words to suggest
his company on her walk and anticipated him by waving her
stick and hurrying along toward the drive.

It was just after she had turned off into the narrow grass-
grown rocky road up Glenbristle that Myrtle saw the
coruscation of the Macmillan and Buchanan tartans, and at
once decided that the two kilted figures walking towards her
were the young men Carrie had sent her to warn against the
vengeance of Ben Nevis. If the slightest doubt remained it
vanished when she came face to face with Alan Macmillan.

"Pardon me," she said. "But I have a letter for you
two gentlemen from my sister-in-law, Mrs Royde. At
least, I have a letter for Mr Buchanan. Which is Mr
Buchanan?" Myrtle asked, trying to look as if she really
had not the slightest idea.

A weight descended upon the soul of James Buchanan as he put out his hand for the letter. He told himself he had known all the time that the hundred-dollar bill had been a mistake for a ten-dollar bill. Even that was five times as much as the largest voluntary donation he had yet received for the Scottish Brotherhood of Action.

"Mrs Royde is so very sorry she couldn't give you the warning herself," Myrtle said as James passed the letter to Alan.

"It's very kind of her," he said, "but my friend and I are not at all in awe of people like Mr MacDonald of Ben Nevis."

"Not at all," Alan said emphatically, his blue eyes kindled to what Myrtle found an entrancing fire by the flame of poetic action. "We appreciate very much the trouble Mrs Royde has taken, and the trouble you have taken," he added with what Myrtle found an entrancingly awkward bow, "but I think I may say that Ben Nevis has more to fear from us than we from him."

"A great deal more," James Buchanan muttered grimly.

"But I don't think you two realize what kind of a man Ben Nevis is," said Myrtle. "Will we sit down for a few minutes and discuss the matter? I'm dying to sit down for a few minutes."

A suitable bank of grass was discovered and the three of them paid homage to Scotland's national pastime by going into committee.

"Now first of all I must make my own position clear," said Myrtle. "I'm devoted to Ben Nevis." She found the scowl on the poet's brow so entrancing that she repeated her assertion with great emphasis for the pleasure of seeing it deepen. "And Mrs Royde is also devoted to Ben Nevis," she went on, with a sidelong look to see the effect of that statement on the scowl. Either it was already as deep as he could make it or the announcement of Carrie's devotion had no more effect than the announcement of her own. "At the same time," Myrtle continued, "my sister-in-law is terribly worried because she's afraid you will think she may have said something to Ben Nevis about the plan you told her you had to kidnap him."

"We gave up that idea as soon as we heard Ben Nevis was a friend of Mistress Royde," James Buchanan said.

"Well, of course, I don't want to say anything that

might sting you into longing to show that you could kidnap
Ben Nevis, but . . . oh well, I won't say it. All I want to
have you realize is that Ben Nevis is the toughest thing in
kilts since Robert Bruce."

" Bruce didn't wear the kilt," both young men contradicted simultaneously.

" Well, whatever he wore, I guess he was tough all right.
And so's Ben Nevis, believe me. While you and my sister-
in-law were having your quiet afternoon together yesterday,
I was with him up on the moors, and if you'd seen the way
he laid about a camping party and shut them up in the
dungeons of his castle you'd know just how tough he is.
Well, somebody brought him word that you two were
camping out somewhere around on his land, and this afternoon he aims to have you both thrown into the nearest loch.
That's what's worrying Mrs Royde. She enjoyed your
hospitality yesterday in your camp, and she just can't bear
the idea of a watery grave for both of you. And now I've
met you both I can't say I'm tickled to death at the notion
myself. So put our minds at rest by moving away from Ben
Nevis's hunting-grounds, and when I see Mrs Royde at lunch
I'll be able to tell her my mission has been successful."

" Are you seriously suggesting, Miss Royde, that this
swollen-headed, Anglicized, degenerate laird will try to
throw my friend and me into a loch ? " James Buchanan
asked.

" It's not a suggestion at all. He certainly will," Myrtle
declared.

" Did you ever hear the like of that, Alan ? " James
asked.

The question acted like a pitchfork on the bard's shock of
fair hair, tossing it in every direction.

Myrtle thought she had never seen hair glint so cunningly.

" But I tell you he will," she insisted earnestly. " You
didn't see him charge those campers yesterday. I did."

" A mob of Cockney hikers, I suppose," said the bard
contemptuously.

" I don't know where they came from, but I do know he
shook them one after another like so many rats."

" Let him try to shake me," said James Buchanan, his
round head weaving the air like a boxer's. " I'll pull his
lugs for him."

" His what ? " Myrtle asked.

" His ears. Ay, and his nose. Shake me, will he ? "
James threatened.

" He might shoot you," said Myrtle. " He shot a crooner
in a portable radio."

" This is a really great chance for poetic action," the
bard observed, a dreamy smile quickening upon his rowan-
red lips.

" It's a great chance for action of any kind, poetic or
otherwise," James Buchanan declared. " Shake me, will
he ? Man, I hope fine he just tries. You're sure the ploy
is to start this afternoon, Miss Royde, because I have to go
back to Glasgow to-morrow and I don't want to miss this
shaking ? "

" But you forget, Mr Buchanan, that Ben Nevis has
keepers and beaters, not to mention his two sons," Myrtle
said.

" So big a Chieftain's sure to have a tail," Alan Macmillan
scoffed. " Well, maybe he and his tail will be able to throw
James and me into the nearest loch. But if they do I promise James and I will come back with a tail of our own and
throw him and his sons and his keepers and his beaters into
every loch he owns, one after another."

" You know, I'm crazy about Scotland," Myrtle declared,
gazing into Alan's eyes. " You're *all* so fierce. It makes
Chicago seem kind of slow and sleepy. And you're so
much what my idea used to be about poets, Mr Macmillan,
until I met two or three of them and found them sissie or
highbrow. Well, I suppose if you're set on shooting it out
with Ben Nevis nothing I can say or do will change your
mind. I don't know what I'm going to tell my sister-in-
law when I see her. I guess she's going to call me the
world's worst diplomat. She'll be sure that if *she* had given
you the warning you'd have listened to her. Perhaps you
would," Myrtle added softly, with a sidelong glance from
beneath her long-lashed lids at the poet, whose rose-browned
complexion caught a deeper rose as he replied in a carefully
indifferent tone that nobody could persuade him to run
away from Ben Nevis.

James Buchanan caught Myrtle's sidelong glance, and his
brow puckered. Two of them, within twenty-four hours, he
reflected. However, this one was not married. He wished
he did not have to go back to Glasgow to-morrow. If
Alan stayed here in defiance of those ' No Camping ' notices,

it looked as if things would be amusing.

" Are you rested now, Miss Royde ? " he asked. " Would you like to see our camp ? "

" I'd adore to see your camp if it isn't very far," Myrtle assured them. " But I have to be back by half-past one to lunch. Oh, I know, perhaps I'll be picked up by the car. I'm getting pretty good at walking, but I'm not a world-beater yet."

" It's about a mile further up the glen," she was told.

" I guess I can crawl as far as that."

Myrtle was right. She did manage to reach the camp, where the two little green tents were pitched on the level sward in the shelter of the granite escarpment.

" I'm devoted to Ben Nevis as I told you, but I can't for the life of me see why he objects to two cunning little green tents like these," she commented. " Why, they hardly take up any more room than a couple of lettuces." She turned to Alan Macmillan. " Which is yours ? "

He showed her and she peeped in to admire the sleeping-bag.

" Is that some of your poetry ? " she asked, pointing to an open exercise-book, the manuscript in which was covered with erasures and corrections.

" It's something I'm working at, yes," the bard admitted unwillingly.

A picture presented itself to Myrtle's mind, the picture of herself living in a little green tent like this and listening some of the time to birdsong and the rest of the time to poetry inspired by herself, a melodious and carefree exist-ence. She looked at her watch, one of the most expensive that ever came out of Tiffany's.

" Oh dear, I'd like to stay, but I suppose I ought to be getting back to Glenbogle if I'm not going to miss that ride back in the car," she sighed.

." What's the matter, Miss Royde ? " the lawyer asked.

" Oh, I don't know. I was just thinking what a false existence we most of us lead. This is real life."

" It's all right when it's fine," the bard allowed.

" Yes, I dare say if it's pouring with rain you might feel it was just a little bit too real." She sighed again. " It seems a pity you shouldn't be allowed to enjoy this lovely weather. Would your pride be terribly hurt if I were to ask Ben Nevis as a special favour to let you camp here in peace? Mind you, I can't be absolutely sure he'd give you permission, but I've a notion he *would* listen to me."

"James is going back to Glasgow to-morrow, anyway," said the bard. "And I'll accept no favours from a man like Ben Nevis. It's against my political principles."

"How rigid you are! But what are you going to do if Ben Nevis really does get violent? I mean to say there are only two of you. You couldn't hope to win in a fight. I've seen what he can do with sixteen hikers, and eight of them women. And when Mr Buchanan leaves you to-morrow, what will you do, Mr Macmillan?"

"I am not going to run away from Ben Nevis," the bard declared. "I'll not do that for anybody."

"I'll tell you what you might do, Alan," said his friend. "You might move up to that cave on Ben Cruet. They're not likely to find you there."

"Uaimh na laoigh," the bard muttered, paying such great attention to the correct pronunciation of the Gaelic that Myrtle thought he was groaning.

"Oh, you're in pain," she exclaimed with quick sympathy. The bard looked at her in astonishment.

"No, I'm not."

"But you groaned as if you were in pain."

"I wasn't groaning," said the bard indignantly. "I was saying the name of the cave in Gaelic. Uaimh na laoigh. The Cave of the Calf."

"Pardon me. That's where I lag behind my sister-in-law. She knows Gaelic."

"Not very much," the bard commented.

"Oh well, of course I can't criticize," Myrtle said, aware of a slight pleasure in the fact that Carrie did not know very much Gaelic. "But I think this plan for you to go and live in a cave is very good. Is it terribly far away from where we are now?"

"If you can get a little way up the brae at the back I can show you more or less where it is," Alan volunteered.

James Buchanan nodded agreement with some reflection of his own.

Scrambling up to a point whence the whereabouts of the cave could be pointed out involved a good deal of help from Alan's hand for Myrtle, who thought it must have been the long walk from Glenbogle Castle which had made her a little stiff.

At last they reached a level grassy ridge from which Alan pointed out a mass of stone some seven or eight hundred feet up the slopes of Ben Cruet on the other side of which was the Cave of the Calf.

" It's quite an easy climb," he assured Myrtle.

" And I'm getting better and better at climbing every day," she told him. " How long do you think you'll camp in that cave ? "

" I've only provisions for three days."

" Only for three days ? And then what will you do ? "

" I'll have to camp somewhere nearer to where I can buy provisions."

" And how long will you stay there ? "

" I promised my mother I'd be back in Glasgow in another week. She wants to go and stay with some friends in Perth and I said I'd go with her."

" Why doesn't your father go with her ? "

" My father's dead."

" Oh, I'm sorry. Well, of course you must take your mother to Perth. How long do you think you'll stay there ? I'm asking all these questions because I know Mrs Royde will expect me to come back full of the latest correct information about your movements. She took such a very great fancy to you both."

" I expect we'll be in Perth about a week."

" And then ? "

" Oh, I expect I'll go back to Glasgow."

" That reminds me. Mrs Royde wants your address and Mr Buchanan's address. She liked Mr Buchanan so very much. She spoke with such deep admiration of his grasp of statistics."

" I'll give you our addresses when we get back to the tents."

Myrtle sighed.

" Why do you sigh ? " the bard asked.

" I was thinking how sad life was so often. I mean to say, look at us. Ships that pass in the night, and speak each other in passing. Only a look and a . . . and a . . . how does it go on ? "

" I'm afraid I don't know."

" Well, it doesn't matter. You understand what I mean. I'll go back to America at the end of next month by the latest. And you're going to Perth next week. Of course I might see you again while you're living in your cave. But I might not. This may be the last time we ever meet."

"I hope not," said the bard, and his eyes were now a melting blue that Myrtle found even more entrancing than when they were lighted by the flame of prospective combat.

"Do you really hope not?"

"Yes, really."

"Well, of course Mrs Royde and I might come along together either to-morrow or the next day. My sister-in-law's so very romantic. I think she'll be crazy to see your cave. Now, I'm not romantic at all. I suppose that shocks you as a poet?"

"Not in the least," said the bard. "I am extremely anti-romantic myself."

"You are? Well, that's another link between us because I pride myself on being intensely practical. But that isn't quite fair to Carrie—Carrie is my sister-in-law. She is romantic, but she is also intensely practical. Perhaps not quite as practical as me. I'm so practical you could almost call me hard-boiled."

"Well, being very practical myself," said the bard, "I only admire practical women."

"Didn't I hear your friend Mr Buchanan call you 'Alan'?"

"Yes, that's my name."

"Strange. It has always been a very favourite name of mine. I don't know why at all. I never knew any Alan I had a crush on. I don't remember any Alan in a book I liked very much. And yet I've always been kind of fond of that name. Oh well, we mustn't stay chatting here. I'll have to get back to Glenbogle. So, I suppose it's good-bye, Mr Macmillan."

"James and I will walk with you as far as the end of Glenbristle."

"That's very sweet of you."

It was even harder for Myrtle to scramble back down to the level where the two little green tents were pitched. She had to hold the bard's hand almost all the way.

"I told Miss Royde we would walk along with her as far as Glenbogle, James," said the bard.

"And we must walk very quickly," Myrtle added, "or I'll miss the car."

It was already a quarter to one when Myrtle and her escort

reached the signpost at the entrance to Glenbristle.

" I'd love to have you walk along with me a bit more of
the way, but I think the sight of you both in Glenbogle
might stir up trouble," she said. " And I do want Mrs
Royde and myself to have the pleasure of visiting you in
your cave before your provisions run out," she added to the
bard. " Tell me the name of it again."

" Uaimh na laoigh."

" I do think it's the most melancholy sound I ever heard.
I'm sure the poor calf it was called after never managed to
make such a heartrending moo when it wanted mother. I'll
have lots of fun trying to have Mrs Royde tell me what it
means. Will you write it down on the envelope with your
address ? "

The bard obliged.

" And those three words make a noise like that ? " Myrtle
asked in awe. She emitted a melodious groan. " Is that
anything at all like it ? "

" Ooav na. . . ." the bard choked. In his endeavour
to make the ' laoigh ' sufficiently guttural the ' gh ' broke
away from the preceding vowels and entered his windpipe.

" Oh, you haven't sprained your throat ? " she asked
anxiously.

" No, it's perfectly all right. As a matter of fact ' laogh '
—that's the nominative—is one of the great test words in
Gaelic pronunciation."

" I'll say it must be. I hope there's a more comfortable
word for ' veal.' Otherwise, I think one's table manners
wouldn't be considered too good. Well, I suppose we have
to part. Good-bye, Mr Buchanan. I won't see you again.
Good-bye, Mr Macmillan. Mrs Royde and I will try our
hardest to visit you in your cave. If I were you I'd move
right up there now just in case Ben Nevis goes on the warpath
in Glenbristle."

" I'll camp up there with you to-night, Alan," James
Buchanan offered. " I'll take the bridle-path across to
Glenbore to-morrow morning and catch the Fort William
bus from there. I think it saves sixpence. I'm not sure
about that, but I think it does."

" Oh, I'm so glad yu've decided to move too, Mr
Buchanan," Myrtle said. " That will be such good news
for Mrs Royde."

" Mind you, I'm not moving because I'm afraid of a

shaking from Mr MacDonald of Ben Nevis," James Buchanan announced truculently.

"Surely not, Mr Buchanan. You're moving to oblige Mrs Royde and me, which is most chivalrous of you."

Myrtle shook hands and set out towards the Castle. The two young men sat down on a bank above the road and watched the trim figure disappear round a bend.

"A nice wee lassie," James observed. "Och, I like these American women a lot better than I like Englishwomen. They make you feel at home with them much more quickly. Losh, Alan, there's not many Englishwomen could have made me agree to move up to yon cave because that clown of a laird has been blethering away what he's going to do with campers. I felt it was a bit weak right enough, but och, I hadn't the heart to refuse the wee lassie. You know, I made sure she had come along to say that hundred-dollar bill was a mistake. I was a bit relieved to find she hadn't, I tell you. Twenty pounds is a lot of money for a treasurer to be asked to hand back. I'd been building a good deal on that twenty pounds, Alan. But you'll need to watch your step pretty well."

"Why?"

"I'm telling you."

"What are you telling me?"

"I'm just telling you. You'll need to watch your step."

"Why?"

"I'm telling you, Alan."

"You're not telling me."

"You know fine what I mean."

"I haven't the remotest idea."

"Ach, get away with you, Alan. Do you mind Annie Duncan?"

"Of course I do."

"And Jeanie Duncan?"

"Of course."

"Well, that's what I said, I'm telling you."

"The circumstances are entirely different."

"Och ay, the circumstances are different, but the root of the matter is just the same."

"Neither Annie nor Jeanie was married," Alan pointed out. "And they were sisters."

"Well, I'll admit that you were in a more difficult position with them. Still, though neither of them managed to hook you, it started a family row which has lasted ever since. So all I'm telling you is ' watch your step.' If you start trying to teach yon wee dark-eyed lassie how to pronounce Gaelic you'll be in trouble with the other. And I don't want to lose Sister Carrie's voluntary donations. Besides, she may buy this property up here. She's what the S.B.A. has been looking for."

" Imphm! " the poet grunted in agreement.

" Imphm! " the lawyer echoed.

Then they lit their pipes and lay back on the grassy bank, staring at the cloudless sky. A quarter of an hour passed in silence, at the end of which time they sat up to look at a car go by in the direction of the Castle.

They did not hear Ben Nevis bellow, " Scottish Nationalists, by gad! " though the bellow was so loud that those inside the car might have been forgiven for supposing it was heard by the people in the streets of Inverness and Fort William, by the monks of Fort Augustus, by the patients in the Kingussie Sanatorium, and even a faint echo of it by the spinsters and the knitters in the sun on the marina at Oban.

However, the passing of the car stirred them to get up and walk back to their camp in Glenbristle.

" My god! " James exclaimed. " Somebody has gone off with the tents."

Alan ran across to where his sleeping-bag was still lying upon the grass at the foot of the rocky escarpment.

" My poems are all right," he shouted.

" What good are they ? " James yelled back indignantly. " We can't sleep under a blasted exercise-book."

" We'd better take the rest of our stuff up to the cave right away," Alan suggested, when his friend reached the scene of the raid.

" But who can have taken the tents ? " James demanded.

The answer to that question was given not to the owners of the tents but to the guests of Ben Nevis assembled in the dining-room at the Castle, when at twenty minutes to two Catriona and Mary MacDonald, crimson in the face with the exertions they had made to be back in time for lunch at half-past one, came heftily in and before their father could tell them that they were ten minutes late, like two hunters flinging down the skins of the wild beasts they had slain, flung down on the floor beside him two little green tents.

" Found them in Glenbristle," Catriona growled.

" We'd taken the bridle-path," Mary growled.

" Wanted to see if we could put up a record in this dry weather," Catriona explained.

" We should have done if we hadn't spotted these tents," said Mary. " But lugging them with us took the stuffing out of our final spurt."

" Sorry we're late for lunch, father," Catriona growled.

" But we thought you'd like these trophies," growled Mary.

" These tents must belong to those Scottish Nationalists we saw loafing about by Glenbristle," said the Chieftain. " Well, that gives us the beat for this afternoon."

Carrie and Myrtle were eyeing one another across the table in consternation when into the dining-room there floated from without the sound of choric booing.

" What the deuce is that wild hullabaloo ? " Ben Nevis shouted.

Toker hurried to the window.

" Some kind of demonstration appears to be proceeding, sir," the butler informed him.

" Proceeding where ? "

" It doesn't appear to be proceeding anywhere, sir. It's just proceeding in the courtyard. It's some kind of gathering."

The chieftain jumped up from the table and looked out of the window. The sight of him swelled the gathering from a pimple to a fiery carbuncle. The booing doubled and redoubled in volume and above it were heard such derisive epithets as ' Fascist bully,' 'Scotch landgrabber,' 'Old Bluenose,' ' Tartanface,' ' Mussolini,' and ' MacBlimp,' accompanied by arpeggios of shrill and mocking female laughter.

" Donald, Donald," his wife begged, " don't expose yourself to this kind of thing. It does no good. Pay no attention and let us get on quietly with our lunch."

" You infamous riff-raff," Ben Nevis leant out of the window to bawl at the hikers, who shook their fists at him with cries of ' Fascist hound,' ' Fascist crook,' ' Dirty Dictator,' ' Stinking Blackshirt,' and amid catcalls, groans, and hisses, ' we want Mosley ! '

The furious Chieftain was now leaning out of the window like Punch in one of his paroxysms, leaning out so far indeed that the anxious Toker was standing by, ready to snatch at his kilt if necessary to save him from diving head foremost into the courtyard.

"Murdoch! Iain!" Mrs MacDonald exhorted. "Do get your father away from that window. Hugh! Mr Royde! Please use your influence. Mr Fletcher, you know what those dreadful hikers are capable of. Couldn't you most kindly go down into the courtyard and quieten them?"

"Best thing is to turn the hose on them," Mary growled.

"Mary, I'm astonished at you," her mother boomed reproachfully. "After what I said to you and Catriona yesterday evening."

But above the maternal boom resounded the paternal bellow.

"I defy you, you Bolshie scum! You won't get off so easily next time."

Mrs MacDonald now rose from the table and went across to lay a soothing arm upon her furious lord.

"Donald, please remember your dignity and do not argue with these people."

"But you didn't hear what they said to me, Trixie. They said they were going to make me learn the meaning of democracy. They actually had the infernal impudence to threaten me with reprisals."

The memory of this flooded him with fresh rage, and shaking off his wife's restraining arm he rushed to the window again.

But apparently by now the hikers had said what they had to say. They had hoisted their knapsacks and camping equipment and with bowed backs they were moving off across the courtyard toward the gates.

Few sights offer to the tender-hearted observer so poignant an illustration of man's weary pilgrimage through this vale of tears as that of hikers overloaded with equipment moving from their camping-ground to the nearest railway-station at the end of a holiday. Perhaps the only rival among the spectacles of human misery is that of hikers overloaded with equipment streaming out of a railway-station toward their camping-ground at the beginning of a holiday.

"Poor things," sighed Mrs MacDonald. "They do look so tired."

"Poor things?" her husband echoed wrathfully. "They'll look a good deal more tired before I've done with them. But come along, let's finish our lunch first."

" Donald, what are you proposing to do now ? "

" I'm going to keep them on the move with the lorry all the way down Glenbogle," the Chieftain declared, and the expression upon his countenance was the expression of a Caligula gloating over the prospect of some gladiatorial enormity.

" Then do we give a miss this afternoon to these Scottish Nationalists ? " Chester Royde asked. The question was not in fact prompted by blood-lust, but by the new owner of Knocknacolly's desire to get a closer view of the Macmillan and Buchanan tartan, the glimpse of which he had caught from the Daimler having inspired him with a greater respect than ever for the possibilities of Highland dress.

" Oh, we can deal with those brutes to-morrow," said Ben Nevis. " Or the next day."

" I hope not the next day," said Mr Fletcher gently. " The next day is Sunday."

Carrie and Myrtle looked at one another. Both of them were thinking what a good day that would be to visit the poet.

Chapter 9

THE CAVE OF THE CALF

OF the way in which Ben Nevis with a motorized column consisting of the lorry, the Daimler, Kilwhillie's seven-year-old Austin, and Murdoch MacDonald's two-seater harried those sixteen hikers for eight miles down Glenbogle the victims shall tell presently. It is enough at this point to say that he returned from the operation in boisterous good-humour and, much to the relief of Carrie and Myrtle, seemed to have forgotten about the Scottish Nationalists in the excitement of planning to shoot the Knocknacolly moors next day.

" Mind you, it's not for the birds you've bought Knockna-colly, Royde. It's for the stalking," he warned the new proprietor. " You've not killed your first stag yet. I hope you're going to do that next week So you mustn't expect the birds we should have had on Drumcockie if they hadn't been scared by those disgusting hikers."

" There should be plenty of birds," Kilwhillie put in modestly. " Of course Knocknacolly is not Clacknaclock and it's not Drumcockie, but you should have some good sport."

" Ah, but I want to get him after a good stag at the back of Ben Goosey," said the Chieftain. " I can't tell you how much I'm looking forward to initiating you into the king of sports, what ? "

" I'm looking forward to it myself," said the young financier.

" I don't want you to go away with the idea that harrying hikers is the only sport we can offer you in the Highlands."

" My dear Ben Nevis, I wouldn't want to spend a more thoroughly enjoyable time than I spent this afternoon hust-ling those hoodlums out of Glenbogle. It was great."

" You haven't seen Knocknacolly yet, Myrtle," said her host, a genial glow warming his eagle's beak. " I tell you what. Murdoch shall drive you in his car to-morrow."

" Oh, that'll be very exciting," said Myrtle. " But I don't think I ought to monopolize Murdoch. I know Carrie would like to drive in the two-seater."

" But I'm not going to-morrow," said Carrie quickly.

" Carrie! " her sister-in-law exclaimed.

" Well, I've a whole heap of letters to write."

" So have I," said Myrtle. " I believe I ought to stay home too."

" Oh, Myrtle, you haven't seen Knocknacolly yet."

" But I'd like to see it with you. I want to hear your plans for it."

" But I'd like to hear your ideas after you've seen the lodge. Then we can see if your ideas are the same as mine. I think it would be a pity for you not to go to-morrow just because I have a whole heap of letters to write. Besides, I want to work at my Gaelic."

" Oh, you do ? "

" Yes, I really do, Myrtle. When I start something I always like to stick to it."

" Yes, I know how very persevering you are."

" Well, now we've bought Knocknacolly I do feel I ought to be able to speak Gaelic. Don't you think I'm right to persevere with my Gaelic, Ben Nevis ? "

" I do indeed. Only wish I could speak it as well now as I could when I was a four-year-old," said the Chieftain. " I used to rattle it off to my nurse in those days. I've always regretted I didn't keep it up."

" And I want Chester to learn too," Carrie went on. " He's very good at languages."

" That's right. You mastered Red Indian, didn't you, Royde ? " Ben Nevis asked. " You ought to be able to tackle Gaelic."

" I picked up a bit of the Carroway language," Chester admitted modestly.

" Rather like my Gaelic, I suppose. You don't speak it, but you understand it."

" I understand a word here and there."

" Oh, I don't understand every word in Gaelic," Ben Nevis continued. " But if I know what they're talking about I can follow perfectly what they say. What you want to do is to get hold of a few simple expressions one's always using up here like ' Half luke ' and ' Half ewer,' and then when they start talking back you smile and nod and they're awfully pleased."

" Half luke ? What's that mean ? "

" Half luke : it's wet. Half ewer: it's cold."

" Half luke. I must remember that," said Chester.

8

" I'll spell it for you, Chester," said his wife. " It comes in the first exercise of *Gaelic Without Tears*. T-H-A-E-F-L-I-U-C-H."

" What's that mean ? "

" It's wet."

" But Ben Nevis said ' it's wet ' was ' half luke.' "

" That's what I spelt for you."

" And you'd have me learn Gaelic ? "

" I certainly would, Chester."

" Well, I've thought of another way of shewing my appreciation of Scotland, Carrie."

" What's that ? "

" You'll see presently," said her husband, a dreamy look in his eyes.

" I believe I'll learn Gaelic," said Myrtle.

" What do you want to learn Gaelic for ? " asked her sister-in-law.

" Goody, why shouldn't I, Carrie ? "

" You aren't Scottish."

" Well, you don't have to be French to learn French," Myrtle protested. " No, ma'am, you certainly don't."

" Oh, if you want to learn Gaelic there's no reason why you shouldn't."

" I don't think so either," Myrtle said in a voice that made Carrie more determined than ever that her sister-in-law should go to Knocknacolly to-morrow and that she herself would stay at home to write letters.

But when the Knocknacolly party had left, Carrie felt it was a pity to waste such lovely weather indoors over letters and told her hostess that she thought she'd explore Glenbristle again, and have another picnic lunch by herself.

" Isn't there a cave somewhere near Glenbristle where Prince Charlie hid from the redcoats ? " she asked.

" Oh, my dear child, Prince Charlie's cave is away on the other side of Glenbogle half-way up Ben Booey. You'd never find it by yourself even if you could walk as far."

" I suppose I must have dreamt about this cave near Glenbristle. It seems so familiar somehow. But I have these strange dreams about the past, Mrs MacDonald."

" Do you, dear ? " her hostess boomed placidly. " You should drink a cup of camomile before you go to sleep. it's an old-fashioned remedy, but these old-fashioned remedies are often the best."

"But I like dreaming, Mrs MacDonald."

"I can't say I do. I dislike so much the feeling of not being able to control one's movements, which is such a feature of most dreams."

When Carrie received her sandwiches from the hands of Toker she asked him if he knew anything about a cave near Glenbristle.

"I'm afraid I don't, madam, but if you wouldn't mind waiting for a minute I will endeavour to ascertain from one of the gillies if such a cave exists. It is certainly well within the bounds of probability that it does. Excuse me, madam."

Toker withdrew from the hall in search of information, and when he was gone Carrie caught sight of the two green tents that Catriona and Mary had brought back as trophies yesterday. They were lying neatly folded under the table on which the MacDonalds parked their bonnets. The spirit of the Scottish Brotherhood of Action animated its latest member with the resolution to return the tents to their dispossessed owners. But when she pulled them out from under the table she found it was beyond her power to manage both tents. Even one would not make walking easy. She lacked the heftiness of the MacDonald girls. Just then the butler came back.

"I have made enquiries, madam, about this cave, and it would appear that there is a cave on the lower slopes of Ben Cruet overlooking Glenbristle. I'm afraid I could not venture to make any attempt to pronounce the name of the cave in Gaelic. I have been in the service of Ben Nevis for twelve years, but although I have read all Sir Walter Scott's wonderful novels and take an intense interest in the legendary lore of the Highlands I have no Gaelic."

"I'm learning Gaelic now, Toker."

"Are you indeed, madam? May I respectfully express my admiration? You have indeed set yourself a task. But to return to this cave. It would appear that the most convenient way of obtaining access to it from here is via the old bridle-path to Glenbore. When you reach the gate of the drive instead of carrying on along the road down Glenbogle you should bear up the slope, or brae as they call it here, to the left and follow this path. The cave would appear to lie some five miles further along, quite an appreciable walk in fact and by no means any too smooth."

"I'll take it very easy."

" Precisely, madam, and the view as you come round the shoulder of Ben Cruet and look down into Glenbristle and across over Glenbogle is said to be exceptionally fine. Probably you will choose this point of vantage to consume your lunch."

" It sounds the very spot. Oh, and that reminds me, Toker, I thought I'd take one of these tents with me."

" Pardon my apparent density, madam, but what would be your object in doing that ? These are the tents belonging to two campers which Miss Catriona and Miss Mary brought back at lunch yesterday."

" Why, I thought one of these tents would be so nice to sit on for my lunch."

" You would not find a plaid more commodious, madam ? I will procure a light one for you, if you desire."

" No, I'd rather have one of these tents. There's no objection to my taking one of them ? "

" None whatever, madam. They are at present very much in the position of articles in a lost-property office. I could not say if there would be any probability of your meeting one of the owners, but I should surmise that would be a far stretch even for the proverbially long arm of coincidence."

" Well, if I did bump into one of the owners I could say I found it," Carrie suggested.

" That would undoubtedly offer a perfectly feasible explanation, madam. Shall I fold the tent for you as handily as possible ? "

" Thank you, Toker, if you will, please."

The butler set about his task with the gravity of a high priest performing a solemn rite.

" I have made as good a job of it as I could, madam, but I fear it's an awkward bundle, except for the back, which is the method adopted by hikers for what may be called without the least irreverence, I trust, taking up their beds and walking. Are you quite sure, madam, that on second thoughts you would not prefer me to fetch you a plaid ? "

" No, I think you've made quite a convenient bundle for me, Toker, thank you."

" I appreciate the compliment, madam, though I venture to think I hardly deserve it. I hope you will have an agreeable day, madam, and that the cave will repay you for the long and somewhat arduous walk."

" I'm sure it will."

Carrie put a loop of the tent round her cromag, swung the cromag over her shoulder, and set out.

" Well, the more I see of Americans, Mrs Parsall, the queerer I think 'em," Toker presently observed to the housekeeper. " There's Mrs Royde now. Nothing would please her but she must take a tent to sit on. Gone off with it over her shoulder like a blooming Dick Whittington."

" Americans ? " Mrs Parsall echoed. " Don't talk to me about Americans, Mr Toker. Good English milk gone sour, that's what Americans are."

The particular American whose oddity had been the occasion of this observation by the Glenbogle housekeeper had never felt less American than this morning when she was on the way to strengthen the mystical bonds of race that linked her to that attractive young poet. The acquisition of Knocknacolly had changed the outlook a good deal. It meant that for the next two or three years at any rate she and Chester would be coming over to Scotland regularly. It meant that Knocknacolly could become the centre from which the regenerative activities of the Scottish Brotherhood of Action might exercise a benign influence over the whole country. It meant, putting politics on one side, that she might become the patroness of Scottish art. The future was so full of promise that it was some time before Carrie realized what an awkward addition to a walk was provided by a folded tent. She was tempted to deposit it beside the bridle-path and leave it to Alan Macmillan to rescue if he felt inclined. Then she recalled her racial background. Ancestrally she had wandered barefoot along these slopes, her back bent beneath a creel of peats. Was she, a degenerate MacDonald of to-day, going to falter beneath the weight of a portable tent ?

Carrie had been toiling along in laborious progress for about an hour when the repeated changes she had been making in the way she held the tent at last broke down Toker's careful arrangement of it in a comparatively neat bundle, and the green canvas, after trying to wrap her up in itself, began to drag behind her in an unwieldy train. Once again the temptation to leave the tent beside the path assailed her, but she called upon the spirits of her ancestors and stooped to conquer.

Preoccupied with the task of trying to refold the tent,

Carrie did not hear anybody approaching and was much startled when she heard a gruff voice say:

"No camping is allowed here."

She swung round to see gazing at her over her shoulder a gaunt, unshaven, wall-eyed man in brown tweed with a powerful cromag and a gaunt, matted, wall-eyed retriever.

"I'm not camping," said Carrie.

"No camping is allowed here," the gaunt man repeated.

"But I'm not camping," she insisted.

"No camping is allowed here," the gaunt man repeated yet again, and as if vexed by the strain that was being put upon his master's speech the wall-eyed dog gave a low growl.

Those who have tried to argue with a wall-eyed man, or for that matter with a wall-eyed dog, will recognize at once the disability under which Carrie laboured. So much does the wall-eye always dominate the other eye on such occasions that every remark is addressed to it, with the result that a despair of establishing rational intercourse asserts itself and one surrenders to the irrational.

"I don't expect you know who I am," Carrie said, smiling, she felt hopelessly, at the wall-eye.

"No, I don't know who you are," the gaunt man agreed, and the assertion of his ignorance must have carried with it an indication of hostility, for the dog growled again.

"Tha è blath," Carrie observed.

"I don't know that name at all," the gaunt man replied.

"You're not a Gaelic speaker then?"

"Are you a Gaelic speaker?"

"I'm learning to speak it."

"Were you speaking to me in Gaelic then?"

"Yes, I said ' it's warm.' Tha è blath."

"When you are after saying it in English first I know what you are after saying in Gaelic. Yes, it is warm. It's very warm. But camping is not allowed here."

She was up against that wall-eye again.

"But I told you, I'm not camping here. I'm staying at the Castle. I'm staying with Ben Nevis. I suppose you are one of his keepers?"

"Yes, I am one of the keepers. And you are staying at Glenbogle Castle?"

"I certainly am."

The wall-eye contemplated the outspread tent for a

moment, and then fixed its opaque glance on Carrie.

" If you are staying at Glenbogle Castle, why are you camping here ? "

" But I tell you I am not camping here."

" That is a camping-tent."

" Yes, that's a camping-tent."

" If you are not camping here, why do you have a camping-tent ? "

Carrie was in a quandary. If she said the tent belonged to a friend to whom she was taking it, this gaunt, wall-eyed man was capable of following her until she reached the cave, and that might make things awkward for Alan Macmillan.

" Well, I don't know if Ben Nevis would approve of one of his guests being questioned like this by one of his keepers, but the reason why I have this tent with me is because I wanted something to sit on while I was eating my lunch."

The gaunt man shook his head.

" It's not at all what I would be thinking anybody would do," he said sceptically. Then he doffed his cap and gazed across to the Three Sisters of Glenbogle for counsel. " Well," he said at last, turning to Carrie, " you've put me into a very difficult kind of a situation. I'll just have to walk down to the Castle and receive my instructions. And I'll have to ask you to stay where you are till I am after receiving them. Ben Nevis's orders about campers are very strict. If he was to hear I had let a camper get the better of me, my place would be gone to-morrow. I'm sorry, mistress, to disconvenience you, but if you are a friend of Ben Nevis you'll know the kind of man he is and understand I'm only doing my duty. I'll leave my dog with you. There'll be no harm in him if you stay where you are, but you'll please understand it's his business to see you don't move from where you are."

With these words the gaunt man said something in Gaelic to his dog and then strode off at a rapid pace along the path leading back to the Castle.

Carrie sat for ten minutes in a fume of indignation under the horribly steady glare of that milky pale-blue eye. The ancestral memories which should have illuminated with a sense of human continuity her present situation at the mercy of a tyrant forsook her. Then she tried to make friends with her gaoler, calling him ' good old fellow ' and

' nice old dog '; but no epithet tender or fulsome availed
to clarify to the semblance of canine kindness that opaque,
remorseless eye.

" Oh, well, I may as well eat my sandwiches," she murmured to herself.

After she had munched away three or four she fancied
she discerned a glimmer in that agate which eyed her and
flung a sandwich to the dog. It did not even sniff it. It
merely growled censoriously. Cerberus was more venal and
his three heads less deterrent than this solitary milky wall-eye.

" I'd like to wring your neck, you darned coyote," Carrie
told him.

He settled his nose between his paws and growled a
surly defiance.

It says something for Carrie's devotion to an ideal that
during the hour and a half which elapsed before the gaunt
man came back she had worked through two long exercises
in *Gaelic Without Tears*.

" I must apologize, Mistress Royde," the keeper said,
doffing his cap. " Mr Toker is after telling me that you'll be
looking for *Uaimh na Laoigh*. I'll take you there myself."

" What am I looking for ? "

" *Uaimh na laoigh*. The Cave of the Calf."

" Wait a minute. I'll have you say that again when I've
found the words in my book. I've got it; *uamh*, cave.
What's calf? I've got it. *Laogh*. Genitive, *laoigh*. Now
say it again, will you ? "

The gaunt man did so. Carrie tried to imitate him,
and the dog growled fiercely, receiving a blow on the
haunches from his master's cromag and a Gaelic oath.

" You're saying it very well, Mistress Royde. It's very
difficult to say well."

" You didn't seem to think much of my Gaelic pronunciation when I said it was warm, and that's a darned sight
easier to say than uaimh na laoigh."

" Will we be going along there now ? "

Carrie shook her head.

" Why, no, I don't think I'll go there this afternoon.
I'll go right along back to the Castle. You can carry that
tent for me," she added quickly, for it occurred to her that
if she left him here the keeper and his dog might go and
fix Alan Macmillan with their wall-eyes. " What's your
name ? " she asked.

" Neil Maclennan. I hope you'll make a complaint about me to Ben Nevis, mistress."

" You do ? "

" Yes. He'll be hearing then what an eye I'm keeping on me for these hikers and campers and he'll be very pleased. I'm sure of that. Och, yes, he'll be very pleased indeed."

" Oh, you think he'd like to hear you'd handed over one of his guests to that lovely-looking dog of yours. What's his name ? "

" Smeorach."

Carrie searched the vocabulary of *Gaelic Without Tears*.

" But that means ' thrush.' That's a bird. What a queer sort of a name to give a savage animal like that! "

" Och, he's not at all savage."

" Oh, he's not ? "

" No, no; he's very gentle. Very kind."

" That·shows what very wrong ideas we can get into our heads about animals. But don't worry, Neil, I'll tell Ben Nevis that Smeorach and you together are the most savage things I've seen in this part of the world."

The gaunt man looked grateful.

" He's a very fine gentleman is Ben Nevis," he said fervidly.

" He's all that, and then some," Carrie agreed. " I suppose you'd lay down your life for him ? "

The gaunt man stopped, dropped the tent upon the path, and turned round to Carrie with a puzzled expression.

" Lay down my life for him ? " he repeated. " Was it die for him you were wanting to say ? "

" That's right," Carrie said encouragingly.

" I wouldn't want to die for anybody," said the gaunt man. " Och, I don't take to the notion of dying at all. It's very difficult to know what is going to happen. I wouldn't mind death so much at all if I was sure his friend Satan wasn't waiting round the corner just behind him. It's a terrible business that, right enough. The minister was preaching about it last Sunday morning. It was a very powerful sermon. It lasted for all but a quarter of two hours, and when we came out of the church we were just burning with the good man's words as if with the flames of Hell. Big Duncan—that's the headkeeper—he grew so hot that the packet of black-striped balls he keeps in his pocket melted with the heat and when he put his hand in

his pocket to find a black-striped ball for his grandson Willie
to suck, his hand just stuck inside the bag and he had to give
Willie two because he could not pull them apart.   Och, no,
mistress, I wouldn't be putting myself forward to die for
anybody."

"Doesn't the old clan loyalty survive?" Carrie asked.

"Och, there's no clans left now," said the gaunt man.
"The clans were finished long ago."

"And I suppose you think the fairies are finished too?"

"I never saw the fairies myself," said the gaunt man,
picking up the tent and continuing along the path toward
the Castle.   "But I wouldn't like to be so positive there are
none of them left.   Och, I'm not saying there *are* any of
them, but there might be."

Carrie found Toker distressed about the interruption of
her walk.

"It was quite all right," she assured him, "I was feeling
pretty tired when I was made to sit down and behave
myself."

"It's very good of you, madam, to take the unpleasant
business so philosophically."

"And after all he wasn't to know that I wasn't a hiker."

"I'm afraid I cannot accept your kind excuses for him,
madam.   It is the business of a gentleman's servant to
know these things.   It should be second nature, as they say."

When Myrtle returned from Knocknacolly she was full
of what a delightful place could be made of it if the present
lodge were pulled down and a modern house built on the site.

"It's a pity our boy friend isn't an architect, Carrie.
We might have gotten him a good job to keep him amused
till we came back next summer.   How did you find him in
his cave?"

"I didn't find him."

"You didn't?" Myrtle exclaimed.

"No; I had all those letters to write."

"And you wrote them?"

"I certainly did."

"But Mrs MacDonald said you took your lunch with you."

"So I did.   But I didn't go to the cave.   I just sat around
and dreamed for awhile and then came back here."

However, at dinner that night Ben Nevis gave the show
away by revealing that one of his keepers had suspected
Carrie of being a hiker.

Alone among the audience Toker preserved an expression of restrained disgust. The remainder of the party found the matter comic and laughed uproariously, particularly the victim's husband.

" Say, that's a peach, Ben Nevis," he declared. " I'll bet you were mad, Carrie, weren't you ? "

" Oh, I didn't mind at all," she replied. " I realized he was only doing what he thought was his duty. In fact his greatest anxiety was to have Ben Nevis know what he had done."

" Hark at that now," the Chieftain woofed with gusto. " Well, they may laugh at us up here for our old-fashioned notions of loyalty, discipline and obedience, but when one finds it I must say it warms the cockles of the heart. Don't you agree with me, Hugh ? I say it warms the cockles of the heart."

" Oh, very much so," Kilwhillie agreed. The cockles of his own heart were in a responsive condition to warmth that evening because Chester Royde had enjoyed his day with the Knocknacolly grouse so much that he hàd insisted on adding £500 to the purchase price and this meant the late owner would be able to buy a new car which ought to last him for another seven years. He was dreaming now of Royde's first stalk on Monday and of his killing a stag with such a forest of antlers that he would insist on adding yet another £500.

The next morning at service in the Castle Chapel Mr Fletcher preached on the text ' Be thou faithful unto death,' while the Chieftain cleared his throat from time to time in a manner as near to ejaculating ' hear, hear ' as left no doubt of his approval.

" Capital preacher, isn't he ? " he said to his guests. " And what I like particularly about his sermons is that he never gives one unless I ask him to. Can't stand this idea some clergymen have that a sermon is always welcome."

Carrie and Myrtle had planned to go for a walk together that Sunday afternoon and visit the cave, for they had both quickly realized that neither was going to be able to shake off the other. When the time came for them to start, however, they were discouraged to find that Murdoch and Iain were proposing to accompany them.

" We heard you wanted to see that cave on Ben Cruet," said Iain. " So as there's nothing for us to do, being Sunday afternoon, Murdoch and I thought you'd like us to show you just where it is."

"Oh, that's angelic of you, Iain," said Myrtle. "But there's no reason why you should put yourselves out for Carrie and me. We'll enjoy exploring the way for ourselves."

"Yes, indeed," Carrie added. "And besides, I think the cave is too far away for a Sunday afternoon walk. So please, don't bother; we'll just take a little walk by ourselves."

"It's no bother," said Murdoch solemnly.

"And we really have nothing to do this afternoon," Iain added. "We'd enjoy a walk."

"It's terribly sweet of you both," Carrie said. "But Myrtle and I couldn't think of dragging you out on such a hot afternoon. And it's looking very much like rain."

"I like a good tramp in the rain," Murdoch declared.

"I'm not so fond of rain myself," said Myrtle. "I'll tell you what, why don't you two boys take Carrie for a walk, and I'll stay home and write some letters?"

"Right-oh," Iain agreed, without a trace of disappointment in his reception of the news of Myrtle's defection.

"I don't think I want to get wet just to see a cave," said Carrie quickly. "Anyway, I'm not really so anxious to see this cave at all. I just had an idea yesterday that it would make a good object for a walk as I was by myself. And then Myrtle thought the cave sounded kind of cute. And we just thought we'd wander along and perhaps find it. But if it's going to rain I think I'll stay home."

Murdoch thumped the glass.

"Doubt if it'll rain before the sun goes down," he decided with nautical knowledgeableness.

"I wouldn't dream of setting my opinion against yours in the matter of weather," Carrie broke in, "but I believe it's going to rain this very afternoon. So I think the wisest plan is to give up visiting the cave to-day and go there some day later in the week. I'm sure I don't know what put this idea of a cave into my head?"

"You may have read about it in my little volume, *Echoes of Glenbogle*," said the chaplain.

"My, are you a poet too? I mean are you a poet, Mr Fletcher?" Carrie exclaimed.

" I have ventured to commit one or two little indiscretions in verse," the chaplain confessed.

" And you've written a poem about this cave. Oh, please read it to us, Mr Fletcher," Carrie begged.

" Oh, do, please, Mr Fletcher," Myrtle added earnestly. " I think it'll be so much nicer to hear Mr Fletcher's poem about the cave than walk all that way to see it, don't you, Carrie ? "

" I'd just adore to have Mr Fletcher read us his poem."

The chaplain smiled modestly and going to the bookcase took down the slim volume of his verse from which he began to read:

> Hark how the wind from Cruet's icy peak
> Wails through the corries to the glen below,
> The while within a cave a fugitive
> Shivers and shrinks to see the swirling snow.

> Through the long week the redcoats, a grim band,
> Glenbogle and Glenbristle for their prey,
> Had searched, and eke Strathdiddle and Strathdun,
> To reach the slopes of Cruet yesterday.

> The fugitive had heard their fierce halloos,
> But hidden in a dark and friendly cave,
> Had hitherto escaped their vigilance
> And laughed to think how wildly they would rave,

> Did they but guess how near he was to them
> And to their brutal and relentless grip.
> But ah, they knew it not, and so the band
> Passed by and brought a prayer to his lip.

> But why, when now the redcoats are away,
> Shivers and shrinks he in the swirling snow ?
> Why doth he hearken to the wild wind's howl
> As if it were the howling of the foe ?

> Alas ! it is because his Mary dear,
> Mary Macdonald of the nutbrown hair,
> Had promised him to come this very night,
> And bring provisions to his secret lair.

He gazes from the entrance of the cave
Into the fearsome night of storm without,
And when he cries in anguish, ' Mary mine ! '
He fancies he can hear an answering shout.

Into that fearsome night the fugitive
Rushes to seek her, but when she is found,
His Mary's lying in a shroud of snow,
A corpse upon Ben Cruet's cruel ground.

The chaplain closed the volume.

" Is that all ? " Myrtle asked.

" That is all."

" My, I think that's the saddest poem I ever heard. I don't think I could visit the cave this afternoon, could you, Carrie ? "

" No, I wouldn't want to visit it right now. But I thought it was called the Cave of the Calf."

" So it is, Mrs Royde. It was already called the Cave of the Calf when this young Jacobite fugitive had the sad experience which I have tried to express in poetic form."

" It's a true story ? " Carrie asked.

" Perfectly true," the clergyman replied. " His name was Alan Macdonald."

" Alan what ? "

" Alan Macdonald."

" And her name was Mary ? "

" Yes, Mary Macdonald. They both came from Glenbristle."

" And my great-great-great-great-grandfather would likely enough have known them both," Carrie exclaimed in awe. " Do you believe in reincarnation, Mr Fletcher ? "

" I'm afraid that is not an accepted Christian doctrine."

" Isn't that too bad ? We're very very interested in reincarnation over in the States. Several of my friends are just crazy about reincarnation. A classmate of mine had a revelation after she left college and found she was Catherine de' Medici, or was it Catherine of Aragon ? Myrtle, do you remember Katie Van Stiltzkin—Catherine Arkwright that was ? "

Myrtle nodded.

" Was it Catherine de' Medici or Catherine of Aragon she was the reincarnation of ? "

" I think it was both."

" Don't be foolish, Myrtle. You can't be the reincarnation of two people at once. That goes right against the whole principle of the thing. However, it doesn't matter about Katie Van Stiltzkin. It just occurred to me that perhaps I was the reincarnation of Mary Macdonald. Certainly when I was sitting up there yesterday afternoon and gazing away across Glenbogle I did feel a kind of hidden presence warning me to be careful."

" That must have been the keeper's dog," said Myrtle.

" I'm afraid my sister-in-law's terribly prosaic, Mr Fletcher. But do please read us some more of your poems."

" I'd like to hear the one about Alan Macdonald again," said Myrtle. " I don't know why, but Alan has always been a favourite name of mine."

" It has ? " Carrie asked suspiciously.

" Yes, ever since I can remember," Myrtle assured her with complete conviction.

Chapter 10

THE MUCKLE HART OF BEN GLASS

IT was the custom of Glenbogle for Angus MacQuat or another of the pipers to rouse Ben Nevis every morning at eight by playing beneath his window the ancient *Iomradh Mhic 'ic Eachainn* or *Fame of Mac 'ic Eachainn*, in which the virtue, nobility, valour and generosity of the chieftain of Ben Nevis were celebrated with what the less imaginative Southerner might have thought a certain amount of exaggeration. The tune, however, had a fine lilt and possessed a persuasive drive to energetic action which the shrilling of an alarm-clock lacks. Even the guest who had not been warned about the significance of this aubade often sprang out of bed to look out of the window and see what was being killed.

On that Monday morning in mid-August the skirling of *Iomradh Mhic 'ic Eachainn* was heard at the top of its power played by two pipers at six o'clock, and when the skirling of the pipers began a housemaid entered and drew the blinds to reveal a sky the grey expanse of which displayed a determination to rain as soon as it could, the kind of sky which makes fishermen stare with distasteful surprise at the fellow-guest in an hotel who remarks that the weather does not look too promising.

" He's getting us out good and early, Carrie," said her husband. " Will you go along to the bathroom first or will I ? "

" Why, I don't believe I'll come, Chester," she replied, yawning from the depths of the bedclothes. " It sounds a kind of a tiring business the way Ben Nevis described it last night at dinner. Besides, I wouldn't want to kill a lovely stag even if I were near enough for a shot at it."

" I forgot to tell you last night, but we've settled not to go stalking over at Knocknacolly. Ben Nevis wants me to have a shot at some particular stag he's had news of between Ben Booey and Ben Glass."

" Oh, then I certainly won't come, Chester."

" The only thing is I told Kilwhillie you'd like to have some time with him at Knocknacolly. I mean to say if we're

taking on the place right away I think you want to get
wise to the conditions there. After all, we'll have to make
quite a few arrangements before we go back to the States
next month. I want to get hold of an architect and have
him hustle next winter."

" I don't see that Kilwhillie will be much use over choosing
an architect, Chester. And what about the legal part of it ? "

" Why, I thought I'd have our London solicitors put that
through."

" Don't you think it would be better if we employed a
Scottish lawyer ? Scottish law is quite different from
English law, you know."

" How's it different ? "

" I don't know exactly how, but I know it's much better
and much cheaper."

" But do you know any Scottish lawyers ? "

" I heard of a young Scottish lawyer the other day who
was very highly spoken of. James Buchanan was his name.
I have his address in Glasgow. Wouldn't it be a good plan
if I asked him to come up here to take your instructions ?
And he might know of a good architect. I think we ought
to employ one of the younger Scottish architects, don't you,
Chester ? "

" I don't mind how young he is if he doesn't try to make
me live in one of those frozen cheeses like we saw on Friday.
Gee ! That was terrible."

" I want to have one of the artists of the Scottish Renaissance. I don't suppose you've heard about the Scottish
Renaissance."

" Can't say I have. What's it stand for ? "

" The rebirth of the whole country."

" That's O.K. by me. Only I'd like to use reborn artists
who have been weaned if it's all the same to you. But see
here, honey, I want you to have all the fun you can get out
of this little place. It's yours. Got me ? "

" Oh, Chester ! "

" Yes, you're to be the owner of Knocknacolly."

" Chester, how sweet of you ! "

" Well, I guess I'll go and dress myself now for this stag-
hunt. If you don't want to go over to Knocknacolly with
Kilwhillie, you'll have to tell him yourself."

" All right, Chester. But I'm not going to get up yet
awhile."

9

"Get up nothing," said the young financier. "I wouldn't be jumping around in pajamas at this time of the morning if I didn't think Ben Nevis would be singing *Kathleen Mavourneen* to me in a minute."

Carrie dozed off again, but was awakened about seven o'clock by Chester's coming back into the room.

"Say, this deer-stalking seems to be a pretty serious business," he announced.

"What's the matter, Chester?"

"I've been sent back to put on different clothes."

"What's the matter with your clothes?"

"That's what I asked Ben Nevis when he took exception to them at breakfast."

"I think they look very good."

It is true that her husband looked like an even more brightly-coloured full-page advertisement in *Esquire* than he had on the Twelfth, but Carrie thought men ought to look like that when they were indulging in country sports and pastimes.

"It seems they're too bright," said Chester. "Ben Nevis says I'll never get within a mile of a stag dressed like I am."

"But you're not wearing anything as bright as his kilt."

"That isn't what he thinks. Oh, he was very nice about it. He blamed it more on the stags than on my clothes. He said stags were exceptionally nervous animals and need to be humoured. It was my pullover which worried him most. He asked if it was made by the Indians."

"Made by Indians?" Carrie echoed indignantly. "Why, that's the pullover I gave you last Christmas, Chester. It's a genuine Fair Isle product. I paid thirty dollars for that pullover."

"Well, Ben Nevis looked at it the way he looked at the shirts of those hikers. But the whole rig-out wasn't his idea of the way anybody ought to be dressed for stalking stags. He said there was a big tradition behind this business of stalking and he wanted me to start in the steps of this tradition right away. Well, what's it matter anyway? I'll be stalking by myself presently on the Knocknacolly forest, and I'll wear what I like there. What I like," he repeated.

He came back a few minutes later in a suit of darkish green tweed.

"I didn't know you had a suit as quiet as that, Chester," said his wife.

" I didn't know it myself.   That's the advantage of a good
valet.   He makes it his job to be prepared for emergencies.
Well, seeing I'm dressed for a funeral I hope we'll kill a
pretty big stag.   I'll look kind of foolish if we come home with
only a couple of rabbits."

" When do you think you will be back, Chester ? "

" I don't know at all.   But there's a look in Ben Nevis's
eye which makes me think he intends to kill a stag to-day
even if involves killing me to do it."

" Perhaps I'll go over to Knocknacolly with Kilwhillie or
perhaps I won't.   It looks to me as if we'd have a downpour
before long."

" It doesn't look too good, does it ? "

" That'll mean you'll give up stalking and come home ? "

" Give it up ? " Chester exclaimed.   " Not Ben Nevis.   I
guess Ben Nevis would be the biggest disappointment to a
deluge since old man Noah.   Any deluge that thinks it can
stand between Ben Nevis and shooting a stag had better start
in to think again and remember what it felt like to be a
puddle."

The stalking novice left his wife and went down to join his
host.

" Ah, there you are.   That's better.   I hope you didn't
mind my suggesting you toned down your colour scheme,
what?   I mean to say, I'm a very old hand at this game and I
do want to give you some idea of what a grand sport stalking
is.   You'll hear the young people to-day running it down.
Why?   Laziness.   Sheer unadulterated laziness.   It's those
confounded motor-cars.   What they want now is to be driven
practically to the butts and then have the birds driven to
them, with a loader standing by.   Then a rich lunch and be
driven to the next moor and if they don't kill at least a
hundred brace each they think they've had a poor day's
sport.   Sport?   That's not sport.   That's nothing but luxury.
Of course, fellows like that aren't up to a long day in the
hills.   But you're different, Royde.   You want real sport
and I'm going to do my best to let you have some.   But you
mustn't mind my giving you advice.   You've just bought the
best twelve-head forest in Inverness-shire, and by gad, you
bought it for a song.   However, Kilwhillie got twice what
he ought to have got from that bounder Dutton for Glenbore,
and there's no doubt Knocknacolly Lodge isn't what it was.
It never was as a matter of fact, but luckily you can afford to

put it in order. I'm hoping to get a cable from my boy
Hector to-day to say he's got his leave. Now, he's just as
keen on stalking as I know you're going to be, and I taught
him the whole art of it. Because it is an art. You'll hear
people talking about painting and poetry and all that sort
of thing, but of course if it comes to real art they're not in it
with stalking."

The majestic splendours of the Three Sisters of Glenbogle
have been hymned too often to encourage a late comer in the
field of Highland romance to venture upon an encore. It is
enough to say that by nine o'clock that morning Ben Nevis,
Chester Royde and big Duncan Macdonald were in the midst
of them. The sky was heavily overcast, but the rain still
held off.

Duncan slowly swept with his glass the craggy and precipi-
tous horizon, the sides of which were green-striped with
the courses of innumerable burns descending to the
great flat where they were standing beside a small black
lochan.

" There's a hell of a lot of flies and gnats and midges
around here," Royde remarked.

" Rain on the way," said Ben Nevis. " Well, we can do
with it. The country's parched."

" It's not so darned parched as all that," his guest replied.
" I've been up to my knees half a dozen times already in
bog. Blast these midges! "

" They'll get used to you in time," Ben Nevis assured him.

" Hell, I don't care whether they get used to me. The
question is, ' will I get used to them ? ' "

" You're fresh blood," Ben Nevis explained.

" Oh, I knew I was some kind of a prize-sucker all right.
Oi! "

" What's the matter ? "

" Why, some flat grey brute of a fly landed on me and
planted the needle of his syringe about an inch into my hand.
Gosh, the sunnavabitch has drawn blood. What would you
say to that now ? "

" It must have been a cleg," Ben Nevis decided. " You'd
better light up a cigar."

Chester Royde took his host's advice and had just lighted
a big Larrañaga Corona when Ben Nevis with a muffled bark
bade him throw himelf down on the ground. As he seemed
inclined to question this order, the Chieftain flung an arm

round his shoulder and by falling prone himself fetched his guest down with him.

"Say, what's the big idea?" asked Royde, whose Larrañaga Corona had planted itself between a couple of bog-asphodels.

"A stag," said Ben Nevis.

"Where?"

"Duncan has seen his antlers above Drumstickit, the ridge rising west from Ardoo."

"Ah, do what? I can't do more than I'm doing with my nose routing about in this god-awful marsh. Still, stalking's stalking and I'll do anything you like."

"You mustn't mind if I seem a bit ceremonious, Royde," the Chieftain said. "We keep very strictly to traditional methods at this sport."

"Oh, I see. Flinging me down on the ground like that is an old ceremony, is it? They had some queer ceremonies among the Carroways. There was one, I remember, when the Chief put two fingers in the butter and hoicked out a great blob of it which he popped into my mouth before I could stop him. I was just going to spit it out when the fellow who was taking me around the reservation dug me in the ribs and whispered the Chief was paying me the highest compliment a Carroway Chief can pay anybody. He said what I had to do was to swallow the butter, rub my belly, turn up my eyes to express a sort of delirium of delight, and if possible eructate. He said if I could manage even the feeblest little eructation I was a blood-brother of the Carroways for life. But could I contrive even the merest hint of an eructation? No, sir, I could not. I was as dumb as a flute in the window of a music-store. If I'd been told I'd be scalped unless I could produce a suitable response to that blob of butter I could never have arranged . . ."

"Hush, Duncan wants us to crawl along and hear his plan of action," Ben Nevis interrupted. "Keep as flat as you can. Now you see why I was so anxious for you to change your clothes."

"Not half as anxious as I'll be to change them when I've crawled along a bit further like this."

"We may have to crawl a mile or so like this," said Ben Nevis.

"A mile?" his guest ejaculated. "Isn't deer-stalking more of a sport for crocodiles than human beings?"

Presently they reached the spot where Duncan was survey-ing the ridge running along the horizon from the great black precipices of Ard Dubh.

" It's himself," he said to Ben Nevis, awe, exultation and greed mingled in the tone of his voice.

" Not the muckle hart of Ben Glass ? "

" It's himself," Duncan repeated. " I would know him if the eyes of me did not know anything else at all."

Ben Nevis turned to his guest.

" You're in luck, Royde. I heard he'd been seen feeding between Ben Booey and Ben Glass the last week or so. We've been trying to get that hart for the last five years. It was an old gillie from the Findhorn country first called him the muckle hart. They don't use that word any longer around here."

" What's it mean ? "

" The big hart or stag. You'll never have a finer head if you live as long as Methuselah. Well, I'm glad something warned me to give Knocknacolly a miss to-day. Mind you, I never hoped that at your very first stalk you really would have a chance at the muckle hart of Ben Glass, but there you are, beginners' luck, as they say. We're going to have a stiffish stalk, but if you can get a fair shot at him before dusk this is going to be a day you'll never forget."

" Before dusk ? " Royde echoed in accents that verged on consternation. " We surely aren't going to crawl along on our faces like this for another ten hours ? "

" Not all the time," Ben Nevis replied encouragingly. " But we have to take advantage of all the cover we can to cross this flat. I don't know whether Duncan proposes to get round to the corrie between Kincanny and Ardoo and climb up Ardoo . . ."

" I told you just now, Ben Nevis, I'll do anything you like," Royde interrupted with a touch of fretfulness, for a fat gnat had just stung his left eyelid with lustful savagery, and it was swelling rapidly. " You needn't keep saying, ' Ah, do! "

Ben Nevis laughed boisterously until he was glared at by Duncan, who shook his head in reproof of such noise.

" You'll please to remember, Ben Nevis, that the less noise you are making the nearer we may happen to come to him-self."

" Yes, I apologize, Duncan. I'm setting Mr Royde a very bad example." Ben Nevis turned to his guest. " The old man's quite right to remind me not to make too much noise, but I couldn't help being tickled by your thinking I was saying ' Ah, do ' when I was saying ' Ardoo.' "

" What's the difference ? "

" Ardoo—A-R-D D-U-B-H—means black height. You see those black precipices ? "

" And we're scheduled to climb up them ? "

" Oh, there are other ways up which offer no problem to the man with a steady head. But Duncan may prefer to make a wider detour and scramble up to the end of Drumstickit—that's the ridge on the other side of which himself is lying down just now. Which side are we going to approach him from, Duncan ? "

The old stalker looked at the sky.

" There's no wind. It makes no difference for the wind. He won't get the scent of us one side more than another. I think the rain will begin about eleven o'clock, and when it does it will rain hard, right enough. That will make the climb up by the Ard Dubh a little difficult the way the water will be streaming down."

" You think we ought to go round and take the long crawl along Drumstickit ? " Ben Nevis asked.

" Ay, I believe that will be the best way of it," Duncan replied. " It'll be plenty long and plenty wet right enough. But on the Ard Dubh the gentleman might be swept off a ledge and know nothing about it till he was brought up before his Creator."

" Well, we don't want that to happen, Duncan, even to get a fair shot at the muckle hart of Ben Glass," his chief told him.

" I feel pretty much the same way about it as you feel, Ben Nevis," said Chester Royde. " I know I'll have to meet my Creator one day, but I don't want to butt in on Him when He's busy."

" The Lord is never too busy to judge a sinner," Duncan proclaimed sternly.

" Why, I know He holds the biggest one-man job anywhere," said Royde. " But that's no reason why I should butt in on Him before I'm expected. I think we'll give 'Ah, Do ' a miss to-day. Say, Duncan, if I light up another cigar will that beast over there get a whiff of it ? "

" I wouldn't say but what he mightn't, Mr Royde. And we'll have to keep very low for the next two hours before we reach

the far end of Drumstickit. You'll hardly be able to keep
your mouth out of the moss so as to enjoy a good smoke as it
ought to be enjoyed. And I'm not the one to ask a gentleman to waste the gifts the good Lord has given to him. Now
you see yon big crag away over there to the west of where
himself is lying?"

"I see a big grey mass of stone about two miles over to the
left. You don't mean that?"

"That's it, right enough. It's you that have very good
eyes, Mr Royde."

"And we're going to crawl on our bellies as far as that
mass of stone?" Chester Royde asked incredulously.

"That's the first thing we have to do. I hope we'll reach
it just before the rain begins to get really heavy."

There are many tracts among the mountains of the North
which cast a weariness and a disgust upon those who have to
tramp across them. The view of the encircling bens may be
sublime, but the sublime can become tiresome when exactly
the same aspect of it is presented during an hour's plodding
over featureless bog furrowed by burns every one of which
takes the same dreary course and makes the same monoton-
ous burbling. Such a tract was Achnacallach, the great flat
which the stalkers had to cross to reach the westerly shoulder
of the ridge known as Drumstickit. To walk across it was a
penance; to crawl across it was purgatorial.

"Never mind, Mr Royde, you'll find it easier as you get
used to it," said Duncan, with kindly encouragement.

"I will, will I?" Royde grunted sceptically, raising a fat
crimson face already considerably increased in bulk by the
attentions of the cloud of gnats and midges which hovered
above his head in a satanic aureole.

"Keep your head down, Royde. Keep your head down,"
Ben Nevis adjured him. "It's going to rain pretty hard soon
and then you won't be bothered at all by the midges. This
flat is called Ackernercallick, which means the field of the
old woman."

"You can't tell me any woman lived to be old in this piece
of country," Royde said emphatically.

"She was a witch," Ben Nevis recounted. "That's right,
isn't it, Duncan?"

"Ay, she was a bad witch right enough. She would be
flying out here by the light of the moon and doing all sorts of
devilment on her neighbours."

" She couldn't have had many neighbours around here,"
Royde put in.

" No, no, but she would be flying from here down into
Glenbogle and away over down into Strathdiddle and
Strathdun to be putting all kinds of illness into the cattle.
She lived beside those stones. They call them Carn na
Caillich to this day. And it was there that Donald shot
her."

" Take a breather for a moment, Royde, while Duncan
finishes his tale," Ben Nevis advised.

" I'd enjoy my breath more if half the flies around here
didn't follow it into my mouth," said Royde.

" Don't worry about the flies. They'll clear off when it
rains. Go on, Duncan, tell Mr Royde the story of Donald
Cam."

" Well, it was this way. Donald Cam was terribly put
about by the way this old witch was plaguing all the animals,
flying about in the night and nobody knowing whose byre
she would not be lighting on next. The minister in Strathdiddle preached a great sermon against her, och, a very
powerful sermon by what they still tell of it. But it was all
to no purpose. No purpose at all. The old witch seemed
to take a pure delight in spiting the minister's holy words.
Now, Donald Cam was a very religious man. Indeed, I
believe he was an elder; but if he wasn't an elder he was
certainly a deacon. So being full of zeal for the work of the
Lord he loaded his gun with a crooked sixpence and two
silver buttons that belonged to the King of Scotland, and
when the witch was away at her devilment he waited for
her by the carn where she lived. Nobody knows to this
day what happened exactly, but in the morning they found
Donald Cam lying asleep on his back with a dead crane on
top of him—heron some call the bird. Och, it was the old
witch right enough, because she was never seen again and
when they cut the crane open they found the crooked sixpence and the two silver buttons inside. Donald Cam was
very pleased they found the buttons, because the King of
Scotland gave them to his grandfather, and he would have
been missing them sorely from the box where his grandfather put them. Ah, indeed, yes, it shows that the Lord
does not turn His face from the godly man who keeps His
commandments. And ever since the place has been called
Achadh na Caillich. The Field of the Old Woman."

" But how came this guy Donald to lie there with this bird
on top of him ? " the American asked.

" It was never rightly known," Duncan replied. " Donald
himself had a notion that the witch put a spell on him just
as he fired. But others said it was the whisky he was after
drinking to keep his courage up. Well, if it was the whisky,
no man had a better right to it than Donald. There's no
man alive to-day in these parts who would sleep a night in
Carn na Caillich, even if he had a bottle of Haig's Gold Cap
in each pocket."

" Would you sleep there yourself, Duncan ? " his chief
asked.

" I wouldn't like it, Ben Nevis, and that's the truth I'm
telling you. Herself may be dead, but that's not to say the
spirit of her will not be flying around still. But we mustn't
stay blethering like this. Here comes the rain."

And indeed there did come the rain with a vengeance.

" Well, this is the first time water wetted my seat first
since I used to sit down in puddles when I got tired of walking
and wanted my nurse to take me home," Chester Royd
declared. " Say, Ben Nevis, is that the big idea about the
way a kilt is made ? "

" What ? "

" Why, pleating it all around the behind like that. I'll
bet you haven't had a drop of rain through yet."

" No, I'm all right."

" Of course you are. I thought at first it was just a
picturesque bit of hooey like those feathers the Indians dress
you up in when they adopt you into their tribe. War-
bonnets they call them. But I'm beginning to grasp the
design of the kilt. I see now it's the only wear for up here.
These breeches I'm wearing are no manner of use at all
against rain like this. I'm just a crawling aquarium. Say,
Ben Nevis, you don't think that big stag is going to sit up
there much longer in this rain ? He's the biggest moron in
antlers if he does."

" Not he. He's enjoying it," Ben Nevis declared.

" That stag must have the nature of a hippopotamus,"
Royde commented.

It was about noon when they reached the cairn and found
a dry recess in the stones where they could eat their sandwiches and refresh themselves for awhile after the long crawl
across Achnacallach.

" Say, do my eyes look kind of funny, Ben Nevis ? " his guest asked.

" They do look a little puffy. That's the midges."

" Well, they don't feel like eyes to me at all. They feel more like a couple of currants somewhere in the middle of a cake. And they're sinking deeper in all the time. I guess I won't be able to see to aim my rifle when the time comes."

Chester Royde had some reason to enquire anxiously about his eyes, and his host's description of them as a little puffy was far from adequate. There was in fact very little indeed of them now visible because, through the swelling of the lids from the bites, Chester's cheeks, naturally fat, had swelled to nearly twice their size and now threatened to engulf not merely what was left of his eyes but his ears as well.

" It's not raining so heavily now," Duncan announced after taking a look round the savage landscape.

" You want us to start ? " Ben Nevis asked.

" It might be as well," the old stalker suggested. " We will have a long long crawl along the top of Drumstickit."

" Not on our bellies ? " Royde exclaimed.

" Not all the way. Och, we'll be able to move along perhaps for quite two miles upon our hands and knees, and we'll have good cover from the rocks till we get to the top of Drumstickit."

" You know, Royde," said his host enthusiastically, " I believe you're going to get this fellow this afternoon."

" You do ? " the other countered dubiously. " Well, I can't say I feel quite so confident about that. In fact I've a hunch I'm not going to get this fellow this afternoon."

" Oh, you mustn't take up that attitude. You mustn't really," the Chieftain begged. " Confidence is half the battle in stalking. What you want to say to yourself all the time as we crawl along Drumstickit is, ' I'm going to get that hart. I'm going to plant my bullet in his shoulder.' Now then, forward ! We have a long way to go yet."

There were many moments during that endless crawl along the top of the narrow ridge known as Drumstickit when Chester Royde wondered why he had bought Knocknacolly for the sake of the twelve stags he was supposed to shoot upon its forest every year. There were many moments when he wondered what it was that had so fascinated him about life in the Highlands of Scotland. There was one bitter moment when, in crawling over what looked like a patch of bright short grass, he had sunk into it like the hippopotamus in whose nature he had discovered a kinship with the muckle hart of Ben Glass, and had asked himself what mad impulse had led him to book a state-room for himself and Carrie in the *Ruritania* in which to cross the Atlantic when they might have spent a perfectly good holiday in Vermont.

" Hush, don't make so much noise," Ben Nevis whispered hoarsely. " We're getting pretty near now."

" But my mouth's full of some kind of vegetable matter," Royde protested. " I'm only expectorating."

" You'd better swallow it," Ben Nevis advised. " It won't do you any harm. And keep down closer than ever up this rise. We ought to sight him when we get to the top. You're going to have one of the great moments of your life in another few minutes."

" If I live to see it," Royde muttered to himself, combing bits of moss off his tongue with his teeth.

But when, drenched to the skin, aching in every bone, and itching acutely, Chester Royde Jr. peered over a clump of heather to get his first sight of the muckle hart of Ben Glass there was no sign of him on what was left of Drumstickit before the long ridge was absorbed by the steeps of Ard Dubh. It was idle for Duncan to clap his spyglass to his eye and sweep it round. There was no stag.

" That's extraordinary," Ben Nevis exclaimed. " That hart's uncanny. He couldn't have winded us. It must have been sheer instinct which made him move."

" I never thought he would be such a moron as to sit fooling around here in that rain for us three mutts to shoot him. I guess that stag was wise to us before we ever started crawling across that flat stretch about ten o'clock. It's half-past three now. That stag's curled up comfortably somewhere two or three miles from here as dry and warm as I wish I were. Well, what do we do now, Ben Nevis ? "

" What do you say, Duncan ? " the Chieftain asked.

" I don't know what to say, Ben Nevis, and that's the truth," Duncan replied disconsolately. " It's very disappointing right enough. We might go round behind the Ard Dubh and get to the westerly shoulder of Ben Booey where you'll often find them feeding about four o'clock.

I'd like Mr Royde to have a chance at a good stag after
his disappointment. If we don't find one there, I'm afraid
we'll have to give up for to-day. We'll be a good two hours,
and maybe a little more, maybe more like three before we
can get to where the car is waiting, and the rain's coming on
hard again."

"What do you say, Royde ? Shall we go round behind
Ardoo ? "

"Well, I'd hate to have you call me no sportsman, Ben
Nevis, but I think I'm going to say ' Ah, don't.' "

"Well, then we'd better make for the car," said Ben
Nevis regretfully.

"We don't have to crawl on our bellies after that ? "
Royde asked.

"Ha-ha," Ben Nevis guffawed. "I'm afraid you're
rather irreverent about the greatest sport in the world.
Well, we'd better foot it. And you can light up your cigar
now without fear of the consequences."

"If it will keep alight in this rain. But I don't believe
Popocatepetl would keep alight in rain like this," said
Chester Royde.

Even the sanguine spirit of Ben Nevis was damped by
the double effect of the disappointment over the stag and
this tremendous downpour. He found nothing to say to
counteract the moroseness of his guest who, soaked to the
skin and with a face that if they had been invented at this
date could well have been compared to a barrage balloon,
trudged across the dreary flat known as Achnacallach,
across which he had crawled that morning accompanied
by a cortège of flies, gnats and midges.

Then suddenly he plucked from his mouth the Larrañaga
Corona that was contending with the rain and flung it away,
unable to stand the reek of it any longer, so much more now
did it resemble a damp leaf from a November bonfire
than a Larrañaga Corona.

"You know, I don't believe that guy ever did shoot that
witch," he said to Duncan.

"Och, yes, Mr Royde, the incident was well known at
the time all round about Strathdiddle and Glenbogle.
I've heard my grandfather tell about it many a time."

"I believe she's still moving around and up to her tricks.
I believe it was her you saw sitting up there on the top of
Drumstickit."

"But it had horns, Mr Royde. I saw them with my spyglass."

"Hasn't the Devil got horns?"

"Och, never say such things, Mr Royde. You're not telling me it was Satan himself I saw sitting up there on Drumstickit this morning. That's a terribly fancy to put into a man's head."

"Well, I leave it to you, Duncan. It was either the witch or her master the Devil. You can choose between them."

"Ach, no, Mr Royde, it was the great stag himself, right enough. I know the antlers on him as well as I know my own two hands. It was unlucky he would take it into his head to go away like that. But never fear, Mr Royde, I'll come for you one morning and we'll go for a stag together. Just you and I. We were too noisy to-day?"

"You're not saying I'm too noisy, are you?" the Chieftain asked.

The old man stroked his superb beard judicially.

"Och, yes, you're too noisy altogether, Ben Nevis. You've always been the same since you were a bairn. You'd make more noise than twenty buzzards before you were five years old. Screaming about the place, you would be, och, yes, screaming and shrieking and whistling."

"Well, I don't scream about the place now."

"No, you don't scream nowadays, Ben Nevis. But you talk twice as loud as anybody else. You can't help it. You don't know you talk so loud."

"Are you seriously trying to tell me my voice frightened that stag?"

"Ach, I don't know. It's impossible to say what frightened it, but I'd like to take Mr Royde out by himself. He's had a very disappointing day."

"Yes, I wish we'd gone after those Scottish Nationalists now," Ben Nevis spluttered.

Then he fell into a moody silence as the rain managed mysteriously to come down harder than ever. They had still two hours of hard walking before they reached the road where the car was waiting for them.

Chapter 11

PEATY WATER

THE stalk after the muckle hart of Ben Glass was repeated back in Glenbogle by Carrie and Myrtle Royde, but much more successfully, for they tracked their quarry to his lair before the heavy rain began.

Carrie had been tempted to try to give Myrtle the slip, but on reflection she had decided that in the matter of Alan Macmillan Myrtle held a stronger position as the sister of Chester than she as his wife. After all, she told herself, the fact that the poet was a very attractive young man should not be considered anything more than an agreeable reward for her response to ancestral demands upon her allegiance. The situation had been changed by Chester's acquisition of Knocknacolly and his presentation of it to herself. It would not be fair to Chester or herself to let Myrtle suppose that her plan to make Knocknacolly the centre of a Scottish renaissance was inspired by the *beaux yeux* of Alan Macmillan. And if she gave Myrtle an impression she was trying to sidestep her over Alan Macmillan that was just what she would think.

"Myrtle dear," she said to her sister-ih-law after breakfast, "I do feel we ought to see Mr Macmillan to-day if we possibly can. I was talking to Chester this morning and he agrees with me it'll be much better to have a Scottish lawyer do the business about Knocknacolly. So I think Mr Buchanan would be the very one, don't you?"

"Sure."

"And then we must have an architect, and I expect either he or Mr Macmillan will know of a good young architect. That will mean they can all go and camp out in the lodge, which will make it so much pleasanter. I'm so afraid if we don't see Mr Macmillan before he goes he may not want to come back to this part of the country. And I think it will be wiser not to say we know who took their tents, don't you? I mean, their pride might be upset and they might want to revenge themselves on Ben Nevis. They're so high-spirited."

"It was you who started off trying to give them back the tents."

" I know. It was too impulsive of me. I am very impulsive, Myrtle. That's my Celtic blood."

" Yes, your feminine Celtic blood."

" But you will come with me this morning, Myrtle ? Please do. I want to take Mr Macmillan some provisions, because I'm sure he's run out of them by now."

" Sure, I'll come with you. But how are we going to get hold of any provisions ? "

" Why, I thought if you asked Mrs Parsall the housekeeper to make you up lunch and tea for two, I'd ask Toker to make me up lunch and tea for two."

" Won't that seem a little funny ? " Myrtle suggested.

" Oh, they'll just think we each thought the other wasn't going to do it. We can pack everything in my lunch-basket."

Myrtle looked doubtful.

" I'm positive they'll think it kind of queer."

" But they expect Americans to be queer," Carrie pointed out.

" How about it if Murdoch and Iain MacDonald tag on to us the way they did yesterday ? " Myrtle asked.

" Oh, I've thought of a splendid plan to get them out of the way. Yes, I'm going to ask them to take the full measurements of Knocknacolly Lodge, and I'm going to ask Kilwhillie to go with them."

" And what about Catriona and Mary ? "

" Oh, they don't like us, Myrtle. They despise us, darling, for being so effeminate."

Myrtle sat pensive.

" Why so thoughtful all of a sudden ? " Carrie asked.

" I was thinking what a man would feel like walking out of church with one of those two and knowing it was no use, he just had to go through with it. I guess it would be easier to marry the Venus of Milo. She's big and she's hard and she'd be pretty cold, but she hasn't any arms."

" I don't think you ought to think thoughts like that when you're not married."

" That's the time to think them, angel child. It will be too late afterwards."

After asking Toker to make up a lunch packet for herself and Myrtle, Carrie found Kilwhillie and the two MacDonalds in the Great Hall.

" Oh, isn't this fine," she exclaimed. " Just the very

people I wanted. I wonder if you three very charming gentlemen would do me a favour."

Kilwhillie tugged at his moustache and bowed with what he believed was the kind of courtliness a middle-aged bachelor should show to a young married woman."

" I'm sure we shall be delighted."

" I was wondering if you would all three go over to Knocknacolly and bring me back the measurements of the Lodge so that I can plan out the alterations we want to make. It would be so very kind and helpful."

" But I thought I was going to drive *you* over there this morning," said Kilwhillie, a little ruefully.

" Well, that's just it, but I feel sort of dull and heavy and headachy. I guess it's the weather. So I'm going to be mean and cry off. And that's why I wondered if you'd come to my rescue," she added, turning the full power of her greenish eyes on Murdoch and Iain.

" I'll do any measuring you want," the sailor volunteered.

" So will I," the undergraduate echoed.

" I know I'm asking a lot, but I want the full measurements of every room and the garden and all the outhouses. I expect it'll mean rather a long business. I've just asked Toker to make up a packet of sandwiches for Myrtle and me because we thought you could drop us where the road turns off to Glenbristle. Will I ask him to prepare three packets of sandwiches for you in case you can't get your measuring done before lunch ? "

" Oh, don't bother," said Kilwhillie. " We'll . . ."

" It's no bother at all," she interrupted " Surely I can do a little thing like that when you're being so kind and helpful. Myrtle and I will be ready for ten o'clock if that's all right for you."

She hastened lightly from the Great Hall, flashing back a grateful smile for the chivalry with which she had been treated.

" Oh, Toker, I'm so sorry to worry you again, but I wonder if you'd make up another three packets for lunch and tea. Mr Cameron and Lieutenant MacDonald and Mr Iain are going over to Knocknacolly in Mr Cameron's car, and Miss Royde and I are going with them."

" Quite an expedition, madam."

" Yes, I do hope the rain will keep off."

" I fear not, madam. I always dislike adopting a pessi-

10

mistic attitude, but I never saw a sky look so determined
to rain."

" That's too bad. But never mind, we'll have good shelter.
I'll bring down my lunch-basket if you'll put the five
packets inside."

When the butler informed the housekeeper of the addi-
tional picnic fare required she told him he must have made
a mistake.

" I seldom make mistakes, Mrs Parsall," he reminded her,
with cold dignity.

" Well, what does Miss Royde want two packets for ? "
she asked. " Is it a school-treat ? "

" Probably Mrs Royde and Miss Royde each thought the
other was giving the necessary order."

" Oh well, I've given Mrs Ablewhite her instructions now.
It'll only cause more confusion if I alter them. If there's
two packets too many there must just be two packets too
many. Mrs Ablewhite will be quite enough annoyed at
everybody trapesing out to picnic on a day like this. The
whole arrangements for lunch will now have to be altered.
Well, I hope it rains good and hard. It will serve 'em
right," Mrs Parsall ejaculated bitterly.

It was half-past ten when Kilwhillie pulled up at the corner
of the Glenbristle road to let Carrie and Myrtle alight.

" Weighs quite a lot," Murdoch observed as he deposited
the lunch-basket in the road.

" Oh, we'll carry it between us," said the owner cheerfully.

" You'd better change your mind and come with us to
Knocknacolly, Mrs. Royde," Kilwhillie put his head through
the window of the car to advise. " I'm sure we're going
to have a drench of rain presently."

" Oh well, if it does, Myrtle and I will just have to go
back home. We can always leave the basket under a rock
and have somebody pick it up going past in a car. I'd
adore to come with you, but I know if I go for a long drive my
headache will start again."

Kilwhillie's ancient Austin rattled on its way, and the
two young women picked up the basket between them.

" My, it does weigh quite a bit," Myrtle exclaimed.

" I'll say it does," said Carrie triumphantly. " There
are seven lunches and seven teas in it."

" Carrie ! "

" I told Toker to put in three for our late escort."

" And they think they'll find their lunch and tea in the car. What'll they do when they find it isn't there ? "

" Come home, I guess."

" Carrie, you're ruthless."

" You have to be ruthless when you join a cause."

" What cause have you joined ? "

But before Carrie could answer, the red and yellow of the Macmillan tartan flashed upon the grey midge-infested air of the morning, and they saw the bard swinging down through Glenbristle toward them.

" You know, I think he's terribly attractive," Myrtle sighed. " I'm not surprised you've fallen for him even though you are married to my brother."

" I haven't fallen for him in that way," said Carrie quickly. " Ours is a political and literary friendship."

" Just that," Myrtle murmured in a far-away reflective tone of voice. " Oh well, I'm not interested at all in politics."

" Hullo," the poet exclaimed, with a genuinely glad smile. " I was afraid I wasn't going to see you both again. Somebody pinched our tents and we moved up to Uaimh na Laoigh last Friday."

" Isn't that the most melancholy sound you ever heard, Carrie ? It's like one of those sad noises you hear out at sea in a fog. Say it again, will you, Mr Poet ? "

" I wish I could pronounce Gaelic as well as he does," Carrie sighed. " Well, we want to see your cave. And I've got a lot of business to talk. I only wish Mr Buchanan hadn't gone away on Saturday."

" But he didn't go away," said the bard. " He's up in the cave now. He twisted his ankle. We're both going to-morrow morning. I was just off to Kenspeckle to get some food. We're clean out of it."

" We've brought you some provisions. So you can put that basket on your shoulder and lead the way to your cave. I guess we've saved you getting a terrible drenching. There are spots of rain already, and aren't these flies terrible! "

The bard lifted the basket and they set off along Glenbristle.

" It's a bit of a climb," he warned them when they reached the spur of Ben Cruet, eight hundred feet up which was the cave.

" I don't believe we'd have dragged that lunch-basket up there," Carrie said.

" Never," Myrtle agreed fervidly.

However, they managed to scramble up themselves, though Myrtle had to do without the help of the poet's hand owing to the attention he had to pay to the lunch-basket. The entrance of the cave was reached just as the rain started to come down in earnest.

" Haven't you found a divine place to camp in! " Myrtle exclaimed.

There was indeed some excuse for her rapture. The cave was dry and airy. The view on either side of the hump of stone that marked the entrance was superb, looking down into Glenbristle and away across Glenbogle to the three mighty Sisters—Ben Booey, Ben Gorm and Ben Glass. While the two young women were extolling it, the husband of one and brother of the other was about half way across the dreary flat of Achnacallach. Not the most powerful telescope would have revealed him, for between him and the view commanded by the cave lay the ridge of Drumstickit about five miles away as the crow flies, but very many more as Chester Royde was crawling. Soon the rain sloping across Glenbogle in great ladders dark as crape obliterated the view, and the two young women turned to the more cheerful sight the interior of the cave presented. The occupants had had time to make divans of dry heather on which they had spread their sleeping-blankets. A convenient venthole at the back of the cave allowed a turf fire to shed a friendly glow of warmth without stifling the inmates. Carrie noticed that the poet's notebook was lying open on his bed. Through the un-romantic mind of Myrtle danced a butterfly thought that life in a cave like this with so personable a caveman would be very good. And what mattered the rain without when this cave was lighted within by the radiant tartans of Clan Macmillan and Clan Buchanan ?

" It's such a very lovely surprise to find you still here, Mr Buchanan," Carrie exclaimed.

" I wrenched my ankle like a clown and had to stay here, but I'll be able to get along to the bottom of the glen to-morrow if I take it quietly. And then we'll catch the bus to Fort William. The trouble is we've eaten ourselves clean out of food. Did Alan tell you ? "

" Fortunately Myrtle and I have brought you enough food to last you till to-morrow. It's mostly sandwiches but there's some tea and some cake and fourteen hard-boiled eggs, so it'll keep you from starving. You can leave the basket in the cave and we'll fetch it away sometime."

" It's awful kind of you, Mistress Royde. We're awfully obliged to you. We really are."

" And now I want to talk to you about a little matter of business," Carrie began.

Once again James Buchanan experienced that sinking feeling, due not to shortage of victuals but to the dread that he was going to hear the hundred-dollar bill had been a mistake.

" Yes," Carrie went on, " I want you to act for me in a business matter."

James Buchanan gazed at her in something like stupefaction.

" It's over this property which my husband has bought, and which he wants to present to me. I told him I knew of a very clever Scottish lawyer and explained that Scottish law over real estate was quite different from English law, and of course so very much better."

The gaze of James Buchanan was no longer something like stupefaction: it was stupefaction.

While Carrie was discussing the niceties of legal representation Myrtle and Alan sat on improvised hassocks of heather at the entrance of the cave.

" Did you know there was a terribly sad story about this cave ? " she asked. " Wait a moment, what is it in Gaelic ? "

" Uaimh na laoigh."

" Are you musical, Mr Macmillan ? "

" Well, I like music, but I'm no piper."

" I wasn't thinking of the bagpipes. That's a special kind of music I haven't gotten accustomed to yet. But I am pretty musical, and I buy quite a few highbrow phonograph records. I've a Victor recording of a clarinet quintet by Brahms and when I hear you say Ooav and what you say after that I could just imagine it was the clarinet on this Victor record. But I was asking you if you knew there was a terribly sad story about this cave."

" No; I've not heard it."

" Well, it seems there was once a young fugitive from the redcoats hiding in this cave."

" Not Prince Charlie ? " the poet asked suspiciously.

" No, not Prince Charlie."

" I'm surprised to hear that. There's hardly a cave in the Highlands in which he isn't supposed to have hidden from the redcoats," Alan Macmillan scoffed. " If he'd slept one night in every cave in which he's supposed to have slept he'd have spent three years hiding from the redcoats instead of less than five months."

" Oh, this really is a true story. His name was Alan Macdonald . . . your name's Alan, isn't it ? "

The owner of the name nodded.

" I think I'll call you Alan if you don't mind. It's a name I've always been fond of, and now I've met somebody called Alan it seems a pity to waste the chance of using it. You don't mind, do you ? "

" Of course I don't mind," the poet answered, with a blush.

" That's sweet of you. But if I call you Alan you'll have to call me by my name. I expect you've forgotten what it is, haven't you ? "

" Myrtle."

" Oh, you hadn't forgotten," she exclaimed, with gentle gratification. " Isn't that very encouraging! "

She relapsed into a dream from which Alan roused her by asking for the rest of the story.

" Oh yes, the rest of the story," she said. " Well, this Alan Macdonald loved a girl in Glenbristle called Myrtle."

" Myrtle ? "

" Did I say Myrtle ? Goody, isn't that strange! No, her name was Mary. Fancy me calling her Myrtle! Well, this poor girl set out one night to bring her Alan provisions and she was caught in a blizzard and frozen to death. The chaplain at Glenbogle Castle made a poem about it which he read to us. It was terribly sad. I felt I wanted to cry."

The more modern poet made a scornful noise.

" I expect it was a ghastly poem."

" Well, it was an old-fashioned kind of a poem," Myrtle admitted. " I mean to say, when he'd finished reading you knew just what had happened."

" As you would after reading a paragraph of a newspaper," Alan said derisively. " I thought you told me you weren't romantic."

" I'm not romantic. I'm terribly practical. I'm more practical than you are."

" How do you make that out ? "

" Well, while you were sitting around writing poetry, you forgot you'd run out of food, and if it hadn't been for Carrie and me you'd have been walking along Glenbogle now in all

this rain to go and fetch it, and your friend Mr Buchanan
would have had to wait till about five o'clock this afternoon
for his lunch. You ought to write a poem about that."

"Well, I'll tell you something, Myrtle, I did write a
poem about you."

"You did? Oh, Alan, I'm thrilled to death. Nobody
ever wrote a poem about me. I guess the only poets I ever
knew were all too sissie. Is it a long poem?"

"No, it's very short."

"Could you . . . would you say it to me? What's it
called?"

"I call it *Peaty Water*."

The blue eyes of the poet burned as he gazed in front of
him and intoned in a voice from which the faintest breath of
dramatic expression had been ruthlessly eliminated:

> " *The heather,*
> *The fading heather,*
> *Is spread like the robe of a dead king*
> *Upon my country,*
> *Upon my dying country.*
>
> *I do not lament therefore, but laugh*
> *When down through the stale dead purple*
> *Dances the peaty water*
> *Warm with the sharp sun of the high tops,*
> *Prickt by the sun of the high tops,*
> *The prattling peaty dark-brown water,*
> *The warm dark-brown water of life.*"

"Yes, go on," said Myrtle when the poet stopped and
looked at her intensely.

"That's all. I'm afraid you'll think it rather old-
fashioned. Imagist poetry has not kept its hold upon contemporary expression, but I would justify it by the old-
fashioned circumstances in which it was written."

"But I thought you said you'd written a poem about me?"
Myrtle asked in a puzzled voice.

"That poem is about you."

"Do you mind saying it once again?"

Once more the poet gazed fiercely in front of him from
blazing blue eyes and intoned *Peaty Water*.

" I suppose you'll think me just a poor sap, Alan, but I can't see where I come into that poem."

" You prefer the reverend gentleman's newspaper paragraph in verse about Myrtle Macdonald ? "

" Oh, Alan! "

" What ? "

" Why, you've said it yourself now. It was Mary Macdonald."

" I meant Mary," said the poet with a blush.

" And now you're blushing."

He blushed more richly, and scowled.

" You mean to say," he began in tones which his embarrassment rendered ferocious, " you mean to say you can't perceive the image in that poem ? "

" I can see all sorts of images in it, but I can't see my own."

" The warm dark-brown water of life," he urged, blushing again.

And then she too blushed, their blushes seeming more vivid because they were flaming against those sombre ladders of rain sloping from the leaden sky to the glen below.

" Say the poem again," she murmured.

And this time he forgot the rigid principles imbibed from the gospel of Willie Yeats and allowed dramatic expression to enter into his recitation of *Peaty Water:*

> " *The heather,*
> *The fading heather,*
> *Is spread like the robe of a dead king*
> *Upon my country,*
> *Upon my dying country.*

> " *I do not lament therefore, but laugh*
> *When down through the stale dead purple*
> *Dances the peaty water*
> *Warm with the sharp sun of the high tops,*
> *Prickt by the sun of the high tops,*
> *The prattling peaty dark-brown water,*
> *The warm dark-brown water of life.*"

Myrtle sighed.

" And you really wrote that about me ? "

" I did."

"It's like a wonderful secret," she sighed again. "Say it to Carrie. She'll never guess it."

Myrtle was right in presuming that her sister-in-law would not connect the poem *Peaty Water* with herself. She listened to it with a rapt expression in her greenish eyes that turned them to beryls.

"I think that's a perfectly wonderful poem, Alan," she said. "And the peaty water is S.B.A. of course."

"S.B.A. ? " Myrtle asked, a little sharply, for she had not heard Carrie call him Alan before. "Who's S.B.A. ? "

The other three looked at one another.

"It isn't a person, honeybunch. It's a . . ." Carrie stopped. "I think she ought to be told, don't you ? "

"Certainly," Alan agreed, with a fervour that won him a flash from Myrtle's dark-brown eyes.

"Och ay," James Buchanan confirmed. "Miss Royde is fully entitled to be told." The treasurer was thinking of more voluntary donations to the fighting fund.

"S.B.A. stands for Scottish Brotherhood of Action," Carrie revealed. "It's a secret society aiming at the revival of the national spirit of Scotland."

"Does it want all that reviving ? " Myrtle asked. "I haven't been here quite a week yet, but I haven't seen much sign of collapse."

"The country's practically dead, Miss Royde," James Buchanan assured her earnestly. "Do you realize the rate at which our industries are being moved south ? It's really fearful. When I tell you that in Kilmarnock no less than . . ."

"Don't start giving statistics now, James," his friend interrupted a little irritably. "Miss Royde is American. She has no interest in Scottish politics."

"Oh, but that isn't true, Alan. Since you said your poem and I've learnt that the dark-brown water of life is the image of the Scottish Brotherhood of Action I've become terribly interested in Scottish politics."

James Buchanan's bullet-head swung round. So she was calling him 'Alan' already, and by the look in the other one's eye the other one wasn't too pleased about it. He would have to warn Alan again. She was a nice wee lassie, but she was not the owner of Knocknacolly, and it was Alan's duty to do nothing that might endanger the latter's interest in the S.B.A.

"Myrtle, how can you say that?" Carrie exclaimed. It was true she had failed to identify her sister-in-law with the dark-brown water of life, but she was under no illusions about her sudden interest in Scottish politics.

"But, Carrie, I am. There's something about the atmosphere here which seems to illuminate my real ego. And I think Chester feels it too. I'm wondering if we haven't perhaps Scotch blood . . ."

"I wish you wouldn't say Scotch blood as if it was broth or whisky," Carrie interrupted. "Anyway, Chester never suggested you had Scotch blood. The ancestor he's proud of is that Hungarian great-grandmother of yours."

"Marka Tiktok. Yes, well, she was a very very exceptional woman and kind of took the shine out of the rest. But there's a lot more great-grandmothers and great-great-grandmothers, and the more I think about it the more positive I feel that one of them came from the Highlands."

"The more you think about anything the more you can think what you want to feel," Carrie pointed out.

"I don't know why you're so grudging about my Scottish blood. Chester would be tickled to death to find he had Scottish blood. For all you know, Carrie, that may have been the attraction which brought you two together."

Myrtle was tempted to suggest herself as a member of the Scottish Brotherhood of Action, but she did not want to ruffle her sister-in-law's red hair by trespassing upon her private romantic property and she refrained. After all, a young man whose attraction Carrie had discovered first had written a poem about herself. She could afford to be generous. And Carrie was very sweet. If Alan wore well and if she herself should decide it was something more than the beginning of a pleasant summer flirtation Carrie would be helpful and understanding. That was certain.

"A curious thing happened after Alan and I went back to our camp in Glenbristle last Friday," James Buchanan was saying. "While we were talking to you, Miss Royde. . . ."

"As we've all gone so far with Christian names," Carrie put in, "I don't see why you have to call Myrtle Miss Royde, James."

"That's a matter for Miss Royde to decide, Mistress Royde . . . I should say Carrie," said the lawyer.

"Oh, James, I'd adore to have you call me Myrtle.

But go on with your story. What happened when you went back to your camp? "

" We found somebody had walked off with our tents."

" Good gracious, what did you do? " Myrtle asked.

" There was nothing we could do except take the rest of our equipment up to this cave."

" Say it, Alan."

" Uaimh na laoigh."

Myrtle gave a little laugh of delight deep in her throat as the coo of a dove.

" I'll just have to learn Gaelic," she cried.

Carrie felt that her hair was brightening to the red in the Macmillan tartan, but she controlled herself admirably and said how much she should enjoy doing exercises in *Gaelic Without Tears* with Myrtle.

" Is Gaelic a good language for love? " Myrtle was asking now.

" The emotional variety is rich—very rich," Alan informed her.

" What is ' I love you ' ? "

" Tha gaoil agam ort."

" Oh, another nice clarinet noise? And what's ' kiss ' ? "

" Pog."

Myrtle blinked.

" I don't think that's quite so good. Do you think that's quite so good, Carrie? "

" I guess no nation thinks any other nation's word for kiss is quite so good," her sister-in-law replied, with that in her voice which made James Buchanan hastily return to the tale of the vanished tents.

" We thought your friend Mr MacDonald of Ben Nevis must have taken them," he said darkly. " I was waiting for him to come along and try to shake me. Ah, I'd have liked fine for him to come along and try to shake me."

" Oh, I don't think the disappearance of your tents had anything to do with Ben Nevis," said Carrie. " I guess a dog must have been nosing around and gone off with them."

" A dog go off with two canvas tents? " James exclaimed. " No dog could go off with even one. They're awkward things for a body to carry, leave alone a dog."

" Oh, they're awkward, are they? " Carrie asked, her greenish eyes innocent as water.

" Alan and I were so sure your wild laird had taken them that if we had not thought it would make it a bit awkward for you we would have gone to the Castle and asked what the blazes he thought he was playing at."

" Oh, I wouldn't bother to do that," said Carrie quickly. " You wouldn't bother to do that, would you, Myrtle ? "

" No, indeed I wouldn't," Myrtle urged. " He is so very violent, he really is."

" So you think he'll shake *me* ? " James demanded.

" Oh, no, James, I don't think he'd do that, but I wouldn't put it past him to pull a gun on you. I wouldn't really. Besides, if you're going to put through this real estate deal for Carrie, you may have to come to the Castle some time, and you wouldn't want to start off talking business the way they do in a wild west film."

" Myrtle's right," Carrie said. " You'll spoil everything, James, if you start quarrelling with Ben Nevis. My husband won't understand it."

" Och, that's all right, Carrie. Don't fash yourself about my behaviour. I know when to be professional."

" I'm sure you do. Well, I'll write to you in Glasgow and give you full instructions."

" I'll need to know the name of Mr Cameron's lawyer."

" Yes, I'll find that out. But now there's another thing. Do either you or Alan know of a really good young Scottish architect ? I guess we'll pull the lodge to pieces quite a lot, and it would probably mean a good job for him."

" What about Bob Menzies, James ? " Alan asked.

" I was just thinking the very same."

" Is he young ? " Carrie asked.

" No, no. Robert Menzies is about the same age as myself," said James. " Twenty-six."

" Oh my, aren't you old! " Myrtle exclaimed. " You're not so old as that, Alan ? "

" I'm twenty-three."

" Same age as me," said Carrie.

" Three years older than I," Myrtle added.

" And is this Mr Robert Menzies a good architect ? " Carrie asked.

" He's very modern," said Alan.

" Oh dear, will that mean he'll want us to live in a kind of cross between a conservatory and a prison ? " Carrie asked anxiously.

"You needn't be afraid he'll suggest any kind of design that will violate the spirit of the place. He's modern, but his modernity is an expression of contemporary Scotland."

"And he's a member of the Brotherhood," James added. "I don't want to make that a reason for giving him the job, but if you wish Knocknacolly to be an expression of the new spirit in Scotland I don't believe you could get a better architect than Robert Menzies. He's an awful nice wee man too. I think you'd like him."

So finally it was settled that as soon as possible the architect should go and camp at Knocknacolly when, if Carrie and her husband approved of his ideas, he could be entrusted with the job, with James to look after the business side during the winter.

"And perhaps after you've taken your mother to Perth, you'll come and camp at Knocknacolly too?" Carrie asked Alan.

"I don't see what use I'll be," he demurred.

"But of course you'll be terribly useful," Myrtle declared. "Won't he, Carrie?"

"Indeed yes, I should say he would. I'll need your advice, Alan. And I want to get a little runabout, and you could drive it back to Knocknacolly after I'd had a busy day with plans."

Alan blushed.

"I'm afraid I can't drive a car."

"What?" Myrtle exclaimed. "Oh, I'll have to teach you, Alan. I mean Carrie and I will have to teach you. What's the Gaelic for car?"

"They have a synthetic word which I can't remember. But no Gaelic speaker ever uses it. They just say 'car'."

"Oh, well, I've learnt one Gaelic word anyway," said Myrtle. "And now what about eating a little lunch? James looks terribly hungry."

So they ate lunch, Carrie and Myrtle very sparingly because they wanted to leave as much as possible for the two young men, and after lunch Alan read a good deal of his poetry, which was not easy to follow: but he looked so attractive on his rostrum of heather that neither Carrie nor Myrtle bothered in the least about the words.

After a time, however, James Buchanan protested.

"I don't see why you want to read poetry as if you were a stirk trying to silence a stirk on the other side of a dyke,

Alan. When I read your poetry to myself I can make quite a lot of sense out of it here and there, but when you read it I can't understand one word. It's a daft way of reading."

" I am reading in the way poetry should be read," Alan asserted severely.

" Who said so ? "

" It's the traditional way of reading poetry."

" I thought you were so modern."

" My work is modern."

" Then why do you read it like an ancient Druid ? "

" What do you know about poetry, James ? "

" I never will know anything about poetry if I have to listen to you hooting it at me like an owl in a tree. Suppose I were to get up in court and hoot at the sheriff like that, what would become of my case ? "

" The parallel is ridiculous."

" Do you or do you not want to make yourself intelligible ? "

" It depends what you mean by intelligible."

" Do you want your poetry to make sense ? "

" Poetry is not intended to make sense. You're confusing it with prose."

" Then prose is sense and poetry is nonsense ? "

" If you like."

" And you're going to spend your life writing nonsense ? Losh, no wonder Scotland's going downhill."

" I think I understand what Alan means," said Myrtle, remembering the secret of *Peaty Water.*

" That's right, Myrtle. Encourage him. He's been spoilt all his life by encouragement," James groaned in disgust. " The only reason he's learning Gaelic is because he wants to add a few more incomprehensible noises to the ones he can make already in English."

" No, no, James, that isn't fair," Carrie interposed. " Alan is learning Gaelic because he knows that the life of a nation is its language."

And this started another argument, and so with arguments and plans for the future and a few statistics from James and an early tea it was four o'clock, and with the rain seeming to abate Carrie and Myrtle decided they ought to be going back to the Castle.

" My dears, you're drenched," Mrs MacDonald boomed

in dismay when they arrived home. " Where have you been ? "

" We found a cave to shelter in," said Carrie. " Mr Fletcher told us about it. And we had a lovely, lazy day. It's only now coming home that we got so wet."

But when Chester arrived back about a quarter-past seven it seemed absurd for her or Carrie to talk about being wet.

" Oh, Chester, I've never seen anybody so wet. Did you fall into the river ? And oh my, Chester, what have you done to your face ? My dear, it's bigger than a pumpkin."

" I'll tell you when I've had a bath," he replied.

" Did you kill a stag, Chester ? "

" Not yet. But I'm sure going to. I've taken a kind of dislike to stags. You can arrange Knocknacolly as you like, Carrie, but I want one biggish room set apart for me. I aim to cover the walls of it with stags' heads."

" And is stalking good sport ? "

" Stalking isn't a sport at all, Carrie, but killing stags is a duty."

" Do go and bathe your eyes, Chester."

" If I can get at them," he said, moving in the direction of the bathroom.

Downstairs in the Great Hall Ben Nevis, quite as wet as his guest but unmarked by a single midge's bite, was waving a cablegram and shouting to everybody who came in that Hector had been given his leave and hoped to be home by the twenty-eighth.

" My, isn't that splendid! " said Myrtle.

" You'll like him, Myrtle. He takes after me in every way. Voice, figure, features and general outlook on life. Well, we had rather a disappointing day, but what of it ? There are plenty of other days. Fill up your glass, Hugh."

The laird of Kilwhillie came over to Carrie.

" We managed to get the measurements you wanted."

" Oh, isn't that kind of you, Kilwhillie! I really am terribly obliged. And I was so sorry about your lunch. I didn't realize all the lunches were in my basket. What did you do ? "

" Oh, it was quite all right. We got a snack at my house."

" I'm writing off to our lawyer to-morrow. So will you

let me have the name of yours? I'm longing to feel Knocknacolly is really mine, and I shall want your advice about so
many things."

Kilwhillie tugged at his moustache, and bowed.

" I will always be at your service, Mrs Royde."

" Fill up your glass, Hugh, fill up your glass," the Chieftain
exhorted. " Yes, we had a disappointing day. However,
we only just failed to get the finest stag in this part of the
country. An historic animal really. The muckle hart of
Ben Glass, Hugh."

" By Jove, Donald, the muckle hart himself! "

" Yes, but the beggar slipped us. We had pretty nearly a
four-mile crawl on our hands and knees, and some of the
time on our tummies."

" Chester crawled four miles on his tummy? " Carrie
exclaimed incredulously.

" Like a good 'un," Ben Nevis declared with enthusiasm.
" Well, I must go and get into some dry clothes."

He swallowed one more hefty dram and strode from the
hall, his kilt clinging to him like the draperies of a Rhine
maiden or Nereid.

The rain that started on that Monday fell heavily and
almost incessantly for the next five days and not quite so
heavily and somewhat less incessantly for another five days
after that. For a time even the hardiest sportsman was
deterred from activity, but nevertheless the time passed
pleasantly enough. Kilwhillie went back to Kilwhillie
House. James Buchanan was put in touch with his lawyers
Messrs Macbeth, Macbeth and Macbean of Inverness, and
the meticulous process of selling a landed estate in Scotland
was set in motion. Carrie, who had felt guilty over Kilwhillie's lunch, had suggested to her husband he should
add another 2,500 dollars to the purchase price of Knocknacolly.

" But I've already added that, Carrie."

" I know, Chester dear, but I'd feel so much happier if he
had what he'd said to himself he would take, and that was
eight thousand. That's roughly forty thousand dollars,
isn't it? "

" Well, if it pleases you, it's O.K. by me," said Chester.

" Oh, Chester, you're so big-hearted. But I do think
Knocknacolly is worth forty thousand dollars."

" It certainly is if it's giving you so much pleasure."

" Oh, it is, Chester. I can't tell you what pleasure it's going to give me. And when the architect comes I'll have him pay particular attention to this room for your stags' heads. Oh, and, Chester, I'd like to have a little runabout so that I can run over to Knocknacolly when I feel inclined."

" A two-seater ? "

Carrie hesitated. The temptation was strong.

" No; I think it had better be a four-seater," she said, conquering it.

" I'm going into Inverness to-morrow. I'll probably find there what you want."

" Will I come with you, Chester ? "

" No, don't you bother, dear. I have a little business to attend to. Oh, by the way, which do you like best, purple or orange ? "

" Purple or orange ? What for, Chester ? Neither suits me. Well, I suppose purple would, but I don't want to think about purple for a few years yet."

" Why not ? "

" It's so ageing."

" Is that so ? " said Chester pensively. " But I wasn't thinking about a frock for you. I was just asking which colour you like best."

" Oh, as a colour I like orange—definitely."

" Yes, I believe I do too."

" By the way, Chester, I'm arranging for the architect to camp up at Knocknacolly. I want him to soak himself in the atmosphere."

" He'll do that all right if it goes on raining like this. But if he wants any more soaking I'll take him with me when I start getting my own back on stags. What's his name again ? "

" Robert M-e-n-z-i-e-s. But it's pronounced ' Mingies.' "

" For the love of Mike, why ? "

" I don't know why, but it is. And I suggested Mr Menzies should have a couple of friends with him. One of them will be Mr Buchanan the lawyer, who wants to get thoroughly conversant with conditions at Knocknacolly, and as he'll have to manage all the business part of it while the alterations are being made after we go back home this fall, I think that's a good idea, don't you ? "

" This lawyer of yours can't have much of a business if he

11

can afford to go camping out at Knocknacolly with an architect."

"But I told you, Chester, he's quite young. I think it's much better to have a clever young lawyer who can give your business more of his personal attention."

"Where did you get hold of him?"

"I met him in—in Edinburgh when I was waiting there for you to come up from London."

"Well, it's your house and it's your country. You do what you like. Who's the third in the party?"

"A young Scottish poet called Macmillan."

"A poet? Holy snakes, are you going to turn Knocknacolly into a National Park? What's the poet going to do?"

"He's going to give me the benefit of his advice."

"A poet is?"

"Sure."

"It's lucky your Mr Buchanan has plenty of time on his hands."

Later Carrie told Myrtle how sweet and understanding Chester had been about her plans for Knocknacolly. She also explained that she had led him to suppose she had met James and Alan in Edinburgh.

"So of course you won't have met them, Myrtle, till I introduce you."

"Is that a warning?"

"Warning of what?"

"A warning I'll have to be good as gold and sweet as pie if I ever am to be introduced."

"Oh, Myrtle, no. You couldn't think I'd be so mean."

Myrtle looked at her sister-in-law.

"Of course I don't, honey," she said, laughing softly and patting Carrie's shoulder.

Pleasant indeed and full of happy prospects and activities was Glenbogle in spite of the rain. The Chieftain and his wife were contemplating the leave of their eldest son. The keepers and gillies and workmen were looking forward to the Gathering on August 28th. The children were practising reels and sword-dances for the great annual event with indefatigable zeal. The pipers were hardly ever silent in their resolve to defend the music of Glenbogle against all competitors. Murdoch and Iain MacDonald had proclaimed their intention of tossing the caber and putting the stone for the honour of Glenbogle's muscles against whatever

brawny outsiders should venture to challenge their power.
Catriona and Mary MacDonald were volunteering to bicycle
into Fort William at the slightest excuse to fetch extra yards
of ribbons for rosettes. Carrie and Myrtle were driving over
to Knocknacolly in the ten-h.p. Austin which Chester had
bought in Inverness with the energetic Widow MacDonald
who was scrubbing out some of the rooms, and also making
expeditions to Fort William for various domestic articles.
Chester Royde Jr. was much in the company of Kilwhillie,
with whom he paid two or three visits to Inverness, the
object of which was not divulged. Kilwhillie's moustache
under the effect of that unexpected extra £1,000 had to be
tugged at continually to prevent its sweeping up like a
cow's horns and thus contravening what Kilwhillie considered
the suitable habit of growth for a laird's moustache.

The happy inhabitants of Glenbogle were as innocent as
once upon a time the inhabitants of Glencoe that down in
London an enemy was plotting their ruin.

Chapter 12

OUSE HALL

BRITISH democracy has many glories, not the least of which is its ability to produce liberal-minded and progressive peers who instead of sulking about the burden of taxation get in touch with the people and keep in touch with the people. Such a peer was John Henry Charles Bunting, seventh Earl of Buntingdon, also Viscount Ouse and Baron Bunting of Buntingdon, of Ouse Hall, Buntingdon, Beds, and 201 Belgrave Square, S.W., the President of the National Union of Hikers. Many readers will be familiar with the photograph of Lord Buntingdon in shorts and shirt holding his hiker's staff, his benevolently domed head hatless, liberty, equality and fraternity twined in the smile that wreathes his large melon-shaped face of the Rugby not Association type of melon. Underneath this representation one may here read, ' Bachelor peer says everybody should hike,' or ' Earl says hiking is shortest cut to true democracy,' or ' Hundreds of hikers yesterday acclaimed the Earl of Buntingdon when he presided at the Annual Hikery held in the grounds of Ouse Hall, his picturesque Bedfordshire seat. Lord Buntingdon in thanking the members of the National Union of Hikers for again electing him as their President stressed the moral, mental and physical value of hiking in preventing Britain from becoming a C.3 nation.'

Just about the time on that Monday when Duncan sighted the muckle hart of Ben Glass, Lord Buntingdon came in from a walk round his tortoise enclosures at Ouse Hall—he had the finest collection of tortoises in the world—to receive from his butler a telegram:

> *Can you possibly come London to preside at very important indignation meeting of N.U.H. at Astrovegetarian Hall, Villiers Street, Strand next Friday at eight? Your presence would be intensely appreciated. Prew ready to come immediately to Ouse Hall if you desire further information*
>
> *Buckham*

" When did this come, Maple ? "

" It has just this moment been telephoned through from the post-office, my lord."

Lord Buntingdon went into the library and wrote his reply:

> *Percy Buckham, 15 Quilting Gardens, Primrose Hill, N.W.*
> *If my presence considered absolutely necessary will preside at meeting but shall be glad if Prew will come to Ouse Hall and explain full circumstances stop I shall be glad to put him up to-morrow or Wednesday night stop Please telegraph time of train's arrival*
>
> *Buntingdon*

Such a telegram was typical of that progressive peer. His quick sympathies reacted immediately to the appeal oi Percy Buckham, the Acting President of the N.U.H; but the blood of Whig and Liberal ancestors famous in English politics ran in his veins and with it the caution such an inheritance brought. Hence he answered the appeal, but at the same time was determined to know in advance exactly what his action would let him in for.

Later that day, just when Lord Buntingdon was returning from a second visit to his tortoise enclosures where his progressive mind, ever eager to leap ahead, disciplined itself by the contemplation of nature's Fabians, Maple handed him another telegram:

> *Grateful thanks for your spirited attitude. Will arrive Buntingdon 7.26 to-morrow evening*
>
> *Prew*

Lord Buntingdon's oval brow became slightly elliptical at the epithet 'spirited.' It had not occurred to him there was anything particularly spirited about his proposed action. It was rather a bore, certainly, going up to London in this hot August weather, but overcoming his own indolence was as much credit as he could take in the circumstances.

" The story you have just told me, Mr Prew, is certainly astonishing," said Lord Buntingdon when he had listened at dinner the following evening to what the Secretary of the N.U.H. had to say about the adventures of the hikers in Glenbogle. " Do you suppose this Mr MacDonald is a Fascist ? "

" No. Enquiries we have made do not indicate that there is any connection with Fascist activities, Lord Buntingdon.

It would seem to be a case of unbridled individualism," Mr
Prew went on primly. " Indeed, one might almost say
demented individualism."

" I understand his annoyance about the grouse . . . but
that does not mean I sympathize with such a deplorable loss
of self-control."

" Oh, I can assure you, Lord Buntingdon, that if he had
pointed out we were spoiling his shooting arrangements and
asked us to take our tea elsewhere we should have complied
with such a request immediately. Oh, but immediately,
Lord Buntingdon."

" Quite, quite. As you know I do not preserve game
myself, but consideration is owed to landowners who do."

" We always impress that on our young people, Lord
Buntingdon," said the Secretary earnestly. " I always say
if you're on private property you must behave as if you were
in somebody else's house. But we were given no opportunity
to apologize and withdraw. This Mr MacDonald literally
charged at us and when I tried to explain what the N.U.H.
was he gripped me by the collar and shook and shook and
shook and . . ."

" Yes, you've already made that clear," Lord Buntingdon
interrupted. " Fill up your glass, Mr Prew," he added,
pushing the decanter of port towards his guest.

" Thank you, no, Lord Buntingdon. I find that more
than one glass of port tends to aggravate my rheumatism."

" You suffer from rheumatism, do you ? "

" Yes, in the knees, Lord Buntingdon. Ah, well, anno
domini, anno domini. One must accept it."

" You get it in the knees, eh ? That's where I get it
sometimes. I *have* wondered whether we're wise to wear
shorts at our age."

" Oh, Lord Buntingdon," the Secretary exclaimed,
" don't say that ! My own idea is that if we didn't wear
shorts as often as we could we should have much worse
rheumatism. I think shorts are the healthiest garments any
man can wear, or any woman for that matter."

" Not *any* woman, Mr Prew. The faintest touch of
steatopygy is fatal to the successful wearing of shorts."

" Yes, I suppose it would be," the Secretary agreed,
wondering what on earth steatopygy was. " But surely
that's a rare complaint ? "

" Not so rare as all that among women."

" I must admit I'm a little ignorant about certain aspects of women, Lord Buntingdon. A bachelor, you know."

" I'm a bachelor too, don't forget."

" Yes, indeed, so you are, Lord Buntingdon. Shall I strike a jarring note if I call it a blessed state ? "

" I've never regretted it. But then of course I've had so many interests," the peer went on dreamily. " The League of Nations, and promoting the culture of the soya bean, and basic English, and spelling reform, and hiking, and of course my tortoises."

" I know, Lord Buntingdon, I know. The variety of your interests is truly phenomenal. Oh, that reminds me, we were approached the other day by the Nudist Ramblers Society asking if we would accept them as an affiliated branch of the N.U.H. The Committee rejected the application."

" Quite right," said Lord Buntingdon decidedly.

" I'm glad you endorse our attitude. What we felt was that, although at present the Nudist Ramblers only ramble about over one or two strictly private estates the owners of which have granted their permission, it would not do to create confusion in the mind of the general public between nudists and some of our jolly young people who, revelling as they quite rightly should in their own youthful bodies, wear actually very little in the way of clothes. We did in fact have slight trouble a fortnight ago when two of our most energetic young lady members were asked by the Vicar of Bustard Abbas in Dorset to leave his church. Oh yes, he addressed them from the pulpit in the very coarsest biblical language . . . one would think a clergyman would know better in these days. But I always say if one wants to find old-fashioned bigotry one must look for it in church. The girls were lightly clad, yes. But for the Vicar to complain that his choir broke down in the middle of the Venite through staring at them when they came into the church was a reflection, had he stopped to reflect, not upon the poor girls, but upon the nasty minds of himself and his badly-trained choir. The whole business was most unpleasant. One old woman, an inmate of the Bustard Abbas almshouses, was seized with a form of hysterics and had to be led out of the church in convulsions of laughter, and according to the Vicar continued to laugh ungovernably at intervals for nearly a week, which seems to have exasperated one of the other almswomen into emptying a cup of tea over her. In fact Bustard Abbas appears to be one of those remote and peaceful country villages which is literally seething beneath the outwardly beautiful surface with the rankest and basest animal passions. You'll pardon my strong language, Lord Buntingdon, I hope? And, dear me, I'm wandering from the real question at issue. This degraded mediæval superstition which still lingers always rouses my ire."

"Come along, we'll go into the library and have our coffee," said Lord Buntingdon soothingly. "But I'm glad you choked off those nudists. A bachelor's state may be blessed, but we can't be too careful, and I don't want to be associated with nudists. Anyway, I don't like 'em. I came upon a colony of them once in Germany, skating. It was a most unpleasant sight. They looked like chilled meat."

In the library Mr Sydney Prew returned to the subject which had brought him to Ouse Hall.

"Of course, it was open to me to take out a summons for assault and battery against Ben Nevis."

"Against Ben Nevis?" Lord Buntingdon gasped, his oval brow suffering another ellipse.

"That is what they call this Mr MacDonald in Invernessshire."

"A nickname, do you mean?"

"No, he is known as MacDonald of Ben Nevis."

"Oh, I see, he's one of those Highland chief fellows. Go on."

"As I was saying, I could take out a summons against him for assault and battery, and so could young Tom Camidge for shooting his portable wireless set as well as assaulting him personally, and so could all the rest for the assault, and the shutting them up in those dungeons; but Mr Buckham feels that the only lesson to give Mr MacDonald is a lesson that will teach him the power of the National Union of Hikers rather than the power of British justice, which no doubt he knows already."

"What form does Mr Buckham propose his lesson should take?" Lord Buntingdon asked.

"He wishes the N.U.H. to declare war on Mr MacDonald and make his life a burden to him until he sues for peace."

"How does Mr Buckham propose to wage war?"

"He wants volunteers from the N.U.H. to camp on Mr MacDonald's land, to pull down the notice-boards, to

annoy him in every possible way and possibly even to seize
and occupy Glenbogle Castle. He proposes to assume
command himself of the operations. The meeting is being
held on Friday to rouse the feelings of the Union. Mr
Buckham will address the meeting. So will Tom Camidge.
His fiancée, too, Miss Winifred Gosnay, will relate the
experience of the girls shut up in the dungeon. And finally
I shall tell of the way this Highland bully shook and shook
and shook . . ."

" Yes, yes," Lord Buntingdon interrupted, " that will be
what you will tell the meeting."

" And also I shall relate the really horrible tale of the way
we were driven out of Glenbogle by lorries and motor-
cars."

" But what do you want me to do ? " Lord Buntingdon
asked, a little dubiously.

"We want you, our much revered and, if I may say so,
much loved President to take the chair and lend the weight
of your name to what we feel will be one of the most impressive demonstrations of democratic solidarity and determination this country has witnessed for many a long day. I
know how strongly you feel on the subject of collective
security, and this seems to me, if I may venture to say so,
a phenomenal opportunity to display a most convincing
example of the advantage of collective security."

Lord Buntingdon remained silent. He was pondering
the motto of his house. *Festina lente.* He was reflecting
upon the gait of his tortoises. He was asking himself whether
it was wise to involve himself in what amounted to an
incitement to the members of the N.U.H. to take the law
into their own hands. The Gordon Riots! The Buntingdon Agrarian Outrages ? The Buntingdon Raid ? A
vision passed across his fancy of himself at Madame Tus-
saud's—of himself in shorts and shirt leaning upon his hiker's
staff, with waxen brow and waxen knees and glass eyes,
staring at the crowds that read the number attached to him
and turned to the catalogue to find out that this was the
famous Earl of Buntingdon who had ravaged the Highlands
of Scotland with an army of hikers.

" I don't think I ought to take the chair, Mr Prew," he
said at last.

" You don't, Lord Buntingdon ? This will be a grievous
blow to our Acting President, Mr Buckham. Must we take

it you disapprove of the action we plan against Mr Mac-
Donald ? "

"By no means, Mr Prew, in my own house. But there
is a great difference between commending your energetic
proposals in private and commending them upon a public
platform. My brother peers already disapprove of me very
much. The speeches of few noble lords are received so
frigidly as mine. But so far I have not directly attacked
the sacred rights of landed property, and as a landed proprietor myself I am in rather a delicate position. You
must see that ? "

"Yes, I do see that, Lord Buntingdon, but I also see that
you are one of democracy's doughtiest champions and I feel
that your absence from the platform on Friday next will be
a bitter disappointment to our splendid young people who
look up to you as a leader."

"I can assure you, my dear Mr Prew, that I am acutely
aware of my responsibility toward these splendid young
people, but I confess I am apprehensive of what the Press
may make of my open encouragement of what undoubtedly
is lawlessness, however much we may recognize that such
lawlessness was provoked by the previous lawlessness of Mr
MacDonald."

"But we can exclude the Press," Mr Prew urged. "In
fact we ought to exclude the Press. It's not a public meeting.
Nobody will be admitted who cannot show his or her card
of membership. Of course if you decide that you cannot
take the chair we must bow to the inevitable, but at the risk
of committing a nuisance . . . I should say rather of being a
nuisance," Mr Prew hastily corrected in answer to the surprised expression on Lord Buntingdon's melon-shaped face,
"at the risk, I say, of being too persistent I must beg you to
change your mind and agree to take the chair on Friday
evening. You have taken the chair on all the momentous
occasions in the Union's history. It was you who put to
the vote the question of supplying hotels with green sign-
boards painted N.U.H. in white letters under our device of
the crossed staffs and our motto *Hike On—Hike Ever*. It was
you who signed your name at the head of the protest to the
Editors of the *Concise Oxford Dictionary* because the word
' hike ' was not yet included in their columns. Lord Buntingdon, please, please recall the great Annual Hikery,
growing in size and importance every year, which is held in

the park of Ouse Hall and try to imagine what it would mean
to those splendid young people if their beloved President
failed to lead the Hikers' Song,

> " *Hike, hike, hike along the high road,*
> *Hike, hike, hike along the low,*
> *Hike across the bens, hike across the fens,*
> *Hike, hike, hike, never ride a bike,*
> \ *And carry with a smile your load,*
> *Boys and girls, hike, hike, as fast as you like,*
> *And hike, if you like, as slow.*
> *Boys and girls, hike together, for it's always hikers' weather,*
> *And sing the hikers' song as you go.*"

Mr Sydney Prew's prim voice did not do justice to the
Hikers' Song, but Lord Buntingdon in fancy heard it rolling
from the voices of happy young people massed upon the great
lawn at Ouse Hall. The spirit that led the first Earl of
Buntingdon to whistle James II out of England and himself
into an Earldom abode in the seventh Earl of Buntingdon.

" Very well, Mr Prew, I will take the chair on Friday,"
he said.

" Oh, huzza! " the Secretary exclaimed with prim
enthusiasm. " I wonder if I may use your telephone, Lord
Buntingdon ? "

" Certainly."

" I know Mr Buckham is hanging on to the other end, as
the picturesque phrase hath it, hoping to have word with
me that you will take the chair on Friday."

" No Press," Lord Buntingdon reminded him.

" No Press. Except a great press of young people, I
hope," Mr Prew added archly, as he tripped out of the
library to telephone the Acting President.

Mr Percy Buckham has been described in *Boost*, the
advertisers' advertiser, as one of the live wires of the wireless
world. This paradox meant that Percy Buckham, the
managing director of the firm which made the portable
wireless-set known all over Great Britain as Buckham's
Little Songster, spent a very considerable sum annually on
advertising. It is perhaps superfluous to describe him.
Who does not know those dark compelling eyes, that out-
thrust chin, that masterful mouth and concentrated frown
beneath the curly hair of a he-man with the heart of a boy ?

No matter the pages of what paper you turn you will not find it easy to escape Buckham's talks under the heading *Lend me Your Ears*. He is as anxious to borrow the ears of readers of *The New Statesman* as those of *Secrets and Flame* that he may return them filled with facts about his Little Songster.

'Buy Buckham's Little Songster and carry the world round with you in one hand.' 'The Four B's of Music— Bach, Beethoven, Brahms and Buckham.' 'Wouldn't it give you a thrill if Mr Baldwin walked into your room and talked to you? Buckham's Little Songster will bring Mr Baldwin into your room.' 'Have you ever dreamed that the world's great singers sang for you alone? Buckham's Little Songster will make your dream come true.' 'Henry Hall's Band will play hikers up the steepest hill if they carry Buckham's Little Songster in their knapsacks.'

It would be wrong, very wrong, to connect Percy Buckham's interest in the National Union of Hikers with his interest in the Little Songster. He presided as enthusiastically over the hiker without a Little Songster as over the one who never hiked four miles without one. On the other hand, it would be dishonest not to admit that his desire to avenge the treatment of the sixteen members of the N.U.H. was stimulated to the point of fury by the news that Ben Nevis had emptied both barrels of his gun into Tom Camidge's Little Songster.

"Don't prosecute, Tom," he urged. "I'll give you another Little Songster. This has become a personal matter for me. I'm in with you over this up to the hilt. I'm going to show this Highland bully what it means to put Percy Buckham against him. We'll carry the war into the enemy's country, Prew. I hope Lord Buntingdon will support us."

So on this evening the creator of the Little Songster was waiting anxiously in his house on Primrose Hill for news of this support.

"Hullo! Is that you, Prew? Yes? He *will* take the chair? That's splendid . . . what's that? No Press? But you know I always give the Press their chance. This would be splendid copy for them . . . well, of course, if the old boy's adamant. . . . I suppose it will have to be limited to members of the Union. But I think it's a pity to lose the publicity. After all, it is a unique occasion. There's been nothing like it since the sort of thing you read of in history

books. . . . Oh, I agree it adds very much to the strength
of our position if Lord Buntingdon presides over the meeting,
and you were quite right to give way over the Press . . .
yes, as you say, it isn't as if it was a meeting open to the
general public. By the way, Prew, will he be wearing
shorts ? . . . well, you might ask him, will you ? . . ."

Buckham held the receiver to await Lord Buntingdon's
decision.

Mrs Buckham, a plump blonde of about thirty-five with
china-blue eyes and the winning smile of a successful business-
man's wife, smiled encouragingly at her husband.

" You're pleased Lord Buntingdon has agreed to take the
chair, Percy ? "

" Very pleased," he rapped out, his chin making passes at
the receiver.

Mrs Buckham looked so conventional that it was rather
surprising to find her apparently taking for granted her
husband's intention to start a civil war. The explanation
was that she always attributed any eccentricity of Percy's
to its publicity value, and his success in business seemed to
her an answer to every criticism.

" Is that you, Prew ? What does he say ? . . . he thinks
it better not to wear shorts ? Why ? . . . yes, well, perhaps
he's right. We'll none of us wear shorts on the platform,
then. You'll have to let the speakers know. You'd better
come round to my office to-morrow morning. We'll lunch
together and discuss any details we've not arranged yet.
Thank Lord Buntingdon from me for his assent. Say how
much we all appreciate it. Good night, old man."

Buckham hung up the receiver.

" Funny how timid these lords are, Ethel," he observed
to his wife. " I don't think if I was the Earl of Buntingdon I
should be afraid of the Press."

" I'm sure you wouldn't, Percy."

" If this war starts it means washing out that cruise in
September, unless you'd like to take Maud Runcible."

" I'd love to take Maud Runcible."

" Would you ? All right, you'd better arrange it. I
hope we get good weather. Are you coming to the meeting
on Friday ? "

" Do you want me to come, Percy ? "

" I shall be making a speech. I think you ought to hear it."

" Then of course I'll come."

Chapter 13

THE EXTRAORDINARY MEETING

THE Astrovegetarian Hall in Villiers Street, Strand, is one of several such edifices erected in London to house the opinions of the sect or philosophical society or collection of cranks which has subscribed to build a temple of its own. They usually consist of a fairly large central hall with a number of smaller lecture-rooms attached, and the sect or society by letting out these rooms and the main hall itself often derives a handsome return on the investment in the shape of rent.

The Astrovegetarian Society itself used its hall only on certain dates like the Summer and Winter Solstice connected immemorially with the influence of the heavenly bodies upon the fertility of the earth, and such was its broadmindedness that if a Butchers' Friendly Society had desired to use the hall for some celebration it would have been let to them for the fixed fee.

On this Friday evening in August the lecture-rooms were experiencing the effect of the holiday season, but even so, besides the booking of the main hall for the National Union of Hikers, rooms had been booked for the Society for the Promotion of Non-metallic Gramophone Needles, the Birth Control Crusade (Shock Troops Debating Society), the Root and Branch League, the Friends of Wo Ho Wo, the Edible Fungus Club and the London Animist Association. It was remarkable with what accuracy the janitor directed the members of these various gatherings to the right room almost before they had time to name their particular objective, for outwardly they all looked much the same mixture of dowdiness and defiance.

Naturally the great majority of those turning into the Astrovegetarian Hall that evening were members of the National Union of Hikers, and by ten minutes to eight the central hall was already full of healthy happy sunburnt young people, with a sprinkling of equally healthy happy sunburnt slightly older people, all singing the Hikers' Song interspersed with some of the favourite songs of the First Great War. It might be said that they made the welkin

ring, for the dome of the Astrovegetarian Hall was gilded
with planets and stars on a cerulean ground. It was
divided into the twelve signs of the zodiac, beneath each one
of which was a plaster representation of some prominent
vegetable associated with its influence. Nor were the
vegetables ruled by the planets uncelebrated. Thus one
might behold in coloured plaster the spinach of Saturn,
Jupiter's asparagus, the mustard and rhubarb of Mars, the
Moon's cabbages, the beans and parsnips of Venus, Mer-
cury's carrots and the ginger of the Sun. At the back of the
platform was a sort of carved reredos on which symbolical
figures in flowing draperies stood about in æsthetic attitudes
with sheaves and cornucopias.

The last notes of the Hikers' Song had just died away for
the sixth time when, much to the relief of the Shock Troops
of the Birth Control Crusade Debating in Gemini, or more
prosaically, and less ominously from their point of view,
Room 3, a door at the back of the platform opened and the
President, Acting President, Secretary and Honorary
Treasurer of the Union marched in with solemn tread
followed by Tom Camidge, whom we last saw defying Ben
Nevis in his own stronghold, Winifred Gosnay, his fiancée,
whom we last saw zipping up her shorts, and several more of
the sixteen hikers attacked on the braes of Strathdiddle and
imprisoned in the dungeons of Glenbogle.

Amid a volley of cheers, the echoes of which made one of
the Shock Troop debaters in Room 3 get badly mixed up in
the defensive tactics he was expounding, Lord Buntingdon rose
to address the meeting. If he had been in hiker's garb he
would have seemed with his melon-shaped face a fit mate for
one of those fruitarian females on the reredos behind him.
However, as we know, he had ruled against shorts for the
platform party, and his confirmed bachelordom was in no
danger.

" Members of the National Union of Hikers, friends (*loud
cheers*), our energetic and enthusiastic secretary Mr Sydney
Prew (*cheers*) has convened this extraordinary meeting to-
night at very short notice in order to deal with what I do not
hesitate, I say I do not hesitate to call a most extraordinary
situation. In fact I shall not hesitate, I say I shall not
hesitate to call it one of the most extraordinary situations I
have encountered during thirty years of what I hope I may
call public life (*hear, hear*), a life which I have tried to direct

along the path of liberal ideas and democratic progress (*applause*). I am not going to anticipate what other speakers better qualified than myself have come here to-night to tell you. I do not consider it the duty of a good chairman to cut the ground, or may I say pull the chair away from under the speakers who follow him (*laughter, a little uncertain at first, but growing louder when the smile upon the face of the President made it clear that the facetiousness was intentional*)? I recall the story of a chairman that once took the chair for the late Dean Hole of Rochester, who was to give an audience the benefit of his experience as the most enthusiastic and most knowledgeable amateur rose-grower in the country. This chairman, no doubt a most worthy man, was not endowed with the blessed faculty of knowing when to stop, and in introducing the Dean he allowed himself to ramble on for some three-quarters of an hour, at the end of which time he called upon the Dean himself to give the audience his address. ' My address is the Deanery, Rochester,' snapped the Very Reverend gentleman, ' and I am going there now.' (*Loud and prolonged laughter during which Lord Buntingdon reflected what a mercy it was that the chestnuts of his youth were capable of flowering again in his age.*) Well, not wishing Mr Sydney Prew, our most esteemed secretary, to emulate Dean Hole, I have pleasure in calling upon him to address the meeting " (*loud applause, which was renewed when Mr Prew stepped forward on the platform*).

" Mr President, Mr Acting President, girls and boys, I will not, I cannot say ' ladies and gentlemen ' (*giggles*). Do not misunderstand me, girls and boys, I will not say ' ladies and gentlemen,' because I cannot bring myself to introduce into the atmosphere of our great democratic pastime the artificial, meaningless and stuffy epithets of a mercifully decaying and hidebound conventionality. Nobody who has enjoyed the privilege of serving in however humble a capacity under that great champion of progress, our revered President, Lord Buntingdon (*loud cheers*), could bring himself to bow the knee to the household gods of an outworn and discredited social creed. But make no mistake about it, girls and boys, those tawdry household gods are not yet overthrown. Only last week sixteen members of our Union were given literally concrete evidence of their still potent sway over the hearts and heads of some of our fellow-citizens (*shame*). You cry ' shame ' now, but what will you cry when you hear all the facts ?

"A fortnight ago to-morrow sixteen of us entrained at
Euston and detrained the following morning at Perth. We
had promised ourselves the pleasure of hiking through the
romantic Highlands of Scotland as far as Inverness-shire and
thence westward by way of Fort William through Glencoe
and on to the bonny bonny banks of Loch Lomond, expecting
to entrain again at Glasgow to-morrow night, returning
refreshed in mind and body after our fortnight's holiday to
our work in London. To our delight—and will my Scottish
friends in the audience forgive me if I add to our surprise?—
we detrained early in the morning at Perth under a sky of
cloudless azure. I shall not take up your time by dwelling on
the beauties and absorbing interest of our route, on Birnam
wood familiar to students of Macbeth or on the gorge of
Killiecrankie where the romantic Dundee met his end.
Let it suffice to say that on the night of Wednesday, August
11th, we pitched our camp on the northerly banks of lovely
Loch Hoo. Lovely, do I say? Yes, lovely indeed save for
one object which defiled the beauty of the scene. That
object was a blatant freshly-painted notice-board inscribed
with the words with which so many of you are so painfully
familiar. No camping. (*Loud cries of 'shame.'*) Shame
indeed! Shame upon the man who erects such a notice-
board and thereby proclaims to the world his anti-social bent
and his anti-democratic bias! You who have been privileged to wander carefree adown the pleasaunces of Ouse
Park, have your eyes been revolted by such a notice-board?
(*Loud cries of 'No.'*) Where over the many broad acres
owned by your revered President will you find such a notice-
board? (*Cries of 'Nowhere.'*) Nowhere indeed! And why?
Because Lord Buntingdon regards his ownership of some
eleven thousand acres in Bedfordshire less as ownership than
as a sacred trust. (*Loud cheers, during which the owner himself
pondered gratefully on the absence of reporters.*) You will not be
surprised to hear that we paid no attention to the forbidding
notice-board, and you will signify your approval in the
usual manner when I tell you that we actually pitched our
camp right round this preposterous scarecrow. (*Applause and
laughter.*) We had no jugs of wine, but we had jugs of water
filled from a babbling stream close at hand. We had loaves
of bread, but we had cheese also. And in some cases thou
wast—or shall I say wert?—beside me in the wilderness. No
matter. For all of us wilderness was Paradise enow. And

to add the last touch to our enjoyment we had with us our Little Songster, which under the expert eye of our friend Tom Camidge discoursed sweet music until the whole party, pleasantly tired by the long day's hike in halcyon weather, expressed itself ready for sleep.

" We were so captivated by the site of our camp that on the vote being put to the party it was decided nem. con. to prolong our sojourn there for another night and to spend the day in comparative idleness preparatory to a formidable hike of twenty-five miles the following day through some of the most majestic mountain scenery in the British Isles. In the morning we bathed in the clear invigorating waters of Loch Hoo. In the afternoon we decided to wander up the braes of Strathdiddle and take our tea in the bonny purple heather, as the song hath it. The kettles were singing on the spirit-lamps. Note that, please. We were faithful to the rule of the N.U.H. which exhorts members to abstain from lighting fires where the lighting of such fires may cause the faintest risk of damage to the countryside. The kettles, I say, were singing on the spirit-lamps. The Little Songster had just been tuned in to Crooner's Corner, that very popular new feature on which the B.B.C. is so much to be congratulated because by instituting such a feature it shows it is not afraid to stand up for popular taste against the would-be tyranny of musical highbrows. Not that I condemn musical highbrows as such. Far from it. I am something of a musical high-brow myself. I positively revel in Grieg's *Peer Gynt* Suite for instance, but I do not want to ram Grieg's *Peer Gynt* Suite down the throats of those who prefer Bing Crosby or Henry Hall. But I am digressing. Well, there we were in the bonny purple heather doing no harm to anybody or any-thing, waiting for the kettles to boil and listening to one of Henry Hall's crooners on the Little Songster, when suddenly a line of kilted figures armed with guns appeared on the sky-line. When I tell you that these were the first kilts we had seen since we stepped out of the train at Perth five days earlier, and when I remind you that our hearts had recently beaten high at the tale of Killiecrankie and the death of Bonny Dundee, you will understand how excited we were by what seemed a vision of the glamorous past. Those of us who had cameras had hastily trained them upon the advanc-ing line, when suddenly one of the kilted figures charged forward ahead of the rest and in the voice of a bull of Bashan demanded to know what we were doing on his land.   I as the senior of the party and Secretary of the N.U.H. stepped forward to explain the scope and objects of the Union, but before I was able to utter more than a few words this Mr MacDonald of Ben Nevis as he calls himself seized the collar of my shirt and shook me—I will not say as a dog shakes a rat because I absolutely refuse to admit the justice of such a comparison.   But no matter.   He was a bigger man than myself and he did not scruple to take a mean advantage of his strength and size.   Then he dropped me in a sudden access of fresh rage and fired both barrels of his gun into Tom Camidge's Little Songster.   I shall leave Tom Camidge to tell his own story.   It is enough to say now that when he protested at the brutal treatment of his portable wireless-set this bully MacDonald turned on Tom and shook him as violently and brutally as he had shaken me.   This naturally roused Miss Winifred Gosnay, who with great courage like a real Joan of Arc attacked the infuriated landowner with her staff.

" Girls and boys, in that moment for the first time in my life I was tempted to regret that I was a bachelor, so inspiring was the sight of this noble-hearted girl, heedless of all save that the man she loved was in danger, dashing recklessly to his help.   The vigour of her attack was such that the minions of Mr MacDonald of Ben Nevis were alarmed.   A hefty young woman, who we learnt afterwards was one of his own daughters, gripped Winifred Gosnay by the back of her shorts and flung her on the ground with cowardly ferocity. A moment later and we were all being attacked, and attacked by men armed with guns, mark you, by men prepared, moreover, to use those guns, as was shown when the owner of the land shot Tom Camidge's Little Songster. Well, we put up a great struggle against impossible odds, but at last we were surrounded, disarmed and forced into a lorry which drove us at high speed to Glenbogle Castle, the residence of this so-called MacDonald of Ben Nevis.   You will perhaps laugh when I tell you that his servile dependants fawn upon him by calling him Ben Nevis as if he were in all sooth actually the tallest mountain in the British Isles instead of a common Fascist bully tricked out in a kilt and the unworthy proprietor of some of the finest scenery in the land.

" When we reached the Castle, the male and female members of the party were torn apart, and both were dragged off to separate noisome dungeons. Girls and boys, you may well ask if you are listening to a tale of something that happened during the Wars of the Roses. But you are not. On the evening of yesterday week, August 12th, in this twentieth century of ours, sixteen members of the N.U.H. were incarcerated in dungeons by a kilted Fascist bully. (*A storm of boohs, hisses and catcalls.*) You are shocked. You may well be shocked. But let me continue. Apparently the wife of this Highland gentleman (*boohs*), the wife, I say, was touched by the plight of those unfortunate girls, some of whose experiences in the dungeon you will presently hear from the lips of Miss Winifred Gosnay, and Mrs MacDonald caused them to be released by the hands of the private chaplain. I do not wish to say a word which can offend the religious susceptibilities of anybody present, but I must declare that a clergyman who accepts the employment of a man like this MacDonald of Ben Nevis degrades his cloth. Beside such a man the turbulent priests of the Middle Ages like Friar Tuck and Thomas à Becket were orderly God-fearing members of society. Not only did Mrs MacDonald cause the girls to be released, but she also provided them with cold supper. I wish to say all that can be said for the other side; I am no atrocity-monger. Meanwhile, the chaplain and the head-keeper, a bearded giant of a man and the creature of MacDonald, proceeded to release the men of the party, who were incarcerated in a kind of underground bowl. But we were ready for them, yes, we were ready for them, and in a trice it was they who were the prisoners and we who were the freemen.

" Well, to cut the story short, we joined up with the girls and forced our way into the castle lounge where MacDonald and his guests were carousing together. There Tom Camidge and I warned him that he had not heard the last of the matter. I was about to expatiate further on the power of our great Union when MacDonald's pipers sounded the charge and we were driven out of the Castle by his hireling bullies and braves armed with axes. After that we tramped back to our camp and the next day we arrived at the Castle mustered in the courtyard, and challenged MacDonald to show himself. He did show himself from the safety of a window, and we hurled execrations at him.

" You think I have finished. There is worse to come. We were hiking our way out of Glenbogle when after about three miles we were overtaken by a lorry and three motor-cars filled with fiends in human shape who literally drove us before them for eight miles. Sometimes one or other of us would fall from the road on either side into the grass. Did our tormentors care ? No, they laughed. To them it was great sport. To them we were of less importance than their grouse or their stags or their rabbits.

" I have nearly done. We reached the end of Glenbogle literally battered to pieces by these cars and utterly worn out by the speed at which we had been compelled to move along one of the roughest roads in the kingdom. We were quite incapable of hiking another step. So it was decided to take the bus to Fort William, which involved a wait of three hours for half the party who could not be accommodated in the first bus. Then we decided to take the train back to London and bring our case before you. You will hear from our Acting President what action it is proposed to take against the forces of Fascist reaction. Nothing remains for me except to sit down and allow other speakers to take up the case."

The Secretary resumed his seat amid thunderous applause, and the cheering was redoubled when Lord Buntingdon leaned over and shook him by the hand to congratulate him upon his eloquence and commiserate with him on his ordeal.

Then the President rose and called upon Miss Winifred Gosnay. By this time, however, poor Miss Gosnay was suffering acutely from stage-fright. She had frequently spoken at the Debating Society of the great London store in which she worked, and when she was invited to relate her experiences in the dungeons of Glenbogle she had heedlessly consented. But the sight of that audience of four or five hundred excited hikers was altogether too much for her self-confidence. Perhaps if she had been wearing shorts and grasping her staff she might have managed to summon up the necessary courage, but in her best summer frock and sauciest hat she was paralysed.

The Acting President went across to encourage her to rise, but she shook her head almost hysterically.

" I couldn't, Mr Buckham. I couldn't really. I wouldn't be able to say a word. I'd just make an exhibition of myself. Ask Elsie Vyell. She was in the dungeon too."

The Acting President beckoned Tom Camidge to try his power of persuasion.

" No, Tom, please. I couldn't really. Don't go on. I'll burst into tears in a minute. I didn't think it would be like this when I said I would."

Tom Camidge, from the long emotional experience of a two years' engagement to Winifred, advised the Acting President it would be dangerous to press his fiancée further.

Mr Buckham went over to Elsie Vyell and invited her to give the audience an account of what she and her companions had suffered in the dungeon.

" Oh, I couldn't, no, no, I really couldn't, Mr Buckham," she declared, a nervous giggle striving to free itself from a fog of blushes.

" But Lord Buntingdon is particularly anxious that you should tell the story of the mouse," Mr. Buckham pressed.

Poor Elsie Vyell, torn between the embarrassment of disobliging Lord Buntingdon and of addressing the audience, surrendered and was led to the front of the platform by Mr Buckham.

" I've really nothing to say," she assured the audience, who by an encouraging cheer made her more nervous than ever, so nervous indeed that the convulsive movement she gave seemed the preliminary to a dive from the platform into the middle of the people in the front seats.

" You're doing splendidly, Miss Vyell," came the suave voice of the Honorary Treasurer, who was the officer of the Union seated nearest to her. In private life the Treasurer was Mr Fortescue Wilson, affectionately known as Cutie Wilson to the outlying northern suburb in which he practised as a dentist. " Don't be afraid. Just speak up."

Now Miss Vyell lived in the same suburb as Mr Wilson and was a patient of his, and she responded mechanically to the quiet confidence of the voice that bade her ' speak up ' as she had often obeyed the same voice bidding her ' open, please.'

" Well, now I'm here," she started off breathlessly, " I may as well tell you what happened to Winifred Gosnay in this horrible place where we were all shut up in the dark. It was a sort of coal-cellar, only there was no coal. I was using shocking language (*sympathetic cheers and laughter*) and one of the girls told me to shut up and another girl said what of it and she said what I said was what it was. And then there was a most shocking shriek and Winifred Gosnay called out something was walking up the inside of her leg. Well, of course that started all of us off shrieking and Winifred got a bit annoyed because it wasn't walking up us and then she screamed again because it was biting her, and when we struck a match we couldn't see anything and then the clergyman came with a lantern and let us out and just as he came in Winifred screamed again and a mouse jumped out of her shorts."

The feminine part of the audience, which was quite half of it, emitted a loud gasp of horror, and stifled shrieks were heard from different parts of the hall. Miss Vyell was dimly aware that any tale of atrocity she could relate after the mouse would be an anticlimax, but she had no notion how to retire from the platform, and stood there, twisting her handkerchief and heaving helplessly.

Once again Mr Fortescue Wilson came to her rescue.

"Thank you, Miss Vyell," he said in that tone of quiet confidence in which he had often congratulated her upon keeping her mouth open so patiently and at last gave her leave to shut it.

She turned quickly and went back to her seat, and while the auditorium rang with applause he leant over to the table on the platform and poured her out a glass of water which he handed her as he had handed to her so many glasses of water.

"Well done, Miss Vyell," said Lord Buntingdon benignly, and if Miss Gosnay felt a prick of jealousy it ceased to smart almost at once when her fiancé Tom Camidge began to address the audience. His speech and the two others that succeeded added little to what Mr Prew had already related, and the chairman was beginning to look rather bored. One of the most powerful weapons in the hands of evil is that after a time the basest and most barbaric actions under repetition get accepted as normal occurrences and fail to shock. Moreover, the experience gained from debating such topics as the advantage of collective security at the weekly meetings of this or that local debating society was inadequate to provide the technique required to hold the attention of as large an audience as this. The expressions of indignation grew gradually fainter as successive members related their experience, and it was evident that a more galvanic oratory was required if the National Union of Hikers was to be stimulated into effective action.

Fortunately Mr Percy Buckham was at hand to administer

such a stimulus. He possessed, indeed, all the attributes a demagogue requires. His voice was as insistent as a mechanical drill, but the timbre was nevertheless pleasing. He had a chin which gave to his countenance the kind of romantic determination that a cowcatcher gives to the locomotive of a prairie express. He had a forefinger which when pointed at his audience had the admonitory force of a loaded pistol. He was as warm and fluent as the hot-water tap of a hotel bath, as self-confident as an Orangeman contesting a seat in County Down, and as full of catchpenny emotion as an illustrated daily.

" My lord, fellow-members of the great National Union of Hikers, lend me your ears," Mr Buckham cried, and the meeting came back to life, with cheers and laughter for that phrase which by now was associated in the mind of the general public much more closely with Percy Buckham and his Little Songster than with Mark Antony and his funeral oration.

" I look round me at this magnificent gathering and I ask myself if it is imaginable that the young men and young women who have heard the story they have heard to-night will not exact an eye for an eye and a tooth for a tooth from this proud tyrant who has dared to question their right to freedom. And as I watch your muscles grow taut, your mouths grimly set and your eyes flash, I know that it is not imaginable. Freedom! Is there any word in this wonderful English language of ours except the word ' mother ' which can win a comparable response from our hearts? Freedom! Do you remember, some of you, that day in June when a party of us hiked to Runnymede on the anniversary of the signing of Magna Charta? Do you haply recall the few words I had the privilege of addressing to you on that sacred day in the annals of democracy? Did I not urge you then to give up everything, even life itself, rather than surrender one jot, one tittle or one iota of your precious freedom? (*Loud and prolonged cheers from the audience, most of whom were chained to office-stools or counters for fifty weeks every year.*) I hear in that noble outburst of spontaneous cheering the answer. No, you will not renounce your freedom, any more than your forefathers would renounce it at Runnymede, at the threat of Castile's dark fleet, at the bidding of James II, or even for the great Duke of Wellington himself."

This last allusion puzzled the audience, who supposed

that the great Duke of Wellington had won a conspicuous
victory for freedom by defeating Napoleon at Waterloo.
Mr Buckham perceived with the demagogue's quick instinct
that his last allusion had missed its mark and hastily reloaded.

" The great Duke of Wellington who, after gloriously
freeing Europe from the tyranny of Napoleon Bonaparte,
lost touch with the people as he grew older and sought to
hamstring the onward strides of democracy by impeding
the progress of the Reform Bill. And why did the Duke of
Wellington lose touch with the people ? Because he lost
touch with youth, and a hundred years ago the future of this
country of ours was as much in the hands of youth as it is
to-day. Well, perhaps not quite as much, for never in the
history of the world has the future depended so much upon
youth as it depends to-day. (*A loud ' hear, hear ' from
Mr Sydney Prew.*) Our energetic secretary agrees with
me, I am glad to find. Youth! Is there any word in
this sublime English language of ours except the words
' freedom ' and ' mother ' which can make our hearts
beat so fast ? Why does hiking occupy the position it does
in the esteem of sagacious men of rank and experience like
our President ? Because it is essentially a youth movement.
Lord Buntingdon in his wisdom knows that it is to youth
we must look if we are to weather safely the storms which
already threaten our horizon. So it is to you, the youth of
Britain, that I appeal now to assert your right to breathe the
same air as this proud tyrant, MacDonald of Ben Nevis. I,
Percy Buckham of Primrose Hill, speaking as the Acting
President of the National Union of Hikers and in the name
of all my fellow-members, defy him. I claim the right to
breathe the same air as he breathes. I claim the right to
hike across the ground he owns. I demand the hospitality
of that ground for our sleeping bodies.

" MacDonald of Ben Nevis with two cowardly shots from
a double-barrelled gun disabled a portable wireless-set
whose merits I have had the honour to proclaim to the world.
When MacDonald of Ben Nevis struck at the Little Songster
he struck at Buckham of Primrose Hill. (*Cheers and excited
laughter.*) Buckham of Primrose Hill will strike back.
Buckham of Primrose Hill this night calls for volunteers to
carry the war into the enemy's camp, and let me tell him
that notice-boards inscribed ' No Camping ' will avail
him nothing to protect that camp. MacDonald of Ben

Nevis drove sixteen of you through Glenbogle with lorries and cars filled with his hirelings.   Buckham of Primrose Hill with his volunteers will drive MacDonald of Ben Nevis from one end to the other of his own glen.   (*Loud cheers.*) MacDonald of Ben Nevis immured sixteen members of the National Union of Hikers in his noisome dungeons.   I declare here and now that I Buckham of Primrose Hill will lock MacDonald of Ben Nevis into his own dungeon with his own key which is now in my possession."

And amid rapturous cheering the Acting President of the N.U.H. waved above his curly head the keys of the dungeons which Ben Nevis had expected to be brought him with his coffee that night of the Twelfth of August.

" We shall enlist volunteers to-night.   The Secretary will take the names of all who are able and willing to join in this tremendous manifestation of Youth, Freedom and Democracy against the forces of Reaction and Fascism (*boohs and catcalls*).   I know that many of you have already taken your holidays for this year.   Those of you who have will regret their inability to share in the fight like the gentlemen who King Harry said would regret being absent from the glorious field of Agincourt.   Those of you who have not yet taken your annual holiday will rejoice, I know, to avail yourselves of the opportunity that presents itself to strike a blow for Youth, Freedom and Democracy.   And do not let our young Joan of Arcs hold back.   We want the army that marches against MacDonald of Ben Nevis to be truly representative of our great Union.   I have myself cancelled my berth for a month's pleasure cruise in the Mediterranean in order that I may devote the whole of my holiday to making this roystering bully bite the dust.   (*Loud and long cheers.*)   No doubt Mr MacDonald expected our injured members would meekly sue him in a court of law.   No doubt he expected to counter-sue for trespass and damage to his property.   I venture to prophesy that we shall surprise him by our prompt and resolute action.   I do not propose and you will not ask me to give you the details of our campaign.   When we can estimate the strength of which we can dispose I shall call a council of war.   I hope that within a week the vanguard of our Expeditionary Force can march.

" I have little to add.   This is a critical evening in the history of our great Union.   I venture to say that upon the response to my call for volunteers the whole future of hiking in this country depends. If we fail our glorious pastime, why then, the sooner we go back to bicycling the better."

As he uttered this fearful taunt the Acting President of the N.U.H. thrust his forefinger at the audience as you may see it out-thrust in many a paper to demand your attention for the merits of the Little Songster. Then he slowly and gravely lowered his arm and, after bowing to Lord Bunting-don, resumed his seat.

The President rose.

" Fellow members of the N.U.H., after the fiery eloquence of your Acting President you will not be inclined to listen to any words of mine. You are all eager, I know, to register your names with Mr Prew. It may perhaps savour to you of a certain pusillanimity, but I think it is my duty as your President to counsel a certain moderation in any action you take against this Scotch landowner. The reprisals you take should be strictly confined to personal reprisals. They should not include his game or his crops or his fishing. I know Mr. Buckham will not consider any such action, but I feel it is my duty to give you this counsel and I am sure you will appreciate the spirit in which it is given. Nothing remains for me except to ask you to accord a very hearty vote of thanks to the speakers who have given us such an enjoyable feast of oratory."

While Mr Prew sat at a table writing down the names of the volunteers and the dates on which they would be available for active service, Lord Buntingdon took Mr Buckham aside.

" I hope you didn't mind my giving that little caution, Mr Buckham. I know you would frown upon any type of agrarian outrage, but I felt it would help if I expressed myself strongly against it. Let this be a personal struggle with this MacDonald fellow, but don't damage his property."

" You can rely on me, Lord Buntingdon."

" That's capital. Well, I think I'll be getting back to Ouse Hall. Will you kindly ask somebody to call my chauffeur ? "

Chapter 14

THE GLENBOGLE GATHERING

DURING the week after that meeting in the Astro-vegetarian Hall, of whose weighty decisions not a rumour reached the Chieftain, he was worried by two questions. First whether his son Hector MacDonald, Younger, of Ben Nevis would arrive from India in time for the Glenbogle Gathering on Saturday, August 28th, and secondly whether the sun would shine upon the great occasion.

His mind was put at rest over Hector by receiving a telegram on Thursday to say he would be at Fort William on Friday morning, after which his anxiety was concentrated upon the weather. A dozen times a day he played a tattoo upon the aneroid barometer, and as for Admiral Fitzroy's liquid column, on which the devil's own tattoo would have made no impression, it ran a danger of being petrified into eternal insensitiveness to any atmospheric pressure by the gorgonian glares with which he was continually regarding it.

" I can't understand this infernal weather," he barked. " Can you understand this infernal weather, Hugh ? "

The laird of Kilwhillie was again staying in the Castle to support his old friend as always on any great Glenbogle occasion. It might have been expected that after receiving £1,000 more for Knocknacolly than he had agreed to accept he would have been in high spirits, but he was not. The Celtic melancholy in which he was frequently plunged had never appeared so profound. He was almost like a man brooding over some presentiment of disaster, and when addressed seemed to emerge with a start from some dark world of his own horror-haunted imagination.

" I said, ' Can you understand this infernal weather, Hugh ? ' " Ben Nevis barked more loudly.

" It's the usual weather we get about now."

" I never heard such nonsense."

" I cannot recall more than two Gatherings without any rain at all."

" What a preposterous statement, Hugh! Why, it didn't rain last year."

" That is one of the Gatherings I was thinking of."

" I don't know what's the matter with you. Have you had any bad news ? "

" No, no," said the laird of Kilwhillie, sighing deeply.

" I haven't seen you so gloomy since that champion Belted Galloway cow of yours got bogged and had to be destroyed. You must cheer up. I think the glass has gone up a fraction since morning. We shall probably have a splendid Gathering. Twenty-one coming to lunch, which with ourselves in the Castle will make thirty-four. Royde is keen as mustard on the Gathering."

Kilwhillie looked even gloomier if possible.

" He is, is he ? Did he say why particularly ? "

" Well, it'll be a new experience for him, won't it ? "

" Oh yes, quite. Yes, a new experience. I hope it won't be very sunny."

" Why on earth don't you want it to be sunny ? I hope the sun will blaze down," Ben Nevis declared, and rushing across to the aneroid barometer he drummed on it a roll that should have roused Napoleon himself from the tomb.

" Yes, I think the glass really is inclined to go up at last," he declared.

" Who are coming on Saturday ? " Kilwhillie asked.

" Well, the Lindsay-Wolseleys of course, and Bertie Bottley and Jack Fraser and Rawstorne, and oh, well, the usual crowd. Macintosh was coming, but he has some ploy of his own. Lochiel can't come either. Nor can Dunstaffnage. Ross was coming, but he wired me this morning he wouldn't be able to manage it."

" The Duke, you mean ? "

" Yes. Did you mutter, ' thank God,' Hugh ? "

" No, I was only clearing my throat."

" I always thought you liked Ross."

" So I do," said Kilwhillie warmly. " I like him and respect him. I consider him the greatest living authority on Highland dress. You're sure he's not coming ? "

" No; I told you he wired me this morning. He has to open a sale of work at Strathpeffer. He'd promised and couldn't get out of it. What a strange fellow you are, Hugh. A minute ago you were in a state of utter gloom, and now you're humming to yourself."

" I often do that, Donald. I caught the habit from my

dear old mother. She used to hum over her patience, and then I used to hum."

" I never heard you hum before," said Ben Nevis, a little suspiciously. At that moment Chester Royde came into the Great Hall, and the Chieftain's attention was diverted from Kilwhillie's humming.

"Hullo, Royde. The glass has gone up a fraction since this morning. I believe we shall get it fine on Saturday."

" That's corking," said the American guest enthusiastically. " But I give you fair warning, Ben Nevis, I'm going to enjoy myself, wet or fine."

Presently he drew near to Kilwhillie and said in a low voice:

" It's arrived. It's up in my dressing-room now."

" Oh, that's splendid," Kilwhillie gulped.

" Some time to-day or to-morrow I'd be mighty glad if you'd come along up to my room. I'd like to dress myself from top to toe and have you give me the O.K. for Saturday."

" Of course, I'll be delighted." Kilwhillie gulped again.

" What are you two plotting over there ? " their host barked genially.

But at that moment a piece of blue sky about the size of the flag over the Cambridge University Boathouse appeared in the sky, and he went charging out into the courtyard to gloat up at it.

" I'm afraid it is going to be fine on Saturday," Kilwhillie murmured to himself.

" Afraid it is going to be fine ? " Chester Royde exclaimed.

" Did I say that, Royde ? I meant I'm afraid it's *not* going to be fine."

" Well, I don't give a darn either way, Kilwhillie. I guess this orange kilt of mine will look fine if it's a second deluge."

" Orange kilt ? " Kilwhillie gasped. " But you decided on a purple one."

" Oh, I'm having a purple one as well, but it's the orange one they've sent along from Inverness. I told the tailor if he couldn't get both of them made in time to put all his work into finishing the orange one."

" And he has ? "

" He certainly has. It's a peach. Say, why don't you come up and have a look at it ? "

"I think I'll wait till you have it on," said Kilwhillie in the voice of a man under sentence of death.

"But don't breathe a word to Carrie about it. I aim to give her a little surprise on Saturday morning."

"I don't think you'll miss," Kilwhillie commented, with a touch of the sardonic in his tone.

The morning of Friday was the finest since the rain started on the day Chester Royde went stalking. Ben Nevis, excited by the prospect of a really brilliant day for the Gathering and the arrival of his eldest son, went barking all over the place with such persistency that his guests retreated to some of the more remote rooms in the Castle, unable to deal with the noise so early in the day.

Carrie and Myrtle retired to the room in the North Tower, to discuss whether or not to send word to Alan Macmillan to bring the architect from Knocknacolly and come to the Gathering, or whether to wait until James Buchanan arrived with the deeds early next week, before presenting them all at Glenbogle.

"I wouldn't like it if Ben Nevis was rude to Alan," said Carrie.

"Indeed, no, nor would I?" her sister-in-law affirmed.

"And perhaps as they're arriving to-morrow," Carrie went on, "they might find the walk from Knocknacolly a bit tiring."

"I believe they would. I think we'll drive over to Knocknacolly in your funny little runabout on Sunday," said Myrtle. "I think that will be more fun. Besides, there's no need for Chester to meet them till James Buchanan comes. And if this architect turns out to be a nice boy we can have a party of our own."

Carrie agreed a little dubiously. She had a notion that Myrtle intended to start her right off on architecture.

At that moment the noise of what they supposed was the barking of Ben Nevis reached even this remote room. In point of fact it was the sound of Old Ben Nevis and Young Ben Nevis barking at one another, for Hector had just driven up to the Castle.

The Chieftain had not exaggerated when he said his eldest son was his second self. To be sure, Hector was neither so florid nor so weatherbeaten as his father, and though his nose was the authentic eagle's beak of Mac 'ic Eachainn it lacked as yet the rich deep hues of amaranth

and damson which could flood his father's. He was slimmer
too, naturally, and was indeed a fine figure of a young man;
but he had the same choleric blue eyes, and already even
at twenty-five the same rumbustious voice.

Carrie observed, a little gladly it may be added, that her
sister-in-law was obviously agreeably surprised by Hector
MacDonald, Younger, of Ben Nevis.

" He's had a good trip. You had a good trip, Hector,
didn't you ? " Ben Nevis bellowed.

" Absolutely tophole," Hector bellowed back. " The
Colonel wasn't too keen on giving me leave. I won't be
able to take more than the inside of a week."

" Oh, well, one can do a lot in a week. Now, would you
like some more breakfast ? "

" No, thanks, I had a very good breakfast in the train.
But I think I'll go and get out of these clothes, and have a
bath."

" That's the stuff."

And as Hector MacDonald, Younger, of Ben Nevis strode
off towards his room, Angus MacQuat piped before him
Mac 'ic Eachainn's Return to Glenbogle.

On the morning of August 28th Carrie awoke to the agreeable thought that Ben Nevis had been granted his desire
and that it was a gloriously fine day As a matter of fact
it was a fine day, but the rich glow that filled the room was
caused not by the sun but by her own husband, who was
standing at the foot of the bed wearing a kilt that was not
so much orange as flame-coloured, a doublet of amber tweed,
and a heavily-brassed leather sporran.

" Chester! That's why you asked me whether I liked
orange or purple best. But why didn't you wear my tartan
—the Ben Nevis Macdonald ? "

" Listen, sweetheart, I went into the whole business of
tartans with Kilwhillie, and he ruled right out the idea of
wearing a wife's tartan. By what I could make out those who
know about these things calculate no man can do anything
much dirtier than sport his wife's tartan. Kilwhillie classed a
man who sported his wife's tartan with cattle-rustlers and
kidnappers and communists. He wanted me to have a grey
kilt, but I said ' nothing doing.' And then he admitted
that some guy in the eighteenth century used to wear a
purple kilt. And that was my first idea. In fact there's a
purple kilt being made for me right now in Inverness. But

you remember those Scottish Nationalists who got Ben Nevis's goat?"

"I remember a whole lot of foolish talk about Scottish Nationalists, yes."

"All right, honey, don't you get peeved now. But one of those Scottish Nationalists was wearing a red and yellow kilt which took my eye as we drove past in the car. And I said to myself right then I'd have an orange kilt."

"A red and yellow kilt? That sounds like the Macmillan tartan. Mr. Macmillan, the young poet I told you about, wears a red and yellow kilt. Or at least he did when I met him in Edinburgh. By the way, I'm expecting him and Mr Menzies, the architect, to reach Knocknacolly to-day, and I thought Myrtle and I would drive over to-morrow and see how they're getting along."

"That's fine. But you haven't said what you think of my costume?"

"Why, Chester, I think you look a perfectly good Highlander."

"Are you pleased I've shown my appreciation of your ancestral territory like this?"

"Chester, you've been just as sweet as you could be about my country."

"I was a bit worried at first I'd look too fat in a kilt, but the tailor told me he'd far sooner make a kilt for a figure like mine than for one of those thin fellows. Wilton was a bit obstructive about it." Wilton was Chester Royde's English valet.

"He was?"

"Yes: I think he was annoyed because I dressed myself yesterday afternoon and asked Kilwhillie to look me over."

"And Kilwhillie said it was all right?"

"I don't think he's tickled to death by the orange kilt. He said it was brighter than he thought it would be. He said he'd have advised a saffron kilt, the kind some of the Irish use, if he'd known I was going all out on orange. He put me wise, too, about the sporran."

"How?"

"Why, I thought it would be more convenient to wear it on one side like a trouser pocket. But it seems that for a fellow to wear his sporran on one side tells against him pretty heavily in Highland society. I suppose I'll soon get used to walking about like a kangaroo with a pouch in front of me, but I still think the place for a pocket is on the side. I asked him if there was any objection to me carrying an extra sporran on the hip, but that suggestion upset him a lot. He wouldn't hear of it. Still, there's no question about it, Carrie. The kilt's pretty comfortable."

Chester Royde took a turn round the room to demonstrate the ease with which he could carry the unfamiliar garment.

" You look very comfortable," his wife assured him.

Chester stopped suddenly and gazed at her gravely.

" Say, Carrie, what do you suppose I'm wearing underneath this kilt ? "

" Why, I don't know, Chester. Little panties ? "

" Little panties nothing. I'm not wearing a darned thing underneath except the tails of my shirt."

" Didn't the tailor send them ? "

" Nobody wears anything underneath a kilt."

" Chester, I don't believe it."

" Well, would I be such a mutt as to go about like a nood statue hung around with a curtain unless it was what they were all doing ? "

" Chester, you *must* have made a mistake."

" No mistake at all. The tailor told me some folk wore tartan trews when they were going to a dance. They're the kind of panties old maids used to wear. But when I consulted Kilwhillie he said he wouldn't agree even to that. He said if I'd made up my mind to wear the kilt I must wear the kilt properly, or he'd take no responsibility in the matter."

" He's taken on a much bigger responsibility as it is," Carrie declared.

" Aw, don't worry. I'm not going to fall down on this business."

" I hope not. If you start falling down the sooner you go back to your own clothes the better."

" You're not nervous about me, are you, Carrie ? "

" Well, I rather wish you hadn't told me about wearing nothing underneath. I'll feel a bit nervous even about Ben Nevis now. But, look here, you're dressed or as much dressed as you can be. You'd better go on down to breakfast and let me get dressed."

" It isn't breakfast-time yet ? "

" What time is it ? "

Chester looked at his watch.

" Twenty-five after seven."

" What ? " Carrie gasped indignantly. " And you're up and dressed already ? "

" I wanted to dress myself before Wilton came up. It gives me a kind of kick to keep him in the background over this kilt business. I don't think he thought I was serious when I said I was going to wear it to-day."

" What are you going to do till breakfast ? "

" I'm going outside to practise walking about by myself."

Just after eight o'clock when Angus MacQuat was playing the customary aubade beneath the window of his chief, for the first time in twenty years he played a false note in the middle of the *Iomradh Mhic 'ic Eachainn.* It was caused by suddenly catching sight of Chester Royde coming round the corner of the North Tower.

Ben Nevis rushed to the window to let his piper know his mistake had not escaped his ears and received his first sight of Chester Royde.

" My god, Trixie," he turned to shout at his wife, " there's a Scottish Nationalist in the Courtyard."

" Well, you can't do anything about it in your pyjamas, Donald," she boomed placidly from the four-poster.

The Chieftain rushed to the window again to demonstrate that he could do something about it and this time recognized his cherished guest.

" Hullo, Royde," he bellowed down, " this is a very sporting effort on your part. By Jove, it is! All right, Angus, you needn't go on playing."

The piper saluted and retired. Just before he vanished round the Castle walls he threw a backward glance over his shoulder, and then with a puzzled shake of the head proceeded on his way to his porridge.

" I can't quite make out what that tartan is," Ben Nevis was calling down.

" It isn't a tartan at all," Royde replied. " Kilwhillie advised me to steer clear of tartans. This is his idea of a good substitoot."

" Do you know what I thought you were at first ? I thought you were a Scottish Nationalist. I did, upon my soul. Well, I must say it was jolly nice of you, Royde, to think of this way of paying a little tribute to the Gathering. And by Jove, what a day, eh ? "

" Some day."

" I knew it was going to be fine. We always get fine weather for our Gathering. Last year it was lovely. Well, I must go and get dressed myself. See you presently at breakfast."

Back in his room Ben Nevis turned to his wife. " I can't understand why Hugh advised Royde to get an orange kilt, Trixie."

" An orange kilt ? " Mrs MacDonald boomed in equable astonishment.

" Well, it's really more a kind of orange-scarlet. I cannot understand why Hugh chose such a bright colour. He hates bright colours. That Erracht Cameron tartan he wears is pretty dull, but even so he always buries a new kilt for two years in a bog before he'll put it on. I really can't understand it. Well, we've got an absolutely glorious day for our dear old Glenbogle Gathering, Trixie."

" I'm so glad, dear."

" And I think that pretty little Royde girl took quite a fancy to Hector, didn't you ? I noticed her smiling at him a lot last night at dinner."

" Well, it would be a very wonderful match for her if Hector did take a fancy to *her*," said Hector's mother.

" I wish that silly Colonel of his had given him more leave. But Rose-Ross always was a silly fellow. Talking of Ross I wish the Duke was coming to-day. I'd have liked to hear what he had to say to Hugh when I told him Hugh advised Royde to get that orange-scarlet kilt."

However, any speculations in which Ben Nevis was tempted to indulge about Chester Royde's kilt or his son's ability in the time at his disposal to secure the hand of Myrtle Royde were soon ousted from his mind by the claims of the Glenbogle Gathering upon his attention. Those familiar with the West Highlands and the slight inclination in that part of the world toward the romantic timelessness which is prosaically called unpunctuality will appreciate what a struggle the Chieftain had every year to begin the Games not more than two hours after the printed announcements hung up even as far as in the shops of Fort William advertised that they would begin. This was ten o'clock, but the remoteness of Glenbogle made it difficult to muster many spectators from outside the glen by that time. Therefore, naturally, those who lived in and round about the Castle took it for granted that not many would have arrived

before eleven o'clock at the earliest and usually started to
get ready themselves at that hour. Since the introduction
of summer time the tendency had been to get ready even
later than that because, as they argued, it was not really
eleven o'clock but only ten o'clock. They were still devoted
to Mr Lloyd George on account of old-age pensions, but
their devotion did not extend to according what was called
Lloyd George's time an equality with God's time.

The combination of Harrow and Cambridge with his
own natural impetuosity had given Ben Nevis that passion
for punctuality of which we have already had a taste in his
irritation when dinner was postponed on the night of the
Twelfth of August ; and if the march headed by himself and
his pipers to Achnabo, the field where the Gathering was
held, did not leave the courtyard of the Castle by half-past
eleven and thus allow the games to start before noon he grew
fierce.

The exhilarating prospect of a cloudless day and the
presence of his eldest son made him more than usually
anxious this year to reach the field as soon as possible
and more than usually boisterous over the preliminary
marshalling.

" You're rather late, Wolseley . . . glad to see you, Mrs
Wolseley . . . we're just just forming up in the courtyard
. . . the ladies are going on ahead . . . ah, there you are,
Bertie . . . you'd better take up your place . . . if any
of the visiting pipers who are competing want to join you,
Angus, you'd better get them lined up . . . ah, Rawstorne,
where's Jack Fraser ? . . . has anybody seen Jack Fraser ?
. . . oh, there you are, Jack, you're rather late . . . Hugh!
Hugh! Hugh! . . . where the deuce is Kilwhillie ? . . .
ah, there you are, Hugh . . . look here. I want you to
march on the right of Royde . . . I'm going to put him on
my right . . . Hector will be on my left . . . I want nothing but kilts in the front line. . . . Wolseley, will you and
Bottley muster the second line round you . . . now, we'll
give the ladies another five minutes . . . Angus! Angus!
Angus! . . . where the deuce is Angus MacQuat ? . . .
ah, there you are, Angus . . . now, you know what you
have to play us down with . . . *Mac 'ic Eachainn's March
to Sheriffmuir* until we approach the field, and then break
into *Clan Donald is Here* . . . Catriona! Mary!! . . .
Good Lord, haven't you started down to the field yet ? . . .

Where's your mother ? . . . Trixie !! Trixie!!! . . . I'm
sorry, Trixie, I didn't see you were just behind me . . .
but do make the ladies move along . . . Mrs Wolseley and
Mrs Rawstorne and Lady Bottley went on five minutes
ago . . . oh, you're waiting for Carrie and Myrtle . . .
ah, there they are . . . come along, young ladies. We
can't begin our march until you're on the field. . . ."

At last the group of thirty or so friends, relations and
dependants privileged to accompany Mac 'ic Eachainn on
this glorious occasion was marshalled and waited only the
command of Ben Nevis to march. He donned the high
bonnet with the two eagle's feathers of a chieftain in which
Raeburn had painted his great-grandfather, and which he
wore only on the day of the Glenbogle Gathering.

" Now, are you all ready ? " he bellowed. " Very well,
then, on we go! "

The skirling of ten pipers rent the air as they stepped out
to the tune of *Mac 'ic Eachainn's March to Sheriffmuir*, followed
by the honoured guests, every man with a cromag nearly as
tall as a window-pole.

" Enjoying this, Royde ? " Ben Nevis asked.

" Why, I should say I am," replied his guest, who had
added to the brilliancy of his appearance by carrying an
orange plaid over his shoulder. In fact to a casual glance
it might have seemed for a moment that the right side of
Ben Nevis was in eruption.

But not even that rumbustious voice could compete with
ten pipers blowing full blast three or four yards in front of it,
and the Chieftain was silent until he had taken his seat on
the mound which overlooked the arena.

Then he observed as he had observed at the beginning of
every Glenbogle Gathering for the last twenty-five years:

" Not so many here yet as there ought to be."

There never had been and there never would be enough
people with faith that games advertised to begin at ten
o'clock would begin much before one o'clock. In any case
except to piping experts the earlier part of the proceedings
was a little dull, consisting as it did of the same example
of *ceòl mór*—the classical music of the bagpipe—played by
twelve pipers in turn on a wooden platform before which sat
the judges with notebooks and pencils, marking the faults
and merits of each performer's grace-notes, slides and
doublings. Kilwhillie was one of the judges; Colonel

Lindsay-Wolseley was another; the third was a former pipe-major of the Clanranalds called Farquhar Macphail. It was noticeable that both Kilwhillie and the Colonel always ascertained his opinion of each performance first, and then after the very faintest camouflage of expert hesitation proceeded to agree with it. If Pipe-major Macphail had been a cynic he might have lured Kilwhillie or the Colonel into expressing a positive opinion of some performance before he gave his; but Pipe-major Macphail was not a cynic. Through twenty-one years' service with The Duke of Clarence's Own Clanranald Highlanders (The Inverness-shire Greens) he had preserved a simple belief in human nature.

" You're not looking quite so well this beautiful morning, Kilwhillie," he observed in an interval of silence while one of the competitors was intent upon his tuning slides. " No, sir, you're not looking so well as usual."

" I'm quite all right, Pipe-major," said the laird, giving a listless tug at his moustache. He could not explain that a light remark of his lifelong friend and neighbour Ben Nevis was weighing very heavily upon his mind. Pipe-major Macphail was not to know that Ben Nevis had said he could not understand why he had advised Chester Royde to choose an orange kilt, and then had added, " You'll have Ross on your trail, Hugh, when he hears about it."

Kilwhillie was not inclined to hero-worship, but the Duke of Ross he had long worshipped not for his rank but for his infallible judgment on any question connected with Highland dress, jewellery, use, custom, lore, genealogy and coat-armour.

And as if in answer to his unspoken thoughts Colonel Lindsay-Wolseley asked him at this moment why he had allowed that American fellow to rig himself out in that extraordinary get-up.

" It's not my business, Wolseley," Kilwhillie snapped. " I'm not his tailor."

" No, no, of course not," said the Colonel soothingly. He had never heard Kilwhillie bite like this at a remark. " I just thought with a great authority like you at hand he'd have taken the chance of a little good advice. I wish the Duke had been able to come to-day. I can just imagine what he would have said."

The Colonel chuckled to himself, and then concentrated

on the eleventh performance of the pibroch chosen for the
competition.

Kilwhillie hunched himself moodily in his chair. On
many a previous morning when Glenbogle gathered he had
sat wrapped in his plaid while the rain poured down, listening much more cheerfully to the same composition played
over and over again.

In another part of the field the competition for putting
the stone was proceeding, to describe which would be even
more tedious than to watch it.

This, indeed, was the hour of the Glenbogle Gathering,
when those who were wandering round the field asked
themselves why they had arrived only two hours late. The
friends from Fort Augustus or Fort William they were expecting to meet and with whom they were hoping to enjoy
a fruitful gossip had not yet arrived. Even from Kenspeckle
only one busload had been delivered as yet.

Myrtle Royde, catching the prevailing mood, was thinking
how pleasant it would be if among the spectators the red
and yellow of the Macmillan tartan, brighter even than that
tango kilt Chester was wearing, should suddenly flicker into
view, when a voice barked in her ear:

" Enjoying yourself? You're looking very thoughtful."

She turned to see young Ben Nevis smiling down at
her.

" I was wondering just exactly what they were doing with
that stone."

" Putting it."

" Putting it where ? "

" As far as they can. Iain's ahead now with his second
put. I think myself he'll win, though old Murdoch usually
fetches up a bit of extra beef for his third put."

" I can't pretend to be terribly excited, Lootenant."

Young Ben Nevis blinked. His father had pressed upon
him the immense advantage it would be to consider Myrtle
Royde as a prospective Twenty-fourth Lady of Ben Nevis,
but like his brother Murdoch before him he was a little
startled to be addressed as Lieutenant with the pronunciation
' Lootenant.'

" I say, don't call me that," he begged.

" Well, what do I call you ? Ben Nevis Junior sounds
kind of awkward to me."

" Couldn't you manage ' Hector ' ? "

"Why, I dare say I wouldn't find it terribly difficult, Hector."

"That's topping. Look here, you'll give me the first eightsome to-night?"

"The first what?"

"The first eightsome reel."

Myrtle still looked blank.

"It's a dance."

"But I don't know how to dance it."

"I'll teach you before dinner. You'll learn it in no time. I think we'll manage one or two sixteensomes to-night. But we shan't get a thirty-twosome. Not enough of us."

"Isn't that too bad? Tell me, Hector, what do you think of my brother in his kilt? I think he looks cute, don't you?"

"Yes, but I don't know why Hugh Cameron made him get an orange kilt."

"I'd call that colour more of a tango than an orange."

"Personally I should have advised him to get a grey one."

"But Chester's crazy on colour."

"Oh, great put, Murdoch! Bravo!" young Ben Nevis barked. "I thought old Murdoch would call up some extra beef for the third round. He's a good foot beyond Iain now. Oh, good one, Kenny!"

"Who are you cheering now?"

"That's Kenny Macdonald, our blacksmith. He's an inch or two better than Murdoch, I fancy. Yes, I thought so."

A light crepitation of applause from the few who were watching the putting was audible above the piping.

"Now it's Iain's last put. Oh, jolly good, Iain! Jolly good indeed!" the eldest brother exclaimed. "Did you see that last put, Dad?" he shouted across the field to the Chieftain enthroned on the mound.

"Jolly good!" the Chieftain bellowed back.

The two or three competitors left failed to come within a couple of feet of Iain, who emerged from the contest as the winner amid general enthusiasm.

"We'll probably go back to the Castle now for lunch," said Hector.

"That'll be more exciting, won't it?" Myrtle suggested.

" Oh, putting the stone's pretty exciting," Hector insisted.

" Is it ? " Myrtle asked doubtfully. " Well, I wasn't terribly thrilled by it. It's about the least exciting thing I've seen since I came to Glenbogle."

Far different was the scene on the field of Achnabo when Ben Nevis and his guests returned to it after lunch. Omnibuses and cars from Fort William and Fort Augustus, and even from lordly Inverness itself, had discharged their sightseers. The battered Fords and Morrises and Austins of many a village and clachan had brought gossips old and young, male and female. Former pupils were asking former schoolmasters and schoolmistresses if they recognized them. Shepherds were discussing gloomily the latest low level to which the price of wool had sunk. Crofters were exchanging tales about the misdeeds of the Department of Agriculture. Farmers were shaking their heads over the prospects for store-cattle at the next sales. Tea was being swilled in half a dozen tents and insides were being plastered with slices of chalkwhite Glasgow bread. Toward one tent with the Committee's cardboard sign a procession of slightly surreptitious figures, all with the same expression of elaborate purposelessness, was ever wending, and from the same tent another procession of figures whose tongues sometimes peeped from pursed satisfied lips but whose eyes had the innocent look of children beholding life for the first time was ever emerging. It is a remarkable tribute to the enduring influence of John Knox's ethics that in a country where enough whisky has been distilled and drunk during the four centuries of Presbyterianism to flavour every loch in Scotland, natives who take one dram of it at a public festivity like the Glenbogle Gathering should still be able to romanticize the little indulgence with the flavour of mortal sin.

Within the rope ring that enclosed the arena the change was not less remarkable. Runners were tearing round amid the excited exhortations of their supporters to win or lose races. Massive figures in kilts and vests whose muscles stood out like the bumps in the mattresses of remote Highland inns were tossing the caber and throwing the hammer. And on that platform, where for three seemingly endless hours piper after piper had marched up and down playing the same example of *ceòl mór*, half a dozen little girls whose velvet doublets jingled with medals were dancing reels and strathspeys and jigs and as they leapt higher and higher displaying beneath their kilts a lather of frilly underclothes. Laughter and chatter and cheers resounded upon the sunny air, and in all that merry throng only Kilwhillie and Colonel Lindsay-Wolseley and seven pipers looked sad, the seven pipers because they had not won a prize, Kilwhillie and the Colonel because the piping had only just finished and they had not yet lunched.

" You're not one of the judges for the dancing, Hugh ? " the Chieftain asked.

" I think Wolseley and I have done enough judging for the present," Kilwhillie answered reproachfully. " We haven't had any lunch yet, and there will be another hour or two later with the piping."

" You'd better toddle back to the Castle. Toker will look after you. Who won in the Coalmore ? "

" Angus."

" Oh, he did, did he ? That's good news." He looked across to where Mrs MacDonald was sitting on the mound, almost as massive a female shape as the great statue of Liberty. " Trixie! Trixie! " She looked up and acknowledged his hail with her parasol. " Angus has won in the Coalmore! "

Mrs MacDonald tried to express gratification over the result of the *ceòl mór*, which was difficult partly on account of the distance between her and her husband, but chiefly because she had been the recipient of this announcement at about this time of the afternoon in every one of the last fourteen years. True, she was carrying a parasol this year instead of an umbrella for the first time.

" Hullo," said Ben Nevis, " that's a big busload of hikers from Fort William."

A number of young men in khaki shorts and the usual polychrome of shirts were alighting from an omnibus which had just driven up to the field of the Gathering.

" You're not going to order a general attack, I hope," said Colonel Wolseley with a smile.

The Chieftain guffawed genially.

" Not to-day, Wolseley. Glenbogle is Liberty Hall to-day, what ? Delighted to welcome everybody here to our Gathering. Even hikers. But look here, Wolseley. You and Hugh really must go and get some lunch."

The laird of Kilwhillie was drawing one half of his moustache across his mouth in a manner that suggested he should eat part of it as a hors-d'œuvre if he and the Colonel did not soon sit down to a substantial meal.

They set out for the Castle, and Ben Nevis wandered patriarchally about the field. This was perhaps the hour in all his year he most enjoyed, this opportunity to meet the old friends of a lifetime, farmers and tradesmen, crofters, shepherds, schoolmasters and gillies. The enjoyment of his patriarchal promenade was much enhanced to-day by the perfection of the weather. The wrinkled faces of Donaldinas and Kennethinas, of Kirsties, Morags, Floras, Peggies and Ealaisaids usually smiled up at him from beneath dripping umbrellas. On this superb afternoon whatever moisture bedabbled them was caused not by rain but by the warmth of the blazing sun.

" Hullo, how are you, Jemima ? "

" I'm feeling fine, thank you, sir. And how is yourself, Ben Nevis ? "

" Grand, Jemima. Splendid gathering, isn't it ? "

" Beautiful, Ben Nevis. There never was a better, I'm sure."

" Have you had a talk with Hector yet ? He's back from India."

" No, I haven't had a talk with Master Hector yet. From India ? Fancy that now. It's very warm in India, they say."

" Jolly warm in Glenbogle to-day, what ? "

" Och, indeed, yes, it is warm right enough."

" And how's the bottuck ? "

Jemima managed to grasp that he was enquiring after the *bodach* or old man, and answered solemnly, " My father's fine. He has the rheumatism sometimes. But och, he'll be ninety-five next week, and that's a great age for a man like my father."

" Well, tell old Rory I was asking after him, Jemima."

" I will indeed. It's himself that will be pleased when he hears Ben Nevis was asking for him."

" I don't suppose I'll ever see ninety-five, Jemima, what ? "

" Och, it's you that will be seeing more than ninety-five, Ben Nevis. Och, yes, indeed, and perhaps a hundred whatever."

Ben Nevis took a snuff-box from his pocket and offered it to old Jemima Macdonald, the widow of a former shepherd

of his. She took a hefty pinch of which the expressed keen
appreciation, and the Chieftain bellowed a greeting to an old
man with a beard of snow over a face like the ruins of Petra,
' rose-red and half as old as time.'

" Hullo, how are you, Alasdair ? "

" Ah, well, well, well, what a beautiful day, Ben Nevis, and
what a beautiful Gathering ! "

" Yes, it's one of the best I ever remember. I was sorry
Sandy didn't manage to do better with the caber."

This was the grandson of the old gentleman.

" Och, he was tossing like a clown. Just a clown. Nothing more. It's better not to be speaking about it. You're
looking very well, Ben Nevis."

" I'm feeling very well, Alasdair. Did you hear about
our little affray up at Drumcockie on the Twelfth ? "

" Yes, yes, indeed, we were all hearing about it. Terrible
people, those hikers. Worse than the Chermans, I believe.
But some people like them."

" They do ? "

" Och, yes, there's my neighbour, Mrs Macfarlane who
lives three miles away up Strathdun just where the road
comes into it. She's daft for hikers. Bed and breakfast and
eggs and milk and teas. They're round her like bees in the
heather."

" Good god ! But she hasn't one of my crofts ? "

" No, no, she has one of the Department holdings."

" There you are, Alasdair. There's Government inter-
ference for you. Poking their noses into the Highlands, and
the only result is hikers. Well, I'm going to devote myself
to stamping out hikers in Inverness-shire. I only wish I could
stamp them out all over the Highlands, but we get no kind of
co-operation from Argyll in this sort of thing. Of course, the
truth is they're all so many Mrs Macfarlanes in Argyll.
They batten on them, the County Council included. I'm
glad to see you at the Gathering and looking so well, Alasdair. Have you talked to young Hector yet ? "

" Och, yes, I had a word with him. Fancy flying all
the way from India. What a time we live in ! Where will
we be flying next ? "

" You and I will be flying to Heaven, I hope."

" Not in an airioplane, Ben Nevis. No, no. It might
break down and we would be finding ourselves in the wrong
place."

" Well, take care of yourself, Alasdair. I may be over in
Strathdun soon, and I'll look in and have a crack. How's
the old lady ? "

" Och, the *cailleach*'s very well, but she would never
admit it. She's like all the women that way."

Ben Nevis waved a patriarchal arm and passed on to chat
with another crony. If anything was lacking to make his
day a success it was supplied when after an hour of such
gossip he noticed that Hector was sitting by Myrtle on the
mound and apparently keeping her very well entertained.
A glow of pride suffused his being. Murdoch and Iain might
be able to toss the caber, throw the hammer, and put the
stone, but it was his eldest son and successor who knew what
was really vital to preserve the glories of Mac 'ic Eachainn's
line. A great lad, Hector MacDonald, Younger, of Ben
Nevis. The Chieftain was roused from such fond patriarchal
reflections by the voice of Chester Royde at his elbow.

" Ben Nevis, have you noticed the head guy among that
bunch of hikers ? "

" I haven't been looking at them. I welcome the brutes
to Glenbogle on the day of the Gathering, but I can't bring
myself to look at them. If I look at a hiker for more than a
minute I get a curious kind of buzzing in the top of my head."

" Chance the buzzing for once and take a look at him,"
Royde urged.

" Do you mean the fellow with the chin ? "

" That's the guy I mean."

" His face is familiar to me somehow. Was he among that
crowd we dealt with on the Twelfth ? "

Chester Royde shook his head.

" I can't recognize any of them from that bunch of hoodlums. This is a new gang. They've been staring at me quite
a lot. Particularly that stiff with the chin. Now what are
they staring at me for ? "

" I expect it's your kilt."

" Hell, there are plenty other folk around in kilts. I
don't see what they want to pick on me for as a close-up."

" A close-up ? "

" Yes, that guy with the chin, which invites punching,
keeps nodding in my direction, and then one of these hikers
strolls along and stares me up and down as if he wanted to be
sure of knowing me again. If I hit one of them, would that
spoil your notion of a happy day ? "

" I sympathize with you, Royde. But I'd rather you didn't hit any of these brutes this afternoon. I mean to say, Glenbogle is Liberty Hall to-day. Highland hospitality and all that sort of thing, don't you know ? It's a tradition with us in Glenbogle. In the old days we even welcomed Macintoshes who came to the Gathering, and normally of course we cut the throat of any Macintosh at sight."

" I don't want to break up tradition, Ben Nevis, but if that guy with Cape Cod tacked on to the lower part of his face sends any more of his young friends to stare me up and down I don't believe I'll be able to keep from hitting him."

" Look here, Royde, the prize-giving will start in another few minutes. You don't want to wait for that. It takes about an hour with the speeches, and it'll be very hot in the tent. Why don't you stroll along back to the Castle and have a drink ? I'd suggest your going into the Committee tent, but it's full of flies and you hate flies."

" I went into the Committee tent. Major MacIsaac kindly offered me a highball. But every time I looked up one of these hikers was peeping in at me around the flap."

" I never heard anything so outrageous," the Chieftain declared warmly. " I tell you this, Royde, if a single hiker dares show himself in Glenbogle after to-day I'll have him thrown into the Bogle."

" He won't find me standing by with a hook to fish him out," the indignant Royde vowed.

" That fellow's face is curiously familiar to me," said Ben Nevis, looking again at the man with the chin, who it is hardly necessary to say was Percy Buckham himself. " I've seen him somewhere. But where, that's the question ? " Just then another old crony who had not yet had a chance of a gossip came up, and when Ben Nevis looked round again Chester Royde had wandered off.

During the prize-giving Mrs MacDonald and her two daughters, who stood on either side to hand her the prizes for presentation to the embarrassed winners, must have lost between them not less than seven pounds of weight, so furiously hot was the inside of the tent, crowded with people who had not won prizes and through whose serried ranks those who had won prizes were compelled to fight their way to get within reach of Mrs MacDonald's gracious hand. After this the Chieftain made his annual speech and was dug in the back by his daughter Catriona because he began as usual, ' Fellow clansmen and clanswomen, and all my good friends, in spite of the weather . . . I mean thanks to the glorious weather, I think we can say that of the very many great gatherings this dear old glen of ours has seen, the Glenbogle Gathering of this year has surpassed all its predecessors . . ." But there is no need to continue, for such speeches whether made by the Squire at a flower-show in Hampshire or by the Highland Chieftain upon his native heath are all essentially the same.

" Well, Carrie," the Chieftain asked when they were all back in the Great Hall and he had just drunk a highball as high as Ben Booey itself and a great deal more yellow, " well, Carrie, how did you enjoy your first Glenbogle Gathering ? "

" Oh, it was marvellous, Ben Nevis."

" Where's the MacRoyde ? " asked the Chieftain, whose wit had been stimulated by that majestic highball.

" I don't know. I haven't seen him for a long while."

But it was not until Carrie went up to dress for dinner, and found no sign of Chester in his dressing-room and Wilton, his man, with what she called that British look on his face, that she began to wonder if anything had happened to him.

" Where's Mr Royde, Wilton ? "

" I don't know, madam. Is he not downstairs ? "

" I haven't seen him since before we left the field."

" I'll go downstairs, madam, and make some enquiries."

Presently the valet came back to inform his mistress that nobody had seen Mr Royde.

" It's mighty queer, Wilton."

" It is indeed, madam."

Carrie went along to her room to dress, but when dinnertime came and she joined the rest of the house-party in the Great Hall there was no Chester.

Chapter 15

THE FIRST PRISONER

THE disappearance of Chester Royde cast a gloom over what should have been as festive an evening as Glenbogle Castle had ever known. Hector had found Myrtle an apt pupil in the eightsome reel which they had practised together in the library for half an hour before dinner, but what sister could have the heart to dance reels when her only brother had vanished?

Ben Nevis expressed the mood of all the guests when he said that after a very quick dinner they must send out search-parties.

" My theory is the poor chap's sprained his ankle," he declared, in a tone that Einstein might have used to announce his Theory of Relativity.

" But, Ben Nevis, why should he have sprained his ankle? " Carrie asked.

" He may have been a bit confused by his kilt. It was the first time he'd worn a kilt, remember. Of course, he *may* have broken a leg."

" But if he'd sprained his ankle or broken his leg," Carrie argued, " surely he'd have been able to call for help. There were so many people about."

" But he may have wandered off into the hills."

" What would he do that for? " Myrtle objected. " He hasn't gone wandering off up into the hills any other day."

" Ah, but he wasn't wearing the kilt," Ben Nevis pointed out sagaciously. " I'm sure it was the feeling of freedom the kilt gives a man that made him walk further than he meant. We'll find him all right. He can't have walked very far."

" I saw him leave the field round about half-past five," said Kilwhillie, without adding that the sight of that orange kilt moving off the field had removed a weight from his mind.

" I know," said Ben Nevis, " he was annoyed by those hikers. They would keep coming up and staring at him. It was I who advised him to go back to the Castle. He wanted to hit one of them, but I explained that on the day of the Gathering Glenbogle was Liberty Hall and that I

even gave a welcome to hikers. He understood my point
of view perfectly and said he wouldn't hit any of
them."

" Perhaps one of them followed him off the field and he
did hit him," suggested Catriona.

" Oh no, Catriona," Carrie said positively. " If Chester
gave his word to your father that he wouldn't hit one of
them, you can be sure he wouldn't. Chester never breaks
his word, does he, Myrtle ? "

" Only in Wall Street. Never in private life, of course,"
Myrtle replied.

" Ah, well, business is different," said Ben Nevis. " Break-
ing your word is what business really means."

" Hullo, Dad, you're getting very cynical," Hector barked
affectionately.

" What I was going to say," Catriona managed to
interpose, " was that if Mr Royde had hit one of the hikers
the others might have set on him."

" Don't believe it. Don't believe it," the Chieftain
scoffed. " Don't believe hikers would have the courage to
set on anybody. Look at the miserable resistance they
offered to us the other day on Drumcockie."

" I must say I think you were very lucky, Ben Nevis, not
to be involved in any unpleasant legal business," said
Colonel Lindsay-Wolseley, who was one of those who had
stayed on to dinner at the Castle.

" Never thought they would attempt any legal tom-
foolery with me," the Chieftain replied. " Shouldn't have
minded if they had, but I knew they wouldn't. I'll tell
you what, Wolseley, you missed a jolly fine bit of sport by
going off like that."

" I still think you were lucky," the Colonel maintained.

Ben Nevis exhaled contempt for the initiative of hikers in
a great gusty ejaculation, and turning presently to Kilwhillie
he expressed his unalterable opinion that of all the many
obstinate men he had met in his life Lindsay-Wolseley
was without doubt the most obstinate.

" I suppose it's all that time he spent on the North-west
Frontier. Hope they won't send the Clanranalds to
Peshawar. I don't want Hector to grow obstinate and be
unable to see anything except what lies straight in front of his
nose."

Kilwhillie might have commented that with such a nose

even so restricted an outlook would be wider than that of many.

"As a matter of fact absolutely between ourselves," his old friend continued, "if things go as I rather think they will go I shall advise Hector to chuck the army."

He looked across fondly to where his eldest son was trying to convince Myrtle that her brother might have taken it into his head to drive down the glen in one of the omnibuses for the sake of the walk back and misjudged the distance.

Just then Toker came in to announce dinner, which the host said must be eaten as quickly as possible, and with a view to securing speed he hushed the pipers and stopped Mr Fletcher from saying grace, after which he began to arrange plans for the various search-parties that were to set out the moment the meal was over. He had already given orders that all his tenants and dependants who were being entertained at the Castle were to start looking for the missing guest immediately.

It was a pity her master could not hear what Mrs Ablewhite had to say about him to Mrs Parsall.

"Six good days it's taken me to prepare for this evening, and now just because that Mr Royde isn't back in time for dinner He must want to charge through my dinner like a bull in a china-shop. Disgusting isn't the word for it. What *are* you doing with those peas, Flora? For goodness' sake, girl, go away and do nothing if you can't do something better than anything. Well, really, Mrs Parsall, these Highland girls are enough to try the patience of an angel in heaven. Tell Mr Toker, Alec, it's not a bit of good him fidgeting and fretting me. No dish can be served quicker than what it can be served. Consideration, Mrs Parsall? He doesn't know the meaning of the word. After that lunch I had to prepare for thirty-four! And now dinner's shovelled into them quicker than anyone could shovel coal into a range! Maggie, if you're going to stand gaping like that, go and gape outside of my kitchen, girl. Why doesn't Mrs MacDonald stop Him, Mrs Parsall? But it's always the same at every one of these blessed Gatherings. They just go to His head."

In the dining-room Ben Nevis was hoping that Carrie did not feel it was heartless of them all to be enjoying their dinner while she and for that matter all of them were so anxious to be off in search of her husband. Had anybody been watching Toker at that moment he would have noticed that at the word ' enjoying ' his face contracted like the face of one who had bitten recklessly at a chocolate under the impression that it was filled with fondant and found too late from an exposed nerve that it was filled with caramel.

" Iain, you're through with your fish. I wish you'd go round to the back and muster the first party. The moon's already up. You won't want more than one or two lanterns to give Royde a chance of sighting you and giving a shout. I suggest you cross by the bridge and comb the other side of the river. And look here, Murdoch. I think you'd better take a party with pitchforks and see if by any chance he's in trouble with the bull."

" Oh, Ben Nevis! " Carrie gasped.

" I don't think he is for a moment," he assured her. " But it just occurred to me he might have crossed over the Bogle to get away from being stared at and wandered into the bull's field. Ordinarily that shorthorn is as decent and docile a beast as you'd meet anywhere, but your husband's plaid may have excited him. Of course, it wasn't red, but the bull may have thought it was red, if you see what I mean ? Don't you think that's possible, Hugh ? "

" Very possible indeed," the laird of Kilwhillie agreed with conviction.

" Don't listen to Donald, my dear," the hostess boomed reassuringly. " If there had been any unpleasantness with the bull, people on this side of the river would be sure to have seen. Donald dear! "

" What is it now, Trixie ? "

" Don't let yourself get too excited, will you ? You're making Carrie and Myrtle nervous."

At this moment Catriona and Mary rose from the table simultaneously.

" Mary and I are feeling as fit as be blowed. We propose to foot it to the entrance of the glen and then beat both banks of the Bogle all the way back."

" Catriona," her mother protested, " you won't be home till five or six in the morning if you do that."

" That's all right, Mother," Mary growled. " We'll take some grub with us."

" Good girls, good girls," their father applauded. " Don't worry, Trixie. It's a thoroughly sound scheme. When on earth is the next course coming, Toker ? "

The butler approached his master's chair and murmured some words in his ear. " Well, why does she let herself get fussed ? I don't let myself get fussed."

At this moment one of the gillies made a sign to Toker from the doorway that he wished to speak to him.

Mrs MacDonald seemed oblivious of what Sir Hubert Bottley on her right was saying to her. She was watching Toker. Her mighty bosom heaved slowly like the Atlantic at the approach of a storm. She was wondering if the request of Catriona and Mary for grub to carry with them to Glenbogle had been that last straw to break the camel's back of Mrs Ablewhite's endurance, and if Toker was to be the bearer of an ultimatum. She saw him receive a note from the hands of the gillie, and after a momentary hesitation bring this letter to the Chieftain. She saw her husband tear open this letter and read it, and as he read she saw his countenance illuminated by a crimson fluorescence, his nose darken to the purple of a Himalayan potato, his ears smoulder, his eyes grow globular and luminous, his left hand grasp a handful of air and squeeze it into a vacuum.

" Something's happened to Chester! " Carrie exclaimed.

" Ben Nevis, what is it ? " Myrtle cried. " Oh, tell us the worst."

" Donald! " his wife boomed, and tolled him back to his sole self.

The Chieftain threw the letter across the table to Kilwhillie.

" Read it, Hugh. I shall burst if I try to read it myself."

Kilwhillie took his spectacle-case from the pocket of his mulberry-velvet doublet, put on his glasses and pored upon the letter.

" Not to yourself, Hugh," the Chieftain bellowed. " Read it aloud."

And in the fashionably unemotional voice of a barrister reading a love-letter in a breach of promise suit Kilwhillie read:

NATIONAL UNION OF HIKERS,
702, GOWER STREET,
W.C.2.

" *Sir,*

" *This is to notify you that by a unanimous vote of the Union taken at an extraordinary general meeting convened on August 20th at the Astrovegetarian Hall, Villiers Street,*

*Strand, the President of the Union, the Rt. Hon. the Earl
of Buntingdon, occupying the chair, the outrageous action taken by
you on August 12th last against sixteen members of the Union including the Secretary, Mr Sydney Prew, was declared an intoler-
able infringement of democratic privilege.   In the opinion of the
meeting any redress through legal channels was found inadequate
and by another unanimous vote it was resolved to set in motion
against you the full powers of the Union for offensive action on a
level with your own.*

"*Misled by the apparent success of fascist methods in
Foreign Affairs you have attempted to imitate such methods in
England . . .*"

" England! " Ben Nevis exploded.   " The ruffian thinks
Glenbogle is in England!   Do you hear that, Hugh ? "

Kilwhillie decided to treat this question as purely rhetorical,
and went on reading . . . " *but you will find that when a great
democratic institution decides to take offensive action it can
act with greater vigour, effect, speed, and ruthlessness than
any dictator.   The war declared upon you, MacDonald of
Ben Nevis, by the National Union of Hikers, began this afternoon when one of your accomplices in the dastardly aggression
committed by you against the collective security of the afore-
said Union was seized by the Union's armed forces.   To
him will be meted out the same treatment as was meted out
by you to sixteen members of the Union.*"

" They've kidnapped Chester ! " Carrie cried.

" Well, what would you say to that ? " Myrtle asked.
" Oh, pardon me, Kilwhillie, you want to finish reading.
Carrie and I interrupted you."

" *Furthermore the same treatment will be meted out to every one
of your accomplices including yourself.   You have asked for
war, MacDonald of Ben Nevis, and you shall have war, ruthless war until you sue humbly for peace.   The National Union of
Hikers will then decide the terms upon which its members will
grant you peace.*

> *Percy Buckham,*
> *Acting President.*"

" There you are, you see, Ben Nevis," said Colonel
Wolseley, shaking his head.   " This is what comes of taking
the law into your own hands."

" What do you mean, Lindsay-Wolseley ? "

The Colonel recognized by being addressed with both his surnames that his host was angry, but in his position as Convener of the Police Committee of the County Council he felt bound to express his opinion even if such frankness should lead to a temporary breach between Ben Nevis and himself.

" I mean exactly what I say," he replied. " Your action on the Twelfth was responsible for what amounts to a threat of plunging this part of Inverness-shire into anarchy."

" Are you seriously trying to argue with me, Lindsay-Wolseley, that this impudent epistle is on the same level as my drastic but completely justifiable attempt to solve the hiker problem in the Highlands once and for all ? I never heard a more preposterous comparison."

" What is the difference ? " the Colonel pressed.

" The difference is that I had a perfect right to give a lesson to those hikers trespassing on my land," Ben Nevis declared angrily.

" That way lies anarchy," the Colonel retorted.

" Look here, Lindsay-Wolseley, I don't often lose my temper, but if a guest at my own table is to sit there and call me a Bolshevist I warn you I may not be able to keep my temper."

" My dear Ben Nevis, you are the very last person in this world to whom I would apply such an epithet. What I said was that if you arrogate to yourself the right to take the law into your own hands you are inviting other people to do the same, the result of which will be anarchy."

" I suppose you'll argue next I have no right to take immediate steps to rescue my guest from the hands of these detestable Cockney brigands ? I suppose you expect me to notify that beetroot-headed police constable at Kens-peckle and ask him to do it for me ? "

" Constable MacGillivray is one of the best fellows we have in the County Police," said the Colonel warmly. " I take strong exception to your describing him as beetroot-headed."

" He is beetroot-headed. His face is the colour and shape of a beetroot, and any brains he has are the brains of a beet-root."

" Surely I'm in a better position to assess his qualities than you ? In fact I have so high an opinion of MacGillivray that I've just pressed for his promotion to Sergeant, promotion which he thoroughly deserves."

Ben Nevis snorted.

" You might as well press for the promotion of a beetroot, Lindsay-Wolseley. Anyway, I'm not going to notify MacGillivray that one of my guests has been carried off by hikers. I know exactly the sort of silly expression he'd have on his beetroot-face after riding up from Kenspeckle on that bicycle of his."

" Well, what are you going to do, Ben Nevis ? " the Colonel asked.

" I'm going to beat the glen for hikers all to-night and to-morrow : . ."

" Don't forget to-morrow's Sunday, Ben Nevis," put in the chaplain, who, though no Sabbatarian himself, knew what a tremendous sermon any beating of the glens and straths and bens of Mac 'ic Eachainn's country would evoke from the Reverend Alexander Munro of the United Free Church in Strathdun.

" Look at that now, Lindsay-Wolseley. And yet you can bring yourself to sympathize with brutes who deliberately take a mean advantage of my being handicapped by a pompous little ass of a minister like Munro. Anyway, the question of Sunday doesn't arise yet. Sufficient for the day is the evil thereof, what ? We'll beat Glenbogle and Glenbristle for hikers to-night. And the sooner we start the better. Look here, Toker, I think we'll cut out the rest of the dinner. I'm sure everybody's had enough. You've all had enough, haven't you ? We'll all have to change into proper clothes for the beating of the glens. Hector, you'd better drive Myrtle in that curious contraption of Murdoch's he calls a car. Where's Angus ? Oh, look here, Angus. I'm sorry to upset the pipers' evening after the splendid way they upheld the honour of Glenbogle to-day, but I want them to go and play in different parts of the glen and to listen carefully about every five minutes."

" What would they listen for, Ben Nevis ? " his piper asked.

" Why, to hear if they hear anybody shouting for help. Don't you realize Mr Royde has been carried off by hikers ? "

" What would they be doing that for, Ben Nevis ? "

" I can't waste any more valuable time explaining the whys and wherefores of this business."

" Very good, Ben Nevis," said his piper, retiring with a puzzled expression on his long lean face.

" Now, look here, Wolseley, I refuse to quarrel with you over this wretched business. Two old friends and all that sort of thing. But I don't want . . . what's the name of that bounder who wrote to me, Hugh ? . . . Buckham ? . . . yes, well, as I was saying, Wolseley, I don't want to involve you if I catch this fellow Buckham and decide to have him thrown into Loch na Craosnaich. I mean to say if he were drowned or anything, you might have to resign your seat on the County Council. So I think you and Mrs Wolseley ought to go home."

The rest of the guests who had been invited to the dinner and the dance hastily said they thought they should be going. The prospect of being summoned before the Procurator-Fiscal's deputy lacked attraction.

" I feel terribly bad about spoiling the lovely time we were having," Carrie told her host when the last of the guests' cars had gone sweeping down the drive.

" My dear young lady, what have you done to spoil it ? "

" I feel that perhaps if Chester hadn't taken to wearing the kilt all of a sudden like that this wouldn't have happened."

" Not a bit of it! Don't you worry your pretty little head any more, except of course about poor old Chester. The extraordinary thing to me is that a man like Colonel Lindsay-Wolseley, who's spent half his life chasing Afghans and all that sort of thing about the hills of the North-west Frontier, wouldn't insist on leading one of the search-parties. But they're all the same, these old soldiers. Their livers get congested, I think. What Wolseley likes is bringing up petty points at a Council meeting. That's his idea of excitement nowadays. Awful, isn't it ? I hope Hector'll soon find the right girl and get married. He's been in the Army just about long enough. In fact between you and me, Carrie, I wish he and Myrtle would make a match of it."

" Oh, you think they'd suit one another ? " Carrie asked, with a touch of dubiety in her tone.

" Don't you ? "

" Well, Myrtle is a girl who'll choose for herself, that's sure."

" I'm very glad to hear it. I mean to say a young fellow like Hector wants to feel he's been chosen, not just picked out of a drawer like a handkerchief. But look here, I must get along and change. Will you join my rescue-party ? "

Carrie hesitated.

" Don't you think I'd be wiser to stay home ? " she suggested. " If I weren't home when Chester came back with his rescuers he'd feel he'd have to go out again and look for me."

Mrs MacDonald coming along at that moment overheard this remark of Carrie's, which she acclaimed as profoundly sensible. She was not given to making demands on the sympathy of her guests, but a brief interview she had just had with Mrs. Ablewhite, during which she had not received the support she might have expected from Mrs Parsall, had left her with a desire to confide in another woman.

So when the various noises connected with the dispatch of the search-parties by Ben Nevis had died away in a medley of shouting, piping, whistling, and tooting, Mrs MacDonald asked Carrie to come and sit with her in that room that was for ever England in spite of still being called the Yellow Drawing-room. There she spoke to Carrie of the temperamental peculiarities of Mrs Parsall and Mrs Ablewhite and even of Toker. And in her turn Carrie talked to Mrs MacDonald about Wilton's British oddities and the French excitability of her own maid Célestine.

" But still I have so much to be thankful for, Carrie. It's only very rarely that Mrs Ablewhite gets quite beyond herself as she was when I went down to see her after dinner this evening. And there's no doubt she had taken a great deal of trouble about our dinner to-night. However, I think everything will be all right when she and Mrs Parsall and Toker have had a night's rest."

" I was telling Ben Nevis a while back how much I felt to blame."

" My dear child, you ? What possible blame can attach to you ? I think you've been most considerate in not making any fuss about your poor husband. I have the greatest admiration for your courage. No, no, it's my dear Donald who's entirely responsible for the little uncomfortableness. He lets himself get too excited. Just like a child indeed. If I could only get him to drink a cup of chamomile tea every night. But he won't. He says he'd sooner pour hot-water on the clippings of the lawn-mower and drink that. I'm afraid Hugh Cameron is a bad influence."

" Kilwhillie ? Oh, surely not, Mrs MacDonald ? "

" Yes, yes. And the tragedy of it is that at one time there was nobody I welcomed more gladly to the Castle. I used to say Donald never slept so soundly and so peacefully as when Hughie Cameron had dined at Glenbogle. But of late he has seemed to take a delight in egging Donald on. I blame him entirely for that first affray with the hikers."

" Well, it's true it was Kilwhillie who persuaded Chester to get an orange kilt. I know Chester was intending to get a purple one."

Mrs MacDonald shook her head.

" Dear, dear, dear! And Hugh Cameron used to be so quiet in every way—quiet in his tastes and quiet in his habits. But he's never been the same since he saw the Loch Ness Monster last spring. He's never really recovered from the excitement of it. I do hope he won't egg Donald on to do anything desperate to-night if by chance they come into contact with the hikers."

Mrs MacDonald and Carrie sat on talking until Carrie felt that a sameness was creeping into the conversation. She told her hostess she was going up to the room in the North Tower, the windows of which afforded the widest view of any in the Castle.

" I'm going to play Sister Anne for a little while, Mrs MacDonald, up in the tower-room."

" You'll probably find Mr Fletcher up there. That's his favourite haunt."

" Maybe we'll hear some news of Chester soon."

Mrs MacDonald patted Carrie's shoulder.

" Don't fret too much, my dear. I feel convinced that nothing serious has happened to Mr Royde."

With the sweet sad smile of the young matron in some fragrant old-fashioned tale of the knightly days of yore, Carrie left the Yellow Drawing-room.

Mrs MacDonald had been right. The Reverend Ninian Fletcher was in the tower-room, reading in a grandfather's chair beside a glowing peat fire.

" Ah, Mrs Royde, this is a welcome and unexpected visit."

" I came up here, Mr Fletcher, because I thought I might see something down in the glen."

" Let me pull the curtains," the chaplain suggested.

They stood for awhile gazing out upon the moonlit scene,

but there was no sign of so much as a lantern. Carrie asked
the chaplain if he would mind the night-air from an open
casement, and receiving his assurance that he slept every
night with his window wide open she leaned out and
listened.

"What was that ? " she asked when a melancholy hoot
was heard. " Isn't that Chester's voice calling for help ? "

But Mr Fletcher assured her it was an owl, and a moment
later the great white bird itself swept past the casement on
silent wings.

" Goody, that scared me," Carrie exclaimed, and she
hastily shut the casement. " It was like a ghost."

" They are uncanny birds," the chaplain agreed. " Better
come and sit by the fire. I'm sure we shall soon be getting
news of your husband."

" I hope so, Mr Fletcher. But of course you yourself
had a nasty experience with those hikers, didn't you ? "

" It was rather unpleasant, but at any rate Mr Royde is
not in Mac 'ic Eachainn's Cradle."

" What makes you say that ? "

" Because the door is still off its hinges, and from what
I know of this part of the world likely to remain off its
hinges for a long, long time to come. Doors that are broken
in the West Highlands don't get mended so quickly as all
that," the old chaplain chuckled.

" Mr Fletcher, I wish you'd read me some more of your
poetry. I think there's nothing so soothing as poetry when
one's feeling anxious the way I'm feeling about my poor
husband right now. I do wish we could have some news of
him."

The chaplain went to the bookcase and came back with
Echoes of Glenbogle. Turning over the pages, he chose a
poem and began to read it, explaining that the verses were
spoken alternately by a daughter and her mother:

> " ' *O where is my Ronald, my bonny young Ronald,*
> *O where have they hidden my Ronald so true ?*
> *'Tis a week since he bade me farewell in the gleaming,*
> *A week since he kissed me a tender adieu.*'

> " ' *Oh, ask not, sweet Flora, where Ronald is hidden,*
> *'Tis better the tidings thou never should'st hear,*
> *Thy Ronald slain foully by one of Clan Chattan,*
> *Fares home to Glenbogle this morn on his bier.*'

" ' *My Ronald slain foully by one of Clan Chattan ?*
Now tell me, oh, tell me, which one did the deed ?
Was it Iain, the Red Macintosh of Loch Stuffie,
The foulest of all of Clan Chattan's foul breed ? '

" ' *Yes, Flora, sweet Flora, 'twas Iain of Loch Stuffie,*
Who stabbed with his sgian thy Ronald's true heart,
For jealous was Iain of thy love for young Ronald
And made up his mind two fond lovers to part. '

" ' *Oh mother, dear mother, I hear the pipes wailing,*
Oh, mother, dear mother, the coffin is here,
Why didst thou not . . . ' "

" Oh, please, Mr Fletcher," Carrie interrupted, " I really
don't think I can listen to any more of that poem. It's a
little bit too appropriate."

" But this happened more than two hundred years ago,"
the chaplain explained with a reassuring smile, " though
they do say that the ghost of Ronald MacDonald still haunts
the spot where Iain Roy Macintosh murdered him. Flora,
who was a daughter of the MacDonald of Ben Nevis of that
time, killed herself, as I tell in the rest of the poem. Shall
I go on ? "

" No, please, I'd rather you didn't, Mr. Fletcher. It's
so terribly realistic."

" But I've tried to preserve a happy mean between romance and extreme realism. What I forgot to tell you was
that this was Flora's bower and it's said that her ghost is
sometimes seen making its way from the tower to keep a
tryst with the ghost of her murdered lover."

" Oh, please, Mr Fletcher . . ." Carrie was protesting
again when she stopped abruptly and cried:

" Hark! That's not an owl."

" No, no," the chaplain agreed, " that's definitely a
deeper note than an owl's, and more persistent."

Persistent was perhaps rather lacking in colour as an
epithet for the almost continuous howling that seemed to
come through the floor of what had been the ill-fated
Flora's bower of long ago.

" That *is* Chester's voice," Carrie declared, after listening
intently for a while. " It's the noise he used to make when
he was a cheer-leader at Yale. I didn't know him in those

days, but I heard him howl like that for the Carroway Indians in Canada and they said it made their traditional war-cry sound kind of tame. Hugging Bear, the Carroway chief, asked Chester if he'd mind terribly if they used it as a new war-cry for the tribe and Chester said it was O.K. by him so long as they didn't come and do it at New Haven during the match against Harvard." She listened again. "Oh, yes, that's Chester sure enough, but where is he?"

She ran across to the window and flung open a casement. "You can't hear it so well from here," she said. "It must be somewhere inside the tower."

"I wonder," said the chaplain, "I wonder if the noise can possibly be coming from the dungeon where the young women hikers were shut up."

"I never saw that dungeon. Where is it?"

"Immediately underneath where we are now, though there are two rooms in between. If that noise is Mr Royde, he must have exceptionally powerful lungs."

"Oh, he has," said Carrie eagerly. "You wouldn't think it to hear him speak ordinarily, but Chester has one of the biggest voices anywhere. I suppose that's why he was a cheer-leader at college. Oh, Mr. Fletcher, do let's go and let the poor boy out."

"But that's the problem," the chaplain replied. "The keys of the dungeon have been missing ever since the night of the Twelfth. Ah, wait a moment. I'm on the track of the solution. The hikers carried off the keys with them. Dear me, dear me, what an exceedingly cunning revenge."

"Revenge?" Carrie cried. "Oh, they haven't done anything horrible to Chester? They haven't cut off his nose or blinded him or anything like that?"

"He would never be able to make a noise like that unless he were in possession of all his faculties," the chaplain declared emphatically.

"But how are we going to get him out?" Carrie fussed. "It's nearly eleven o'clock and he must have been shut up since this afternoon. I can't think how nobody heard him calling."

At this point the howling from below took on a fresh intensity of sound.

"Mr. Fletcher, Mr Fletcher, we must get him out. Oh, dear, why did everybody go off to look for him in the glen when he was here in the Castle all the while? Think what a

terribly long business it was to get you out of the other
dungeon. What *are* we going to do ? "

The chaplain smiled benignly.

" We are going to release Mr Royde in a very few
moments," he announced.

" But we'll never break in the door."

" We're not going to break in the door ; we're going to
use the secret passage."

" Secret passage ? "

The chaplain went across to a cabinet set in the wall.
He turned a handle to open what was in reality a door
and disclosed the narrow stone stairs of Gothic romance.

" I'm afraid you'll find the descent will mean sweeping
off a good deal of dust and cobwebs," said Mr Fletcher.
" But I dare say you won't mind that in such a good cause."

" Oh no, of course I won't, Mr Fletcher. Oh, listen to
poor Chester now."

With the door at the head of the stairs open and a channel
to conduct the sound the noise was certainly impressive.

" Come along then. I have a taper here which I use
for my sealing-wax. I don't think we need a lantern."

They went slowly down some eighty steps in a spiral that
was by no means adequately illuminated by the chaplain's
taper until they reached a door, the rusty bolts of which took
some time to pull back. However, at last they pushed it
open to enter a vaulted cellar that reverberated with the din
of Chester Royde's shouts.

From this cellar they passed through into another and
beheld the captive sitting on a packing-case, throwing back
his head from time to time to produce a still louder yell.

" Chester! It's Carrie," his wife cried, running across
the cobbled floor to embrace him. " Chester, why didn't
you call out before ? "

" Why didn't I call out before ? " the captive echoed
indignantly. " How the hell . . ."

" Chester, please. Mr Fletcher's with us."

" Oh, I'm not so easily shocked as that, Mrs Royde,"
the chaplain put in.

" How could I call out before, Carrie, when I was
gagged ? "

" Gagged ? "

" Sure, I was gagged. I'd be gagged now if a mouse
hadn't run up the inside of my kilt and made me give such

a jump that the darned gag bust. I understand now why
women can't stand the idea of mice. I used to laugh at
them, but that was before I took to the kilt."

" Oh, Chester, your hands are tied behind your back."

" Sure, they're tied behind my back. You don't think
I wouldn't have beaten hell out of that door if they hadn't
been. My ankles are tied too."

The chaplain produced a penknife, and Carrie cut the
cords round her husband's wrists. Then she knelt down
and severed those that bound his ankles.

" Gee, that certainly feels good," he declared.

" And now tell us what happened," Carrie begged.

" Wouldn't Mr Royde tell his story more comfortably
by a good fire ? " the chaplain suggested.

" Why, yes, how wise you are, Mr Fletcher," Carrie
agreed.

At this moment Mrs Parsall had just entered the Yellow
Drawing-room to inform Mrs MacDonald that the emotional
tension in that part of the Castle she ruled, which had only
just been allayed, was now more acute than ever because
Flora MacInnes and Maggie Macphee had come running
along from their bedroom into the housekeeper's room,
screaming that one of the Castle ghosts had chased them
with a horrible roaring noise.

" And that's set Mrs Ablewhite off again, ma'am. She's
withdrawn the withdrawal of the month's notice she gave
me after Mr Toker brought word that dinner was over before
the crême brulée she'd made was served. And that's how
matters stand. As soon as I tell Florrie and Maggie to go
back to their rooms they just sit down on the floor and
scream. And they've nothing on but their nightdresses and
bare feet."

" Dear me, Mrs Parsall, I'm afraid you're having a
very difficult time with the staff." Mrs MacDonald sighed.
" Which room are Florrie and Maggie in ? "

" They sleep in the room off the passage that leads to the
door down into the dungeon under the North Tower.
That's the trouble. It seems that the body of a hunch-
backed pedlar who'd been murdered and robbed in the
glen was hidden in this dungeon a hundred years ago or
more, and the silly girls think it's this hunchback that's
after them, though as I said to them whatever did they think
he'd want to chase them for even if it was his ghost and which

of course is nonsensical. But I do not want Mrs Ablewhite to leave us, ma'am, and if she gets ghosts on top of all her other worries, that's what she will do."

" I wonder if some chamomile tea . . ." Mrs MacDonald began.

" You'll excuse me, ma'am," the housekeeper interrupted impatiently, " but things have gone beyond anything chamomile tea can do. I dislike causing you trouble, ma'am, but the only thing is for you to come down to my room and try and alleviorate matters a little."

Mrs MacDonald rose with a sigh.

" Very well, Mrs Parsall. I'll see what I can do. It would be sad if Mrs Ablewhite left us."

" It would indeed, ma'am. Mrs Ablewhite has her faults. We all of us have if it comes to that, but take her all in all we should find it very hard to replace her."

The Lady of Ben Nevis and her housekeeper were on the way to the latter's room when down the stairs from the corridor leading to the room in the North Tower appeared Carrie and Mr Fletcher, both of whom were covered with cobwebs, and Chester Royde.

" Mr Royde! You've been found! " Mrs MacDonald boomed.

" Mr Fletcher and I found him," Carrie said proudly. " The hikers had shut him up in the dungeon, and we heard him shouting for help."

" There's your ghost, Mrs Parsall. I think you can put matters right now." Mrs MacDonald sighed with relief. " And ask Mrs Ablewhite to be kind enough to send up some dinner for Mr Royde, and particularly some of her always delicious crême brulée. He must be famished. Unless of course you think it wiser to arrange something for Mr Royde without consulting Mrs Ablewhite."

" Oh no, ma'am, Mrs Ablewhite will be gratified to think there's somebody in the Castle with an appetite."

In the Yellow Drawing-room Chester Royde recounted his adventure:

" I'd noticed these hikers following me around on the field, and it got my goat, but Ben Nevis asked me to remember it was a special occasion and not to take any notice. So after a while I walked back to the Castle. Everything was pretty quiet. I went into the Great Hall and poured myself out a highball. And then I felt I'd let myself be annoyed

unnecessarily by these hikers and I decided I'd stroll back to
the field. Well, I went out, and the next thing I knew was
my head was in a sack and I was being run along as if I was a
bad man being run out of a mining-camp. I think I know
who the guy was that got his hand around the back of my
neck, and believe me, I'm gunning for him till I get him, and
if I don't change the shape of that chin of his into something
the nose above it won't recognize I'll resign my blood-
brotherhood with the Carroway Indians.

" Well, they tied me up and gagged me and left me
sitting in that dungeon, and if a mouse hadn't run up inside
my kilt and made me jump and bust the gag I'd be sitting in
that dungeon now."

" Dreadful! " Mrs MacDonald boomed dolorously.

" That's what happened to one of the young women
hikers," said Mr Fletcher. " There must be quite an
appreciable number of mice in that dungeon."

" You've never had a mouse run up your leg, Mr
Fletcher ? " the released captive enquired.

" No, I can't say I ever have," the chaplain replied.
" On one occasion many years ago when I was taking duty
for the Bishop of South-east Europe at Taormina a scorpion
got into my tooth-glass, which was very unpleasant,
but . . ."

" Well, I always did like cats," said Chester. " But
when I go back to the States I'm going to found the Chester
Royde home for stray cats. And. Carrie, it'll be some
home."

Chapter 16

BUCKHAM'S CAMPAIGN

BEN NEVIS allowed himself to be dissuaded next day from attacking the hikers, apparently in deference to the Sabbath, actually because it was not yet known where their camp was, and he felt disinclined to indulge in vain reconnaissance after the long day of the Gathering and the restless night of searching for his kidnapped guest.

" I do often get a little irritated by our Highland Sunday," he admitted, " but there's something to be said for it after a day like yesterday. All the same, if they want to have a quiet day once a week I wish they wouldn't drag religion into it. Religion always makes for bitterness. Don't you agree with me, Mr Fletcher ? "

" It should not," said the chaplain, a gentle deprecation in his voice.

" Oh, I'm not suggesting that's the whole object of religion, though, by Jove, after arguing at council meetings with one or two of those ministers from the West, I might be excused if I did think so. No, all I mean is I think religion should be kept out of ordinary life. But I'll always maintain religion's the finest thing in the world in its proper place. I've always maintained that, haven't I, Trixie ? "

" Always, Donald," his wife replied, with such a glance at the chaplain as the soft pedal of a piano might give did a soft pedal possess eyes.

Not that Mr Fletcher required the warning. He had not lived at Glenbogle for more than ten years to start arguing with Ben Nevis now.

" What about coming for a drive with me in Murdoch's car, Myrtle ? " Hector MacDonald asked. " You don't mind lending me your car, Murdoch ? "

" Not a bit," Murdoch replied, with the yawn of a watch-keeping lieutenant who hears with relief eight bells sound. He intended to doze away this Sabbath afternoon. " You may sight some of those hiker blokes. Visibility is good."

" That's a jolly fine notion of yours, Hector," his father declared enthusiastically. " Jolly fine. And to-morrow we'll get a move on."

" I'd adore to come with you, Hector," said Myrtle, " but I promised Carrie I'd go with her to Knocknacolly and meet the new architect. And didn't you tell me, Carrie, there was a young poet or painter you wanted me to meet ? "

" That's all right," her brother put in. " I'll go along with Carrie. You can meet these folks another time."

" But, Chester, wouldn't you rather rest ? You must be feeling terribly weary after yesterday," his wife urged.

Chester Royde shook his head.

" No, no, I'll come along with you. I want to talk over one or two ideas of mine with the architect."

Carrie with the lightest shrug of a shoulder signalled to her sister-in-law that she did not want to discourage Chester's interest in Knocknacolly, that sooner or later he would have to meet the young men, and that she considered it wiser for Myrtle to give way.

" You realize, don't you, that Mr Buchanan the lawyer hasn't arrived yet at Knocknacolly ? " she asked when with Chester beside her instead of Myrtle she set off down Glenbogle that Sunday afternoon.

" I know, dear, but it's the architect I want to see, not the lawyer."

" Can you move over a little to the left, Chester ? I always feel cramped sitting on the wrong side of an automobile the way they do over here."

" If I move any further along to the left the bulge on this side of your little runabout won't be any too easy to push in again."

" I guess it must be your kilt, Chester."

" What must be my kilt ? "

" You never used to take up so much room before. I think you'd better drive."

So they changed places, and Carrie felt safer, though no more comfortable.

" I wonder why the British build their automobiles for sardines instead of human beings," Chester speculated as they turned round into Glenbore.

" Never mind, it won't be so long now before we reach Knocknacolly," said Carrie.

It may be remembered that she and her sister-in-law had tried to cheer up with bright hangings one of the rooms of the Lodge for the visit of the Scottish Brotherhood of Action. With those hangings and with the lustral energy of the Widow

Macdonald they had faintly lightened the gloom of that
edifice in the baronial style which several years of emptiness
and neglect had deepened. Nothing, however, they had
been able to achieve in this direction was comparable to the
effect achieved by the Macmillan and the Menzies tartan,
the red and white of which was perhaps even more startling
than the Buchanan polychrome.

Carrie need not have worried about the impression the
young poet would make upon her unpoetical husband.
After all, it was the brief glimpse Chester Royde had already
caught of the Macmillan red and yellow from the window of
the Daimler speeding up Glenbogle which had inspired the
orange kilt he was now wearing. He stepped forward and
shook the poet cordially by the hand.

"Mr Macmillan, I'm pleased to meet you," he declared
with a genuine warmth when Carrie had introduced the poet.

Nor was he less cordial when Robert Menzies, a swarthy
little man with fine features, was presented to him.

"My sister-in-law was hoping to have the pleasure of
meeting you this afternoon, Mr Menzies, and you too, Mr
Macmillan, but she'd promised to go for a drive with our
host's eldest son who's back on leave from India and so she
couldn't manage to come along with Mr Royde and myself,"
said Carrie.

It was useless to pretend. Alan's eyes were not quite so
blue when he heard that Myrtle was not coming. She
turned to the architect.

"Mr Royde is anxious to discuss our ideas for transforming
or rebuilding Knocknacolly Lodge, Mr Menzies."

"If you'll come in, Mrs Royde, I have a few rough sketches
I'd like to show you."

Indeed it was useless to pretend. Instead of coming indoors with them to share in the discussion of the sketches
Alan lingered behind and was studying the Austin from
which he had been expecting to see Myrtle alight. Carrie
allowed herself one sigh, and then concentrated upon the
architecture of the new Knocknacolly shooting-lodge.

"There were one or two things you specially wanted to ask
Mr Menzies, Chester."

"Only one thing," he said. "I wanted to ask Mr
Menzies if he'd ever designed a dungeon from which a
contortionist couldn't escape until the man who put him
there let him go."

" No, I can't say I ever have, Mr Royde."

" Get busy, Mr Menzies, and design one. That dungeon and a biggish room to hang up stags' heads in are all I want. Mrs Royde'll let you know what she wants."

" A dungeon, Chester ? " his wife exclaimed.

" I want Mr Menzies to design me the finest dungeon that was ever built. I want a dungeon that'll make Sing Sing look like a bandbox," said Chester Royde sternly.

" A dungeon rather suggests you would like to carry on the tradition of the earlier Scottish architecture before it was so much influenced by the French alliance," said the architect. " I have as a matter of fact a sketch here of a building which would certainly suit the scene here and yet is as modern as some of the latest work of the functional school. The only thing is that it would mean pulling down the present residence altogether."

" Let's have a look at this sketch," said Chester.

Robert Menzies produced from his portfolio a water-colour of a severe and massive keep defying the surrounding bens.

" That is the way it will appear from the north," he explained. Then he produced another sketch. " And this is how it will appear from the south."

This aspect showed as much glass as the other aspect showed of stone.

" In summer all these windows would slide back like this," the architect went on, and produced another sketch which transformed the southerly, south-westerly, and south-easterly aspects of the keep into tiers of loggias.

" I haven't worked out the details," he continued. " So much depends on the number of rooms you want, but my aim would be to expand vertically rather than horizontally, in the way that New York itself has expanded. Referring back to that dungeon, I think you will see the strength of any dungeon in a building like this. However, I'm afraid I'm wasting your time with a fantasy, for of course I realize that a place like this is not practical."

" Why not ? " Chester Royde snapped.

" It would cost too much to build."

" How much ? "

Robert Menzies shook his head.

" I could not say exactly. So much would depend on the size and the number of rooms."

"Well, I'd want to be able to entertain about a dozen guests," said Chester Royde. "And I'd want a big central hall and a library and a big dining-room and a room for Mrs Royde and a room for my stags' heads, and say sixteen bedrooms."

"That would mean at least four lifts."

"Four what?"

"Four elevators," Carrie put in.

"I wonder why you British folk can't use simple ordinary English for simple ordinary everyday appliances," said Chester Royde. "Well, I've given you a rough idea of what we'd want. Give me a rough idea of what it would cost."

"Certainly not a penny less than forty thousand pounds," said the architect. "Transport would be tremendous up here. Oh, I'm afraid my idea is just fantastic."

"Why?" Chester Royde snapped again.

"Well, the cost."

"Don't bother about the cost. If you can satisfy me you have a proposition that will give me value for my money I'm not worrying about the cost. How long will it take to build?"

"At least eighteen months, and even to get it finished in that time would increase the cost."

"How do you like this house, Carrie?" her husband asked.

"I think it might be wonderful," she answered a little vaguely, for she was thinking about Alan's obvious disappointment over Myrtle.

"See here, Mr Menzies. You get to work on a more detailed proposition on the lines indicated, and if Mrs Royde and I approve your design you can obtain an estimate from a builder. I don't want you to go beyond three hundred thousand dollars."

"That's about sixty thousand pounds," the architect murmured in a voice that sounded like the voice of one in dreamland.

"Just about," Chester Royde agreed.

Robert Menzies passed a hand across his brow. He had an idea that it was damp. It was.

"I'll get to work on the plans right away, Mr Royde," he said hoarsely, for the moisture on his brow had escaped there from his throat.

"That's fine," said Chester Royde. Then he turned to his wife. "I guess we don't want to talk about this old lodge. It just wants pulling down as soon as possible."

The architect suggested showing a few more of his sketches, but Royde dismissed the notion.

" No, you concentrate on this little place you have in your mind. I believe it's going to be good. I've taken a fancy to it already. And mind, Mr Menzies, that dungeon must be the toughest thing in dungeons ever built."

Alan Macmillan came into the room and Carrie told him that she and Myrtle would be up soon; but he was obviously still too much disappointed by Myrtle's failure to reach Knocknacolly to-day on account of her date with Young Ben Nevis to respond to so vague a date as 'soon.'

" What's the matter with you, Alan ? " asked Robert Menzies when the Roydes had left.

" Oh, just a feeling that life is a blind alley, that's all," Alan replied morosely.

" Blind alley ? " Robert Menzies echoed. " If I get the job to build this keep . . ." he broke off. " No, I will not believe it's going to happen. Man, do you realize that if it did happen I'd make perhaps three thousand pounds ? Three thousand pounds! It's a fantastic sum of money. But no, no. I just will not believe it's going to happen. I wish Mrs Royde had seemed a little more interested. That's what's worrying me. But her husband's keen, I believe. That's a strange kilt he's wearing. What did you make of it ? "

" I didn't notice it."

" You didn't what ? "

" I didn't notice it."

" Gosh, Alan, no wonder you think life's a blind alley! " Robert Menzies exclaimed in amazement. " We'll have James with us on Tuesday or Wednesday. If I get this keep to build and James gets the business side to look after . . . Alan, it's just incredible. It's like something in a fairy-story. Well, when James told me about that donation of twenty pounds to the S.B.A. I was really staggered, but that was only a beginning. He and I may get anywhere with a start like this. Oh, boy, America's a great country."

" I wish you'd get on with your plans and abstain from platitudinous ejaculation," Alan observed severely.

If Robert Menzies had heard what Carrie was saying to her husband on the way back to Glenbogle in the Austin he would have felt that the likelihood of his plans for the keep being accepted were indeed incredible, for she was asking Chester if he did not think he was making Knocknacolly a much bigger proposition than they had originally intended.

" It's sweet of you, Chester, but I never wanted you to spend so much money on it as that."

" I thought you were aiming to make Knocknacolly the centre of this Scottish rebirth ? "

" Yes, Chester, I *had* thought of doing that."

" If you're going to have a centre you want it to look like a centre, and I guess that building will look like a centre. Anyway, I want a stronghold up here. We can rent a place next summer when we come over, but the year after that I aim to spend three months killing off what stags I don't kill next year and shutting up every hiker I can catch in that new dungeon."

" You'll have forgotten all about hikers by then."

" Never," he declared. " I'll never forget about hikers till I've shut up that guy with the chin in a dungeon alive with mice."

" But, Chester, I don't want mice at Knocknacolly."

" If this Scottish architect of yours builds that dungeon as I want it built not even a mouse will be able to get out of it."

Carrie would have shuddered if there had been room to shudder beside Chester in her runabout, but there was no room for more than the faintest twitch of disgust, and even that was not easy.

" Tell me, Chester," she said presently, " how did you like the poet ? "

" He didn't say a great deal. I thought poets always had a mouthful to say. But I liked that tartan of his."

" He was unusually quiet this afternoon. I guess he must have been thinking about a poem."

" Maybe he was. I don't know what way that takes anybody, but I suppose poetry's something like crossword puzzles, and they keep people quiet except when they're asking fool questions of other people to get themselves out of a dictionary jam."

When the car reached Kenspeckle a party of hikers bowed down by camping equipment were alighting from a Fort William omnibus. Among them was Mr Sydney Prew.

" Why, there's that spider-legged guy Ben Nevis shook

up on the Twelfth!" Chester exclaimed, pulling up and
jumping out of the car without sticking long enough in the
door for Carrie to tug·at his doublet and beseech him to
do nothing rash.

The hikers looked apprehensive. Loaded as they were
with camping equipment, they were incapable of defending
themselves against what they supposed was the Highland
chieftain on whom they had declared war.

The Secretary of the N.U.H. allayed their anxiety and
came forward primly to meet Chester Royde.

" Can I give you any information ? " he asked   He did
not recognize Chester as one of those who had attacked him
on the Twelfth.

" No, you can't; but I can give you some information,"
said Chester truculently.   " I can inform you that you're
safer away from this part of Scotland.   There's a war on up
here, and you may get hurt."

" Oh, indeed ? " asked Mr Prew perkily.   " And may
one enquire if you are one of the enemy ? "

He remembered that the reinforcements he was bringing
to the Acting President were not in a position to offer fight
at the moment, but he did not suppose that this orange-
kilted Fascist bully would venture to attack twelve of them.
Moreover, he noticed from the corner of his eye that
Constable MacGillivray was within hail.

" I had the pleasure of helping to run you out of Glenbogle
just over a fortnight ago," said Chester.   " And I'll have
great pleasure in repeating the operation.   Only, I'll make
you hurry twice as fast next time."

The Secretary turned to his detachment.

" Boys, this is one of them," he said.   " I recognize him
now."   Then he turned to Chester again.   " I do not know
your name, Mr. Mac . . ."

" Mr Mac nothing! "

" Mr MacNothing."

" My name's Royde, not MacNothing," Chester shouted
wrathfully.

" As you please, Mr Royde.   The boys here and myself
are not impressed by either name.   However, I have no
leisure to bandy words with you on the King's highway.
And now, boys, off we go.   We have a long trek before us
yet and we want to pitch our camp before the shades of
night fall fast."

If Chester had been a good intelligence officer he would
have waited to see what direction Sydney Prew and his
reinforcements took, for thus he would have made a valuable
reconnaissance for the defenders of Glenbogle. However,
with the figure of Constable MacGillivray to deter him from
throwing Mr Prew into Loch Ness, he had only one way in
which to relieve his feelings and that was to squeeze himself back into the Austin and drive on to Glenbogle as fast
as possible.

Meanwhile, Mr Prew and eleven heavily-loaded young
men trudged on toward the headquarters camp of the N.U.H.
forces, which was situated in one of the corries of mighty
Ben Booey. It had been dark for a good two hours when
the reinforcements reached their destination.

"You're very late, Mr Prew," said the General Officer
Commanding sternly.

"We may have missed the shortest route," his Chief
of Staff admitted. "Still, I expect we shall muddle through
in the time-honoured way to victory."

Percy Buckham drew himself up proudly.

"There has been no muddling through so far, Mr Prew.
Yesterday afternoon we locked up Mr MacDonald of Ben
Nevis in one of his own dungeons. A very brilliant little
operation for a commencement."

"Oh, huzza, Mr Buckham, huzza, huzza!" cried Mr
Prew as loudly as the exertion of the climb a third of the
way up Ben Booey would allow him.

"Yes, we snaffled him with a sack. I recognized him
by his orange kilt."

"Orange kilt?" Mr Prew echoed "That couldn't have
been MacDonald, Mr Buckham; that must have been
somebody called Royde. I was parleying with him anon.
An American, if one may judge by his accent. But what
of it? As I said, we shall muddle through in the time-
honoured way to victory."

Half an hour later the Chief of Staff was summoned to the
General's tent to hear his plan of action. In ordinary
circumstance a camp of over fifty male and female hikers
would have been resounding with favourite choruses lustily
shouted round the camp fire, but the leader had insisted
that his force should remember it was on active service in
hostile country and behave accordingly. Sentries had
been posted; in the tents the lanterns were masked; the low

murmur of conversation was audible only when drawing near to one of them.

" Come in, Mr Prew," the leader rapped out in a militaristic tone of voice. Whether as command or invitation it was unnecessary, for Mr Prew tripped over one of the ropes at the moment it was uttered and dived into the tent with such velocity that he might have dived right through it if the occupier had not been sitting cross-legged in the way.

" I'm so sorry, Mr Buckham. I don't know how I came to do that. I must have tripped, I think."

" I think so too," the leader said sarcastically. " Well, before you turn in I want you to get at any rate the rough outline of my plan of action."

" The rough outline? Quite. The details of course can be elaborated later."

" Quite," Mr Buckham agreed.

" Quite," Mr Prew echoed.

" Have you your map with you? "

" I have, yes. At least I think I have. Ah yes, I have."

" Your elbow went into my eye then, Mr Prew."

" I am so sorry."

" All right. I'll get my own map out."

It was now Mr Buckham's turn to excavate the hip-pocket of his shorts, but when he and his Chief of Staff tried simultaneously to open their maps the stability of the tent was threatened, and in the end they had to sit cross-legged side by side and study the same map like two pre-Atatürk Turks poring over the Koran.

" This is roughly where we are now," said Mr. Buckham, obliterating Ben Booey with that thumb which always delighted palmists by an almost morbid display of the characteristics associated with self-will.

" Quite."

" The present concentration is fifty-two—thirty-six men and sixteen women. I understand we may expect another twenty-nine, of which seventeen are men, on Saturday and Sunday. Next week therefore will see us at our maximum strength, and I propose to make my attempt to seize and occupy Glenbogle Castle on Tuesday, September 7th. Meanwhile, harassing operations over a wide extent of country will be carried on throughout this week by the force at my disposal, for which purpose it will be broken up into six columns each consisting of six men and two women."

"But that leaves four women unaccounted for."

"They will be used as a mobile reserve. La donna è mobile," Mr Buckham hummed.

"Quite," said Mr Prew, wondering what on earth his commander-in-chief was talking about. "And these harassing operations, what will they entail?"

"Uprooting of all notices of No Camping. Menacing warnings posted up on buildings. Weird noises in the vicinity of the Castle at night. Seizure of hostages whenever and wherever possible. The columns will operate from camps on Ben Gorm, Ben Glass, Ben Cruet, in the country above Strathdun and Strathdiddle, and from where we are now, which will be my headquarters. The commanders of columns will see I receive a daily report of the damage inflicted on the enemy. I will give instructions for the principal operation on Monday, September 6th, when the whole of the present force together with the reinforcements expected next Saturday and Sunday will be concentrated where we are now. I think that's all perfectly clear?"

"Oh, clear as daylight," said Mr Prew.

"You're sure the man in the orange kilt we captured yesterday was not MacDonald?"

"Oh, definitely, Mr Buckham."

"A pity. Never mind, we'll shut him up in one of his own dungeons when we seize the Castle next week."

"Quite."

"You sound sleepy, Mr Prew."

"Perhaps a trifle. Yes, well, we had quite a trek up here from Kenspeckle. I think unless you have anything more to discuss, Mr Buckham, I'll be off to my own tent and turn in."

Mr Prew was half-way through another yawn when the face of one of the sentries, a solemn narrow-headed young man called Arthur Blencoe, appeared in the opening of the tent.

"Hullo, Blencoe, something suspicious on the move?" asked his leader.

"I wanted to know if those shaggy bullocks round here are apt to be at all fierce at night, Mr Buckham."

"I don't suppose so. Why?"

"Well, there's about forty of them nosing about the camp," said the sentry. "They've got horns on them like mammoths. I mean to say it may be all right, but I wouldn't care to interfere with them without I knew they were really all right."

" I sympathize with you, Arthur," said Mr Prew. " I should be inclined to let them alone."

" They're not doing any harm ? " Mr Buckham asked.

" No, they're just nosing about round the tents, and snorting occasionally," Arthur Blencoe replied.

" I think I'd leave them alone if I were you, Blencoe," his leader advised. " They're curious about the tents, that's all it is. They'll move along presently, I expect."

" The moon's pretty bright now," said Arthur Blencoe. " And I thought one or two of them looked at me a bit hard."

" Only curiosity," his leader assured him.

" Yes, I agree with Mr Buckham," said Mr Prew. " Just curiosity."

" It may be," said Arthur Blencoe, doubtfully.

" I think you're perfectly safe to go back to your post," his leader told him.

" Oh, definitely," Mr Prew agreed. " You're not turning in just yet, are you, Mr Buckham ? "

" Not for another half-hour."

" I thought I'd stay and talk over one or two little arrangements. My sleepiness has vanished all of a sudden. No, nò, Arthur, I wouldn't worry my head at all about those bullocks. After all, they are only bullocks, you must remember."

Mr Prew's reassurances were sharply interrupted by a wild shriek the echoes of which among the crags and precipices of Ben Booey were drowned by a louder shriek that made Mr. Buckham's chin quiver like blancmange.

A moment later the ground was shaken by the thunder of hooves and Arthur Blencoe wriggled into the tent like a crocodile taking cover in the Nile.

" Something must have frightened them to stampede like that," said Mr Buckham in a voice which lacked a little of its wonted incisiveness.

Mr Prew peeped out cautiously.

" Yes, they've stampeded right away from the camp. I remember now reading somewhere that these Highland cattle are very easily scared.   But what caused the shriek ? "

By now the camp was a-buzz, and figures were crawling out of the tents into the moonlight on every side.

" We must investigate," Mr Buckham decided, his chin

back to its old jut, his voice as vibrant as ever again. "If you and Mr Prew will move, Blencoe, I'll be able to move myself."

In the furthest corner of the camp a knot of hikers had gathered. The leader walked quickly toward it, and asked what was the matter.

"Oh, Mr Buckham, it's Gladys and Mabel Woodmonger," a young woman babbled excitedly. "A bull put his head into their tent and blew on Gladys's face and when she screamed he caught his horns in the tent and went off with it. I looked out when I heard the scream and the bull charged right past me waving the tent on his horns, and all the other bulls went galloping off like mad things."

"Is that all?" the leader commented with the icy indifference of a dictator who hears that the purge he ordered has been carried out. "Well, you'd better get back to your tents."

"But Gladys and Mabel Woodmonger haven't got a tent, Mr. Buckham. The bull took it away with him."

"They must squeeze in somewhere else. Now, Blencoe, you'd better get back to your post."

And this was the man whom, away across the glen in his castle, the Lord of Ben Nevis, Glenbogle, Glenbristle, Strathdiddle, Strathdun, Loch Hoch and Loch Hoo thought lightheartedly he could expel from his demesne like a stray cat from a backyard.

Chapter 17

FISHING

DURING the next two or three days nothing occurred to precipitate a direct clash with the forces of the hikers. Reports came in of No Camping notice-boards being thrown down or defaced, but none of the Glenbogle keepers or gillies caught more than an occasional glimpse of the elusive invaders. The Castle garrison lost Murdoch MacDonald, who had to rejoin his ship, his leave being over. However, as nobody in the Castle was aware of Buckham's proposal to attack, seize and occupy it, nobody was particularly worried by the departure of Murdoch and his bulging muscles.

Ben Nevis was annoyed by the news about the notice-boards, but he contented himself with giving orders to destroy any camping equipment found on his land and to hale before his judgment-seat every hiker caught trespassing.

This judgment-seat (*Cathair-breitheanais Mhic 'ic Eachainn*) was a prostrate megalith upon a grassy mound overlooking the Bogle about half a mile down the glen.

" From time immemorial Mac 'ic Eachainn has sat here to give judgment," the Chieftain proclaimed solemnly to his guests. " Cahavrayanishvickickyackan we call it in the Gaelic."

" That must have frightened bad men out of this part of the country before there was any need of a posse," observed Chester Royde. " You might click that out again, will you ? "

" Cahavrayanishvickickyackan."

" You know, Carrie," her husband said gravely, " the more I hear of Gaelic the more it reminds me of the Carroway language. That sounds very like ' pleased to meet you ' in Carroway. It sounds a bit like ducks in a marsh too, but then so does ' pleased to meet you ' in Carroway."

" How is it spelt, Ben Nevis ? " Carrie asked. She was sure such a word was right outside the scope of *Gaelic Without Tears*. Indeed, it was a cataract in itself.

" Ah, I'm afraid I can't spell it for you," said Ben Nevis. " As a matter of fact very few people can spell in Gaelic, and I always believe those who say they can only get away

with it because nobody else can, if you see what I mean.
No, I picked up my Gaelic by ear from my nurse. I used
to rattle it off when I was four years old."

" I've got it," Chester exclaimed.

" Got what ? "

" What that word reminded me of. It's not ducks.
It's a machine-gun. Say it once again, will you ? "

" Cahavrayanishvickickyackan."

" Yes, it's just the noise a machine-gun makes in action.
And you picked up that word by ear, Ben Nevis, when you
were four years old ? "

" I did indeed. And my nurse used to sit up there with
me and tell me stories about my ancestors. I always remember what an impression Hector MacDonald, the fourth of
Ben Nevis, made on me. He had a tusk."

" A tusk ? " Chester Royde exclaimed.

" Yes, as big as a walrus according to clan tradition.
Well, this Hector of the Tusk as they called him was an
absolute terror on the judgment-seat. He thought nothing
of hanging or spearing or drowning or burning twenty or
thirty felons in a day. And he had one very curious habit.
When he'd condemned some felon to death he used to nick
the back of his head with this tusk. I suppose the idea was
to prevent confusion. I mean to say, there was nobody in
those days to write down who'd been condemned and who
hadn't. But of course once these felons had been nicked
with Hector's tusk they were marked down for execution.
The nick this tusk made was known as Mac 'ic Eachainn's
kiss. Pockvickickyackan in Gaelic. And the extraordinary
thing is that to this day up in Strathdiddle if anybody gets
a scar the people will say, ' Hullo, I see Mac 'ic Eachainn's
been kissing you.' Of course after the '45, when the heredit-
ary jurisdictions were abolished, the judgment-seat was never
used. But I thought it would be the appropriate place to
try any hikers we catch."

" Pity you haven't got a tusk like your ancestor, Ben
Nevis," said Chester Royde. " I'd give a thousand dollars
to see you nick a square inch out of that hobo's chin."

" Hector of the Tusk must have been an ancestor of yours
too, Carrie," Ben Nevis reminded her.

Three weeks ago Carrie would have been thrilled by the
thought of having such an ancestor, but just now her mind
was concentrated upon the present. It had been made

clear during her last visit to Knocknacolly that Alan
Macmillan was in love with Myrtle. If it had been a case
of which of the two of them he fancied for a summertime
flirtation she would have been jealous at his choice of Myrtle,
but if he had really fallen in love jealousy was out of the
question, and she intended to show herself worthy of her
membership of the Scottish Brotherhood of Action by doing
all she could to help him. Having made up her mind
accordingly, she was not well pleased to notice the amount
of attention Myrtle was allowing Young Ben Nevis to pay
her. It was obvious she was not in the least in love with him,
and her own MacDonald blood did not urge her to do
anything to help in bringing about such a match. On the
other hand, she fancied Myrtle might easily fall in love with
Alan Macmillan, and if she did she was determined to
promote that match. She would persuade Chester to give
Myrtle the Keep of Knocknacolly as a wedding-present
and she and Alan could preside there together over the
accouchement of Scotland's rebirth. Carrie felt as noble
as Sydney Carton when on the Wednesday of that week she
asked Myrtle to come with her to Knocknacolly and fetch
James Buchanan with the deeds.

"I can't, Carrie. I've promised Hector to go fishing
with him."

"Fishing for what? Compliments?"

"No, fishing for fishes."

"You haven't seen Alan Macmillan since he came
back," Carrie remarked, eyeing her sister-in-law keenly.

"I know, but Hector's going back to India on Friday."

"And you want to see if you can make him propose to
you before he goes, just for the pleasure of refusing him?"

"You know, angel child, there are moments when I wish
my dearly loved brother had never met you," said Myrtle.

"Oh, you do?"

"I certainly do."

"Myrtle! Myrtle!" sounded the loud bark of Young
Ben Nevis. "Oh, there you are! Look here, we ought to
be starting. I'm going to use a Redwinged Biffer this
afternoon."

"What's that? A new cocktail?"

Hector guffawed merrily.

"No, no; it's the best fly for Loch Hoch. Always use
Redwinged Biffers there. But I'll take two or three Blue

Spankers as well, because if they won't look at a Redwinged
Biffer, that's the time to try 'em either with a Blue Spanker
or a Smith's Zigzag Nonpareil. Iain! Iain!"

" What is it ? "

" Have you got any Zigzag Nonpareils ? Myrtle and I
are tootling over to Loch Hoch, and I haven't one left."

" Here you are," growled Mary, detaching a couple of
gaudy flies and handing them to her brother.

" Oh, that's very sporting of you, Muggins. Thanks
awfully. Are you ready, Myrtle ? "

" I'm ready."

" Hullo, going off fishing with Hector ? " Ben Nevis
woofed, when he met them in the entrance-hall. " Hope
you'll have good sport. What flies are you taking, Hector ? "

His eldest son told him, and the Chieftain shook his head.

" If you're wise you'll take some Yellow Munks—medium
and large. When you get a day early in September cloud-
ing over about eleven o'clock after a bright morning, Yellow
Munks are the flies for Loch Hoch. That was always
my experience when I fished regularly."

" You prefer Yellow Munks to Speckled Champions ? "
Hector asked.

" Oh, every time, my dear boy, every time. If I couldn't
make 'em look at Yellow Munks I'd try 'em with Fork-
tailed Violets before Speckled Champions any day, or for
that matter Brown Nixies."

" If you suggest any more bugs to Hector, he'll want a
beehive to carry them around," Myrtle said.

" Bugs ? " Ben Nevis echoed in astonishment. " You
never fish with bugs."

" Well, what are we going to do with these rainbow-
coloured bugs if the fish won't eat them ? "

" These aren't bugs. These are flies," Ben Nevis said.

" We call them bugs at home."

" *Do* you ? " Ben Nevis exclaimed in amazement, and
as his eldest son and Myrtle got into the two-seater he shook
his head in what was evidently a sudden apprehensiveness
about the future. Then he recalled the Chester Royde
millions, and his brow cleared like Ben Cruet's peak emerging from the wrack of a passing storm.

When Carrie reached Knocknacolly she found James
Buchanan waiting for her, dressed in a dark grey suit and
wearing a dark grey hat.

" James," she cried, " where's your kilt ? "

" A kilt is not the right way to dress for a matter of business. I have all the papers for Mr Royde to sign."

" But my husband will be terribly disappointed if you don't wear your kilt. I tried to tell him what the colours were in the Buchanan tartan ; but after red, yellow, dark blue, light blue, dark green, light green, purple and puce I couldn't remember any more. I told my husband there were quite a lot more colours in it, and he was very very interested. I said it was really brighter than the Macmillan tartan and he said he couldn't believe that was possible. Oh, how d'ye do, Mr Menzies ? I'm glad to see *you* haven't left off the kilt to work at your plans. How are you getting along ? "

" I'll be able to give you quite a good idea of what I'm trying to do by the end of the week, Mrs Royde."

" I'm so glad. We're both of us so keenly interested."

The fantastic sum of £3,000 once more became credible to Robert Menzies. His dark eyes glittered.

" I was just telling Mr Buchanan I thought it was a pity to put off his kilt the way he has."

" Och, no, Mrs Royde," said James obstinately. " I always draw a sharp distinction between business and pleasure. I wouldn't feel comfortable arranging a matter of business in the kilt, I really wouldn't."

" Where's Alan ? "

James looked round.

" He was here a minute ago. Where did Alan go to, Robert ? "

" I don't know where he went. Will I give him a shout ? "

" Oh, that would be kind, Mr Menzies," said Carrie.

The architect went off to look for the poet, and Carrie turned to the lawyer.

" James, you just have to put on your kilt. I know what I'm talking about. I know my husband. You don't. I want you to make an impression on him. And listen, James, I want Alan to come with us because, when you and my husband and Mr Hugh Cameron of Kilwhillie go to Inverness to settle up everything at Kilwhillie's lawyers, I want Alan to go for a ride with me."

" I'm sorry to disoblige you, Mistress Royde . . ." the lawyer began.

" There you are, you see, James. You can't believe

you're a member of the S.B.A. when you're dressed in those
town clothes. You turn all stiff and awkward."

"Mistress Royde," the lawyer went on, "you've been
kinder to me than enough. You've been kind to all three
of us. I'm grateful to you. I hope you'll believe that.
Very grateful. But all the gratitude I feel could not make
me go to the office of Macbeth, Macbeth and Macbean in
the kilt."

"But Kilwhillie and my husband will be wearing kilts,"
Carrie argued.

"They're clients, Mistress Royde. Clients are in a
different position. I'm a lawyer. Macbeth, Macbeth and
Macbean are lawyers. And they would consider it a very
grave breach of legal etiquette if I were to assist at a matter
like this, wearing the kilt. It would . . . it would . . . well,
I just cannot do it, Mistress Royde, even to oblige you."

Poor James was evidently suffering so acutely that Carrie
had not the heart to plague him longer.

"Very well, James, if you feel as strongly as that about it,
you must do as you like, but it's going to be a disappointment
to my husband."

James grinned his relief, and recovered his dignity by
asking Alan in his gruffest voice what he was at keeping
Mistress Royde waiting like this.

"Waiting for what?" the poet asked, assuming a rival
dignity.

"Did you not ken she's taking you for a ride?"

"I never heard anything about a ride," the poet protested.

"Oh yes, Alan, we arranged that last time I came to
Knocknacolly."

"I must have forgotten," he said.

"You're getting awful absent-minded these days, Alan,"
said his friend severely. "It's a good job Robert and I don't
go about with our heads in the clouds the way you do."

"I'm very sorry, Mrs Royde," said the poet. "But I
really hadn't understood you expected me to go for a drive
with you to-day. How is Miss Royde?"

Carrie shook her head.

"James, I guess you've put the Scottish Brotherhood of
Action into town clothes as well as yourself. Myrtle's very
well, Alan. Come on, we ought to be moving. It's too
bad leaving Mr Menzies behind. But I know he wants to
work at his plans."

" Och, he's back at work on them already," said James.
" He's just living in a dream.   Though if he'd arranged to
go for a drive with a lady he wouldn't have forgotten it,"
James added severely.   " Imphm! I'm telling you, Alan."

When the Austin reached the gates of Glenbogle Castle
Carrie was inspired by the two water-horses mordant on their
pillars to park Alan and the car by a clump of pines and
walk up the drive with James.   Her original intention had
been to bring Alan back to lunch, but she decided it would
be more fun to picnic with him tête-à-tête, and in view of
her proposed self-abnegation she considered that she was
entitled to the pleasure of such a tête-à-tête.

" I'll come back for you when I've introduced James to
my husband.   He'll be having lunch at the Castle, before
they drive to Inverness."

" And you're not going to be there ? " asked James,
aghast at the prospect before him.

" No, I want you business men to get together," said Carrie
firmly.

To her surprise she found Chester had doffed the kilt and
was back in one of his rural costumes from the full-page
colour advertisements of *Esquire*.

" Why, Chester, Mr Buchanan wouldn't wear his lovely
rainbow of a kilt and now you're not wearing yours."

" Well, it was Kilwhillie.   According to him there's a
prejudice in Inverness against anybody they don't know
wearing a kilt.   There's some kind of a Klu Klux Klan
of a Kilt Society, it appears, which takes action against
outsiders.   I couldn't understand what it was all about,
but he set off on such a rigmarole I got tired of it and
changed.   Do you know anything about this kilt society,
Mr Buchanan ? "

" All kilt societies are ridiculous exhibitions of snobbish-
ness, Mr Royde," James Buchanan declared.

" Well, what about beating up this particular one some
day ? " Chester asked.

" It's what it requires," said James sternly.

" I'm glad to hear you agree with me," Chester said.
" I guess if you and I and your two friends at Knocknacolly
went into Inverness in our kilts we'd make that bum society
look pretty foolish."

" Och ay, and it would give the *Inverness Courier* something to write about for a change," said James.

Carrie saw with pleasure that Chester liked her young lawyer, and she slipped away to extract a picnic lunch for two from Toker.

She and Alan ate it together up at the Pass of Ballochy, looking down from a green knoll upon the silver stretch of Loch Hoch and over the wide level of Strathdun. They talked of the Scottish rebirth of which the Keep of Knocknacolly was to be the centre; they talked of the accident of Carrie's walking up Glenbristle that day not yet quite three weeks ago; they talked of Carrie's progress in Gaelic.

" I found out a strange thing the other day. Do you know what *roid* means ? R-O-I-D."

Carrie said she had no idea.

" I looked up *roid* in my dictionary."

" Oh, you did ? R-O-*I*-D without an E, you said ? "

" Yes."

" I wonder what made you look up such a word ? "

" It just came into my head."

" I see. And what does it mean ? "

" That's the extraordinary thing. It means ' bog-myrtle.' "

A slow blush flowed into the poet's face and to shake off his embarrassment he ran down the slope to gather some sprigs of a miniature shrub that was growing in profusion in the moist ground below.

" Crush the leaves. They smell very sweet."

" Alan, they smell delicious."

" Do you remember that poem of mine, *Peaty Water* ? "

" I certainly do."

" I've added to it slightly. This is how it goes now.

" *The sweet breath of bog-myrtle*
Blows on the wind,
And green grow they still,
The leaves of the bog-myrtle.
But the heather,
The fading heather,
Is spread like the robe of a dead king
Upon my country,
Upon my dying country.
I do not lament, therefore, but laugh
When down through the stale dead purple
Dances the peaty water,
Warm with the sharp sun of the high tops,

Prickt by the sun of the high tops,
The prattling peaty dark-brown water,
The warm dark-brown water of life
Whose sweet breath blows on the wind,
Bringing bog-myrtle."

" Yes, you certainly have made it very much clearer now.
I'm wondering how I ever thought the water of life was the
S.B.A.," Carrie murmured half to herself. " We'll go on
soon, will we, and explore around Loch Hoch ? "

Not long before Carrie and Alan reached the loch Hector
MacDonald had decided that the day must be redeemed
from failure by landing a bigger catch than any its waters
could provide. He and Myrtle had been rowed up and
down by a gillie for four hours without persuading a single
fish to pay the slightest attention to Redwinged Biffers,
Blue Spankers, Zigzag Nonpareils or Yellow Munks. It was
after three o'clock, and Hector had had to give up all hope of
catching the trout he had promised to cook for Myrtle's lunch.
" Most extraordinary thing. I've never known Yellow
Munks to fail even when every other fly's been a wash-out.
I expect you're feeling hungry, aren't you ? "
" I believe I could toy with two or three crumbs," Myrtle
admitted.
" Well, what about landing on Ellenanie ? "
" Is she good company ? "
" Is who good company ? "
" Ellen."
" Ellen who ? "
" I don't know, Hector. She's your friend, not mine.
You suggested landing on her."
He guffawed genially.
" Oh, Ellenanie! That's that little island over there. I
thought it would be a good place for lunch."
" Any place sounds good to me with lunch tacked on to
it," said Myrtle. " If we don't eat soon I'll start nibbling
at those bugs the fish refused."
Hector turned to the gillie.
" All right, Lachy, put us ashore on Ellenanie and come
back for us in about half an hour." He turned to Myrtle
again. " There's one fly I haven't tried yet. Hopkinson's
Belted Pinkhead."

"Why don't you try a garden-worm, Hector? I used to catch lots of little fishes with garden-worms in our lake at home."

"I'm afraid that wouldn't be considered very sporting, would it, Lachy?"

Lachlan Macdonald looked at Myrtle as if she were another Lucrezia Borgia, and shook his head in stern disapproval.

"You rather shocked poor Lachy," Hector told her when they had landed on the little island, which consisted of about half a rood of lush grass with a bosket of rowans and elders in the middle.

"He'll get over it," Myrtle prophesied confidently. "My, those sandwiches certainly look good."

They both munched away in silence for a while until hunger had been assuaged.

"I don't believe I care a great lot for fishing," said Myrtle at last. "I think putting the stone and fishing are kind of slow."

"I think fishing is very like life, if you see what I mean."

"Elucidate," she bade.

"Well, I mean to say, some people go through life and catch a basketful and others don't catch anything."

"You're some philosopher, aren't you?"

"Oh, I wouldn't go as far as that," said Hector modestly. "I mean to say we don't get any time for that sort of thing in the Army. But I think a good deal to myself. It's awfully hot in India and sometimes I can't sleep and then I start thinking."

"What do you think about?"

"Oh, I don't think about anything in particular. You know? I just think."

"But you must think about something."

"I don't, really. Unless of course there's something to think about. I mean like what we'd have made if my partner had redoubled in some hand at contract. Do you play much contract?"

"Never."

"You are an extraordinary girl, Myrtle. You must find it awfully dull sometimes, don't you?"

"No; I've kept myself awake all right so far."

"Did you ever think about marrying?"

Myrtle looked quickly at Hector MacDonald, but a

second later she looked even more quickly beyond him across the water to where a red-and-yellow kilt was walking with Carrie beside the banks of Loch Hoch.

"Think about marrying?" she echoed. "Do you mean marrying anybody in particular?"

"As a matter of fact, that's just what I did mean," said Hector, snapping at the hook of the interrogation mark much more greedily than the trout of Loch Hoch had snapped at any of his flies. "I mean to say, could you think about marrying me?"

"Why, Hector, I don't believe I could," she answered, still following over Hector's shoulder the progress of that red-and-yellow kilt beside the banks of Loch Hoch.

"I just asked the question," Hector said. "I mean to say if you can't think about marrying me it's not much use my suggesting we might get married. Or is it?"

"No, Hector, I'm afraid it isn't. After all, we are such very good friends, and I think it would be sad to spoil a friendship by getting married."

"Yes, I see what you mean. And you feel sure it would spoil it?"

"Oh yes, Hector, I certainly do."

"I'd chuck the Army, of course, if we got married. As a matter of fact I am pretty bored with it. Our Colonel's rather a trying fellow. He's worrying about another war all the time."

"Oh, I don't believe we will have another war."

"No, that's what worries him," said Hector. "But as I say, if we got married I'd chuck the Army."

"Oh, Hector, look! There's Carrie!"

"So it is. But what on earth's that walking with her?"

"Surely it's somebody in a kilt. Oo-hoo! Oo-hoo! O Carrie! She's walking away from us. Carrie! Isn't it silly of her not to hear me and turn around," Myrtle exclaimed petulantly.

"I don't know what she's got with her, but it doesn't matter to us, does it?"

"Of course it does, Hector. Carrie! O Carrie! I'm sure she's looking for me. I hope nothing's happened to Chester. She just won't turn around. She is very silly sometimes. Where's Lachy? It's surely time he came back for us."

"I told him half an hour."

" I'm sure we've been on this island more than half an hour. I really do think Carrie can be thoroughly stupid when she chooses."

" We'll row after them when Lachy comes back."

" I don't know why we didn't eat our lunch on the banks."

" I thought you'd prefer the island."

" But islands are so inconvenient, Hector. When you're on an island you can't get off it. And I'm sure Carrie's looking for me."

By the time Lachlan Macdonald arrived with the boat, Carrie was a mile away along the banks of Loch Hoch, and the red-and-yellow of Alan's kilt seemed no larger than a bandana handkerchief.

" It's all right, Myrtle," said Hector. " The Austin is still there. She's evidently only gone for a stroll with whatever it is she's strolling with. Shall we have a shot with Hopkinson's Belted Pinkhead while we're waiting for her to come back ? "

Myrtle danced with impatience.

" I don't want to fish any more, Hector. I'm tired of fishing. It's a bromide sport anyway. You stay here and fling your imitation bugs about. I'm going to walk along and meet Carrie."

Any mortification Hector felt at being thus deserted was forgotten when on Hopkinson's Belted Pinkhead he caught a couple of pounders and a two-pounder in quick succession.

" There you are, Lachy," he roared in triumph. " I knew that was the fly for them."

" Oh yes, she's a good fly, right enough, Master Hector. A pity we didn't try her earlier when the young lady was with us."

" Yes, it was a pity, but you can never tell with trout."

" No, trout are very fanciful, right enough. Very like the women themselves, Master Hector."

" Tell me, Lachy, how are you getting on since you married ? Do you like married life ? "

" Well, there's a great deal to be said for marriage in one way, Master Hector; but there's a great deal to be said against it. Och, yes, you might call it a position for a man betwixt and between happiness and misery. That's what I would call married life."

" Myrtle darling! " her sister-in-law cried when she met them beside the loch. " Where *did* you spring from ? "

" Didn't you hear me calling to you, Carrie ? "

" Was that you calling ? What do you say to that, Alan ? Alan and I thought it was birds."

" You're both of you pretty dumb if you thought that was birds. I guess parrots don't fly around wild in these parts. Do you mean to say you couldn't hear me call ' Carrie! ' ? "

" But Alan and I weren't expecting you down here, were we, Alan ? "

The poet's promise of obedience extracted from him by Carrie before they left the Pass of Ballochy had been severely strained by the command not to pay any attention to Myrtle's voice. He did not think it was fair of her to demand such testimony. His lips moved, but it was his eyes that spoke.

" Listen, honey," murmured Carrie, " wouldn't you like to drive Alan back to Knocknacolly in my funny little runabout ? You remember that poem he read us about peaty water ? Well, he's added one or two lines to it and even if you didn't understand it before I guess you'll understand it now."

" What about Hector ? " Myrtle asked.

" Hector shall drive me home."

Carrie reached him just as Lachlan was unhooking another two-pounder from his line. He had noticed that somebody was approaching along the bank, but the concentration required for the two-pounder had not allowed him to notice the substitution of Carrie for her sister-in-law.

" If you hadn't gone off, Myrtle, you'd have seen what a Belted Pinkhead can do," he shouted exultantly, as he watched the victim's convulsions upon the bank.

" Well, I've been called lots of names," said Carrie, " but I've never been called that before."

" Good lord, it's you! Where's Myrtle ? "

" She's kindly offered to drive a friend of our architect back to Knocknacolly. A Mr Macmillan."

" Oh, that's what that was! I couldn't think what it was."

" What what was ? "

" That tartan. But the Macmillan tartan's notorious. It was always said they invented it to frighten Campbell of Inverneil. But of course nothing could frighten Campbell of Inverneil or any other Campbell off somebody else's land."

" So I'm going to plead for a lift in your two-seater, Hector."

" That's topping."

" My, what lovely fishes! "

" Got 'em all on a Belted Pinkhead," said Hector, gazing at the four trout with fatherly pride. " Young Somerled MacDonald of Ours will be no end bucked when I tell him about it. He always swears by Hopkinson's Belted Pinkhead. We had a terrific discussion about that fly and the Redwinged Biffer one night in the mess at Tallulaḥgabad. Well, I'll be seeing Somerled again pretty soon now. Off back to India the day after to-morrow. All right, Lachy, you can put the fish in the car. I shan't do any more to-day. Good lad, that," he observed as the gillie went off with the catch. " Got married last year."

Hector made a noise like a whale spouting which Carrie recognized as a sigh.

" Why that sigh, Hector ? "

" Took rather a knock this afternoon. What is it old Kipling says ? Can't remember, I'm afraid. But I know he wrote some jolly good lines about the way a fellow feels when he's taken a knock over a girl."

" Poor Hector! And was Myrtle the girl ? "

" Yes. I asked her to marry me just before you buzzed along. I led a heart, but she hadn't got one in her hand and trumped it with a small club, or in other words said she thought friendship was better than marriage. It'll be a blow to the old man. He was convinced that Myrtle and I were made for one another." He spouted again. " Oh, well, such is life! Very like fishing, as I said to Myrtle. One fellow catches a basketful and the other fellow catches nothing. Still, that Belted Pinkhead taught me a lesson. I may cast one over the right girl one day, what ? "

" I'm sure you will, Hector. And I don't really think you and Myrtle were suited to one another."

" You don't ? "

" No. I think you require a softer, gentler kind of a girl. Myrtle is hard as nails."

" By Jove, I believe you're right, Carrie. You know, she actually wanted me to fish with a worm. I must admit that did give me a bit of a bump. Yes, I believe you're right,

Carrie. I don't believe we should ever have seen eye to eye over sport. And that would have created a rift in time."

" It would have created a chasm," said Carrie decidedly.

" And married people can't afford to do that over really important things like sport," Hector observed gravely. " I mean to say you can differ about things like religion because everybody's got a right to their own religion and anyway one doesn't talk about religion in public. But fishing for trout with worms—and garden-worms at that!" He spouted again, but this time it savoured less of a sigh for what he had lost than an exhalation of relief at what he had escaped.

That night Carrie went along to Myrtle's room in her pastel-rose dressing-gown and sat on the bed with her back against one of the mahogany posts.

" Well, did you find out you were right ? " she asked her sister-in-law.

" Right how ? "

" Right in thinking he was your property ? " said Carrie.

" I believe I'll marry him if he asks me."

" Well, if he doesn't ask you himself I'll ask you on his account," said Carrie. " He's probably afraid of your money. Did he read you the poem ? "

" He read me a lot of poems."

" And all about little you ? "

Myrtle nodded.

" What's it feel like to have poetry written about you ? " Carrie asked, her voice just touched by wistfulness.

" It's lots of fun, Carrie."

" He'll have to ask you pretty quick, honey, because now you've refused Hector I don't think we ought to stay on at Glenbogle indefinitely. Anyway, we ought to be nearer Knocknacolly. I suggested to Chester we should furnish some rooms at the Lodge and camp out there till we go home at the end of the month, but Chester's afraid what Wilton will say, and he doesn't want to lose him. However, I guess we'll manage. We can send Wilton down to London."

" You'll have to make it clear to Alan that money doesn't matter," Myrtle said. " What's money anyway ? "

" Just nothing at all, honey, when there's as much of it as you and I have."

Chapter 18

THE PRINCE'S CAVE

BEN NEVIS felt depressed for nearly five minutes when his eldest son told him that he had been refused by Myrtle Royde; but that sanguine disposition was incapable of protracted gloom and by the time Hector left on Friday for India he was as rumbustious as ever, having been particularly elated by the news that two of his gillies with Neil Maclennan had destroyed a small encampment on one of the spurs of Ben Cruet and that Smeorach, Neil's wall-eyed dog, had bitten the leg of the hiker left in charge.

" I hope it was a really good bite, Neil ? " he asked eagerly.

" Oh yes, it was a good bite, right enough, Ben Nevis."

" Not just a scrape ? "

" No, no; it was more than a scrape."

" Good! I'll teach these brutes to threaten me," the Chieftain boasted in his pride.

" That guy's chin would be worth biting," Chester Royde observed pensively. " I reckon he's the leader of the whole gang."

" By Jove, that reminds me," Ben Nevis exclaimed. " Old Duncan sent word last night that this fellow with the chin is camping in one of the corries of Ben Booey. What do you say, Royde ? Shall we try and bag the brute ? "

" Fine. Nothing would suit me better," Chester Royde declared.

" We'll have to do some stalking to get our quarry."

" Stalking ? " Chester repeated suspiciously. " Do you mean crawl along for miles on our bellies the way we did after that darned stag ? "

" Oh, not quite such a tussle as that," Ben Nevis said. " You wouldn't put a hiker on a level with a noble beast like the muckle hart of Ben Glass. No, my idea was to approach the camp fairly cautiously and march them all back to Glenbogle in front of our guns. If this fellow with the chin is the leader and we bag him, that will put an end to the nuisance."

" How ? "

" Why, we'll keep him a prisoner here till every hiker has cleared off my land. But I shan't shut him up in a dungeon this time. I shall shut him up in the Raven's Nest at the top of the Raven's Tower."

" A nest sounds a lot too comfortable for that guy with the chin," Chester Royde objected.

" Oh, it's not really a nest. It's a little room at the top of the tower where the watchman used to keep a look-out for marauding Macintoshes once upon a time."

All that night derisive boohs and catcalls round the Castle indicated that the hikers were growing bolder, as well they might with the reinforcements due to reach them in the course of the next two days.

This act of defiance made Ben Nevis more than ever determined to strike a decisive blow at the enemy's heart, and besides Chester Royde and old Duncan, Iain and a couple of gillies were brought in to strengthen his force. Kilwhillie had gone home two or three days before.

" I'm a little doubtful about that kilt of yours, Royde," Ben Nevis said when the punitive expedition was mustering after breakfast that Saturday. " I'm afraid it'll give us away long before we reach the Black Corrie where these brutes are camping."

" Well, my purple kilt came along from Inverness yesterday. I'll put that on."

" Oh, that's much better," Ben Nevis decided when he saw it. " You'll look like a patch of heather, what ? "

Duncan was waiting for them where the bridle-path that led to the fastnesses of the Three Sisters of Glenbogle joined the road.

" I did not bring the ponies, Ben Nevis," he explained. " It's no more than four miles from here to the Black Corrie."

" You'd better come back for us at one o'clock, Johnnie," Ben Nevis said to his chauffeur. " And tell Archie MacColl to bring the lorry for our prisoners."

Johnnie Macpherson touched his cap and after turning the Daimler with some difficulty drove off.

" Now look here, Iain," he said to his youngest son, " I want you and Lachy and Roddy to work round to the other side of the corrie and cut off the retreat of any of the hikers who get away from us. How many do you think there are in this camp, Duncan ? "

" It was Roddy who saw them on Thursday. How many, Roddy, did you see ? "

" I would say there were six of them," the gillie replied.

" Did they speak to you ? "

" There was a fellow with a huge great chin on him asked me was we having trouble at the Castle. ' What trouble would we be having at the Castle ? ' I said. And he just laughed."

" Come on, Ben Nevis," Chester Royde urged. " What are we waiting for ? "

After the stampede of the bullocks Percy Buckham had moved his headquarters to the Black Corrie and it was there that he was concentrating his forces for the attack he had planned on Glenbogle Castle. The small columns which had been operating during the week against notice-boards of ' No Camping ' had by now all reached the Black Corrie, the only loss suffered having been the destruction of the equipment of one column on Ben Cruet by Neil Maclennan and the bit taken out of the leg of Hiker Charles Cudlipp, who had been left on guard. Instead of the force of half a dozen strong reconnoitred by Roddy Maclean, there were now thirty-six hikers with one casualty and sixteen hiker-esses, two of whom—Margery Pidcock and Gladys Wood-monger—were casualties, the former having been stung on the upper slopes of her thigh by two wild bees and the latter's nerves not having yet recovered from being suddenly awak-ened by a bullock blowing on her face. Moreover, seventeen hikers and twelve hikeresses were expected to join the party in the course of to-day and to-morrow.

" Frankly, I don't see what can stand against us, Mr Prew," said Percy Buckham, fixing his chief-of-staff with two eyes that resembled animated essence of beef.

" No, indeed, Mr Buckham. I cannot see myself."

" What is it, Miss Butterworth ? "

A plump young woman in dark crimson corduroy shorts which matched her countenance was standing all of a tremble like a wine jelly before the leader's tent.

" Please, Mr Buckham,' she panted. " Arthur Blencoe has signalled he can see the enemy approaching."

Percy Buckham leapt to his feet and blew his whistle. Hikers and hikeresses hurried from every direction to gather round and hear his orders.

" Hiker Williamson! " he rapped out.

17

"Here I am, Mr Buckham."

"Take six men and debouch from the entrance of the corrie."

"Very good, Mr Buckham."

"And when you've debouched, don't forget to deploy."

"I won't, Mr Buckham."

"Hiker Hughes, get in touch with Hiker Blencoe. Hiker Rosebotham, get your men up to the ridge. Hiker Hickey, take your column over to the left above the corrie and nip any attempt by the enemy at an enveloping movement in the bud. Mr Prew, muster the mobile reserve and keep in touch with me."

"Where are you going, Mr Buckham?" asked Mr Prew, who was a little annoyed to find himself left in charge of the mobile reserve, a female corps.

"I am leading the attack with the main body. And mind, Mr Prew, if you have to debouch with the mobile reserve, don't forget to deploy immediately."

From the top of the corrie the hikers' leader surveyed with his glasses the advance of the Glenbogle forces a mile away. He observed Iain MacDonald and the two gillies detach themselves and move across to their right with the evident intention of preparing the enveloping movement he planned to nip in the bud. At the same time he saw Ben Nevis, Chester Royde, and Duncan move left toward the entrance of the Black Corrie. With Napoleonic rapidity he decided upon his tactics. He despatched two more columns to support Hiker Hickey, and brought the rest of his force down again into the corrie.

"Now, take cover," he commanded, "and when I blow my whistle, attack and disarm the enemy."

"But suppose they fire at us?" Mr Prew asked. "They have guns, and once Fascism starts it's not easy to predict where it will stop."

"That's the whole point of collective security, and I think you'll admit that my disposition of the force under my command has achieved the maximum collective security. Frankly, I don't believe they *will* fire their guns. Except perhaps in the air. But we shall not be frightened."

"Oh no," Mr Prew declared, with a certain lack of conviction in his negative.

As a matter of fact when Ben Nevis, Chester Royde and Duncan on hands and knees crawled up the rough brae that led to the entrance of the great hollow known as the Black Corrie and the hikers yelling the motto of the N.U.H. as a war-cry—*Hike On, Hike Ever*—swept down upon them from their ambush on either side, Ben Nevis did discharge both barrels into the air, and to judge by the screams of the mobile reserve with deadly effect. However, that was all he was able to do before he and his companions were overwhelmed by weight of numbers and tied up in tents.

On the heights above the corrie the day went equally badly for Glenbogle, for though Iain MacDonald tossed two or three of the hikers farther than he had tossed the caber at the games a week ago, he, Lachy and Roddy were borne down by the superior forces of the enemy. The victory of the hikers was rapid and complete.

And while the prisoners tied up in tents lay waiting for Buckham's decision about their disposal, along the path that led from the other side into the rocky fastnesses of the Three Sisters of Glenbogle there was heard the grand refrain of the Hikers' Song upon the lips of the first body of reinforcements tramping in from Kenspeckle, where they had been deposited by the omnibus from Fort William that met the London train.

Mention has been made of the cave on Ben Booey in which Prince Charles Edward, according to local tradition, spent several nights hidden from the redcoats. Uairah na Phrionnsa or the Prince's Cave was in every way a much more striking piece of natural architecture than the Calf's Cave on Ben Cruet. The view was superb from the rocky terrace in front that ended in an almost sheer precipice of four hundred feet and if Percy Buckham had chosen the view with the express purpose of enraging his enemy he could not have been more devilishly successful, comprising as it did Glenbogle Castle lying among its pines six miles away across the glen and beyond Ben Cruet, in the remoter background, mighty Ben Nevis itself, the Lord of which was impotent in the hands of hikers. It was to the Prince's Cave that Percy Buckham consigned his captives that September day when the sons of Hector suffered the most humiliating defeat in all their long and bellicose history.

At first the prisoners had refused to move from the corrie, but a threat to carry them to the cave tied up in tents persuaded them to give way on this point. On their arrival their arms and legs were bound with ropes, and they were

sitting thus too much dejected to talk when Percy Buckham
came along with a paper, and addressed Ben Nevis:

" I will read you out a letter, which I have composed.   If
you will sign this letter I will give orders for your release,
and hostilities can terminate.   If you refuse to sign I shall
have no option but to keep you prisoners here while I
proceed with my original plan to seize and occupy Glenbogle Castle."

As a cat chatters at a sparrow beyond the range of his
spring, so did Ben Nevis chatter at Percy Buckham when he
heard this insolent threat.   And even as the sparrow safely
out of reach pays no attention to the chattering of the cat,
so did Percy Buckham ignore the chattering of Ben Nevis.

" Here is the letter I propose you shall sign," he began.
" *Dear Mr Buckham . . .*" he broke off.   " I am Percy
Buckham, the Acting President of the National Union of
Hikers."

" One of these days you'll wish you weren't Percy Buckham," Chester Royde warned him.

" Don't bandy words with this blackguard.   Keep cool,
Royde, like me," urged Ben Nevis, whose face was bubbling
like molten lava in the crater of a volcano.

" *Dear Mr. Buckham,*" the leader of the hikers went on
reading, "*I have first of all to express my very sincere regret for
my outrageous behaviour on the 12th ult., when I assaulted and
imprisoned in my dungeons sixteen members of the National Union
of Hikers, including Mr Sydney Prew the Secretary. I must also
express my sincere regret for wantonly firing into the portable radio-
cabinet known as the Little Songster which belongs to Mr Thomas
Camidge and I hope Mr Camidge will be good enough to overlook
my loss of self-control and accept a new Little Songster to replace the
one I destroyed.*

" *In expressing my regret I desire at the same time to offer my
humble apologies to the National Union of Hikers, and in particular
to the President the Earl of Buntingdon, the Secretary Mr Sydney
Prew, the Honorary Treasurer Mr Fortescue Wilson and your good
self.   In order that the extent of my regret and the sincerity of my
apologies may be appreciated I have decided to take down all the
objectionable notices prohibiting camping on my land and I desire
here and now to extend a hearty invitation to all members of the
N.U.H. to camp whenever and wherever they like on my land.
I have instructed my tenants and employees to afford them every
facility they require in the matter of obtaining water and to supply*

them with milk, eggs, fruit and vegetables at a reasonable price.
"*In the hope that you will persuade the National Union of Hikers to accept my apologies and collaborate in future with me in promoting true democratic feeling,*

I remain,

Yours very truly,

" I think you'll agree with me, Mr MacDonald, that considering your behaviour on August 12th you are being let off very lightly. I have a fountain-pen here. If you will sign this letter I will set you and your party free and you can avoid the unpleasantness of having Glenbogle Castle seized and occupied by my forces."

Turner himself would have been baffled to depict the changing hues upon the Chieftain's countenance while Percy Buckham was reading out this letter.

" Give me that piece of paper," he choked.

They unbound his arms and taking the letter he tore it into fragments. Then his mouth opened to breathe in the inspiration that would provide him with the epithet to annihilate the hikers' leader. None of sufficient explosive force was granted to him.

" So that is your reply to my generous offer, Mr Mac-Donald. Perhaps after a night in this cave you will be feeling in a more reasonable state of mind. And that brings me to another matter. I will leave your arms free if you will give me your parole that you will not attempt to escape. In any case I will have your legs untied, for the approaches to the cave are well guarded."

But the Highland pride of Ben Nevis would not allow him to give his parole to a man like Percy Buckham. So he and Chester Royde and old Duncan were left trussed up in the Prince's Cave. Iain and the two gillies were taken down to the camp, for Buckham did not want to maintain too large a guard up at the cave because if by chance one of them should get out of his ropes and set the others free he was doubtful of the guard's ability to hold all the six.

" I feel quite sure we shall soon be rescued," said Ben Nevis when he and Chester Royde and Duncan were by themselves. " There'll be a hue and cry for us down in the glen when we don't come back. You think we shall soon be rescued, don't you, Donald ? "

The old keeper shook his head.

" It rests with the Lord, Ben Nevis. If it please the Lord to set us free we will be set free."

"When Johnnie Macpherson finds we don't come back at one o'clock, he'll wait about for an hour or two, and then he'll go back to the Castle and give the alarm."

" Och, Johnnie Macpherson will go back to the Castle right enough," Duncan agreed. " But what will be the use of that ? He won't be able to tell where we are. We might be anywhere. We might be nowhere at all. Who is to say ? "

" What makes me so mad," said Chester Royde, " is to think that this is the second time that guy with the chin has made a fool of me. It's humiliating."

The afternoon wore away. About five o'clock the prisoners were unbound and given tea.

" It makes my gorge rise to eat their food," said Ben Nevis. " But I suppose we can't starve."

" It's very good tea," Duncan observed. " I wouldn't have believed such people as these hikers could make such good tea as this."

" All tea tastes alike to me," said Chester Royde. " And it's not any too good a taste either."

After the meal they were roped up again and sat in gloomy silence for an hour.

Suddenly Duncan muttered something in Gaelic, and the others looked. At the entrance of the cave a magnificent stag was gazing at them.

" It's himself," Duncan gasped.

" The muckle hart," Ben Nevis whispered hoarsely.

" The muckle hart himself," Duncan confirmed. " Look at the antlers on him."

" Do you mean to tell me that beast staring at us is the beast we stalked in the rain ? " Chester Royde asked.

" The very same, Mr Royde."

" There's not another stag within a twenty-mile radius with a head like that," Ben Nevis declared.

" Well, I don't know," said Chester Royde. " It seems to me I'm the stooge for man and beast in this part of the world. Get away, you brute. Booh! Bang!"

The stag threw up his mighty head, and seemed to sniff at the sound. Then he tossed his antlers, shook his flanks, lolloped away from the cave with a contemptuous lack of urgency.

"Duncan, I believe that stag was laughing at us," Ben Nevis said.

"That was the very thing I was thinking myself," the old keeper agreed. "He'll be on his way back to Ben Glass now with the hinds. He'll be blowing to them all the way he mocked us."

"If I could stick that stag's horns on that stiff's chin or alternatively stick that stiff's chin on that stag's horns I won't worry what kind of a mess Franklin D. Roosevelt makes of Wall Street," Chester Royde declared.

Chapter 19

BOG-MYRTLE

IT was too late when Johnnie Macpherson returned with the empty Daimler to make any effective attempt to rescue the six prisoners of the hikers that day. He and Archie MacColl, the driver of the lorry, had spent one of those afternoons so dear to the hearts of West Highlanders, an afternoon of cigarettes and gossip, completely unaware that the situation called for the slightest initiative on their part. It was not until a certain emptiness reminded Johnnie Macpherson the hour for his tea had passed that he wondered what could be keeping Ben Nevis.

" My goodness, Archie," he exclaimed, " it's a quarter to six by the new time."

" A quarter to six ? " Archie MacColl echoed, shaking his round red freckled face " Look at that now. And I promised Coinneach Mór " (this was Kenny Macdonald the blacksmith) " I'd fetch that broken gate for him this afternoon so as he could get to work upon it on Monday morning."

" What gate is that ? "

" The gate into the bull's field. It's been broken since last October, and it's a big nuisance untying it and tying it up again all the time."

" Och, it's waited so long now it can wait till Monday just as well."

" Och yes," Archie agreed. " Just as well."

" I'd promised to have a look at Mrs Parsall's wireless for her this afternoon," Johnnie announced.

" Is it broken ? "

" Och, I don't know if it's a valve or if the high tension is wrong, but it hasn't been working for nearly three weeks now. She's on at me to look at it every time she sees me. ' What about my wireless, Johnnie, what about my wireless ? ' Och, I got tired hearing about her wireless. So I told her I'd look at it this afternoon, but och, a man can't do everything at once. But that's the way with women. They think a man has nothing to do except be mending a lot of nonsense for them."

" That's true right enough. But they can't help themselves. No, no. They're just made that way."

" Ay, that's just about what it is, Archie. Just made that
way, and that's all there is to it. I wonder what's keeping
Ben Nevis. One o'clock we were to be here, and it's nearly
six o'clock now."

" He may have walked back by the other side of Ben
Booey," Archie speculated.

" Ay, he may have. I never thought of that. Perhaps
we would be better to go back to the Castle and find out if
there's any news of him."

The absence of Ben Nevis made all at the Castle realize
how much they depended on him in an emergency like this.
They recalled the vigour with which he had organized search
parties for his missing guest only a week ago. All that Mrs
MacDonald could suggest was that after he had had his tea
Johnnie Macpherson should drive back to where he had
spent the afternoon waiting for his master. Mrs Mac-
Donald was determined to believe a sprained ankle was the
explanation of the mystery.

" But, Mother, they can't all six of them have sprained
their ankles," Catriona protested. " I think they've been
captured by the hikers."

" I'm certain of it," Mary growled.

Carrie and Myrtle supported this theory, and even Mr
Fletcher, who had spent so many years in avoiding any
difference of opinion either with Ben Nevis or his wife, felt
bound to question the probability of the sprained ankle
theory.

" Oh dear," Mrs MacDonald soughed, " I wish Hughie
Cameron was here." All recent criticism of Kilwhillie was
forgotten in this anxious hour.

At midnight Johnnie Macpherson came back with worse
news than ever. Miss Catriona and Miss Mary had set off
together along the path toward Ben Booey and had not been
seen since they got out of the Daimler about half-past eight.

" But why did you let them go, Johnnie ? " Mrs Mac-
Donald boomed reproachfully.

" How was I to stop them, madam ? " he asked. " They
just jumped out of the car when we reached the head of the
path and were away."

" The hikers must have captured them too," Carrie
declared.

Carrie was right. The hikers had captured Catriona and
Mary. The gallant and hefty girls had marched boldly into

the Black Corrie, and though they put up a magnificent
fight against the mobile reserve they had finally been overwhelmed by twenty young women fighting for the honour of
their sex under the eyes of their male companions.   Back to
back Catriona and Mary had fought, but as fast as they unzipped the shorts of their assailants others took their places,
and though five were unzipped with such heftiness that they
had to retire from the contest, the rest were able to zip themselves up again quickly enough to fling themselves all together against Catriona and Mary and finally to drag them
down to the ground.   When Johnnie Macpherson reached
Glenbogle with the news of their disappearance the two
gallant and hefty girls were lying in a tent, bound securely
with ropes.

" What *are* we to do ? " Mrs MacDonald boomed·deso-
lately.

" We'll have to wait till Monday now and see what can be
done," Johnnie Macpherson said.

" Wait till Monday ? "

" To-morrow's the Sabbath," he reminded her.   " We
might get one or two to have a look for them to-morrow,
but och, we won't get many,   The Minister has been fierce
about Sabbath-breaking for the last four Sundays."

" But surely when Ben Nevis himself may be in danger
there will be plenty of volunteers," said Mrs MacDonald.

Johnnie Macpherson shook his head.

" It's a pity Major MacIsaac went away for his holiday
after the Gathering," he said.   " He might have persuaded
some of them, but they'll never listen to me.   And Big
Duncan, he might have persuaded them, but himself is
missing.   So's Lachy Macdonald.   So's Roddy Maclean.
Archie MacColl would go right enough, being an Episcopalian from Appin, but what would Archie and me do by ourselves ?   They're saying in the bothy there are five or six
hundred hikers camping in the Black Corrie."

" And Catriona and Mary are in the hands of these
people," Mrs MacDonald moaned.

In spite of her own anxiety about Chester, Carrie could
not help winking at Myrtle, who could not contain an explo-
sion of merriment which she apologized for as a sneeze.

" I think we may safely assume they will come to no grievous harm, Mrs MacDonald," said the chaplain.   " The
intention is probably to use them to bargain with."

This notion was too much altogether for Myrtle, who was
seized with such spasms of pent-up laughter that she was
driven into crawling under the table on all-fours to look for
an imaginary ruby supposed to have fallen out of her
bracelet.

"Well, I know what I'm going to do to-morrow morning," said Carrie. "I'm going to drive to Knocknacolly
and consult Chester's lawyer, Mr Buchanan."

"Oh, and I'll come with you, Carrie," said her sister-in-
law, emerging from beneath the table. "That's a wonderful idea."

So on Sunday morning, rather later than they'd intended
because Mr Fletcher took advantage of the Chieftain's
absence to give a longer sermon than usual, they arrived at
Knocknacolly at the moment when Robert Menzies was
making an omelette and his two companions were pointing
out his mistakes, standing one at each elbow.

"For God's sake, you silly pair of clowns, stop your
blethering, and let me make the damned omelette my own
way," the architect was shouting as Carrie and Myrtle
walked into the room, that room which they had taken so
much trouble to make pleasant and cosy for the three young
men and which now after a week of exclusively male
attention was as richly squalid as a Hogarth garret.

"Oh, you're making an omelette," Carrie exclaimed.
"I'm terribly good at omelettes."

"So am I," said Myrtle eagerly. "The secret of a good
omelette is always to . . ."

But Robert's omelette was too far advanced by now to be
interfered with and there were not enough eggs left to show
him how it ought to have been made.

"Anyway, what's more important than omelettes is the
problem of Glenbogle," Carrie said, and she related what
had happened yesterday. "Once upon a time, Alan, you
and James had a plan to kidnap Ben Nevis. Now you've
got to think out a plan to unkidnap him and my poor
husband," she went on.

"If we could get a few of the S.B.A. to Glenbogle," said
James, "we'd soon deal with these Cockney hikers, would
we not?"

The poet and the architect warmly agreed.

"Well, why don't you get the S.B.A.?" asked Carrie.

"Oh yes, why don't you?" said Myrtle.

James Buchanan looked worried.

" It's really a question of finance," he admitted at last.
" Two or three of them could manage right enough, but
most of them are students and they haven't really got the
money to come all the way up here at a moment's notice."

" If that's all you're worrying about, James, you needn't
worry any more. I suppose I have a right to call on the
members of the Brotherhood for action at my expense.
Now see here, I'm pretty practical over matters like this.
My notion would be for you to go and collect as many as
you can and hire automobiles to rush them up to Glenbogle
as soon as possible. How many do you think you could
collect ? "

" I think we might collect a couple of dozen, don't you,
Robert ? But I don't suppose we could get them together
before Tuesday at the earliest."

" Well, let's make it Tuesday afternoon at the Castle
with as many as you can get. Twenty-four aren't very
many against five or six hundred, but twenty-four will be
better than nobody."

" Five or six hundred ? " James gasped.

" That's what they say.   They're camped on Ben Booey,"
Carrie said.

" I don't believe it's possible," James declared.   " Fifty
or sixty perhaps.   But five or six hundred!   It's a ridiculous
figure."

" Camped on Ben Booey, are they ? " Alan put in.   " I'll
bet they have Ben Nevis and Mr Royde shut up in that cave
they say Prince Charlie hid in, which of course is nonsense."

" Why should it be nonsense ? " Robert Menzies demanded
sternly.   He was a fiery Jacobite, and resented a slight even
on a cave hallowed by the Prince's name.

" Och, away with you, Robert, I'm not going to argue
about Prince Charlie, just now," Alan told him.

" Who started the argument, Alan ? "

" No argument *has* started. What's the use of arguing
about Prince Charlie when we have to deal with the present ?
You may be a good architect, Robert, but you're frightfully
unpractical.   You've no conception of poetic action."

" He certainly is a good architect," Carrie interposed.
" I've been looking at his last sketch for the new house, and
it's quite lovely."

" Do you like it, Mrs Royde ? I'm awfully pleased."

Robert Menzies had not had the advantage of meeting Carrie in the romantic circumstances in which his two friends had met her that day in Glenbristle. So far he had been able to behold her only as a possible patroness. He had fancied she was not particularly impressed by his plans for Knocknacolly. Her sudden compliment to his work made him her slave. Carrie wanted the help of the S.B.A., and Robert Menzies made up his mind there and then that she should have it.

" You and Alan and I had better get along down to Glasgow to-morrow morning, James. We'll need all of two days to collect our fellows," he said.

" Wouldn't it be as well if one of us stayed here ? " Alan asked.

And thus it was decided that Alan should be the one to stay.

" It's a pity in a way Robert and I can't catch the train from Fort William this afternoon," said James presently. " We'll have all our work cut out to collect enough of the S.B.A. and be back by Tuesday."

And thus it was decided that Carrie should drive the lawyer and the architect into Fort William, returning later to fetch the poet and Myrtle to Glenbogle.

" How far away we seem from the rest of the world up here," Myrtle exclaimed when she and Alan were sitting on the tangled lawn of Knocknacolly Lodge that looked out across the wide level moor to the mountains all round.

" But it's only seeming, that's the worst of it," Alan muttered. " And at this moment it's the world that's worrying me."

" But why do you let it worry you ? " she asked. " I don't let anything worry me. Of course, I don't like to think of poor old Chester in the hands of those hikers; but it doesn't worry me, because I know nothing really serious will happen to him."

" I suppose it wouldn't worry you in the least to know I love you ? " he enquired gloomily.

" No, it wouldn't worry me," she murmured gently, casting a quick sidelong glance at that rosebrowned face gazing across the moor to where its enemy the world was lurking on the other side of the mountains. " Why should it worry me ? " she added still more gently.

" Why indeed ? " the poet asked, with Byronic scorn for

the feminine wiles he despised even as he succumbed to them.

" It seems to worry you a lot," she said.

" Well, it isn't exactly soothing to fall madly in love with a girl utterly beyond one's reach."

" It doesn't seem to me I'm so far beyond your reach. I couldn't sit much closer to you unless I sat on your knee, and I can't sit on your knee because you're resting your head on your knee and making faces at the poor old world."

" You needn't jeer at me."

" Oh, Alan, I never thought you were quite so dumb. When I met you first I thought you were shy, but that didn't bother me because I liked your shyness. And when you read me that poem about the dark-brown water of life . . ." she sighed. " And then when you read me that poem with what you added about bog-myrtle . . ." she sighed again, and was silent.

" *You* have nothing to sigh about," he observed severely.

" I don't think you've any right to say that about me."

" Why not ? "

" Because I don't think you know enough about me, Alan."

" I'll never have the chance to learn much more."

" It'll be your own fault if you don't. You could learn pretty well all about me by asking one little question."

" And what is that wonderful question ? "

" Oh, you can look after the question, Alan. It's my job to look after the answer."

" There's only one question I want to ask you," he declared sombrely.

" Hadn't you better ask it ? "

" Do you think you could ever love *me* ? "

" Alan," she cried, " you really are too dumb. I thought you were going to ask me to marry you. It's no good asking *unnecessary* questions. That's just wasting time."

" How can I ask you to marry me ? " he demanded indignantly.

" I should think it would be pretty easy even in Gaelic."

" How can I ask you to marry me ? You rich and me poor ! "

" Well, that's a whole lot better than both of us being poor," she pointed out.

And then suddenly the present tripped up the future and nothing mattered except the joy of being together on this tangled lawn, with the wide level moor before them and the the blue mountains beyond. They were still sitting there, when Carrie came back from Fort William. Her greenish eyes looked quickly at the pair of them and brightened.

" So that's settled at last," she said.

Myrtle nodded.

" Carrie darling, I wonder how you understood so well," she murmured.

" I just guessed somehow. Of course I *am* three years older than you," Carrie reminded her.

" I'm glad you're my sister-in-law," Myrtle exclaimed. " For lots of reasons," she added softly.

Carrie smiled. With those four words Myrtle had repaid her own generosity in like measure.

" It's all very well for you two to be so pleased about everything," said the poet. " But what kind of a clown will I feel when I tell Mr Royde ? "

" Oh, don't call Chester Mr Royde," the wife and sister expostulated with one voice.

" Never mind about what I call him," said Alan glumly. " What kind of a clown will I feel when I tell him about me and his sister ? "

" But Chester liked your tartan so much," said Carrie.

" Yes, he adored your kilt," Myrtle added.

" You're not going to marry my kilt. You're going to marry what's inside the kilt."

Myrtle laughed, and the poet blushed.

" You know fine what I mean," he muttered like an embarrassed schoolboy.

" Oh, I've got the most wonderful idea," Carrie ejaculated suddenly. " Oh, it's the most wonderful idea anybody ever heard ! Listen. I know what Alan must do to impress Chester. Somehow or other he must rescue him from the hikers. Oh, it'll be just like one of those books men enjoy reading. Chester coming forward and shaking Alan by the hand and telling him he'll never forget the way he rescued him against fearful odds. And Alan will blush and say it was nothing, but anyway he'd go through worse than that to rescue the brother of Myrtle Royde. And then Chester'll look kind of surprised for a moment and then it'll dawn on him what's happened and he'll squeeze Alan's hand in a brotherly grip and say he only wished he had two sisters so as he could give them both to his rescuer."

" What would he want to give Alan two sisters for ? " Myrtle asked indignantly. " He isn't a Mormon."

" I really am serious about rescuing Chester from the hikers," Carrie insisted. " Didn't you say you thought he might be in the Prince's Cave on Ben Booey ? "

" Yes. Uaimh na Phrionnsa," said Alan.

Myrtle threw her arms round him and kissed him. " Oh, Alan, I do love you when you talk Gaelic. Now say the name of the other cave."

He obliged, and she kissed him again.

" Well, if you have a hunch that the hikers have shut Chester and Ben Nevis and the rest in Uaimh na Phrionnsa . . ."

" No, no, Carrie, you can't do it. I'm sorry, darling, but you don't get that kind of gurgle like the last drop of water running out of a bath."

" Alan, what do you think ? " Carrie went on. " Wouldn't it be worth while to see if your hunch is right ? "

" I'll climb up where the ground drops down in front," said Alan. " I did it the year before last."

But when in the road that branched off from Glenbogle on the farther side of Ben Booey from the Castle he pointed to what at two miles away appeared the sheer precipice in front of the Prince's Cave, Myrtle declared she'd rather leave Chester there as long as Rip Van Winkle than that Alan should attempt such a climb.

" It's not really at all difficult," he assured her. " You can't see the way up from here."

And before Myrtle could argue any more he jumped out of the car, telling them to wait with it, and set off at a rapid pace up the spur of the mighty ben toward the precipice before the cave.

" If anything happens to him, Carrie, I'll never forgive you," Myrtle declared almost tearfully.

" Nothing will happen to him, honeybunch, and think what a story we'll have to tell Chester if he *is* in that cave, and after all Chester Royde Senior and Mrs Chester Royde Senior have to be considered. You'll want a bit of help from Chester when you go home and announce you're going to marry a wild Highlander with an empty sporran."

It happened that, just as the poet scrambled over the top

of the precipice in front of the cave, Percy Buckham was telling his prisoners that when darkness came they would have to move to new quarters on the other side of the glen.

"I want to give you the pleasure, Mr MacDonald, of seeing with your own eyes my forces march into Glenbogle Castle, pull down that flag of yours with half the Zoo on it, and hoist the crossed staffs of the N.U.H. The escort will arrive in an hour."

Buckham turned his back on the prisoners and marching out of the cave came face to face with Alan Macmillan.

"Who are you?" he demanded.

And Alan hit out, catching Percy Buckham fairly on the chin.

"Oh, boy, what a K.O.!" shouted Chester Royde exultantly as Percy Buckham went down on his back.

The congratulations Alan received upon his masterly blow were more than his pugilistic skill deserved. Anybody who hit Percy Buckham was almost bound to hit his chin.

With his *sgian dubh* the poet cut the bonds of the captives, and urged a speedy retreat before Buckham could raise the alarm. There were two hikers on guard further along the narrow path leading round from the cave, but unlike Professor Moriarty they were not prepared to risk a struggle so near the edge of that precipice and scrambled away in the other direction crying, 'Wolla-wolla-wolla!' to summon help from the camp.

An hour later the prisoners had reached the Austin.

"I'll drive you back to the Castle," Carrie volunteered. "Myrtle and Alan will have to walk."

Perhaps their sufferings in the cave had reduced their bulk. Otherwise it is difficult to know how Ben Nevis, Chester Royde and big Duncan Macdonald all managed to get into that little Austin.

"What did Chester say to you, Alan?" Myrtle asked.

"He was pleased about my hitting that fellow on the chin."

"What did he say when you told him about you and me?"

"I didn't tell him about you and me."

"Alan, you really can be terribly dumb, darling. Never mind. I guess Carrie'll tell him all about you and me. Oh, what's that sweet scent on the air?"

"Bog-myrtle," he told her.

"And you and I are wandering along together in the scent of it," she sighed happily.

> "*The warm dark-brown water of life*
> *Whose sweet breath blows in the wind*
> *Bringing bog-myrtle,*"

he whispered.

And they stood there in the gloaming, lost in a long kiss.

Chapter 20

BEN NEVIS FOR EVER

IT was undoubtedly a shock to Ben Nevis when he found that he had been rescued from the cave by a Scottish Nationalist, that the said Scottish Nationalist was engaged to the girl he had fetched his eldest son back from India to marry, and finally that the defence of Glenbogle Castle itself must depend on a body of Scottish Nationalists now being mustered in Glasgow.

" But, Donald, if you feel as strongly about these people as you do, why don't you call in the help of the police ? " his wife asked.

" My dear Trixie, do you seriously think I'll give Lindsay-Wolseley such an opportunity of scoring off me ? I can't say I like the idea of what amounts to an alliance with Scottish Nationalists. It's as if the British Government were to listen to those pestilential Labour fellows and make an alliance with the Bolshies. But sometimes a situation calls for desperate measures, and we must remember that Iain, Mary and Catriona are still in the hands of these foul hikers, not to mention Lachy Macdonald and Roddy Maclean."

" It's really lamentable," Mrs MacDonald boomed plaintively. " I still think it would be advisable to get into communication with the police."

" Trixie, you know what a reasonable man I am. Now please don't make me angry by talking any more about the police. I'd sooner Glenbogle were burnt to the ground than give Lindsay-Wolseley a chance of saying to me ' I told you so.' "

" He seems quite a pleasant young man, this Mr Macmillan," said Mrs MacDonald, steering the conversation away from Colonel Lindsay-Wolseley.

" I don't object to him personally at all," Ben Nevis admitted. " And I really was very glad that he turned up when he did. I was on the point of bursting, I think. It's a fearful strain having to sit and listen to the bragging of a bounder like this Buckham creature. . . . Good God ! "

" Donald, what is the matter now ? "

She might well ask. Lady Macbeth called upon to calm

her husband when the ghost of Banquo sat down in his place at dinner may have been confronted by such an expression of incredulous horror.

" Donald dear, what *is* the matter ? "

For answer Ben Nevis pointed with his finger at a page of the *Scotsman* upon his knee.

Mrs MacDonald leant over to see what in that austere newspaper could have thus convulsed her husband's countenance.

She saw looking round the corner of a wireless cabinet a face. She saw a finger pointed, it seemed, at her personally. She read in large letters LEND ME YOUR EARS. She read on:

" Friends,
    " The other day I overheard my secretary say to a client, ' Mr Buckham will be away on his holiday next week,' and my heart leapt like a schoolboy's at the sound of the magic word. Some of you will be away on your holidays next week. Don't forget to take your Little Songster with you. The good weather I hope you'll enjoy will seem all the better if set fair to music, and if by some unlucky chance it should rain the Little Songster will make you never mind a bit about the weather. Cheerio, folks. Have a good time, and good listening!

                              " PERCY BUCKHAM."

" That's why his face was vaguely familiar to me," Ben Nevis roared. " I must have seen it in an advertisement. But I'm astonished at a paper like the *Scotsman* printing an advertisement like this. I shall write a letter of protest. Oh, well, I knew as soon as they started a page of photographs and a crossword puzzle the *Scotsman* was going to the dogs like everything in this modern world. Fancy opening my *Scotsman* and seeing that bounder's face glaring at me round one of those ghastly wireless contraptions."

" Well, turn over the page, Donald. Don't keep looking at this man's face if it irritates you."

At that moment Toker brought word that Neil Maclennan wanted to speak to Ben Nevis. The chieftain came back presently, looking grave. It appeared from Neil Maclennan's information that the Castle was now entirely surrounded by hikers.

Ben Nevis took out his watch.

"Ten minutes to five. Come along, Trixie, let's go and have some tea."

Chester and Carrie and Myrtle were in the Great Hall with Alan Macmillan.

"We're surrounded," the Chieftain announced as nonchalantly as Leonidas addressing his Spartans the day before Thermopylæ. "What's the earliest you expect your people, Macmillan?"

"I'm afraid they won't be here before to-morrow afternoon," the poet replied.

"Well, we must hold out somehow," said the Chieftain. "By the way, I've found who this fellow Buckham is. He's an advertisement. Mary, go and get the *Scotsman.*"

"Donald, you're forgetting," his wife boomed tragically. "Our poor Mary isn't here."

"Oh no, nor she is. Oh well, we must hope for the best," said the stricken father.

"I'll get your paper for you, Ben Nevis," Myrtle volunteered. "If I'm going to marry over here I guess I'd better begin to practise being a good little wife by British standards."

"I'll get it, sir," said Alan. "Is it in the library?"

"Yes, that's where it is. Thanks very much," said the Chieftain, and when Alan was out of the room he looked benevolently at Myrtle.

"I rather like this young man of yours, Myrtle. He has good manners."

"He has a darned good punch with his left," said Chester.

"He writes lovely poetry," Carrie added.

"Oh well, of course I don't know anything about that, I'm afraid," Ben Nevis barked. "I'm not great at reading at all, as a matter of fact. I mean to say, you start a book and then you put it down, and then when you pick it up again you can't find where you left off. I remember once I read a book twice, and I hadn't any idea I'd already just read this book till I came on a fly I'd squashed in it. Now think what a waste of time that was. Reading a book I'd already read! Heart-breaking, what?"

Alan Macmillan came back with the *Scotsman,* and with him came Kilwhillie.

"Ah, Hugh, you've got here," his old friend bellowed. "Did you see any hikers?"

" Did I see any hikers ? The place is alive with them,"
said Kilwhillie. " They tried to stop my car."

" Good lord, what brutes! Well, I think they'll attack us
to-night."

" You really do ? Hadn't you better get in touch with
the police ? "

" Hugh! I never thought I'd live to hear advice like that
from a Cameron. Do you think I want to spend the rest of
my life watching Wolseley grinning at me down that yellow
nose of his ? "

" What are you going to do, then ? "

" I'm going to fight the brutes. As a matter of fact we
hope to be reinforced by some . . . by some keen young
fellows from Glasgow." He could not bring himself to
confess to Kilwhillie he had made an alliance with Scottish
Nationalists.

" From Glasgow ? " Kilwhillie echoed in amazement.

" Highlandmen, of course. By the way, have you met
Miss Royde's fiancé, Mr Macmillan ? "

Kilwhillie shook hands with Alan, looking dazed. Glenbogle had taken on the quality of a dream-place since he
left it hardly a week ago.

" I thought of using boiling water from the windows of
the first floor," Ben Nevis mentioned casually.

" Boiling water ? What for ? "

" For the hikers, Hugh, of course. What else would I use
boiling water for ? The girls can pour it over the brutes
when they try to force their way in. I'd like to use boiling
oil, but I doubt if we've got enough oil to boil. Have we got
enough oil to boil, Trixie ? "

" Certainly not, Donald," the Lady of Ben Nevis replied
firmly.

However, the attack on the Castle did not develop as
quickly as Ben Nevis expected, though the enemy all through
dinner were very noisy, one particularly objectionable
feature being the repeated singing of the Hikers' Song in the
courtyard.

" I can't stand this much longer," Ben Nevis declared at
last. " I shall have to do something.

" Excuse me, sir," said Toker, " but the blacksmith, the
cowman, the carpenter and two or three of the gillies
attempted a counter-attack a few minutes ago, and it was
not quite as successful as could be wished."

" What happened ? "

" Mrs Parsall and two of the maids are tying up their wounds, which consist of minor injuries inflicted by those long sticks with which the enemy is armed. It would seem that a very determined effort was made to capture Kenneth Macdonald and it was while our side were pulling him by the arms and the enemy were pulling him by the legs that the injuries were inflicted by these sticks."

" The cowardly brutes," Ben Nevis exclaimed.

" In point of fact, sir, it was the young women hikers who used the sticks so recklessly. The men fought more cleanly, if I may use the expression."

The offensive noises continued for two or three hours after dinner and Chester Royde, basing his forecast on his researches into Indian warfare, held strongly to the opinion that an attempt would be made to rush the Castle just before dawn. The Chieftain gave orders that the garrison was to be on the alert all night, the various guards relieving one another at intervals of two hours. He himself did not rest, but stalked about the Castle, encouraging everybody to stand firm for the honour and safety of Glenbogle, like a composite of Macbeth, King Henry V and the ghost of Hamlet's father, a truly impressive Shakespearean shape.

About half-past four loud feminine shrieks were heard coming from the courtyard, and by the dim light of a decrescent moon and the first grey of dawn two massive figures were visible hurrying toward the south postern where Chester Royde was in command of the guard. He seized the pail of soapy water which Ben Nevis had been persuaded to substitute for boiling water, and told Toker who was with him on duty to fling open the postern so that he could make a sally and soak the attackers.

" Hold your fire, sir," Toker begged. Through the casement beside the postern he had recognized the massive figures. " Hold your fire, please, sir. I'm going to open the door. It's Miss Catriona and Miss Mary."

The butler's eyes had not deceived him. Through the open postern the hefty daughters of the house dashed panting and as it closed behind them each threw down upon the floor a wriggling squealing hikeress.

" Got away from the Cave of the Calf on Ben Cruet," Catriona growled. " And bagged those two squawkers by the edge of the larches."

"Well, I do congratulate you girls," said Chester, looking at the two captives in green corduroy shorts who were sitting up by now and scowling at their assailants.

"We had to dash for it good-oh," Mary said. "The Castle's going to be attacked. We overheard them talking about it."

"They're all around us already," said Chester. "Your father's in command. You'd better go along and report with your prisoners."

"Get up, you little blighter," Catriona growled at her prisoner, a small dark young woman. "And if you try to bite me again I'll give you a jolly good welting."

"And that goes for you, you little tick," Mary growled at hers.

"I'm not going to get up before I get a safety-pin," said Mary's captive, a towzled fluffy fair girl called Edith Bassett.

"What do you want a safety-pin for, you little squirt ? " Mary growled contemptuously.

"Never mind what I want it for, you. I'm not going to get up for anybody till I have a safety-pin," said Edith Bassett.

"Where are we going to put these two ? " Catriona asked.

"I know where they ought to be put," Mary replied cryptically.

"Oh, you do, do you ? " said Edith Bassett. "I know where you ought to be put—isn't that right, Minnie ? "

"Yes, and be careful to pull it," said Minnie.

The hefty sisters were not prepared to be jeered at by these two little Cockneys. They bent down and picking up Edith Bassett and Minnie Rogers, put them under their arms and walked off. It was at once apparent why Edith Bassett had demanded a safety-pin.

"Very strong young ladies, sir," Toker commented. "I never did think these hikers would contrive to keep Miss Catriona and Miss Mary long in durance vile, as they say. And I made so bold as to express that opinion to Mrs Mac-Donald when she was inclined to take it to heart so much after they were kidnapped by the hikers. Hullo, sir, look out! I think there's some more excitement coming our way. Yes, indeed, sir, by the living jingo, it's Mr Iain, or I'm a footman. Pardon my excitement, sir, but nobody except Mr Iain could do it like that."

Chester Royde looked out through the casement and by the glimmer of the dawn beheld a burly kilted form tossing hikers about. And then just as half-a-dozen more hikers sneaking up from behind seemed on the point of recapturing him, another kilted form dashed across the courtyard to the rescue and engaged them with his fists.

" Gee, that poet has a lovely punch," cried Chester Royde as he charged from the postern into the fray.

A minute later Iain MacDonald was safe within the Castle.

" Capital bit of work," the Chieftain pronounced. " You hit one of those brutes pretty hard, Macmillan. I don't think you've met my youngest boy, Iain. This is Myrtle's fiancé, Iain."

Iain for one brief instant looked as much surprised as an undergraduate ever allows himself to look, but quickly recovered his normal imperturbability, and nobody could have supposed that he had spent much of the past sixty-six hours rolled up in a tent and tied with the ropes of it and that he had returned home to find one of his father's guests engaged to what unless it had been Glenbogle Castle he would have vowed was a Scottish Nationalist.

" How many hikers do you reckon there are, Iain ? " his father asked.

" Not far off a hundred."

" Oh, is that all ? Kenny Macdonald was putting them at over seven hundred last night."

" He would," said Iain.

" And what's happened to Lachy and Roddy ? "

" They're probably still rolled up in tents."

" Well, you'd better lie down for a few hours and get a bit of rest. We'll wake you if there's an alarm."

" I'm all right, Dad. I've done enough lying down rolled up in that tent to last me for some time," said Iain.

" You'd better go up and see your mother, girls," Ben Nevis said to his hefty daughters, who had just come back from handing over Edith Bassett and Minnie Rogers to the grim guardianship of Mrs Parsall and Mrs Ablewhite, both of whom were drinking tea in the housekeeper's room, an occupation in which they had been almost continuously engaged all night.

" Won't she be asleep ? " Catriona suggested.

" No, no, I don't think so. Every time I've been up to see her she's been awake," said her father. This was not to be wondered at. A visit from Ben Nevis in his present martial mood was only a little quieter than a visit by a squadron of heavy dragoons.

While the garrison of Glenbogle was waiting for zero hour early on that Tuesday morning, the seventh Earl of Buntingdon was turning over restlessly in an L.N.E.R. sleeper, bound for Fort William, and wondering whether he had been wise to respond to Percy Buckham's impassioned appeal to preside at the surrender of Glenbogle Castle to the N.U.H. He switched on the light above his bed, sat up, and took out the telegram which had reached him at Ouse Hall just after lunch on Monday:

After a brilliant little operation in which every unit greatly distinguished itself have honour to inform you MacDonald Macdonald's son American guest headkeeper and two underkeepers were captured on Saturday morning and are now held prisoners stop on Saturday evening Macdonald's two daughters also captured stop am satisfied of ability to seize and occupy Glenbogle Castle on Tuesday and consider it vital to dignity of proceedings you should be present in person to receive Macdonald's apology and accept Magna Charta for N.U.H. from his hands stop have demanded removal of all no camping notices freedom camp anywhere on MacDonald's land and recognized market price for all produce purchased from his tenants stop confident MacDonald will accept terms and give apology demanded stop our casualties so far extremely light only damage being to small quantity of camping equipment and one leg bitten by dog stop secretary and self earnestly hope you will endeavour join us Tuesday for successful accomplishment of expedition's objective as your presence will lend dignity to lesson administered and rouse enthusiasm among members of union who have fought so gallantly in this campaign stop felt your presence at great democratic triumph will serve as notable rebuke to fascist influence everywhere lamentably on increase stop personally realize I am asking great deal but have complete confidence in your generous response stop suggest your wearing of hiking uniform would be intensely appreciated and will send two of our boys to meet train Fort William Tuesday morning with car and bring you to Glenbogle stop unable to receive answer as we are surrounding castle to-night with view to entry to-morrow when you arrive stop salute from every loyal hiker in the field

Buckham.

" A very long and expensive and rather repetitive telegram," Lord Buntingdon murmured to himself. " I wonder

if I am wise in falling in with it. Buckham has always been
prone to excessive optimism."

Lord Buntingdon experienced one of those sudden waves
of home-sickness which sweep over the traveller at moments of
discomfort. The sleeping-compartment was stuffy, and the
application to the top of his head of a draught set in motion
by a switch and directed by a metal slide merely agitated the
stuffiness without providing fresh air. He wondered why
he had been so weak as to forsake the ample tranquillity of
Ouse Hall for this constricted rumbling cell. He thought of
his tortoises, whose leisurely approach to life had so often
checked his more violent progressive impulses to disobey
the motto of the Buntingdons, *Festina Lente*. However, in
spite of these doubts before sunrise, when full morning
arrived and the sleeping-car attendant brought him a cup
of tea and informed him breakfast would be served half an
hour hence, Lord Buntingdon packed away his civilian
clothes and put on the uniform in which he had so often been
photographed at the Annual Hikery held in the grounds of
Ouse Hall.

The other breakfasters could not understand why the
stewards paid so much deference to this elderly hiker with a
melon-shaped face. They did not know he was an earl.

Then somebody suggested it was Lord Baden-Powell, and
though it would have been hard to find two people less alike,
as everybody in the saloon wanted to say he had travelled up
from King's Cross with Baden-Powell the will to believe
asserted itself and the lack of resemblance was ignored.
And when the elderly hiker alighted at Fort William and
was met on the platform by two younger hikers, who
presented arms to him with their staffs, nobody remained in
doubt but that the hero of Mafeking had shared their paste
called cream, their mess of fuller's earth called porridge,
their varnished chips of driftwood called kippers, their tea
called coffee or their coffee called tea, and all those other
luxurious and costly imitations of food that make up breakfast in a contemporary British train.

" Mr Buckham expects the Castle will be in our hands, sir,
by the time our car reaches Glenbogle," Hiker Barlow
informed the President of the N.U.H.

" All going well, eh, Barlow ? "

" Yes, sir, except that Mr Buckham was rather badly mauled
on Sunday night by six of MacDonald's Fascist bullies."

" Dear me, I'm sorry to hear that.   How did it happen ? "

" He was trying to prevent the escape of MacDonald himself whom we had taken prisoner, but he was out-numbered.   Luckily it was only his chin that was rather bruised.   He's leading the assault in person at eleven."

" And that should be over by the time we reach Glen-bogle ? " Lord Buntingdon asked, with a touch of anxiety in his tone.

" Oh yes, sir," Hiker Barlow confidently declared. " We shall see our flag floating over the Castle when we drive up."

There lingered upon the melon-shaped countenance of Lord Buntingdon a trace of that dubiety about the future which had affected his fancy before sunrise, but he shook off presentiment and followed his hiker escort to the waiting car hired for the great occasion.

Away in Glenbogle Mr Buckham, the bruise upon his chin a tartan of leaden blue and livid green and lurid yellow, was addressing his forces on the verge of the assault.

" Now don't forget," he wound up, " the girls will form a mobile reserve ready to throw their full weight into any gap made in the Castle defences by the men.   Do your best, all of you, so that when your President arrives he will greet an N.U.H. victorious all along the line.   I am leading the main assault on the front door.   Hiker Williamson will command the feint against the back of the castle.   Hiker Rosebotham and Hiker Hickey will lead the assaults against the side doors.   Mr Prew will command the mobile reserve and give the order when it is to advance.   Now then, boys and girls, three cheers for collective security and the freedom of the road ! "

Three times did the fifty male hikers fling themselves against the doors of Glenbogle Castle to be drenched from above by pail after pail of soapy water, one of which wielded by Carrie accompanied its contents and temporarily extin-guished Buckham himself and thereby perhaps saved the Castle from being rushed at the third and most vicious assault by diverting the attention of some of the hikers to extricating their leader from the bucket over his head.   Up in the room in the North Tower the Lady of Ben Nevis and the chaplain were the only two inactive members of the garrison, and should they be called inactive whose prayers for the defenders never ceased as the tide of battle ebbed and flowed ?   Once during that third assault the south postern was forced, but

Alan Macmillan, his blue eyes burning with this supreme expression of poetic action, flung Hiker Hickey head over heels back into the courtyard while Chester Royde, Butting Moose of the Carroways, rammed another hiker in the midriff, so that he lay gurgling for breath upon the gravel.

The repulse of that third assault was followed by a lull. The defenders gathered to consult. Reports were unanimous about the strain upon the doors and the unlikelihood of their holding out much longer.

" We'll use the Lochaber axes," Ben Nevis proclaimed. " Get them down from the walls."

Now, the long-handled Lochaber axe is a formidable weapon, and even Chester Royde, who after the Chieftain himself was the member of the garrison most intoxicated by the fighting spirit, looked doubtful about the effect of using it against the hikers. Fortunately, however, something happened to make it unnecessary to disturb the merely decorative existence in which the Lochaber axes had spent nearly two centuries. That something was the sound of the pipes still a long way off, but coming nearer all the time.

" These must be your Scottish . . . your fellows from Glasgow, Carrie," said Ben Nevis.

And then suddenly his brow clouded and the veins in his eagle's beak seemed to run with ink as he cupped an ear to listen.

" Kilwhillie ! Macmillan! Iain! " he gasped. " Am I going mad or are those pipers playing *The Campbells are Coming ?* "

The Cameron, the Macmillan and the young MacDonald scowled in unison.

" What on earth are James Buchanan and Robert Menzies thinking of ? " the poet exclaimed angrily.

" Angus! Angus! " Ben Nevis bellowed. " Tell the pipers to play *Clan Donald is Here* full blast. Full blast, do you hear, Angus ? The Campbells are coming, are they ? Great Scott, I'd sooner hear in my country that ghastly song those hiker brutes were singing last night."

When the strains of *Clan Donald is Here* died down there was no answering skirl from without, and at that moment the full force of the hikers charged for the front door.

" It'll never hold, never ! " Toker was heard to declare. " No door could," he added loyally.

And sure enough at that moment it cracked; but even as it

cracked into the courtyard charged the kilted members of the Scottish Brotherhood of Action, like a tartan catalogue come to life.

" Outside, and at 'em ! " shouted Ben Nevis when the front door gave way.

" Where's that guy with the chin ? " cried Chester Royde, following Ben Nevis as another Chester once followed Marmion.

But at the last moment he was baulked of his heart's desire. He was almost in reach of Percy Buckham when Percy Buckham waved a white handkerchief.

" The yellow-livered coyote," Chester gasped in utter disgust. " He's thrown in the towel."

But it was not respect for his own skin or his own chin which had made a poltroon of Percy Buckham. It was the sight of the Earl of Buntingdon in the hands of the kilted horde whose arrival had snatched victory from his grasp. The person of the President of the N.U.H. was more precious than even its honour.

" It was a mistake, Mr Buckham, to send me that telegram," said Lord Buntingdon when they were driving back to Fort William that afternoon after peace had been signed.

" As it turned out, yes, it was a mistake, Lord Buntingdon. I frankly admit it. But the arrival of those six cars packed with what I understand are all members of a Scottish terrorist society was not to be foreseen by anybody. Without them you would have reached the Castle at the moment when our fourth assault was successful and you would have received from the hands of MacDonald our Magna Charta. Who would have dreamed you would be captured on the road with your guard of honour? "

" Well, well, it can't be helped, Mr Buckham. And at any rate we did obtain from Mr MacDonald a promise that the whole business should be kept out of the Press."

" Yes, in consideration of a document signed by you, Prew, and myself accepting full responsibility for that outrage on August 12th, compensation to MacDonald's employees for wrongful imprisonment, and what is worst of all a solemn pledge that no member of the N.U.H. will ever camp again on the land of MacDonald or this Mr Cameron's land or the land of that most objectionable Yankee."

" Still, I do comfort myself with the thought that the whole business will be kept out of the Press," Lord Buntingdon repeated gratefully. " I hope your chin isn't hurting you very much."

" Oh no, it's nothing and I console myself with the thought that it took half a dozen of them even to do that amount of damage."

" A curious type, that Highland chief," Lord Buntingdon observed pensively. " I'm glad we don't get that kind of thing in Bedfordshire. A man like that would be a great nuisance on the Bench. Well, well, I shan't be sorry to get back to my tortoises. By the way, are we expected to wait for the members to reach Fort William ? "

" Oh no, Prew has been left in charge of the return to London."

The President and the Acting President relapsed into silence as the car turned out of Glenbogle.

Back in the Castle the victory was celebrated with such a feast as Mrs Ablewhite, protesting all the time to Mrs Parsall that it was impossible, loved to provide.

The members of the Scottish Brotherhood of Action left for Glasgow about midnight, all now as firmly convinced that there was something to be said for Highland chieftains of long authentic lineage still in possession of their land, as the Chieftain himself was now inclined to admit that there was something to be said for young men who desired the glory and grandeur of Scotland. In reaching this opinion he was much encouraged by the performance on the pipes of *Mac 'ic Eachainn's March to Sheriffmuir* by Colin Campbell, the student who had been responsible for desecrating the air of Glenbogle with *The Campbells are Coming*. To sit in his own Great Hall and hear a Campbell piping that tune to a Mac-Donald was compensation for many historical events which had taken the wrong course.

James Buchanan and Robert Menzies did not go back to Glasgow with the rest of the Brotherhood. They, like Alan Macmillan, were guests of Ben Nevis. The plans for the Keep of Knocknacolly were approved by Chester Royde, and the lawyer and the architect were bidden to go ahead with the work.

" Well," said Kilwhillie to Ben Nevis, " I never expected to see a cross between the Tower of London and the Crystal Palace at Knocknacolly."

" You never expected to see the Loch Ness Monster, Hugh, but you did."

" That's true, Donald," said Kilwhillie, pouring himself out a second powerful *deoch an doruis*.

Chester and Carrie decided it would be politic for Myrtle to go back with them at the end of the month and prepare Mr and Mrs Chester Royde Senior for Alan's arrival a month or two later.

" Well, I want to be married in November," Myrtle insisted. " So you'd better be ready to sail a week or two later, Alan. And your mother must see the colouring of the trees in our fall."

" Well, when you all come back next year," said Ben Nevis, " you won't find any hikers in Glenbogle. And next Twelfth I'll give you the finest sport you ever had, Royde, on Drumcockie." He raised his glass.

" Slahnjervaw! " he bellowed.

And none had so little of the Gaelic as not to recognize that one who could now truly be called the Monarch of the Glen was wishing them ' slainte mhór ' or ' good health.'

The last word may be spoken by Mr Fletcher in the following little poem which he read aloud after dinner that September night:

> " *Last August the Twelfth on the moor of Drumcockie,*
> *You conquered, Ben Nevis, a barbarous foe;*
> *You eluded his claws on the braes of Ben Booey*
> *And at last in Glenbogle itself laid him low.*

> " *Though hikers may camp in the rest of the country,*
> *Not a tent shall be seen where Ben Nevis is lord:*
> *Ben Booey, Ben Gorm, Ben Glass and Ben Cruet*
> *Will never bow down to that pestilent horde.*

> " *Salute Mac 'ic Eachainn, the brave and the mighty,*
> *The Chief who has routed the Sassenach crew,*
> *The lord of Ben Nevis, Glenbogle, Glenbristle,*
> *Strathdiddle, Strathdun, Loch Hoch and Loch Hoo.*"

" You couldn't write a poem like that, Alan," said Myrtle.

" No, I couldn't," Alan agreed.

" Marvellous, isn't it ? " Ben Nevis glowed. " I simply don't know how it's done. I don't really."